Between
Good and
Evil

Other Books by Rochelle Alers

ROCHELLE ALERS

Between Good and Evil

KENSINGTON PUBLISHING CORP.

kensingtonbooks.com

DAFINA BOOKS are published by

Kensington Publishing Corp.
900 Third Avenue
New York, NY 10022

All Kensington titles, imprints, and distributed lines are available at special quantity discounts for bulk purchases for sales promotion, premiums, fund-raising, and educational or institutional use. Special book excerpts or customized printings can also be created to fit specific needs. For details, write or phone the office of the Kensington Sales Manager: Kensington Publishing Corp., 900 Third Avenue, New York, NY 10022. Attn. Sales Department. Phone: 1-800-221-2647.

Dafina and the Dafina logo Reg US Pat. & TM Off.

ISBN: 978-1-4967-4276-6
First Trade Paperback Printing: January 2026

ISBN: 978-1-4967-4277-3 (e-book)

10 9 8 7 6 5 4 3 2 1

Printed in the United States of America

The authorized representative in the EU for product safety and compliance
is eucomply OU, Parnu mnt 139b-14, Apt 123
Tallinn, Berlin 11317, hello@eucompliancepartner.com

And many among them shall stumble and fall, broken, snared, and captured.

—Isaiah 8:15

Dear Reader,

I have always heard that a writer should write about what they know, and I kept this in mind when I sat down to create the characters for *Between Good and Evil*. For me, it was taking a step back into my childhood when growing up on New York City's Upper West Side, a half block away from Central Park.

The novel is filled with nostalgic events I witnessed and others I heard or read about. It was about a time when kids made friends with those living on the same block or were able to form new relationships whenever they changed schools.

Between Good and Evil is my first attempt to write about male bonding, and I must admit I was overwhelmed with feelings I had never experienced before once I completed the manuscript. My emotions ranged from euphoria, sadness, pity, and regret for characters who occasionally kept me from a restful night's sleep because they wanted me to get up and continue telling their story.

Although Kenny, Frankie, and Ray are figments of my imagination, they embody real young men growing up in a time when America lost its innocence following World War II. Their reaction to the country's racial unrest, the Vietnam War, and the proliferation of drugs destroying lives, ravaging cities, and neighborhoods is also very real. I was a college student when classes were disrupted by anti-war campus demonstrations, and when my three brothers fought in Vietnam—two who received Purple Hearts. They returned alive, but with memories they still refuse to talk about.

The three lifelong friends aren't the only ones who walk the thin line between good and evil. Family members with questionable backgrounds, and women who continue to hold onto secrets at the risk of true happiness, impact the lives of

Frankie, Kenny, and Ray in ways they never could have imagined.

Some of the language is raw, and at times offensive, but this was necessary to make the characters and events more real.

Happy Reading,
Rochelle

Between Good and Evil

PROLOGUE

Newark Trauma Center—Newark, New Jersey—
August 8, 1989

Kenneth Russell knew he was in a hospital because of the distinctive sounds of machines monitoring his vitals. He couldn't talk, was unable to open his eyes, but he could hear and recognize voices. Someone was crying, and he knew it was MacKayla Harrison.

They had been dating for more than a year, when she'd subtly hinted that she often dreamed of becoming a June bride. And Kenneth was ready to make her dream come true. He'd taken the subway downtown to Manhattan's Diamond District to purchase a ring, hoping she would be pleased with his selection.

Kenneth had surprised MacKayla early Saturday morning when he'd called to tell her he was coming to Fort Lee, New Jersey to pick her up before driving down to Atlantic City, where they would spend the weekend taking in a few shows. She had no idea he'd planned to propose marriage.

Everything was falling into place beautifully. He had the ring, traffic on the George Washington Bridge was light, and he felt happier than he'd been in years. Kenneth was ready to begin another phase in his life—that was, until he glanced over at the headline on a stack of newspapers on the passenger seat of his car:

GRACIE MANSION HOPEFUL CAUGHT CROSSING STATE LINE WITH UNDERAGE GIRL . . .
"I Didn't Know She Was Sixteen!"

The headlines from the *New York Times*, the *Daily News*, and the *New York Post* printed variations of New York City's latest political scandal.

Every local television station had covered the story of Michael Boone, a candidate who was campaigning in a primary election against David Dinkins to become his party's candidate for mayor. Michael had been pulled over by Connecticut State Police for a traffic infraction only for the officer to discover an underage girl in the car with him. When questioned about his passenger, Boone denied knowing she was sixteen, because she'd told him she was twenty-two. The girl had been forthcoming when she explained to the officer that they were planning to spend the weekend at a hotel to celebrate her birthday.

There were photos of a handcuffed Boone with his head lowered in shame, and several others with him and his socialite mother during happier times before he'd announced his intention to enter the race for mayor of the City of New York.

A brittle smile touched Kenneth's mouth, and before he could refocus his attention on the road, he veered into another lane and was hit head-on by an oncoming vehicle. He felt the impact of the collision, which flipped his car upside down. He could smell fire, hear screams, and then felt a comforting blackness when he lapsed into unconsciousness.

Kenneth recognized another voice. It was that of his boyhood friend, Frankie D'Allesandro, asking MacKayla how long had he been in a coma. Kenneth wanted to tell Frankie that he couldn't be in a coma, because he was aware of everything going on around him.

"It's been almost a month," MacKayla said. "Ray was here yesterday, and we prayed together that he will recover."

"I would've come sooner," Frankie told her. "But my lawyers asked for a change in venue because several of the jurors perjured themselves. They knew exactly who I was when they were selected to serve."

Kenneth didn't want to believe Frankie had been arrested and indicted under the RICO Act. Three years ago, all the Five Families were on trial and charged with racketeer influence and corrupt organizations. Not only was Frankie not a made man, he also didn't belong to any organized crime family. He could no longer hear Frankie and MacKayla's voices and assumed they stepped out of the room. However, he did hear a voice in his head that he would never forget. And that depended on how long he would live.

I want you to pay the bitches back for ruining my life. I don't care how you do it. Just do it!

Kenneth Russell never forgot his mother's deathbed confession or his vow that he would make those responsible for his existence when they used a young, innocent girl to fulfill their dreams for social and political success. It had taken careful planning and great patience for Kenneth to exact revenge on Precious Boone. Not only had she become a casualty, but unfortunately her son, Michael Boone had ended up as collateral damage.

Once the news got out that Michael Boone was going to be charged with the Mann Act, Kenneth's joy had been limitless. However, after a restless night's sleep, he experienced a modicum of remorse and shame for his involvement in using an innocent man to exact revenge on Michael's mother. He knew his conscience would continue to haunt him and that he'd have to spend the rest of his life atoning for his many sins.

Kenneth didn't want to think about his sins; he just wanted to wake up, marry MacKayla, father children, and live to be an old man. Then he did what he'd never done in his life.

He prayed for forgiveness.

PART ONE

1950s

WEB OF LIES

CHAPTER 1

Mount Vernon, New York—Labor Day Weekend—1951

Precious Crawford Boone examined her face and hair before leaving the bedroom to join her husband on the lawn of their home to greet the guests who had come to celebrate the holiday weekend. She smiled when the reflection of her mother appeared in the mirror.

Lillian Crawford, or Lili to her closest friends, closed the bedroom door. "You look lovely, dear."

Precious turned and stared at the woman who'd spent more than half her life grooming her daughter to marry well. And "marrying well" meant attending a prestigious Negro women's college. Precious had followed in Lillian's footsteps when she was introduced to Negro society at a cotillion ball, graduated Spelman College, and pledged Alpha Kappa Alpha sorority. While Lillian had married the son of a dentist, Precious had trumped her mother when she attracted the attention of a man who'd become a very successful businessman. He didn't have the pedigree Lillian had wanted for her daughter, yet he'd succeeded where the other young men she'd chosen for Precious hadn't. As a Harlem real estate financier, Dennis Boone had become quite a wealthy man. And for a Negro, it definitely was a coup, given the racial prejudice steeped in the fabric of the United States.

Precious rested a hand over her flat middle. At twenty-eight, she'd become the perfect wife and hostess for a man nine years her senior. She was perfect in every way; however, she was unable to give Dennis what he wanted more than the fortune he had amassed. He wanted a son to carry on the Boone name.

She lowered her eyes. "Lovely and unable to give my husband a child." Tears filled her eyes, and she reached for a tissue to catch them before they fell and ruined her makeup.

Lillian approached her daughter and rested a hand upon her shoulder. "I've thought of a way you can give your husband a child."

Precious stared at her mother as if she'd taken leave of her senses. Only Lillian knew why she hadn't been able to get pregnant. Precious had just begun her junior year at college when she met a boy at a fraternity house party. She'd drunk alcohol-spiked punch and ended up in bed with him. Two months later, she discovered she was pregnant. When she told her mother, Lillian reassured Precious she would take care of her problem. Taking care of the problem meant an illegal abortion. She'd gotten rid of her problem, unaware that the backroom procedure would leave her sterile.

She and Dennis had recently celebrated their sixth wedding anniversary, and with each month that passed, her womb remained empty. Precious was beginning to panic after she'd overheard her husband talking to one of his business associates that he was thinking of divorcing his wife because she was unable to give him a child.

"How, Mama?"

"You're going to have to get someone to sleep with your husband, and once she's pregnant and gives birth, then you can claim the child as your own."

Precious began laughing and couldn't stop until she realized her mother was serious. Touching a fingertip to the corner of one eye, she smiled at her mother; then it faded once she met Lillian's eyes. "You are really serious, aren't you?"

Lillian pressed her manicured hands together. Always impeccably turned out with coiffed hair, perfectly applied makeup, and wearing the latest fashions, she slowly nodded. "I'm certain you remember your bible study lessons about Abraham, Sarah, and Hagar," Lillian said in a controlled, modulated tone.

"Of course, but what does that have to do with me and Dennis?"

"You're going to get him to sleep with that young girl who helps clean your house."

Precious's eyebrows lifted. "Are you talking about Justine Russell?"

Lillian nodded. "Her complexion is similar to yours, so folks won't talk if the baby comes out too light or dark."

Precious shook her head. "No, Mama."

"Yes, Precious. You're twenty-eight, and despite having sex with your husband, you still haven't given him a child. And you know he's been talking about divorcing you because you're barren."

Precious's eyelids fluttered. "*We* know why I'm barren."

A scowl crossed Lillian's delicate features. They were features that Precious had inherited along with her mother's thick black hair. "Don't you dare put that blame on me, Precious. If you had kept your dress down and knees together, you wouldn't be in this predicament. But there's no need to cry over spilt milk. What you need to do is listen to what I'm proposing, or you'll find yourself replaced by the next Mrs. Dennis Boone."

Precious sat on the stool at her dressing table; at the same time, Lillian folded her body down on the padded bench at the foot of the bed Precious shared with Dennis. "Okay, Mama. I'm listening."

"You are going to accuse Justine of stealing a piece of jewelry, and rather than report her to the police, you're going to blackmail her into sleeping with Dennis." Lillian held up a hand when Precious opened her mouth. "Please let me finish. You know Dennis always has a drink before going to bed. What you're going to do is slip some of my sleeping pills into his glass, and after he's in bed, Justine can take your place. He'll be so out of it, he'll think he's making love to his wife. Once she discovers she's pregnant, we can set her up in an apartment in the city. I'll hire a midwife to check in on her. Then, you're going to begin eating more than you do so you can put on weight. I'll have Dr. Raitt recommend complete bed rest for the duration of your confinement. And don't worry about his ethics, because I'll give him enough money for him to go along with whatever I propose."

A beat passed before Precious asked, "After she has the baby, then what?"

Lillian flashed a Cheshire cat grin. "Let me handle that."

"I need to know how you're going to handle that, Mama."

"Don't worry, child. Justine will be compensated for her efforts. I'll make certain she will have a place to live, and that she can get a job so she can support herself."

Precious's eyes narrowed. "How long have you been concocting this scheme?"

"From the moment you told me you had overheard your husband talking about divorcing you. You've worked too hard to become the perfect wife and hostess for Dennis Boone for him to discard you like the water in a pail after soaking chitterlings. It's the same with me and your father. I knew I wanted to marry him the moment I saw him at his brother's wedding, and I'd become what folks called a 'brazen heifer' when I chased him until he caught me. You were luckier than me, because Dennis took one look at you and knew that he wanted you. What really helped is your resemblance to Dororthy Dandridge. You lucked out when so many other women had failed when they tried getting Dennis to marry them. So, I'm going to do everything I can to make certain you stay married to him."

A slight smile touched the corners of Precious's mouth. She and her mother had been born into a group of socially and financially respectable New York Negroes who had to pass certain criteria for acceptance. It was through their husbands that they were afforded a status few would ever hope to achieve.

Precious thought about Justine Russell. The pretty seventeen-year-old girl with delicate features in a flawless nut-brown complexion, and thick black hair, had come to work for Dennis to help out her housekeeper grandmother, whose arthritic knees prevented her from standing on her feet for long periods of time to cook and clean the house. Justine, who had moved into a small room off the downstairs kitchen, was scheduled to complete all her high school courses this coming January. She'd told Dennis that she had attended summer school classes to accelerate and graduate six months earlier than her peers. She planned to take time off from her studies before enrolling in college in September with the goal of becoming a schoolteacher. Justine would be the first in her family to graduate high school and also go to college.

Precious resented the young girl, who was as quiet as she was pretty. Pretty enough for Dennis to give her a lingering glance whenever he encountered her. It was something Lillian had noticed and commented on whenever she came to visit. So it stood to reason for Precious that Dennis would be attracted to their housekeeper's granddaughter.

"Okay, Mama. When are we going to make it happen?"

"We'll begin this weekend. Give me that ruby bracelet Dennis gave you for Christmas, and I will hide it Justine's room when she's busy serving guests."

Sighing, Precious closed her eyes, praying what she and her mother were planning would come off without a hitch. They were going to ruin an innocent girl's life to save her marriage. And for Precious, being Mrs. Dennis Boone meant everything, because not only did she not believe in divorce, she knew that as a divorcée she would no longer be welcomed into the elite social circle of prominent Negroes, a prestigious group who had become as essential to her as breathing. She'd become an extension of her husband, and she had no intention of losing that much-coveted status.

Justine Russell couldn't believe what she was being accused of. She'd never stolen anything in her life, and she definitely wouldn't take anything from her employers. But there it was, a delicate gold and ruby bracelet hidden under several full slips in the drawer with her other underwear.

The tears filling her eyes overflowed and streamed down her face. "I swear to you I didn't take it," she pleaded. She looked at Precious, then Lillian, but both women appeared unmoved by her tears.

Precious crossed her arms under her breasts over an off-white silk blouse. "You claim you didn't take it, so how did it get into your drawer? I'm certain it didn't grow legs and walk from my jewelry box into your bedroom."

Justine swiped at her tears with her fingertips. "I don't know," she said, as Lillian shared a look with her daughter.

"Maybe we should call the police and have them question her," the older woman said.

Shaking uncontrollably, Justine feared her knees would give way and she'd collapse to the floor. "Please, don't." She didn't want to get arrested for something she hadn't done, and ruin her chances of graduating high school and going on to college. "I'll do anything you want, but please don't call the police," she continued with her pleas.

"Anything?" Precious asked, her voice deceptively soft.

Justine nodded. "Yes. Anything. Just say it, and I will do it."

"What I'm going to say to you will go no further than this room. And that means you can't even tell your grandmother, or you're going to jail for robbery."

Clasping her hands together in a prayerful gesture, Justine nodded again. "Okay. I promise I won't say anything to anyone."

"I want you to sleep with my husband."

Justine slowly blinked, wondering if she was hearing what she'd just heard. "You want me to sleep with your husband? Why?"

"So he can get you pregnant, that's why," Lillian spat out.

"I don't want a baby. Besides, I'm still a virgin."

"That's even better," Lillian countered. "Once you're pregnant, we'll know it's not some other man's brat. After you give birth, we'll take the baby and then we will make certain you will be compensated."

I can't believe what I'm hearing. These crazy women want me to sleep with a man, get pregnant, then give them my child.

Justine closed her eyes as she attempted to weigh what her employer's wife and mother had proposed against being arrested and possibly going to prison. The Boones certainly had enough money and clout to have her put away for a very long time.

Justine was only seventeen, and she had her whole life ahead of her; it was obvious Precious Boone was unable to give her husband a baby—otherwise, she wouldn't have come up with a crazy scheme to blackmail her into standing in for her.

And she hadn't lied about being a virgin. She didn't even have a boyfriend, because she didn't want to end up like her mother, who'd slept with a man and, upon discovering she was pregnant, he admitted he couldn't marry her, because he was already married. Thankfully her grandmother had stepped in to help raise her, and now that she was faced with a dilemma not of her own choosing, she wasn't able to confide in her.

Now it seemed as if history were repeating itself, because she was going to sleep with a married man; the only difference was that she didn't have to raise the child as an unwed mother. A sense of strength came to Justine she hadn't known she possessed. "You talk about compensating me. What can I expect?"

Precious exhaled an audible sigh, seemingly relieved that Justine was going to go along with their scheme. "Once you know for certain that you're carrying Dennis Boone's baby, you'll be set up in a rent-free apartment in Manhattan. You will be given enough money to buy food, clothes, and whatever incidentals you'll need. A midwife will check on you every month, and she'll be there when you go into labor. She'll make arrangements for you to be taken to a hospital, where you will deliver the baby. And if anyone asks what happened to the child, you will tell them it was born a stillbirth. You will continue to live in the apartment rent-free for another year. During that time, you'll need to get a job that will pay you enough to buy food and other living expenses. You are never to tell anyone about the baby. Not only will we deny it, but I'll make certain you'll be locked away in a hospital for the mentally insane."

"There's no need to threaten me," Justine said, exhibiting a modicum of courage for the first time.

"And there's no need for you to get snippy," Lillian said, frowning.

At this point, Justine was beyond being intimidated. She knew she had to go along with the two scheming women, or they would ruin her life, rationalizing she wouldn't be the first woman to have a baby and then give it up for adoption. Even though she would give up her baby, she had no intention of giving up her dream of becoming a schoolteacher.

"I'm not snippy, Mrs. Crawford. I know what you want, and I'm willing to do it, but I need you to answer one question for me."

"What is it?" Lillian asked with a scowl on her face.

"What do I tell my grandmother once she finds out that I'm moving out?"

Lillian's thinly plucked eyebrows lifted. "You don't have to tell her anything. Mrs. Boone will inform your grandmother that she's sending you to a secretarial school so you can learn enough office skills when it comes time for you to look for a job."

"A secretarial school is not college," Justine countered.

A frown settled into Lillian's features. "Your grandmother can barely read and write, so I doubt if she would know the difference between a secretarial school and a college."

"There's no need for you to talk about my grandmother like that," Justine said, her eyes narrowing.

"And if you continue to disrespect my mother, I *will* call the police and have you arrested for theft," Precious threatened.

Justine knew challenging the two women wasn't in her best interest. She nodded. "When do you want me to sleep with Mr. Boone?"

"Tomorrow night," Precious said. "That is, if you don't have your period."

"I don't," Justine confirmed.

"Good. I want you bathed and dressed in one of my nightgowns, and then I'll come and get you once my husband is in bed. He always has a nightcap before he turns in, so he'll be slightly drunk, and I doubt if he'll know it's you and not me in bed with him."

"What about perfume, Mrs. Boone?"

"What about it?" Precious snapped angrily.

"I'll be wearing your nightgown, but I won't smell like you."

"You're quite the sly little heifer, aren't you?" Lillian drawled. "Not only will you be wearing a silk nightgown, but you also want to wear an expensive perfume."

"She's right, Mama," Precious said. "I'll give you a bottle of my perfume you can keep for yourself. You can also keep the nightgowns."

Expensive perfume and silk nightgowns are nothing com-

pared to what I am going to give you. And there's no guarantee that I could even have a baby, because I've never had sexual relations with a man.

Justine wanted to voice her thoughts aloud. It would serve both women right if she wasn't able to get pregnant. What would they do then? What Justine couldn't understand: why didn't Precious try and adopt a child like so many women who were unable to have children? But it was apparent Dennis Boone wanted his own child and not someone else's castoff.

Justine wasn't totally immune to Dennis Boone, despite his being twenty years her senior. He was wealthy, handsome, and undeniably charming. Under another set of circumstances, she could see herself becoming his mistress if only to reap the benefits of being a kept woman, but that's not what she wanted for her future. She wanted a career before falling in love and marrying and then starting a family—with her husband, not with some other woman's.

"You claim you're a virgin," Precious said, meeting Justine's eyes. "And if you bleed, then I'll make certain to put down a towel to protect the sheet. Dennis always gets on me, then rolls over after he's finished. You can take the towel with you once he's asleep."

"How often do I have to sleep with him?" Justine questioned.

"Two or three times a week. I'll let you know when I want you to take my place. Dennis will never touch me when I have my period, so that's something we will have to coordinate."

Justine waited until the two women walked out of the tiny bedroom that suddenly felt like a tomb. When she'd first moved into the sprawling six-bedroom, six-bathroom Colonial, set on three acres in picturesque Mount Vernon, she felt as if she'd come to another world; it was nothing like the cramped two-bedroom apartment in a Bronx tenement she'd shared with her mother, two aunts, and an alcoholic uncle.

When she'd come to her grandmother crying that she couldn't study because of the constant bickering among her relatives that never seemed to stop, Grandma Flora had asked Dennis Boone if her granddaughter could move in and help her with cleaning and cooking. When he'd given his approval, Justine packed her clothes and books and moved out without a backwards glance. She could still hear her mother accusing her of deserting her, but Justine refused to accept any guilt because she'd wanted a better life.

After sharing a bed with her mother, she would get up early to find discarded beer bottles, ashtrays filled with cigarette butts, and plates of half-eaten food left in the sink, on tables, and sometimes on the floor. She would try and straighten up, put things away before bathing and getting dressed to go to school. On most days, she stayed late, either in the library or study hall, to study for a test or to complete her homework assignments. Her mother would come home exhausted after cleaning motel rooms, and Justine was left to make dinner whenever her aunts worked the night shift in a local city-run hospital's laundry. Her uncle, who'd suffered shell shock during World War II, had sought to erase his demons with liquor. Since he moved in, she'd never seen him sober, and most times she stayed away from him whenever he imagined someone was coming to kill him.

She'd moved out of a home filled with chaos unaware she would be thrust into a situation over which she had no control. Her employer's wife and mother-in-law had concocted a conspiracy where they held her future tightly within their grasp. She would give the scheming bitches what they wanted; then, she'd walk away and never look back.

CHAPTER 2

Justine felt as if she'd been doused with a bucket of ice water. She'd tried rubbing her arms, but it hadn't helped her feel warm. Mrs. Boone had given her several silk nightgowns and a bottle of Chanel No. 5 perfume, and demanded that she take a bath. She told Justine to dab a small amount of perfume behind her ears and between her breasts.

She didn't know why, but she felt like a glamorous actress about to go onstage and listen intently to the director as to what he wanted her to do or say. It wasn't the first time that Justine realized she would've been better off staying in the overcrowded apartment with her squabbling relatives than living on the estate with people who were not only wicked, but lacked a soul.

Justine had become so withdrawn since her encounter with Precious, and even her grandmother had noticed the change in her and asked if she was feeling okay. She hated lying to her grandmother, telling her she was thinking about missing her classmates, since she was finishing high school in January when they had to go until June. She almost burst into tears once Grandma Flora said she was luckier than her classmates, because she'd have her a lot longer before she would take the train from Mount Vernon into Grand Central Station, and then the uptown subway to City College.

She sat at the foot of the single bed and closed her eyes, wondering how much longer she would have to wait before becoming a prostitute. Precious Boone and Lillian Crawford had blackmailed her into offering up her body in order to stay out of jail. The two women had become pimps who were forcing her to have sex with a man; unlike women who sold their bodies for money, she was selling hers to avoid being arrested and charged with theft.

They executed the scheme so smoothly that Justine wondered if it had been their first time. How many other unsuspecting young girls had they blackmailed into sleeping with Dennis Boone, yet he hadn't gotten them pregnant? She wondered, and not for the first time, if Precious's inability to become pregnant wasn't her problem, but her husband's.

Her head popped up when she heard the soft tapping on the door. Pushing to her feet, Justine crossed the room and opened the door. Precious stood there in a matching nightgown, the scent of Chanel No. 5 wafting to Justine's nose.

"Come quickly."

What happened next occurred in slow motion. Justine later recalled going up the back staircase to the second floor. Her bare feet sinking into the deep pile of the carpeting on the hallway floor and stopping outside the open door to the Boones' master bedroom. A table lamp turned to the lowest setting bathed the space in soft golden light.

Justine stood in the doorway, unable to move until Precious gave her a gentle push. "Get into bed with him," she whispered in her ear.

Galvanized into action, she walked over to the bed, and Justine slipped in next to Dennis Boone. She swallowed a groan. He was naked.

As promised, Precious had placed a towel on the sheet where she would lay. The heat from Dennis's body nearly overwhelmed her as he moved closer. Precious hadn't told her what she had to do, so she just lay there waiting. Tears welled up behind her eyelids as she bit her lip and then prayed silently. She prayed it would be over quickly, and she could return to her closet of a bedroom.

Then she heard it—soft snores. It was apparent Dennis had fallen asleep. She had been given a reprieve. Justine didn't know whether to stay in bed or leave. Precious hadn't mentioned anything about her husband falling asleep. Her reprieve was short-lived when Dennis stopped snoring and moved even closer.

Justine held her breath when his hand went under the nightgown, his fingers inching up her thigh until he covered her mound. She swallowed a moan as his thumb massaged her clitoris, and she struggled not to move from the unexpected pleasure sweeping over her body. Justine did not want to believe that she was enjoying him touching her, but then she felt a gush of wetness bathing her folds of her vagina. Then, without warning, he covered her body with his, and seconds later, his erection replaced his thumb as he pushed into her body.

Excruciating pain overlapped what had been pleasure, and Justine clenched her teeth to keep from screaming. She felt as though she'd been ripped in two as he continued to push farther and farther inside her.

"Oh baby, you're so fucking tight tonight," he moaned in her ear. "What the fuck did you do to your pussy, because it's never been this good," he continued, breathing heavily. "I don't want to come, but I can't hold back." The last word had barely slipped past his lips when he rammed in and out of her body like a piston before he growled as if in pain, then collapsed heavily on her.

Justine couldn't stop the tears that flowed down her cheeks and into the pillow beneath her head. The area between her thighs was on fire. And the pain had surpassed her worst menstrual cramps. She counted the seconds when he would get off her so she could flee to her room and wash away all the evidence of what had just occurred. She felt used and dirty. She didn't want to believe her first sexual encounter had been with a married man, one who'd foregone foreplay.

Although she hadn't had sex before, Justine was aware of what it entailed. She'd overheard her aunts whisper about the men they slept with whenever they'd had too much to drink. They would laugh about the ones who couldn't get an erection or a few others who ejaculated before they could get inside them. But then, they would go on and on about those who made their toes curl when they suckled their breasts or rubbed their penises against them, simulating sex until they screamed for them to *just do it!*

Justine felt the rapid beating of Dennis's heart against her breasts. His weight was pressing down on her until she found it nearly impossible to breathe. Anchoring her hand between their bodies, she managed to push him enough where he rolled off face down and began snoring again. She scrambled off the bed, picked up the towel, and ran for the door, unaware that Precious had been standing in a corner of the room, watching her husband make love to another woman.

Cradling the towel to her chest, Justine retraced her steps, using the back staircase to her room. She wasn't concerned that anyone would see her, because her grandmother and the estate's caretaker, the Boones' two permanent employees, lived in the two guesthouses on the property.

She made it to the half bath across the hall from her bedroom. Justine threw the blood-stained towel on the floor of the minuscule shower stall, before taking off the nightgown and leaving it in a hamper. She covered her hair with a plastic shower cap, stepped into the stall, and turned on the cold water. It poured down on the towel, washing away most of the blood, before she turned on the hot water and let it sluice over her body. Tears flowed, mingling with the water when she reached for a bar of soap and facecloth. Justine lost track of time when she washed away the scent of Dennis Boone's body and his wife's perfume. And no matter how hard she scrubbed, she still couldn't feel clean.

It was later, when she lay in bed, that she relived what had occurred between her and the man under whose roof she resided. Justine didn't want to believe her body had betrayed her when Dennis had massaged her clitoris. She had enjoyed the pleasurable sensations that made her feel good. But it was the soreness in her vagina and thigh muscles that had become a constant reminder that she'd given her virginity to someone so unworthy of the gift she'd planned to offer to the man who would become her husband. Now, she was no better than her mother.

Justine wasn't certain whether she could sleep with Dennis Boone again. She didn't want to endure having him push into her body and ejaculate inside her. Perhaps she should've called Precious Boone and Lillian Crawford's bluff and let them contact the police. Getting arrested and possibly going to jail was preferable to becoming a prostitute for two immoral women. And if she were given the opportunity to tell Dennis what his wife and mother-in-law had concocted, there was no doubt he would believe her. Especially if she produced his wife's nightgowns and perfume as evidence. It would serve them right if she were able to turn the tables on the two scheming heifers.

Justine also contemplated packing her clothes and books and running away, but where would she go? She didn't have much money and no means of earning enough where she could rent an apartment or a room in someone's home. Then, she had to think about secretarial school. That was now her priority, because if she were going to attend college night classes, she would need a day job. Baby or no baby, she intended to earn her high school diploma. College would have to wait until after she gave birth.

She rested a hand over her flat belly. She hoped Dennis had gotten her pregnant the first time she'd slept with him, because Justine didn't know how many more times she would be able endure the subterfuge. And if she were caught, then she would sing like a canary. If she were going to be charged with a crime, then she wasn't going to keep quiet about the Boones.

Precious had taken a sip of her second cup of coffee that morning when Dennis walked into the kitchen wearing a silk bathrobe over his pajamas. She had gotten up before dawn, and she was surprised to see him this early. Smiling, she raised her head as he dipped his to kiss her.

"Good morning, my love. You're up bright and early."

Dennis lingered over his wife's head before going to the hot plate and picking up a pot of freshly brewed coffee. He poured steaming black coffee into a cup. "Good morning to you, too. You were magnificent last night."

A hint of a smile reached Precious's eyes. "So were you. I wouldn't be surprised if we made a baby last night."

He glanced at her over his shoulder. "I was thinking the same thing." Dennis walked over to the table and sat opposite his wife. A dark eyebrow, in an equally dark face, lifted. "I don't know what it was, but your pussy felt different. It was tighter."

Precious didn't want to tell her husband it hadn't been her, but another woman he'd slept with. She knew she wouldn't have been able to trick him into believing he'd slept with his wife if she hadn't filled a highball glass with a couple of ounces of bourbon, laced with a small amount of sleep medication. It was enough to dull his senses where he hadn't known whom he was making love to.

"You know I hate it when you refer to my vagina as a pussy," she chastised softly.

Dennis glared at his wife over the rim of the delicate porcelain cup. "A vagina by another name is still a pussy," he said angrily. "And you have to know the reason I married you is because your pussy is the best that I've ever had."

Precious lowered her eyes, knowing Dennis would be turned

on by the demure gesture. She'd learned to gauge her husband's moods and had come to know him better than he would ever know the real Precious Crawford. "I never get tired of you telling me that. If my vagina—my pussy—felt different, it was because I douched with alum. I overheard some women talking about adding a small amount of alum in their douche bags, and I decided to use it to see if it worked."

She'd lied to her husband, but she wasn't about to reveal he had slept with a seventeen-year-old virgin. The only time she'd used alum was on her wedding night. She'd had to convince Dennis that he was marrying a virgin. Not only had she fooled her new husband, but the blood on the sheet from a small cut above her pubic hair served to verify her claim that she'd never slept with another man. And she had her mother to thank for telling her what she had to do to win over Dennis Boone. Lillian Crawford had stepped in again—this time, to save her marriage—and Precious hoped beyond hope that Dennis would get Justine Russell pregnant and give him a son. She didn't want to think of the possibility that Justine could have a girl, because she knew it would be impossible to blackmail Justine again after she delivered the baby if Dennis decided to try again for a boy.

Dennis smiled, his large, straight white teeth a startling contrast against his sable-brown complexion. Precious didn't think her husband handsome in the traditional sense, but still attractive with his strong masculine features and beautifully modulated, deep voice. He was always immaculately dressed, whether in formal or casual attire. Dennis had a standing appointment for a weekly haircut, professional shave, and manicure. There were rumors that her husband, when he'd owned a small grocery store, had been involved in illegal numbers and prostitution before he decided to focus on real estate. He'd begun purchasing foreclosed properties, renovating and selling them for a profit. Now, at thirty-seven, he had acquired the persona of a successful businessman who'd married well. Precious Crawford Boone had the right pedigree to elevate her husband where he'd been accepted and respected among a group of elite New York City Negroes.

"Is it dangerous?" Dennis asked, then took a sip of the steaming brew.

Precious shook her head. "No. I only used a small amount."

"I don't like you putting things into your body that could eventually prove harmful and prevent my getting you pregnant."

"That's not going to happen, darling. I douche with vinegar and water at the end of my menstrual cycle and—"

"Stop with the fucking douching, Precious!" Dennis interrupted. "Why are you messing with nature? It could be the reason why you're not getting pregnant. And don't look at me like that, because you know I can make a baby. I told you about the girl I knocked up before I married you. I told her I would support the child, but she wanted marriage, so she decided to get rid of it."

Precious didn't need Dennis to remind her that he wasn't sterile. She was. And all because a lapse in what had been preached to her as a young girl was forgotten when she opened her legs to a boy because alcohol had dulled her senses where she hadn't insisted that he wear a rubber.

If she had decided to have the baby, then give it up for adoption, she wouldn't have found herself in a predicament where the complications from an illegal abortion had left her sterile. But Lillian wouldn't hear of it. She had no intention of sending her away to have a baby, and then have to explain her daughter's absence. No matter how good her explanation was, there were others who would speculate why Precious Crawford had gone to upstate New York to live with relatives. So having an abortion became the ultimate solution to a problem women had faced from the beginning of time.

"Okay, Dennis. I'll stop douching."

He smiled. "Thank you," he said. And, after a comfortable pause, "I was thinking about us going away for a few weeks."

Precious struggled not to panic. She didn't want to believe

her husband was talking about going away when she'd made plans for Justine to sleep with him. "When and where?" she said, forcing a smile she didn't feel.

"I was thinking about going back to Mackinac Island for a second honeymoon."

Precious loved the island on Michigan's Upper Peninsula, where she and Dennis had checked into a cabin and spent more time in bed making love than touring the island that had been populated by Africans when Michigan was still governed by France.

"When do you want to leave?"

Dennis exhaled an audible breath. "I'm thinking we could leave sometime the first week in October and stay for a couple of weeks."

"Okay."

"Okay?"

"Yes, Dennis. I'll be ready to leave whenever you are." Precious estimated she had almost three weeks for Justine to sleep with Dennis, barring her menstruating, before they left New York for Michigan. "Do you want me to make breakfast for you, or do you want to wait for Miss Flora to get up?"

Dennis waved a hand. "Let Miss Flora sleep. Why don't we get dressed and go out to that diner you like?"

Precious couldn't stop smiling. It was as if she and Dennis were courting again. He would always ask her what she liked and where she wanted to go, and invariably, he would make it happen. It was what she had come to love about her husband. However, there was one thing she didn't like, and that was his using foul language. Inasmuch as she'd tried to correct him, he would revert to the language he'd learned growing up on the streets in Harlem. It was only after he'd made enough money from bookmaking that Dennis decided it was time to sell the grocery store, rent out the brownstone, and move to Westchester County.

Precious always suspected her husband had ties to men who were involved in organized crime, but she hadn't been able to prove it. However, she knew for certain that the company he'd hired to renovate his properties had links to mob activity.

Dennis had reinvented himself as a real estate entrepreneur who lived in a fine house with an educated wife and professional in-laws. The only thing left was the possibility of his running for an elected office. When Precious had mentioned this to him, Dennis rejected the idea, because he had no interest in politics; however, it was something he'd want for the next generation of Boones.

Rising to stand, Precious circled the table and dropped a kiss on her husband's hair. "I'd love that. I'm going upstairs to get dressed." She walked out of the kitchen, silently congratulating herself that she'd fooled her husband into believing he'd made love to his wife. She did not want to think of how many more times Dennis would sleep with Justine before she'd come to her with the news that she was pregnant. Hopefully it wouldn't take too long.

CHAPTER 3

A week before Dennis and Precious were scheduled to drive to Michigan, Justine told Dennis's wife what she suspected.

"I'm late." The two words were delivered in a monotone voice. Justine had slept with the unsuspecting Dennis twice. Now, for the first time since she'd first menstruated at the age of twelve, Justine's period hadn't come on time.

"Are you certain?" Precious asked.

Justine nodded. "I've never been late."

"How late?"

"I should've gotten my period four days ago."

Pacing up and down the carpet in the sunroom at the rear of the house, Precious clasped her hands together. She stopped, turned, and faced Justine. "I'm going to call my doctor and ask him what we should do next. Wait here, and I'll be right back."

Justine sank down to a cushioned rocker. If she was pregnant, then it was over. She wouldn't have to endure Dennis Boone jumping on her, ramming his penis inside her body, grunting like an animal, then ejaculating before pulling out and instantly falling asleep. And she prayed that Dennis's baby *was* growing inside her, if only not to sleep with him ever again.

Justine didn't have to wait long before Precious returned. "The doctor said to collect your urine in a jar when you first get up tomorrow morning. I will take it to him, where it can be tested. Once it comes back that you're pregnant, then I will make arrangements for you to be set up in your own place."

"What about school?"

Precious frowned. "What about it?"

"I'm going to school here in Mount Vernon."

"And?" Precious asked facetiously.

"I wanted to finish high school here."

Justine was hard-pressed to keep the panic out of her voice. She had only two classes, the first beginning at ten in the morning and the second ending at noon. The walk from the high school to the house took less than twenty minutes, which meant she had the rest of the day to herself. After she changed clothes, her chores included making the bed in the master bedroom, then picking up and putting away the clothes. Precious seemed impervious that they belonged on hangers in the walk-in closet. Then she cleaned up the connecting bathroom before going downstairs to dust and run the carpet sweeper over the rugs.

When her grandmother told Justine that she'd gotten approval for her to come and live with her in the big house, she had cautioned her about taking anything, and that included money and jewelry, and whatever she'd overheard was not to be repeated. That's why Mrs. Boone and her mother accusing her of stealing was so far-fetched that Justine had thought they were playing a trick on her, while unaware the two women would trick her into doing something so underhanded and evil that it defied reality.

"There's no way you're going to live here once you start showing."

"If I'm pregnant now, then I probably won't have the baby until next year, sometime around late June. So I doubt if I will be showing that much in January."

Precious's features contorted into a scowl. "You will leave here as soon as the test verifies that you are pregnant. I will make certain all of your school records will be transferred to your new school. And if you're expected to graduate at the end of January, then no one will be the wiser, because the kids at your new school won't know who you are." She paused, glaring at Justine. "I didn't come this far with this plan for you to try and throw a monkey wrench in it."

"Don't you mean you and your conniving mother?"

"You snippy little bitch! If you weren't carrying my husband's child, I would beat the skin off your back!"

At that moment, Justine felt empowered. She had something Precious Boone wanted more than anything else in the world. "Oh, now you think you're the wife of the slaveowner who can beat your slave because they are your property. I am not a slave, and you do not own me. I've allowed myself to be manipulated by two scheming bitches who are going to hell for taking advantage of me. But it ends right here and right now. If I am pregnant, then I'm going to have this baby, because I believe abortion is a sin. I will give you your husband's child, and the instant I push it out of my body, I will curse the day it's born, because it was conceived as a part of an evil scheme. It's nothing but the devil's spawn."

"Keep running off at the mouth and—"

"And what, Mrs. Boone? Justine asked, cutting her off. "You and your mother will renege on all your promises? I don't think so, Mrs. Boone, because right now I have what you want most. And that's your husband's child. So be careful how you speak to me. Are you aware that I have the power to bring this baby to term or do something that could harm it before it's born? Then you would be left with a baby who will be no good to anyone."

Precious's eyes appeared ready to pop out of her head. "What are you talking about?"

A sinister smile lifted the corners of Justine's mouth. "I could begin taking illegal drugs and cause a miscarriage, birth defects, or even a stillbirth."

Precious closed her eyes. "You wouldn't," she whispered.

"Don't tell me what I would or wouldn't do," Justine countered.

Precious opened her eyes. "You scheming little bitch."

Justine smiled. "It takes one to know one."

The seconds ticked by for a full minute before Precious asked, "What do you want?"

"I want to live here until I graduate. After that, I'm willing to move out. By that time, I'll probably be three months along. There's no doubt I'll put on some weight, but wearing larger clothes will do the trick to conceal the changes in my body."

"I have to think about it."

Justine shook her head. "No, Mrs. Boone. You don't have time to think about it. I need to know *now* if I can live here until I graduate high school."

Precious knew when she'd been bested. And by a scheming little bitch who had her spewing curses she never would've said under another set of circumstances. However, a part of her had to admire Justine Russell, not only for her intelligence, but also for her resilience and grit. The initial fear she'd exhibited when accused of stealing the ruby bracelet had been replaced with a resolve to accept her fate, and while accepting it, she had acquired a sense of tenaciousness that would serve her well in the future. The child she carried would no doubt carry the best qualities of its father and mother.

"Okay," Precious said in a quiet voice. "You can stay. But, whenever you're not in school, I want you to confine yourself to the downstairs kitchen."

"That's not a problem," Justine said. "If it's all right with you, I'd like to go to my room, because I have to study for a history exam."

Precious nodded. "Go."

She watched Justine leave, and at that moment, she wanted to curse and throw things to release some of her rage and frustration. The scheme she and her mother had concocted had come close to backfiring, because neither of them had expected their pawn would issue her own demands. Precious knew their cook's granddaughter preferred living in a big house in a suburb rather than in a cramped tenement apartment in a less-than-desirable Bronx neighborhood with rising crime rates, since White residents had begun moving out. It had become the same in many New York City neighborhoods once signs were posted that landlords were willing to rent to Colored people. Once they moved in, services from the city were declined, as if Black folks didn't deserve what had been offered to White folks.

Precious didn't want to dwell on the inequalities between the races, because she had to find a solution to her own personal dilemma. Another woman could possibly be carrying her husband's baby, and Precious had to make certain Dennis would never know that his wife wouldn't be able to bear his children. Gathering her handbag and car keys, she walked out of her bedroom and went outside to the carriage house that had been converted into a garage. Dennis's late model Cadillac wasn't in its normal spot. He'd left the night before to drive to Philadelphia for a meeting with a group of Negro businessmen to discuss building medical clinics in Black neighborhoods where residents didn't have easy access to private or municipal hospitals.

Precious got into the yellow Buick Roadmaster convertible and started the engine. The vehicle had been a surprise birthday gift from Dennis two years before. It had a top speed of 100 mph, and she'd fallen in love with the powerful car when she first saw it in a car showroom, unaware that several months later, she would own it. She headed east to New Rochelle, and when she arrived at her parents' house, she noticed a number of cars lining the driveway. Her father's dental practice was set up in an addition at the rear of the large two-story house, along with a separate parking area for his patients. Judging from the vehicles parked in the driveway, it was obvious her mother was hosting a social event. Dr. Charles and Lillian Crawford were a much-sought-after couple among prosperous and well-to-do educated professional Negroes within the tristate region.

Precious parked her car in the patient parking lot, walked around to the front of the house, and rang the bell rather than use her key. The door opened, and the Crawfords' housekeeper looked at her as if she'd seen an apparition. "Mrs. Boone, I didn't expect to see you."

Precious rolled her eyes at the same time she shook her head. "That's because I didn't know I was required to let you know of my whereabouts."

The woman lowered her eyes at the sharp reprimand. "I'm sorry, Mrs. Boone, I didn't mean for it to come out like that."

"Stand aside, Mamie, and let me in," Precious snapped angrily. She stalked into the house when the woman opened the door wider and headed straight for the parlor, where she knew her mother would be entertaining her guests. The four women, Lillian's sorority sisters, were laughing and playing cards. It was obvious it was her turn to host their weekly bid whist gathering.

She managed to get Lillian's attention, who excused herself, smiling. "I'll be right back after I speak to my daughter."

Reaching for her mother's hand, Precious led her into the library and closed the French doors, where they wouldn't be overheard by the other women. She watched an expression of disbelief settle into Lillian's features as she repeated Justine's demands.

"I said words that I promised myself I'd never say because I hear them much too often from Dennis, but I couldn't help myself," Precious explained. "I can't believe I got down into the gutter with her, Mama."

Lillian flashed a half-smile. "Not to worry, child. We'll go along with her, and the day she graduates she'll be out of the house. And she's right about probably not showing at three months. Of course, she'll begin to eat more than usual, but that will be the reason for her gaining weight. Meanwhile, you'll do the same. The difference is Dr. Raitt is going to recommend complete bed rest for you during your confinement because you'll be spotting. The spotting will be your regular menses that you claim is always light and doesn't last more than two days. He'll also caution Dennis not to have sexual relations with you, or you may lose the baby. And that means your husband will have to take his pleasure elsewhere."

Precious's mouth opened and closed several times before she was able to say, "You're talking about my husband sleeping with other women?"

Lillian waved a manicured hand. "Enough talk about Dennis sleeping with other women, Precious. You didn't have a problem of Dennis sleeping with Justine."

"But that's different, Mama."

"Is it really, dear? What you don't know shouldn't bother you as long as you get what you want, and that is to give Dennis Boone a baby, so he won't divorce you. And I'm almost certain that if Dennis has to step out on you, he'll be discreet. How would it look for a successful Negro businessman to engage in an extramarital affair while his pregnant wife is on complete bed rest? In case you're not aware of it, your husband has worked very hard to gain acceptance among a group of successful Negroes, who are constantly looking for him to slip up."

Precious's eyes grew wide. "How do you know that?"

"Because women talk, and they tend to repeat everything they overhear from their husbands. Meanwhile, I just listen and catalogue whatever they gossip about. It hasn't been proven, but there are rumors that Dennis amassed a small fortune from not only the numbers racket, but also prostitution. Whenever someone brings it up, I just say that my son-in-law is a very astute businessman who has a gift for investing in real estate and leave it at that. He's looked down upon because he's not college-educated, but the mucky-mucks have to accept him because he's amassed a lot more money than some of them had inherited from their fathers or grandfathers. It will be different for my grandson or granddaughter, because you and Dennis will set them up to take their rightful place as the next generation of Boones where folks won't question where they came from."

Precious smiled for the first time in what appeared to be hours. "I hope you're right, Mama."

"I know I'm right," Lillian countered, "but what you have to do is trust me, Precious, and just do whatever I tell you to do, to save your marriage."

"How did you come up with this idea for me to give Dennis a child?" Precious asked after a beat passed. It was something she should've asked her mother weeks ago.

A smile parted Lillian's bright red lips. "What you have to learn to do is be quiet and listen when you get together with your friends. They will invariably talk about things they know and have overheard from their aunts, mothers, and grandmothers. The old folks have done things that will make the dead stand up and come out of their graves. They gossip about women putting a little something in a man's food, so he won't leave them, or giving him a special drink that will restore his manhood."

Precious waved her hands. "Please don't tell me anything else. I'd like to think that Dennis married me because he loved me, not because I put something in his food."

Lillian's expression grew serious. "Don't fool yourself, Precious. I'm not saying Dennis doesn't love you, but he did see you as someone he needed to make business connections as well as elevate his social standing. Otherwise, he would've been known as a former grocery store owner who hadn't gone farther than the eleventh grade."

"Don't forget that he did go back to night school to earn his high school diploma," Precious said in defense of her husband.

"True, but that can't compare with his lack of having a college degree."

"Neither self-made millionaire Cornelius Vanderbilt nor the world's first billionaire John D. Rockefeller had college degrees."

"Times are different, my dear. Most professions nowadays require a college degree. Gone are times when teachers didn't need to go to college, or nurses to nursing school. You are a teacher and I'm a nurse, so we are professional women who don't need to work as shopgirls in department stores or in factories to make ends meet. We are fortunate and have been blessed, because too many young Colored women would love to trade places with us. We live in large houses with live-in help, when so many women are forced into domestic servitude that pay them a pittance of what they're worth for the work they do. My great-grandmother was a house slave, and three generations later, I employ household help. So I don't want to hear you whining about what you have to do to secure the future for the generation of Boones."

Precious felt as if she'd been royally chastised but knew her mother was being truthful. She'd married a successful businessman, lived in a wonderful house where all of her needs were met, and she knew without a doubt that Dennis loved her as much as she did him. He'd become everything she wanted and needed, and she couldn't imagine her life without him.

Three days later, Precious got the call she'd been nervously expecting. Dr. Raitt had called to congratulate her. The test for pregnancy was positive. His patient records had recorded

Precious Caroline Boone, pregnant and with an estimated due date of June 29, 1952. He'd set up an appointment at his New Rochelle office for Precious to come in for a complete examination. The doctor had also suggested her husband accompany her to discuss what to expect during her confinement.

"What are you grinning about?" Dennis asked when he walked into the living room.

Precious bit her lower lip to keep from screaming like someone possessed. It had worked. Dennis was going to become a father! "That was Dr. Raitt on the phone. He called to tell me that I'm going to have a baby, and that when I come in tomorrow for him to examine me, he wants you to come, too."

Dennis clapped a hand over his mouth at the same time he sank down to the sofa. "I can't believe it," he whispered. "We finally did it. We made a baby!"

Precious walked over and sat next to her husband, her arms going around his neck. "Yes, we did, my love." She rested her head on his shoulder. "I hope it will be a boy."

"Boy or girl, darling. It doesn't matter as long as it is healthy."

Exhaling an inaudible breath, Precious smiled. She knew Dennis wanted a son, but she hadn't known whether he'd want a daughter until now. Whatever it was, she would love it to her last breath.

CHAPTER 4

Precious wrapped the lace-trimmed handkerchief around her fingers over and over as she stared out the windshield. Dennis had canceled an important business meeting with his banker to drive her to Dr. Raitt's office in New Rochelle, but said it was more than worth it. Since she'd told her husband that he was going to be a father, Dennis hadn't been able to stop grinning from ear to ear.

"If you don't stop twisting that handkerchief, you're going to rip it to shreds."

It was the first time since her mother had disclosed the scheme—the one she'd concocted to get her daughter into fooling her son-in-law that he had gotten her pregnant—that Precious was not only anxious, but also frightened that she wouldn't be able to pull it off. It took nine months, nearly a year for her pretend she was carrying her husband's child. And a lot of things could happen during that time. Justine Russell's insistence that she live in Mount Vernon until the end of January was risky, while Precious knew she'd made a grievous mistake when she threatened to beat her if she hadn't gone along with her plan. There was something about the teenage girl that reminded her of a dog that decided to attack his master after being beaten by him once too often. However, she could understand why Justine would want to graduate from the local suburban high school rather than move back to the one she'd attended in the Bronx. She was smart, scoring in the top ten percent of her graduating class, and had been accepted as a matriculated student in the City College of New York, where she planned to enroll as a night student. Justine said she would begin looking for employment within days of graduating, because she needed to save money to secure an apartment, buy clothes, pay student fees, and purchase books. Those were her plans before Precious and her mother had blackmailed her into sleeping with Dennis.

"I don't know if I told you, but Mama and I have decided to give Justine a graduation gift for her to attend secretarial school."

Dennis gave her a quick sidelong glance. "But isn't she going to college to become a teacher?"

"Yes."

"If that's the case, then why are you sending her to a secretarial school?"

"Justine is planning to take night courses, because she wants to work during the day. Mama has been in touch with one of her sorors in the city who rents rooms to young female college students, and she claims she's willing to put Justine up until she finds a job."

"What are you going to do to get someone to help Miss Flora once Justine leaves?"

"It shouldn't be a problem hiring someone willing to work as a live-in housekeeper, Dennis. I will ask the pastor at our church if he knows a lady who is looking for work or someone who needs a place to live."

Dennis grunted. "It seems as if you and your mother have really thought of everything when it comes to Justine's future."

Precious decided to ignore her husband's disapproving tone.

"Yes, we have because Justine is the next generation of young Negro women who want to better themselves, and it's up to us to make it easier and not harder for them. It will be the same for you once you have your son or daughter, my love. I know you will do everything you can to build a foundation on which our children will not only thrive but also prosper."

Lines fanned out around Dennis's large dark eyes when he smiled. "You can count on that."

Precious knew she had defused some of his annoyance when she'd called him *my love*. She had learned from the first time she'd garnered Dennis Michael Boone's attention that he was all ego. And she'd used everything in her female arsenal to say and do whatever she needed to become Mrs. Dennis Boone. It hadn't mattered that he wasn't college-educated, or that women of all ages were vying for his attention because he'd made a lot of money.

The first time he'd asked her to have dinner with him, Precious was ready to run in the opposite direction, because despite being impeccably dressed, his table manners were atrocious. He'd held his knife and fork like he was attacking his steak, and she thought she was going to be sick when he talked with his mouth filled with food. Instinctively he knew she was appalled when he asked her why she wasn't eating. Precious knew telling him the truth would probably end whatever relationship she'd hoped to have with him, but decided to be forthcoming, and much to her surprise, he laughed and told her it was a test. It was something he'd devised to judge whether he would continue to see a woman, or their first date would become their last. And because she hadn't been reticent to tell him how much she'd been nauseated, she passed his test.

Dennis further shocked her when he revealed he never would've been accepted into the closed circle of professional, college-educated Negroes if he hadn't learned to mimic their lifestyle. He'd paid a woman to teach him what to wear for different occasions, dining etiquette, and how to dance. Once he completed his transformation, he planned to marry a woman whose status would permit him entrance into an assembly that would have outrightly rejected him no matter how much money he'd earned. It had become a win-win for the both of them. Dennis had married a woman with the right pedigree, and she had a husband with the resources to give her whatever she wanted. Now, she was about to embark on a journey of deceit and subterfuge, and she prayed everyone would come out a winner.

Dennis would become a father.

She would become a mother.

Justine would graduate in January and give birth at the end of June, which left her time to recuperate before she enrolled in college in September.

Precious sat on the table in Dr. Raitt's exam room. His nurse had directed her into the room and helped her exchange her dress for a hospital gown. "The doctor will be with you shortly." The door closed behind the nurse, and seconds later Dr. Raitt walked in, closing and locking the door behind him. She managed a tight smile for the slightly built, middle-aged doctor wearing a pair of rimless glasses. He'd begun losing his hair in his twenties, and his barber had cut what was left close to his smooth, nut-brown scalp.

"Your mother told me everything," he said in a soft drawling voice, his cadence verifying he'd grown up in the South. "I've been reading about experiments in several medical journals about lab rats being injected with a drug that will prevent pregnancy, but the side effects include weight gain and increase in mammary glands, and a few have swollen abdomens."

Precious slowly blinked. "You're saying it mimics the appearance of pregnancy without actually being pregnant?"

Dr. Raitt nodded.

"Are you considering giving it to me?"

He nodded again. "Only if you approve. I wouldn't give it

to you now, but further along in your confinement. Meanwhile, I'd like you to increase your intake of food and try to put on a couple of pounds each month until the beginning of February. Then, when I come to your home, I will administer you an injection of the drug, and within a few weeks, you'll definitely look as if you're carrying a baby."

"Are the side effects dangerous?"

"Yes and no. Once the drug dissipates, the female rats are left sterile."

"I'm already sterile," she whispered.

The doctor smiled for the first time. "So, there's not much for you to worry about. Your mother told me you get your menses every month."

"Yes. But it's very light and doesn't last more than two days."

"Just enough to indicate you may be spotting. That's what I'm going to discuss with your husband."

A wave of panic shot through Precious as she went completely still. "What are you going to tell him?"

"That you should refrain from sexual intercourse, not lift anything heavy, and get plenty of bed rest. I will make house calls each month to check on you. The midwife I've assigned to the mother is first-rate, and she will be monitoring her confinement as closely as I'm going to do with you. Now, you can get dressed and then see me in my office when you're done."

Precious slipped off the gown and slowly put on her underwear, stockings, and then her dress, her mind in tumult. It was obvious her mother had paid the doctor well to violate the tenets of his oath. She knew if she asked Lillian Crawford how much she'd paid Dr. Raitt to go along with her scheme, Precious was certain her mother would refuse to reveal it, even to her own daughter.

Lillian had become the model of a wholly independent twentieth-century Negro woman. Not only had she married well; whatever she'd earned as a nurse, she did not have to share with her dentist-husband, who had inherited the practice from his father. Lillian had also maintained a close relationship with her AKA sorors, who were always available to her whenever she wanted or needed something to cement her status as a much sought-after social doyen.

Precious knew she would never achieve the acceptance or popularity of her mother because of her marriage. It had gotten back to her that although she'd married a man with a sizable fortune, he still lacked the education that would make him their peers. There were those who continued to question how he'd initially made enough money to invest in real estate. A grocery store owner, selling to poor Negroes, mostly on credit, would be hard-pressed to maintain a profit year after year. The ongoing rumors that he had been involved in prostitution and bookmaking for Italian criminals continued to persist, even after Dennis moved from Harlem to Mount Vernon.

Reaching for her handbag, Precious left the exam room and walked several feet to Dr. Raitt's office. Dennis was already there, and he rose to stand along with the doctor when she entered.

He cupped her elbow. "Please sit down, darling. Dr. Raitt was just telling me that based on his calculation, we should become parents in early summer."

"Your husband is right," Dr. Raitt said, as he adjusted his glasses. "However, what I didn't tell him is that the laboratory reported a small amount of blood in your urine, which indicates you may be spotting."

Dennis leaned forward. "Is that serious?"

Dr. Raitt laced his fingers together on the top of his desk. "Not as serious as it is risky. What I mean by that is you have to abstain from sexual intercourse over the duration of your wife's confinement."

Dennis shook his head, seemingly in disbelief. "Are you telling me I can't make love to my wife?"

"Yes. That is if you want her to carry her baby to full

term. Otherwise, there is the possibility that she may miscarry. The choice is yours, Mr. Boone."

A beat passed before Dennis said, "I'll do whatever needs to be done, because I've waited a long time to become a father." Reaching for Precious's free hand, he gently squeezed her fingers. "Both of us have waited a very long time for this moment."

Dr. Raitt smiled. "And because you have, I need for you to go along with my recommendations. I usually ask impending fathers not to share the same bed as their pregnant wives, and that means sleeping in another bedroom, because it's difficult to control temptation. As a young, healthy male, you don't need me to elaborate for you, Mr. Boone."

Dennis also smiled. "I understand exactly what you're talking about, Doc."

"Good. I want your wife to increase her intake of food, because she'll not only be eating for herself, but also the baby. You don't want her to deliver an underweight baby, which can lead to a number of problems."

"No, I don't," Dennis agreed.

"I'm going to come out to your home to check on Mrs. Boone, rather than have her come here to the office. It will be once a month, then twice a month once she's in her seventh and eighth month, then every week during the final month. If she follows my instructions, then you both should welcome a healthy baby boy or girl before the end of June."

Dennis released Precious's hand and extended his to the doctor. "Thank you, Dr. Raitt, for everything. I will make certain my wife follows everything you've told her."

Dr. Raitt shook the proffered hand. "You can thank me later, once I deliver your baby."

"How much do I owe you?" Dennis asked.

"You can speak to my receptionist about the bill."

Precious lowered her eyes rather than glare at the doctor. Her mother had probably paid Dr. Raitt a tidy sum, but the greedy little bastard was probably going to inflate the bill because he knew Dennis would pay it without questioning the amount. She picked up her handbag and followed Dennis out of the doctor's office.

"I'm going to wait in the car, while you settle the bill."

Dennis met her eyes. "Are you okay?"

"I'm just a little tired and I need to rest," she lied smoothly. Precious had read everything she could about pregnancy—fatigue, weight gain, cravings, and mood swings, and she intended to become an award-winning actress in the role of expectant mother. A pseudo-pregnancy was what she needed to decline social gatherings, while lying in bed eating her favorite foods and catching up on her reading. She would also refuse to see visitors. The exception would be her parents. She didn't have to concern herself with a private duty nurse, because her mother would assume that role.

Precious truly had to applaud Lillian Crawford for her ingenious machinations to ensure her status as a grandmother. So many of Lillian's sorors were grandmothers and were constantly questioning why her daughter hadn't given Dennis Boone a child. It had become a point of irritation for Lillian, who knew why Precious hadn't been able to conceive, while she accepted the blame for her daughter's condition.

Well, her plan had become foolproof once Lillian had gotten Dr. Raitt to go along with her ruse. Precious wasn't aware of her mother's relationship with the family doctor, but at this point, she didn't want to think about it or question it. When it came to powers of persuasion, Lillian Crawford was the best. And if she had been a man, then she would've been perfect as the power broker pulling the proverbial strings behind the scenes for a politician seeking an elected office.

Dennis gave her the keys to his Cadillac, and Precious left the one-story building, walked to the parking lot, and got into the vehicle that still had a new car smell. Dennis could be counted on trading in and purchasing a new Cadillac every two years, because he claimed it was a testament to his success as a real estate mogul. Rockefeller had oil, J.P. Morgan banking, Ford automobiles, and Dennis Boone real estate, when he'd secured short-term bank loans to purchase foreclosed properties, renovate them, and then resell them at a profit while repaying the bank loans before their due date.

If Dennis concerned himself with bank loan due dates, it was now the same for Precious. Justine Russell was due to deliver at the end of June, and she prayed the girl wouldn't do anything to harm the baby growing inside her. When she thought about it, Justine would also get something out of the deal. After graduating, she would be given an opportunity to acquire the skills needed to work in an office. Skills that would offer her paid employment, while she was guaranteed to live rent-free in an apartment while she attended night classes.

All Justine had to do was go along with what Precious and her mother had designed for her, and she would be able to continue her life as she'd planned. She would graduate college and become a schoolteacher.

CHAPTER 5

The day Justine received the news that she'd passed the last two New York State Regents tests she needed to graduate high school, her joy was short-lived. She returned to the house in Mount Vernon and was told that her grandmother had died in her sleep. Dennis Boone had reassured her that he would take care of the funeral arrangements. Justine sent her mother a telegram with the news that Flora Russell had passed away and that her employer had scheduled for her to be interred at Woodlawn Cemetery in the Bronx.

Flora Russell was laid to rest on a raw, rainy day in late January with less than a dozen in attendance at the gravesite. Justine had come to the Bronx with Dennis, and once her grandmother's casket was lowered into the ground she returned to Mount Vernon with him to pack for her move to a furnished apartment in New York City.

She'd had little interaction with her boss or his wife once she'd discovered she was carrying Dennis Boone's baby. She'd continued to attend classes, despite experiencing an occasional bout of nausea. However, that paled in comparison to the fatigue that plagued her whenever she needed to concentrate on her lessons.

Her appetite hadn't changed—she didn't feel the need to eat more than usual, and if not for the absence of her menses and the tenderness in her breasts, Justine might have believed she was experiencing a pseudopregnancy. She still wore the same size clothes she'd worn before she'd been with Dennis Boone.

Justine had filled two suitcases with all her worldly possessions and snapped them closed when Lillian Crawford entered her bedroom. "I'm sorry about your grandmother," she said in a soft, controlled tone.

Justine glared at her. She wanted to tell the supercilious woman that she was so sorry that she didn't have the time to attend the graveside service because she'd been too busy looking after her scheming daughter, who spent most of her time in bed eating copious amounts of food.

"Thank you, Mrs. Crawford."

Lillian pointed to the suitcases. "If you're finished here, I will have my man bring them upstairs. He's been given directions where to take you. Once you're in the apartment, he will give you an envelope with enough money to last you for several months. A midwife will check on you every month, and she will give you more money to take care of your personal needs. You don't have to concern yourself with paying rent, electricity, gas, or for the telephone. I suggest you make the best of whatever you're given, because a year to the day after you give birth, you'll be on your own."

Never had Justine wanted to hit someone and continue hitting them until they ceased to breathe. "You and your daughter are going to hell for what you've done to me," she threatened softly.

Much to her chagrin, Lillian smiled. "I may be going to hell, but if you ever tell anyone that you're carrying Dennis Boone's baby, I *will* make certain you end up in jail for a very long time."

Something snapped inside Justine at the same time a rush of rage seared her brain. "I curse you, this house, and everyone in it. And I also curse this evil thing I carry inside me, because it was conceived in sin."

Lillian recoiled as if she'd been slapped across the face. "Get out! Now!"

Reaching for her coat, Justine slipped her arms into the sleeves, picked up her suitcases, turned on her heels, and left the small space that had been her sanctuary since she first moved in. She stood outside in the bitter cold, waiting for the man who would drive her away from a house where she'd been surrounded by people who thought nothing of committing one or more of the seven deadly sins. Mrs. Crawford and her daughter didn't know they'd done her a favor sending her away where she wouldn't be contaminated with their evil. The two women weren't the only ones who'd done terrible things.

Dennis Boone believed paying for her grandmother's funeral had absolved him of the fact that he'd become involved in criminal activity before reinventing himself as a law-abiding businessman. He had purposely ignored rumors that despite his outward appearance, he was still a criminal who lived in a big house with live-in help and had been fortunate enough to marry well. Folks knew that if it hadn't been for his wife, he would've been refused entrance even through the back doors of the homes of most educated Black folks, because he couldn't be trusted. Most of them were doctors, educators, and entrepreneurs, influential people who had attended elite schools while belonging to exclusive social organizations, all achievements Dennis Boone could barely imagine.

Justine did not understand why he drank every night before going to bed with his wife. Was it to dull his senses before he was able to have sex with her? Or perhaps he drank to forget the demons who continued to haunt him for what he'd done in a past life.

Thankfully, she didn't have to wait long for the driver, as a

Ford woody station wagon came up the driveway. Her fingertips were becoming numb despite her wool gloves. The driver came to a stop, got out, picked up her suitcases, and stored them on the rear seats.

"Well, what are you standing there for? Get in the car!" he ordered, holding the door open for her.

Justine got in, sitting behind the front passenger seat, and seconds later the driver slammed the door so hard the vehicle shook. She sat motionless, staring at the rolls of fat on the back of his neck when he hoisted his bulk behind the steering wheel. He was breathing heavily, and she prayed he wouldn't expire until after he'd taken her where she had to be.

Mrs. Crawford had hinted she would live in Manhattan. But where? It would be the second time she would travel to the borough, one of five that made up New York City, but there were so many neighborhoods and Justine hoped she wouldn't be forced to live in a broken-down tenement building with rampant crime.

She shook her head to dispel the possibility. There was no way Precious and her mother would set her up in a less than desirable or dangerous neighborhood and risk her safety, because they wanted the child she carried. It would stand to reason that if they were paying a midwife to monitor her pregnancy, they would want to make certain she would not only carry to term, but also deliver a healthy baby.

Justine felt her eyelids drooping. She didn't know if it was because of her condition, or the heat inside the vehicle, but she was beginning to feel overheated. She shrugged out of the wool coat, unbuttoned her sweater, and then rested her head on one of the suitcases and closed her eyes. The motion of the car over smooth surfaces had lulled her to sleep, but whenever the tires hit a bump or a pothole on the roadway, she was jerked awake.

Sitting up, Justine decided taking a nap, even a brief one, was impossible. She stared out the side window, seeing trees, buildings, and other cars zip past as her driver increased his speed. That's when she noticed it was beginning to snow; she wanted to get wherever the driver was taking her before the snow made driving hazardous.

Justine was finally able to exhale a normal breath when the station wagon came to a complete stop. She was barely able to discern where she was until she peered at a streetlight through the falling snow. The street sign read: 145TH STREET.

"This is your stop, miss," the driver said. He shifted in his seat, then handed her an envelope. "Mrs. Crawford said to give you this."

Justine took the envelope before slipping back into her coat. It was then she saw what had been written on the front of the large envelope. It was the address and apartment number of the building where she would live, and she hoped that in addition to the money she'd been promised, there was a key to her new apartment.

The driver hadn't bothered to get out to help her, so she opened the car door and struggled to get her suitcases and then carried them up the stoop to the building. Justine made it inside the vestibule, and warmth enveloped her like a comforting blanket.

She smiled. At least she wouldn't have to put on layers of clothing, like she'd done when living with her mother, just to keep from freezing to death. There were so many times during the winter months when she'd gone to bed fully dressed whenever the building's superintendent told his tenants that he was awaiting a delivery of coal for the boiler. Justine opened the envelope and saw money, two keys, and a sheet of paper with typed listings. Not only was she grateful for the heat, but the apartment she'd been given was on the first floor. Under another set of circumstances, she would've thanked Mrs. Crawford, but the intense enmity she harbored for the woman and her daughter ran too deep for gratitude or forgiveness. Justine didn't know why, how, or when, but there would come a time when she'd pay them back for what they had done to her.

She put the key in the lock and turned it smoothly. She pushed open the door, picked up her bags, and went inside. There was just enough light coming through the drapes on the windows for her to make out parquet floors.

Justine set down her bags, flicked on a wall switch, and the entryway was bathed in a soft glow from a milk glass ceiling lamp. She closed the self-locking door and walked into the kitchen off the entryway, leaving her coat on a chair and the envelope on a table. She then slowly made her way into the living room that was furnished with a sofa, two matching chairs, and end tables with matching lamps. She continued past the bathroom to a narrow hallway with two doors. She opened one door and looked inside. It was a bedroom with a full-size bed. Then Justine opened the other door to find a smaller bedroom with a twin-size bed. The two-bedroom apartment was a far cry from the little closet of a bedroom in Mount Vernon, and a virtual palace when compared to the apartment where she'd been born and raised in the Bronx.

Justine returned to the kitchen, sat down, picked up the envelope, and emptied its contents. Mrs. Crawford had given her seventy-five dollars—more money than she'd ever had in her entire life. There was also a duplicate key to the apartment, one for a mailbox, and a gold wedding band. And a photograph of a young Black man in an Army uniform. Justine wondered who he was and why it had been given to her. Moments later, she opened a smaller envelope and took out a copy of a birth and death certificate, and a marriage license from the state of Virginia. Her heart beat a double-time rhythm when she realized she was looking at her own birth certificate for the first time. Her mother had listed her father's name as Richard Douglas. Why had her mother registered her in school using her maiden, rather than her birth father's, last name? Then, there was the marriage license with the names of Kenneth and Justine Russell. She stared at the date on the license: July 17, 1951. Suddenly it dawned on her that Lillian Crawford and Precious Boone had falsified a marriage license between her and the man in the photograph. The death certificate documented that Kenneth Russell had died at the age of twenty from a gunshot wound, two months following his marriage.

Justine stared at the two documents, struggling to understand how the two women had not only concocted a scheme to get her pregnant with Dennis Boone's baby, but had also no doubt paid someone to forge legal documents, all with official seals, so she would be viewed as a widow and not an unmarried woman carrying a child.

A wry smile twisted her mouth as she closed her eyes for several seconds. It was obvious they wanted her to answer as few questions as possible once her condition became known. In as much as Justine hated Precious and Lillian, she was grateful that she wouldn't have to prefabricate a story as to why she was pregnant and living on her own. They'd written the script for her. She picked up the single sheet of paper with typed instructions:

A midwife will call you a day before coming to check on you every month. If you're not feeling well, then call her immediately. You will find her number under the telephone in the bedroom. You may use the phone, but at no time will you be allowed to make long-distance calls. The local post office has recorded your name and address for mail delivery. Check your mailbox often because you will get paid receipts for your rent, telephone, and electric, and gas. There is a supermarket on Amsterdam Avenue and several grocery stores on St. Nicholas Avenue. There is also a Chinese laundry, drug store, shoemaker, and drycleaner close by. The beds in the apartment have new mattresses, and you will find pots, pans, dishes, and eating utensils in the kitchen. The refrigerator is new and has been stocked with food items that will last you at least two weeks.

Justine shook her head. It was as if she'd been given her marching orders of what she could and couldn't do. However, she wasn't going to sit and lament the fate the two women had determined for her. She would make the best of what she'd been given, then move on after that. She peered inside the envelope, realizing she'd missed something. Reaching inside, she found a business card with the name and address of the secretarial school she was to attend after she'd given birth.

There were only the sounds of sleet pelting the kitchen window and an incessant ticking of the teapot-shaped clock on the wall as Justine continued to stare at the card. Mrs. Crawford had revealed she'd paid for the six-week coursework in advance, and that meant Justine could enroll at any time. Technical and trade schools, like public and private ones, operated year-round, and she perhaps—just maybe she would sign up now rather than in the summer. Picking up the gold band, Justine slipped it on the third finger of her left hand. It was a little large, but not so much that it would slip off. In that instant, she'd become the widow of Kenneth Russell and the impending mother of his unborn child.

Justine decided to wait a week before calling the school, because she wanted to settle into her new apartment and tour the neighborhood; then she would put into motion a plan that she and no one else would be able to control.

Two days after moving in, Justine met one of her neighbors for the first time. Tall, slender, light-complected with a sprinkling of freckles on her nose and cheeks, and large brown eyes that resembled copper pennies, Pamela Daniels, the mother with two young children, rang her bell and introduced herself as the wife of the building's superintendent.

"I saw you moving in the other day, but I wanted to give you time to settle in before ringing your bell."

Justine smiled. "I'm Justine Russell—and who is this little angel clinging to your neck?"

Pamela dropped a kiss on the braided hair of the toddler on her hip. "This little chatterbox is two going on twenty-two, and her name is Sandra. But everyone, including my husband, calls her Sandy."

Justine opened the door wider. "Please come and rest yourself." She hadn't thought she would make friends or have any visitors aside from the midwife, who was expected to come at the end of the month.

Pamela shook her head. "Perhaps another time. I just came back from dropping my son off at school, and now I have to get Sandy ready for her doctor's appointment." She paused for several seconds. "The only thing I'm going to say is my husband was quite surprised when the landlord told him a single woman was moving in, when all of the apartments in this building are rented to families."

"I'm not single but widowed. I lost my husband in an accident after being married for two months." She rested her left hand over her stomach. "He's gone, but I still have a part of him, because I'm carrying his baby. He was killed when someone tried to rob him, and when he resisted, he was shot in the head."

"Oh, you poor thing."

Justine's eyelids fluttered. "I'm still dealing with his loss. He survived being shot at during the war in Korea, but not here in his own country." She sighed. "It's been difficult, but somehow I've gotten used to not having him." She did not want to believe that she'd become such a convincing actress. If she'd learned nothing else from Lillian Crawford and Precious Boone, it was how to lie. "Even though we'd talked about wanting to wait to start a family, because I was planning to go to college this September, I'm glad we didn't, because I never could have imagined losing my husband this soon."

"When are you due?"

"Late June."

"How old are you, Justine?"

"Seventeen. I'll be eighteen in March."

Pamela slowly blinked. "You're only seventeen, expecting a baby, and living on your own?"

Justine registered the incredulity in Pamela's voice. "Yes," she answered, smiling. "Kenneth and I decided to get married last summer once I realized I would graduate six months earlier than my classmates. He was on leave from the Army, awaiting an honorable discharge when we went to Virginia, got married, then came back to live with my grandmother. A week after he was officially discharged, he was dead." The lies rolled off her tongue as if she'd rehearsed them in advance. They no longer bothered Justine, because she was living a lie.

"What are you going to do after the baby is born?"

"I'm going to live with my grandmother during my ninth month. She has promised to take care of her great-grandson or daughter while I go to college. I told her I would come to see the baby every weekend until I graduate. Meanwhile, I'm planning to acquire the skills I'll need to get a clerical position in an office while I attend classes at night."

"Which college are you going to?"

"City College of New York."

Pamela's eyes grew wide. "Are you talking about the college on Convent Avenue that's only six blocks from here?"

Justine nodded.

"When I look out my window and see people coming out of the subway and walking up the street and turning off on Convent Avenue, I like to imagine myself doing the same, because I've always wanted to be a teacher."

"It's not too late, Pamela. You could go at night while your husband watches your children."

"That can't happen, because I don't have a high school diploma. I got pregnant with my son in my senior year and had to drop out. I'd planned to go at night while my mother babysat her grandson, but when Bobby was a year old, he came down with rheumatic fever, but that was before anyone knew he'd had strep throat. Then I had to scrap my plans and stay home with him."

"How old is he now?" Justine asked.

"He turned six in October and is in the first grade. I have to watch him carefully and not let him become overexerted, because he was left with minimal heart damage."

"Thankfully you didn't lose him."

Pamela nodded. "You're right; it was touch and go for a while. I have to go or I'm going to be late. It takes forever to get this little one into her snowsuit. I have to dress myself before I dress her, or she'll get overheated and start screaming and won't stop until we're outdoors."

Justine wanted to tell Pamela that dealing with a sick baby or dressing one for winter weather was something she wouldn't have to deal with. Once she gave birth, it would all become Precious Boone's responsibility.

She waited for Pamela to leave, closed the door behind her, then walked over to the phone and picked up the receiver to dial the number of the secretarial school. Her call was answered after three rings. Justine gave the receptionist her name and informed her she was pre-registered for six weeks of coursework of typing, shorthand, and recordkeeping.

Her call was transferred to the intake director, and ten minutes later, Justine had committed to begin classes the first week in March. The school had locations in three of the five boroughs, and Justine selected one several blocks north and west of Macy's department store, because it was a direct route. All she had to do was walk across the street and take the downtown subway to 34th Street, then walk four blocks to the school.

Over the past few weeks, Justine had experienced an increase in her appetite, and she needed to purchase outfits in a larger size. She was gaining weight and losing her waistline at the same time. There was another item she wanted to buy in order to save money: a secondhand sewing machine. She'd watched one of her aunts make all of their clothes, from tracing a pattern to pinning the garment together before sewing the seams.

Although Mrs. Crawford had mentioned she would receive money each month from the midwife, Justine wanted to save as much as she could, and along with whatever she'd earned from working, so she wouldn't have to pinch pennies to make ends meet. City College was tuition-free, but she still had to pay student fees and purchase books.

Justine did not have to concern herself with spending a lot on food. Her mother and aunts would cook pots of rice, peas, beans, oxtail and beef stews, and greens with fresh and smoked neckbones to not only feed everyone, but also to last for several days; her favorites were baked macaroni and cheese, smothered turkey wings, potato salad, fried chicken, and pork chops, which were served on Sundays and special family gatherings.

When one door closes, another one opens, Justine thought, smiling. It was as if she could hear her Grandma Flora talking to her. Her life had hit a temporary bump, causing a slight detour, but for Justine it was just that—temporary. She never would've predicted graduating high school six months early had come as a blessing, because if she was going to have a baby in June, then it wouldn't have been possible for her to join her classmates to receive her diploma. Girls who'd found themselves pregnant were forced to drop out and attend night classes.

Justine sat on the living room sofa, listening to the radio. *Search for Tomorrow* and *Love of Life* had become her two favorite daytime soap operas, while she never failed to listen to *Dragnet, Tales of the Texas Rangers*, and *Our Miss Brooks*. Although television was beginning to replace radio as the principal form of family entertainment, Justine still preferred listening to the radio, because it challenged her imagination as to what was happening despite not seeing the images.

A wave of fatigue washed over her where she could barely keep her eyes open. She knew if she didn't get up and go into the bedroom, she would fall asleep on the sofa. Justine forced herself to get up and turn off the radio, and she walked into the bedroom and fell across the bed fully clothed. It was hours later when she woke, refreshed, and went into the bathroom to relieve herself and wash her face.

She stared at the image in the medicine chest mirror on the wall over the bathroom sink, looking back at her. It was as if she didn't recognize herself. Her face was fuller than it had ever been, and her hair, which she straightened with a hot comb, had become even thicker. And that meant she had to go over sections of hair not once, but twice to tame strands before she was able to style it. Once it was straightened, she curled her bangs, then swept her shoulder-length hair in a ponytail and curled the ends. She'd also made it a practice to cover her hair at night before going to bed, with a bandana to keep the edges smooth and straight.

What she refused to do was look at her body in a mirror, despite the obvious changes, because it would serve as a constant reminder of the thing growing inside her. A thing she cursed before it was to take its first breath to live on its own.

CHAPTER 6

Justine met the midwife for the first time at the end of February. She'd called the day before, introducing herself as Miss Cynthia, and she should expect her arrival the next day around noon. That said, she hung up with Justine without giving her a chance to say whether she would or wouldn't be available.

She was available when opening the door to find a middle-aged woman dressed entirely in black, carrying what appeared to be a canvas bag that resembled one used to feed horses. Justine felt slightly uncomfortable when meeting the large gray-green eyes in a face the color of polished mahogany. There was something about the woman with the strangely colored eyes that made Justine think that she was a witch.

"I want you to go into the bedroom and take off all your clothes, then get into bed. I need to examine you."

Justine nodded, unable to speak because the words locked in her throat refused to come out. It would be the first time someone would see her nude body. Even when having sex with Dennis Boone, she'd worn a nightgown.

Turning on her heel, she walked into the bedroom and undressed, leaving her clothes on the top of a dresser, then pulled back the bedspread and got into bed. Minutes later, Miss Cynthia entered the room. She removed her hat, coat, and gloves. She set the bag on the floor near the bed and opened it.

Justine closed her eyes so she wouldn't see the woman when her hands moved slowly over her body as a sculptor would admiring his work of art. She jumped slightly when she felt something round and cold moving slowly over her belly.

"I can hear the baby's heartbeat." There came a pause before Miss Cynthia asked, "Do you know how much weight you've gained?"

Shaking her head, Justine opened her eyes and saw the woman making notations in a small pad. "No. The last time I was weighed in gym class, I was one hundred twelve pounds."

"There's no doubt you weigh more than that now. How's your appetite?"

"It's good. I'm eating more now than I was before becoming pregnant."

"What about nausea?"

"I threw up a few times a couple of weeks after I'd missed my period, but nothing now."

"That's good," the midwife said. She removed a tape measure from the bag and slipped it around Justine's waist. "Even though you're not showing, I would like for you to eat five small meals each day instead of three big ones. That will help to keep you from feeling faint and lightheaded. Stay away from spicy foods that tend to give impending mothers heartburn. And I'm talking about putting hot sauce on your greens, fried chicken, or fish."

Justine wanted to tell the woman she didn't like hot sauce but decided not to let her know that. Since moving into the apartment, she hadn't fried fish, chicken, or pork chops, but had put them in the oven, because she didn't want the apartment to smell like fried foods. Maybe when the weather was warmer, she would be able to open windows to get rid of the smell, and then she would resort to frying her favorite meats. She'd learned one thing from throwing up. It was that smells triggered her nausea.

"It's not going to be long before you feel the baby move, so that's when you'll realize there is something alive inside of you."

"Will it be moving a lot?" Justine asked.

"It all depends," Miss Cynthia said. "Some babies are very active. You probably will notice movement more when you're resting. I'm going to come back again the last Saturday in March to check your progress. Hopefully by then, you will have put on more weight. You don't want to deliver an underweight baby where it would have to stay in the hospital until it gains enough weight before it can be discharged."

Justine wanted to laugh in the woman's face. It wouldn't matter how much the baby weighed, because it wasn't coming home with her. Once she delivered the little boy or girl, the charade would end, while she'd consciously not thought of the child growing inside her as her baby. She wanted no attachment to it, and that meant refusing to look at it once it was born.

Miss Cynthia reached into her bag and removed an envelope, leaving it on the bedside table. "Are you drinking milk?"

Justine nodded. "Yes. The milkman delivers several bottles every week."

The midwife smiled for the first time. "Good, because you need the added calcium."

Justine wondered if the woman knew Mrs. Crawford had taken her to her husband's dental office to have her teeth checked once her pregnancy was confirmed. It was as if Lillian wanted the host carrying her grandchild to be as healthy as possible.

Miss Cynthia returned everything to her bag, walked out of the bedroom, and out of the apartment before Justine was able to put on her clothes. She picked up the envelope and opened it. Tucked inside it was five ten-dollar bills. Justine didn't know if she would receive fifty dollars each month. If she did, then it would be an additional two hundred and fifty dollars on top of the seventy-five she'd been given before. She would be given a total of three-hundred twenty-five dollars in cash before giving birth, and once the baby was born, the monthly payments would stop. However, she would continue to live rent-free in the apartment until the end of June 1953.

Precious and her mother sought to offset their treachery by bribing her, but Justine knew there would come a time when both women would pay for their wickedness.

Winter had loosened its grip on the Northeast, as spring came early with warmer temperatures and longer days of bright sunshine. Justine felt more alive than she had in a while and was looking forward to delivering the baby so she could get on with her life.

She'd learned to type more than sixty words a minute, take dictation, and then transcribe it all perfectly. Once Justine had finished all of her coursework with high marks, the director of the school told her she could recommend placement for her at a number of companies looking for a competent secretary, but Justine knew she had disappointed the woman once she revealed she was pregnant and wouldn't be able to accept any position until the end of the summer. She thanked her and said she had her business card and would contact her once she had the baby and was ready to join the workforce. She'd completed the six weeks of coursework at the secretarial school, confident that she would be able to secure a position in an office that needed a typist and stenographer.

Justine had made two purchases that she thought essential: a secondhand sewing machine and typewriter. She would need the typewriter to type her papers once she enrolled in college, and the sewing machine had proven more than useful once she'd learned to follow a pattern to make blouses and smocks to camouflage her expanding middle. There were times when it was almost impossible to detect that she was carrying a baby. Justine also saved money by not buying lunch when attending classes, because she heated leftovers and filled a thermos with what she would eat during her break.

Miss Cynthia came like clockwork every last Saturday of the month to check on her. She was pleased that her belly was getting bigger and appeared almost gleeful when Justine told her that she'd felt the baby moving. Movement was more apparent whenever she was in bed at night. It was as if the baby were doing somersaults, wanting to come out sooner than its expected due date.

It was obvious the baby knew more than Justine, the midwife, or a doctor, because she began experiencing labor pains in late May. They began intermittently one morning, subsided, then started up again in the afternoon. It was early the following morning when she'd gone into the bathroom to relieve herself because of the intense pressure on her bladder that water gushed into the toilet bowl, and Justine realized it just wasn't urine but that her water had broken.

Reaching for a towel, she shoved it in between her legs as she made it back to the bedroom and called the midwife, telling her that she was in labor. A pain ripped through her body seconds after she hung up. Biting down, she tasted blood where her teeth had cut her lip.

It seemed like hours, but it was only thirty minutes later when the midwife stood over her. She'd asked Justine for a key to the apartment so that she could make a duplicate in case she needed access to the apartment if there was an emergency, and going into labor a month early was definitely an emergency.

The pains were coming faster, harder, and Justine prayed for the baby to be born so they would stop. She felt Miss Cynthia roll her over on the bed, cover it with a rubber sheet, and roll her back before removing her underwear and inserting a hand into her vagina.

"You're fully dilated. It's too late to get you to the hospital, so I'm going to have to deliver the baby here."

Justine lost track of how long she'd been in labor as the pains came and went. The midwife sat next to the bed, monitoring her progress. Seconds ticked into minutes before Miss Cynthia got up.

Standing at the foot of the bed, Miss Cynthia rested a hand on Justine's swollen belly. "I want you to listen to me carefully. When I tell you to push, then you push as if you're having a bowel movement."

Justine nodded; she was in too much pain to speak, and she was unable to stop the tears streaming down her face. There came another shooting pain that felt as if she were being ripped in two. Then she began to pray, asking for forgiveness for cursing the baby inside her. It was because of what she'd said about carrying the devil's spawn that she was going to die during childbirth. The pains were coming faster and faster, overlapping one after another until Justine felt herself slipping away, and she heard the command telling her to push. She pushed again, and that's when she heard a baby crying. Miss Cynthia had slapped its behind before suctioning mucus from its nose.

She drifted in and out of consciousness as she heard the midwife dial the phone and say, "He came early. It's a boy." Justine Russell had just given Dennis Boone his son.

Precious's strident voice could be heard through the receiver when she said, "Bring him to the city office. I will meet you there."

"I will as soon as I finish here," Miss Cynthia said.

"Leave her!" Precious screamed. "I expect to meet you at the office by the time I get there, or you can forget about being paid."

Miss Cynthia's stern expression softened when she looked at Justine lying on the blood-stained rubber sheet. She'd cut the umbilical cord, but hadn't extracted the afterbirth, because it would take precious time away from hailing a taxi to take her to Dr. Raitt's medical office several blocks from Yankee Stadium. Wrapping the baby in several blankets, she repacked her bag, left the spare key on the bedside table, and rushed out of the apartment with the newborn baby boy.

Justine heard the door to the apartment slam behind the midwife, and minutes later, the pain returned. She couldn't understand why she was still in labor when she'd just given birth. Sucking in a breath, she let it out at the same time she pushed again. A weak cry echoed in the room; a chill swept over her once she realized she'd just given birth to another baby. She'd gone into labor a month early because she'd been carrying twins.

Rising up on an elbow, she stared at the tiny baby still attached to an umbilical cord. It was another boy. Sitting up slowly, she bent over and picked up the crying, red-faced infant. Then she began to cry and couldn't stop. With shaking hands, her maternal instincts took over as she rested the baby on her chest, smiling through her tears when his little mouth found her breast and began sucking.

Justine knew she needed medical attention. She managed to reach for the telephone and dialed Pamela's number. When she heard her neighbor's voice, she told her the baby had come early, and she needed her to call an ambulance to take her to a hospital.

"Hang up, Justine. I'm going to call the operator and have her call for an ambulance, then I'll be right over." The building superintendent was given keys to every apartment in the building in the event of an emergency or when any tenant wasn't on the premises.

Justine watched her baby suckle before Pamela rushed in and sat with her until the ambulance arrived. "Your son is beautiful," she crooned. "Have you decided what you're going to name him?"

That was a question Justine hadn't asked herself, because

naming the baby had been taken out of her hands the instant she'd given birth, and once the midwife handed it over to Precious Boone. Precious would never know that Justine Russell had carried not one, but two of her husband's sons, and that presented a dilemma for Justine. She had to move out of the apartment and leave no trace as to where she was going. She'd given up one baby, and she had no intention of giving up another.

"I'm going to name him after my husband and my father. He's going to be Kenneth Douglas Russell." Her son's middle name would be her birth father's last name. At least that wouldn't be a lie.

Precious got out of bed for the first time in days after hanging up with the midwife, got dressed, and then called the caretaker to drive her to her doctor's New York City office. The injections Dr. Raitt had given her to mimic pregnancy had worked. She'd put on weight, and both her breasts and abdomen were swollen. The drug had also triggered headaches that came without warning. They were debilitating, and she was forced to stay in bed in a darkened room as she waited for the pain to subside.

Her moods were so erratic that even Lillian threatened to stay away until her behavior changed; meanwhile, her mother commiserated with Dennis, who'd moved into another bedroom, telling him her daughter's emotional well-being was at risk if she were to become pregnant again. That's when Lillian Crawford recommended Precious undergo a procedure that would result in sterilization following the delivery.

Dennis had balked, declaring he'd wanted more than one child, but Lillian was able to convince him, saying what good would his children be if their mother was committed to a mental hospital? Lillian went on to describe stories of new mothers either hurting themselves or their children because of hormonal changes after giving birth. She told her son-in-law that as early as 700 BC, Hippocrates described women having emotional difficulties after giving birth. Medical professionals called it the *baby blues*, and if he truly loved his wife, he would either sign for her to have the procedure or make certain to use a condom whenever they had sexual intercourse.

Then, she subtly intimated that if he lost his wife, then his social status would also suffer, and the doors that were now open to him would abruptly close, leaving him on the outside looking in. The realization he would be ostracized from a group of people he worshipped from afar from the time he'd been old enough to recognize well-to-do couples dressed to the nines, riding in luxury cars and going to wonderful parties, was enough for him to agree with his mother-in-law. After Precious delivered their baby, he would agree to sign off on the tubal ligation procedure to ensure it would be her first and last pregnancy.

Precious arrived at the doctor's New York City office, then told the caretaker to go back home, and if she needed a ride, then she would call a taxi to take her back to Mount Vernon. He'd given her a puzzled look, then did as he'd been ordered.

A nurse escorted her into an exam room, where Dr. Raitt was weighing and examining her son. "How is he?"

Dr. Raitt, wearing a surgical mask, glanced over his shoulder. "He's a little small, but everything else looks good. I've arranged for you and the baby to check into a private hospital in Pelham. I will recommend you stay until the baby gains enough weight before he can be discharged. Meanwhile, I'm going to give you a shot that will reverse any signs of your pregnancy. It will take a few months before you'll begin to lose most of the weight. However, I caution you against breastfeeding, because the drug has seeped into your milk glands. The baby will have to be bottle-fed formula in the hospital and after you take him home."

Precious nodded. "What about the tubal ligation?"

"It had been scheduled for next month, but now that you've had the baby, I will contact the surgical department to reschedule it for you to undergo the procedure as soon as possible while you're recuperating from giving birth. I'm going to have someone on my staff transport you and the baby to the hospital for admittance. I've already called ahead to let them know I delivered the baby here in my office because you'd gone into early labor. I'll go there later this afternoon to fill out the necessary paperwork documenting the baby's birth. I know you told me that you plan to name the baby Michael Dennis Boone if it is a boy."

Precious nodded again. "Yes. That's what Dennis and I decided if I was going to have a boy." She'd begun to think of the child as hers and her husband's the moment it was confirmed that he was going to be a father. The name Justine Russell was never spoken again once she was banished from her home.

Dr. Raitt finished examining the baby and then called a nurse to come in and dress the infant. Meanwhile, he prepared an antidote to the experimental drug he'd given Precious. Once the baby was dressed and swaddled in a lightweight blanket, Precious carried her son outside, where a driver waited next to the automobile that would transport her to the hospital. She couldn't believe her son was the spitting image of his father.

Sitting in the rear of the car, cradling her son to her breasts, Precious couldn't stop smiling. Her mother's plan had worked flawlessly. Lillian Crawford was right. Once she was reunited with her friends, she would pay careful attention during their conversations rather than attempting to compete with them when it came to talking about her husband's accomplishments. It was something she'd found herself doing much too often, because she knew their husbands had only accepted Dennis because he'd married her.

That would all change now that she'd given Dennis an

heir. Their son would reap all of the benefits that he was entitled to because of his mother's birthright. Her son was not only fortunate, but he was also blessed, because the timing of his birth had come when Dennis was out of town, and when she would see the onset of her menses in a couple of days.

It was perfect.

Everything in her life was perfect.

CHAPTER 7

It was two days after Justine had been admitted to Harlem Hospital that she received her second visitor; the first had been a social worker. Pamela walked into the maternity ward grinning from ear to ear. Justine had been told she'd lost a lot of blood, her son was underweight, and she would remain in the hospital until she was strong enough to be discharged. The attending doctor said there was a possibility that if the baby gained enough weight, they could go home together.

Justine couldn't stop the tears filling her eyes now that her entire world had been turned upside down—because she had given birth to a baby, one she was responsible for taking care of on her own, and because there hadn't been any indication that she'd been carrying twins. Even the midwife had missed the signs there could've been not one, but two heartbeats.

The lies she told were now punishing her, because she'd told Pamela she wouldn't see her during her last month because she was going to go and live with her grandmother. After giving birth, she would stay long enough to recover, then come back to the apartment; and if anyone asked to see pictures of the baby, she would say it had been a stillbirth. The truth was that Mrs. Crawford and her daughter had planned for her to give birth in a private hospital under the name of Precious Boone.

Pushing herself into a sitting position, she smiled through her tears at her friend and neighbor. "I didn't know if you were coming."

"Did you actually believe I wouldn't come?" Pamela pulled the curtain closed around her bed, allowing them a modicum of privacy from the woman in the next bed, and rested her hands on the bed's rails. "How are you feeling?"

"I can honestly say that I've felt better."

"And I can honestly say I was never so frightened when I walked into your bedroom and saw all that much blood. Don't worry about it, because I cleaned up everything."

Justine's eyelids fluttered. "Thank goodness you were around when I called you."

"I was supposed to go grocery shopping, but then I decided to put it off for the next day." Pamela smiled. "It looks as if the good Lord was smiling down on both of us."

"I had planned to go and stay with my grandmother, but that's not going to happen, because my son decided he wanted to come early."

"Are you still going to stay with her?"

Justine shook her head. "Yes, eventually. But for now, I'm going back to my apartment."

An apartment she planned to vacate as soon as the hospital social worker informed her that she'd found one for her. However, that was something she had no intention of telling Pamela.

The middle-aged Black social worker had become the answer to Justine's prayers. When she told her that she was a recent widow, Mrs. Taylor said she would let her supervisor know Justine Russell was an emergency case. That as a widow with an infant, she would become a client under the auspices of the Department of Social Services ADC—Aid to Dependent Children. She would receive a check twice each month to cover rent, food, and clothing. Mrs. Taylor reassured Justine that she would be given an additional check to cover moving expenses.

Pamela slowly blinked. "Are you certain you're going to be okay taking care of yourself and the baby?"

"Women do it every day, Pamela. In some cultures, pregnant women squat down in the field, have their baby, and then a couple of days later they're back working the fields."

"This is not some culture, but the United States, Justine. Women don't give birth in the fields anymore."

Justine met her eyes. "Who are you kidding? You don't think women who work on farms or are sharecropping can afford to lay up for weeks after giving birth? The answer is no. It does happen often enough in the South and also in other rural places in this country." She paused when she noticed a tinge of red suffuse her friend's face. "I'm sorry—"

"There's no need for you to apologize," Pamela countered. "My grandparents were sharecroppers in North Carolina, and my mother said everyone in the family had to work in the fields. That included little kids when it came time for harvesting tobacco."

"Enough slave talk," Justine said. "I'm not certain when I'm going to be able to bring my baby home, but if I'm discharged before he is, then I have to shop for a crib, baby clothes, and diapers."

"You can wait on that. Sandy is almost potty-trained, so I still have a lot of diapers you can have. I'm certain I can find some baby clothes that I packed away after she outgrew them. You can also wait on a crib, because I happen to have a bassinet someone gave me that I never got to use. Ellis wrapped it up and stored it in a room in the basement."

Justine's eyes filled with tears that seemed to come so easily now. She hated deceiving her friend, but there was no way she could tell Pamela the truth about the two women who'd concocted a plan to derail her plans to attend college.

"Thank you, Pamela."

"No, Justine. I should be the one thanking you for all the times you looked after Sandy when I had to take my son to school and then go back and pick him up whenever Ellis wasn't available. Ellis keeps talking about having another baby, but I told him in no uncertain terms that he has a son and a daughter, so that's it for me."

"What do you use to prevent getting pregnant?"

"I'm using a diaphragm, and Ellis will sometimes use a condom." Pamela sighed. "There are times when I question myself why I fell in love with a man who is a super when I could've married one who got up every morning to take the bus or subway to work."

Justine stared at her neighbor as if she'd lost her mind. She'd married a hardworking man who had provided a home for her and their children. At least he'd married her once she discovered she was pregnant with his child. It was something Justine's father hadn't been able to do, because he was already married when Justine's mother told him she was carrying his baby.

"You're married to a good man, Pamela. So, count your blessings."

"You're right. When do you think you'll be discharged?"

"Probably not for another three or four days. I was given a transfusion because I lost a lot of blood. Once my red blood count is up within normal range, then I'll be ready to go home. I'm also hoping my son will have gained enough weight so we can be discharged together."

"Don't worry about your apartment, Justine. I'll make certain you'll have the bassinet, diapers, and some clothes for the baby by the time you come home."

Justine nodded, then averted her face. Pamela Daniels was

not only a neighbor, but a true friend; it pained her that she had to lie to her about her future plans, because she planned to move and leave no forwarding address. What she hadn't decided was whether to leave the furniture or take it with her. The more she thought about it, Justine decided to take everything in the apartment, since she wouldn't have to buy furniture for her new apartment. She would be able to save money; now that she'd delivered Precious's baby, her monthly payments would stop. The only other benefit she'd been offered was that she could continue to live rent-free in the apartment until the end of June 1953.

That also was not an option for Justine, because she didn't want to take the risk that news would get back to Precious that she had another child—a son Justine refused to give up. She'd become a modern-day Rebekah, who'd given birth to fraternal twins Esau and Jacob.

Justine vowed that she would do everything in her power for her son to get what he deserved, even if it meant destroying his brother. Jacob had stolen firstborn Esau's birthright, and history would repeat itself when Kenneth Russell would bring down and destroy Dennis Boone's son sometime in the future.

"I have to go, because I want to be back home to pick up my kids from Ellis's sister. It's not often that she'll volunteer to watch them, because she has four of her own and another one on the way."

Pamela's voice broke into Justine's musings, and she turned to smile at her friend. "Thank you for coming."

"Anytime, Justine. I don't know if I can come to see you again before you're discharged, but you know where to find me."

Justine nodded, then closed her eyes. A wave of exhaustion swept over her, much like the undertow of the ocean that had nearly swept her farther away from the shore the one time she'd gone to Orchard Beach with her family. She'd initially panicked, then allowed herself to relax before a wave came and pushed her to safety.

She didn't feel as physically tired as she was mentally drained. She believed her grandmother inviting her to come to Mount Vernon to live was a reprieve from the upheaval she'd experienced when living with her mother. However, behind the doors of the magnificent white Colonial, Justine had found it to be a house of horrors.

Dennis Boone held court for his friends and business associates like a king holding sway over his subjects, while his wife and mother-in-law were the reincarnations of a fairy tale's evil stepmothers. The two women seemingly had sold their souls to give Dennis Boone what he coveted most—a son and heir.

All she had wished and planned for had been thwarted when she'd been blackmailed into sleeping with another woman's husband. It was as if her life had become a repeat of her mother's. Not only was she unmarried, but she'd bore a married man's child.

Justine still didn't understand how they had come up with a marriage license for her or a death certificate for her so-called husband, but then, people with money could bribe folks to do their bidding. Politicians and gangsters did it every day. It was said that Al Capone had judges and high-ranking police officials on his payroll, and there was no doubt Precious and Mrs. Crawford had used their money and influence to get what they wanted.

She was now eighteen, a high school graduate, and the mother of an infant son. Justine knew she couldn't afford to wallow in self-pity. She had a child to take care of. The social worker had given her the confidence she needed to begin to rebuild her life and eventually her future. She would raise her son *and* become a schoolteacher.

* * *

"I can't believe you're moving."

Justine nodded to Pamela as she cradled Kenny to her chest. It had taken three weeks for a caseworker to find an apartment for her on Manhattan's Upper West Side, less than half a block from Central Park West. It had five rooms on the second floor of a five-story walkup. And this time her name was on the lease.

"I didn't want to tell you because I knew you would be upset. My grandmother decided to rent a two-family house so I can have my own apartment."

"You're right about me being upset," Pamela said at the same time she forced a smile that didn't reach her eyes. "I suppose this is it now that you're moving so far away."

Justine nodded again. "Yeah. Poughkeepsie isn't a subway or bus ride away."

"You will write to me, won't you?" Pamela asked.

"I will as soon as I'm settled." Justine asked herself when was she going to stop lying. It had come as easily as breathing. "I left the keys to the apartment on the windowsill in the kitchen. I have to go now, because the movers have finished loading their van, and I need to hail a taxi to take me to Grand Central to catch the train. The movers are scheduled to deliver my furniture early tomorrow morning." Justine wanted it to be the last lie she told her friend; the movers were instructed to deliver the furniture to her new apartment, and she wanted to get there before they arrived.

"Don't forget to stay in touch," Pamela reminded her.

"I will."

Those were the last two words Justine told Pamela before she walked to the corner and raised her hand to hail a taxi. When one stopped, she got in and gave the driver her new address.

She glanced down at the sleeping infant in her arms and smiled. Kenny was a good baby who only cried when he was hungry or needed to be changed. Now that she was receiving public assistance, Justine planned to stay home with her son until he was ready to attend school. Then, she would find a part-time position to earn enough to supplement her welfare check. Her caseworker had cautioned her that she had to report any money she earned from employment, because then her bimonthly check would have to be adjusted.

Justine resented the restrictions she'd had to adhere to, yet she was willing to follow the rules, because taxpayers were supporting her and her dependent child. She kept up her secretarial skills by taking dictation when listening to radio news, then transcribing them on the typewriter. She wanted to be ready whenever the time came when she would be interviewed and tested for an office position.

The taxi arrived a half hour before the movers, and it took quick work for the three men to unload the van and carry everything up two flights of stairs. Justine sat on a kitchen chair while one man opened boxes with a crib and baby carriage and quickly assembled them. He claimed it was the least he could do for the widow of a deceased soldier. The movers positioned every piece of furniture in the places she indicated to them, and when she opened her handbag to give each man a tip, they vehemently refused to take money from a woman with an infant child.

She placed a blanket-wrapped Kenny on the floor in one of the smaller bedrooms and opened a box filled with baby items. Justine covered the crib mattress with a sheet, then put her son in the crib. She smiled when he stared up at her with large brown eyes that were so much like her own. She didn't know what Precious's son looked like, but there was no doubt Kenny had taken after his birth mother.

Justine fed and changed the baby, and once he'd fallen asleep, she concentrated on unpacking. It was late afternoon when she opened a can of split pea soup, heated it in a saucepan, then ate it slowly to avoid burning her mouth.

After she was discharged from the hospital, she had methodically cooked and used most of the perishable food items, knowing they wouldn't survive unrefrigerated because of the summer heat. She then packed canned and non-perishables like rice, flour, and sugar in tins to transport to her new kitchen.

Justine knew she had to go to the grocery store to buy eggs, butter, milk, and bread. She wasn't as concerned with Kenny's formula because she mixed evaporated milk with water and then added a small amount of cane syrup. She'd grown up listening to Black mothers talk about their babies unable to tolerate cow's milk because it gave them colic. So far, so good when it came to her son's formula made with canned milk. Justine knew she had enough canned foods on hand to sustain her for several days before she had to go out to shop.

There was a small grocery store on the same block as her apartment building and a supermarket on the avenue two blocks away. The apartment the caseworker had selected for her was within walking distance for everything she'd need to sustain her. And having Central Park practically outside her front door made life as she would come to know it complete.

Her new apartment was perfect. It had a large kitchen to the right of the entryway, and a living room that looked out on the street, and Justine was looking forward to people-watching. That was something she couldn't do in her old apartment, because it was at the rear of the building. It had also a bathroom and three bedrooms.

She decided to take a nap while the baby was sleeping; it was going to take a while before she recovered fully from giving birth. Justine made up her bed, kicked off her shoes, and lay across the mattress. She let out an audible sigh. It would be the first time in a long while that she would be able to relax completely without the fear someone would see through the web of lies that now governed her life.

It was if she'd reinvented herself. She was now the widow

of a deceased soldier, and the mother of his infant son. She lived far enough from those who'd known Justine Russell, and only she, and not anyone else, would determine her destiny. Her vow to bring down the women who were responsible for the upheaval in her life was no longer a priority. That would come much later. Now her sole focus was raising a son for whom she'd be proud to be his mother.

PART TWO

1960s

THE FAMILIES

LE FAMIGLIE

LAS FAMILIAS

CHAPTER 8

Kenneth Russell pressed his ear against the closed door, listening for sounds of movement behind it. His mother had gone into the room more than an hour before, after telling him she wouldn't be long, but for a twelve-year-old, more than sixty minutes was a lot more than *not long*. Then, he heard the distinctive tapping of typewriter keys, and knew his mother was working.

It was as if she had two jobs; she worked Monday through Friday as a clerk in a hospital's business office and on the weekends typing papers for college students. Justine Russell admitted that the monies she made from her weekend job occasionally equaled or surpassed her weekly hospital salary. It was cash she'd begun saving for what she termed the proverbial rainy day. Kenny didn't understand what she meant, because it wasn't as if she didn't have enough money to buy food or clothing whenever it rained. He only understood after she'd explained that it was like a savings account; the difference was she hadn't deposited the money in the bank, but it was extra cash on hand in case she needed it for an emergency.

Kenny shifted from one foot to the other. Then he did something he'd been warned never to do. He knocked on the door. The tapping of the keys stopped, and seconds later, the door opened. He experienced a shiver of unease as he stared at a face so much like his own. Folks would say he was a masculine version of his mother. He'd inherited her medium nut-brown complexion, large expressive dark-brown eyes, nose, mouth, and thick hair. His mother had him visit the barbershop every three weeks to keep his hair cropped close to his scalp.

"Whatever it is better be important enough for you to interrupt me when I'm working," Justine Russell said, frowning at her son.

Kenny's head bobbed up and down at the same time he sucked in a breath, holding it for several seconds before exhaling. "I'm sorry to bother you, Mom, but I want to know if I can go with Frankie to his grandmother's house tomorrow afternoon."

A beat passed before Justine asked, "Where does she live?"

Please don't let her say no once I tell her where it is. "It's on Pleasant Avenue."

Justine's eyebrows nearly met as a frown flitted over her features. "Pleasant Avenue in East Harlem?" Kenny nodded. "I've told you before that I don't want you going to the East Side."

His shoulders slumped. "I'm not going by myself. Frankie also invited Ray, so there will be three of us."

Justine shook her head. "I don't know, Kenny. Other than Frankie and Ray, I know nothing about these people. I'd like to talk to Frankie's grandmother to get more information from her."

"She doesn't speak a lot of English. Whenever Frankie talks to her, it is in Italian."

"Is there anyone in that house who speaks English?"

"Yes. What if I have Frankie call one of his uncles and then have him call you?"

"Okay, but don't get your hopes up, because if he doesn't agree to what I want, then you're not going."

Kenny curbed the urge to kiss his mother. He remembered the last time he'd done it, he felt awkward, because all of the boys he knew tended to put some distance between their mothers whenever they attempted to kiss them. Not only had he grown several inches over the summer, and now was taller than his mother, but he was also changing physically. Hair had sprouted under his armpits and pubis. And there were times when his penis became so hard that it was both painful and pleasurable at the same time.

Mr. Morrison, his gym teacher, had taught a class about what to expect during the onset of puberty, and while most of the boys laughed and joked, Kenny had listened intently, because he'd heard stories about boys becoming fathers as young as thirteen and fourteen. He'd grown up without his father, and he had no intention of becoming one unless he was married. There was no doubt that his mother truly loved his father, because even after his death, she'd continued to wear her wedding ring.

Kenny practically ran to the living room to dial Frankie's number, and when Mrs. D'Allesandro answered, he introduced himself and politely asked to speak to her son. Francis was the oldest of the four D'Allesandro children, and the only boy; he'd complained bitterly that his three sisters refused to get along, and he couldn't wait to grow up and move out of his house. It was different for Kenny, because as an only child, he didn't have any siblings to fight with. His other friend Ramon Torres was one of six children who lived in a three-bedroom apartment with his parents and elderly grandmother.

Kenny, Frankie, and Ray had become inseparable once they'd found themselves in the same seventh grade class at their junior high school. Even if you didn't see the three to-gether, you rarely saw them alone.

They were in math class when they'd heard the news that John F. Kennedy had been assassinated. At first, none of them could understand why teachers and staff were crying until Kenny arrived home and watched the footage on television. His mother had bought the television with the monies she'd earned typing a thesis for a graduate student and a disserta-tion for a history professor studying for his doctorate. When Kenny asked her how she'd connected with people who wanted to use her services as a typist, she said she'd befriended a patient who had come into the hospital's business office to settle a bill. When he saw her typing, he said he would post a notice for anyone needing typing services at a college's stu-dent building with her name and telephone number.

When someone contacted Justine by phone inquiring about her typing papers, she'd make arrangements for them to meet her at the New York Public Library's Bloomingdale Branch. Kenny always sat at a nearby table while his mother dis-cussed her fee and the timeline when she would be able to complete the project. He'd witnessed Justine's negotiating skills when she asked for a deposit beforehand. Most times, her customers offered to pay whatever she charged upfront, to ensure her promise to deliver what they'd paid for. It was as if Justine Russell became another person when she had to conduct business. She always made eye contact, spoke in a quiet voice, and her face was always expressionless. Aside from purchasing typing and carbon paper, erasers, and rib-bons, she was able to make a profit for her time and skills.

"Hi, Kenny."

Frankie's voice broke into his musings. "I told my mother about going to your grandmother's house tomorrow, but she wants to talk to someone about the party. I know you said your Nonna doesn't speak very good English, so could you have someone talk to her?"

"Hold on. My cousin Tony's here. I'll go and get him."
Kenny placed his hand over the mouthpiece. "Mom! Come here!" He handed his mother the phone, then stood several feet away, watching her expression as she listened to the person on the other end of the line.

"I'm going to give him permission to go now that you're telling me you'll pick up my son and drop him back home." She nodded, smiling. "Thank you, Mr. Esposito. Goodbye."

Kenny couldn't stop smiling when his mother hung up the phone. "Thanks, Mom."

Justine smiled. "You're welcome. I hope you'll complete your homework today or tomorrow morning before you leave, because I'm not going to allow you to stay up late Sunday night to work on it."

"I only have math homework. I'll do that today."

"Okay. Now, if you don't need me for anything else, I'm going back to work. If you get hungry, there's chicken and potato salad in the refrigerator."

"Thanks, Mom."

Justine nodded. "You're welcome."

Turning on her heels, Justine walked back to the small room she had set up like her office with an old rolled-top desk and a couple of bookcases she'd bought from a store selling secondhand furniture. A gooseneck table and floor lamps provided enough light for her to work during the evening hours. She'd replaced the heavy drapes with lacy ones that allowed an abundance of light during the daytime. Several potted green plants lined the windowsill and tops of bookcases; framed prints of ancient maps on two of the four walls cheered up and added color to the space.

Almost all of her weekend hours were spent typing, and occasionally transcribing diction from a professor who preferred using a tape recorder to writing on legal pads. Despite having to rewind the tape several times because she had a problem understanding his German-accented English, she preferred listening to him, because it was nearly impossible for Justine to read his illegible handwriting.

Although she had sacrificed not attending college until her son graduated high school, Justine hadn't regretted it, because the joy she derived from becoming a mother was more rewarding than she could've ever imagined. If she hadn't been on welfare, she didn't know how she would've been able to survive, because then she would be forced to work and pay someone to watch her son when she wasn't at home. The bimonthly checks were enough to cover her rent, utilities, and food. Justine had become quite adept as a seamstress when she was able to make most of her clothes from the patterns she'd purchased from a store selling fabric and notions. These savings allowed her to buy new clothes and shoes for Kenny.

She and Kenny were inseparable the first six years of his life, until it came time for him to attend first grade. Justine had taught him to read and count before enrolling him, and when she'd met his teacher for back-to-school night, Mrs. Connolly recommended he skip a grade. Justine had rejected it, because she felt her son wasn't socially mature enough to be with older kids. Her rationale was if he was academically gifted, then he would always rank at the top of his class. She hadn't disclosed to Kenny's teacher that she also had been an above-average student.

Justine made good use of the hours when Kenny was in school. She'd taken the subway downtown to the Barnes & Noble bookstore to purchase used books on English lit, psychology, sociology, history, math, science, and early childhood education; a stack of spiral college-lined notebooks were filled with notes covering each subject as she read the books from cover to cover. Her fervent wish to become a schoolteacher did not end once she'd become a mother. In fact, it was stronger than ever.

A month before Kenny was scheduled to graduate from

the sixth grade, Justine spoke to her caseworker about seeking employment. She wanted to earn enough money so she wouldn't have to rely on the city's welfare checks. After her caseworker warned that teenagers needed close monitoring when left at home alone, the woman was able to secure a position for Justine at St. Luke's Hospital in Morningside Heights, and if Justine was interested, her hours would be eight in the morning until two in the afternoon. She was interviewed, given a typing test, and was hired a week later. She would leave the house before Kenny; however, she'd be home before his classes ended at three o'clock. Her beginning salary wasn't enough for her to be taken completely off of the welfare rolls, but she would receive a lesser amount for her to maintain her current lifestyle.

Justine had felt as if she were finally in control of life, with a new job and her son entering junior high school. She had lectured Kenny about not allowing kids in the house when she wasn't there, and he was to make certain to take his key and lock the apartment before leaving for school.

She deliberately hadn't befriended any of the tenants in the building, because she didn't want to repeat the lies she'd told Pamela Daniels. There were times when she thought about her former neighbor and her children, experiencing a modicum of guilt for losing contact with her. But when she'd moved, it was to begin life anew without the web of lies that she feared had been spinning out of control.

Now her life was on an even keel with a job she loved and a son who made her proud to be his mother. He was a straight-A student, and he made friends with boys who also were good students. The first time he asked if Frankie and Ray could come over to study for a science exam because there were too many people and noise in their apartments, Justine had given her approval. The first time she saw Francis D'Allesandro, she thought she was looking at a young Tony Curtis because of his brilliant blue eyes and dark hair. Ramon Torres was equally attractive with his swarthy complexion, large dark eyes, and curly hair. She'd heard talk around the neighborhood that girls were constantly flirting to get their attention.

Justine was forthcoming when she spoke to Kenny about keeping his distance from girls who wanted him to be their boyfriend, because it would lead to disaster if he were to have sex with any of them. She told him she'd only married after finishing high school, and planned to go to college, but she had to forfeit that plan once she discovered she was pregnant. What she hadn't planned on was losing her husband so soon after their marriage, leaving her to raise their son on her own. Justine hated lying to her son about his father, while she promised herself that there would come a time when she would reveal the truth about his birth.

She would wait until he was old enough to decide whether he wanted to exact revenge on the women who, with their money and influence, had blackmailed her into having a child they'd planned for her to carry, then turn over to them. No one—not Precious Boone, Lillian Crawford, or even the midwife Miss Cynthia—had known she was carrying twins. She may have been forced to give up one baby, but not the remaining twin. She would do everything possible to keep and raise him, because after all, she was his biological mother.

She closed the door, sat down at the desk, and rewound the tape recorder, her fingers paused on the typewriter keys. Justine had been contemplating purchasing a new IBM Selectric to replace the outdated manual. A smile flitted across her face. She'd made enough money from typing papers to purchase a new electric typewriter. It would be a gift to herself for her thirtieth birthday. After making her own clothes and buying secondhand and used items, it was time she began to think she deserved better. And because of all she'd gone through, she now deserved owning something that was brand new.

CHAPTER 9

Frankie D'Allesandro put his hands over his ears to block out the yelling and screaming coming from his sisters' room, and he wondered when it would ever stop. They argued and fought about everything: clothes; if one stayed too long in the bathroom; whose turn it was to help their mother wash dishes or clean the apartment.

It was a wonder that he could keep up with his schoolwork with the chaos that seemed to escalate every day. Whenever he had to study for a test, he'd pack up his books and go to the public library, or he would ask Kenny if he could come to his house so they could study together. Kenny told him he felt different from the other kids because he was growing up without his father. However, Frankie had to remind his friend that his father had been a soldier and fought in a war to stop the spread of Communism.

There were times when he'd gotten so sick of hearing talk about Communism and the Red Scare. Kids his age shouldn't have to concern themselves whether they would be blown up by bombs like the Japanese during World War II. The photographs he saw in a magazine of people after the atomic bombs had been dropped on Hiroshima and Nagasaki had triggered nightmares for weeks. The images were something he didn't believe he would ever forget.

Frankie just wanted to be a kid who enjoyed going to school and playing with his friends, but it was now May 1964, and adults still continued to talk about the assassination of President John F. Kennedy, along with the persistent rumors of a government conspiracy and cover-up. Some hinted it was a mob hit, while others blamed it on Cuba's Communist dictator Fidel Castro.

The ongoing talk of doom and gloom was the reason social studies was Frankie's worst subject. He refused to read the newspaper, listen to or watch the nightly news, and his textbook had remained unopened even in class. Frankie had come to rely on Kenneth Russell to help him pass the subject. His dislike of social studies was offset by his love of math. Numbers had come so easily for Frankie when he was able to solve a problem within seconds of the teacher writing it on the blackboard, while he was a B-plus student in English and science.

His other friend Ramon Torres had become known as the *mad scientist*. Ray's obsession with science ranged from anatomy to zoology. He was able to identify and name every muscle and articulated bones in the human body. He, Ray, and Kenny had become best friends and unofficial blood brothers in and out of school, and whenever they studied together, they confidently knew they would pass all of their exams.

When any of Frankie's relatives asked if he was going to work in his father's grocery store once he graduated high school, he told them of his plan to go to college to become an accountant. He'd known by Gio D'Allesandro's expression that he was disappointed that his only son had chosen not to take over the business he established as a small vegetable stand before he added canned goods, milk products, and deli meats; no number of threats or pleading from the elder D'Allesandro could get Frankie to change his mind. However, he did have the support from his uncle—also his godfather and namesake, known in his neighborhood as Frankie Delano—that once Frankie became an accountant, he would have him oversee his East Harlem business ventures.

Just when he was ready to go into his sisters' bedroom and tell them to stop fighting, he heard his father's voice as he pounded on the closed door. It wasn't often that Gio got up early on Sunday morning, because it was the only day he allowed himself to sleep in late. Opening the grocery store at six in the morning and closing around seven at night, six days a week, Gio declared Sunday as his day of rest. The year before, he'd stopped attending Sunday mass with his wife and children, because he found himself falling asleep during the priest's homily. His snores had embarrassed his wife Kathleen, who suggested he stay home rather than embarrass her. Pushing off his chair, Frankie walked to the bedroom door and opened it just enough to hear what his father was saying to his sisters.

"How many times have I told you about making all that racket when I'm trying to get some sleep? Is what I'm saying going in one ear and out the other? I warned you the last time you were fighting with one another that I'm going to enroll you in Catholic school so the nuns can teach you right from wrong, because you refuse to listen to your mother."

"Please no, Poppa," Elizabeth pleaded. "I'll stop fighting with Mandy."

"Lizzy is always taking my clothes," Amanda said.

"I don't care who's doing what to the other. Once this school term is over, you won't have to fight over clothes, because you all will be wearing uniforms. Your mother will go to Holy Name tomorrow and register you for September. And if I hear another argument or fight, the three of you will spend your entire summer vacation in this very room. You will only be allowed to come out to eat and use the bathroom."

"We can't watch television, Poppa?" asked six-year-old Carolina.

"No television. I swore I would never beat my daughters because I saw what my father did to my sisters, but I swear by all that's holy that I will take a belt to all of you if you don't learn to get along. We're all going to Nonna's later this afternoon, so if you don't behave, then I'll have Miss Townsend come over and watch you."

Frankie couldn't stop grinning as he closed his door. It was about time his father had stepped in to chastise his daughters, because his wife had declared she was at the end of her rope with them. Her husband had refused to hit their daughters, and while she disagreed with him when it came to child-rearing, she had gone along with him because he was man of the house.

Kathleen D'Allesandro was two months pregnant with her fifth child, and she hoped it would be her last. Her first four children were born two years apart, and after she delivered Carolina six years ago, her menses had stopped completely; she attributed it to early menopause. But now, at thirty-one, she was pregnant again.

Although Frankie loved his parents, he had no intention of repeating their lives. His mother was eighteen and his father nineteen when they married. He was born a year later; then came three more children, every other year. Not only did his mother appear to be overwhelmed taking care of four kids, but with another on the way, Frankie knew it wasn't going to be easy for her.

He wanted to graduate college, get married, and then buy a large house with a backyard and enough rooms for his kids to have their own bedrooms. Although his father owned and operated a neighborhood grocery store, he still wasn't able to compete against the local Safeway and A&P. Gio claimed he was happy that he'd earned enough to pay his bills and take care of his family, but admitted the business didn't bring in enough for him to set up a college fund for his kids. Frankie knew he would have to earn the grades and focus on attending a public college; and if he wanted to go to a private one, then that meant he would have to secure a scholarship. The commotion in his sisters' room had stopped, and Frankie was finally able to complete his algebra and science assignments. Now, when he went to visit with his relatives, the notion that he wouldn't have to come home and stay up late to do homework was no longer a reality.

"Where are you going, and how do you know these people?" Ramon Torres stared at his grandmother's reflection in the mirror as he brushed his hair. "I'm going to Spanish Harlem with Frankie and his family." He knew that whenever he left the house, his grandmother would question where he was going and with whom.

His grandmother's penciled-in black eyebrows lifted. "Spanish Harlem?"

"*Sí, abuela,*" Ray answered in Spanish.

"*El barrio is peligroso,*" Carmen Torres said, mixing English and Spanish, as did a lot of Puerto Ricans on the mainland. "You have to watch out for the Latin Kings, Ramon."

Ray set down the brush. "Where I'm going is not dangerous, and there aren't any Latin Kings." He didn't tell his grandmother that if there were gangs, then they were Italian holdovers from the turn of the century, when large numbers of Sicilians congregated between 106th and 116th Streets along the East River, but over the years many relocated to other neighborhoods; the ones who'd stayed continued to hold onto their language and culture.

"I just want you to be careful."

"I will be careful, *abuela.* Frankie's cousin is going to drive me there and back. He's a cop."

Carmen made the sign of the cross over her chest. "*Está bien.*"

Ray agreed with his grandmother. It was good. When Frankie had called to say his police officer cousin was picking him and Kenny up, he knew they would be safer than taking the crosstown bus to and from East Harlem. Frankie inviting him to meet his relatives was a first, because other than his parents and sisters, Ray had never met any of Frankie's large extended family, many who lived across town.

"Well, well, well. Look at you," crooned Delores Torres, as she walked into her brother's bedroom. "Who's the lucky girl?"

Ray frowned. "There's no girl, Delores. Kenny and I are going with Frankie to his grandmother's house."

His fifteen-year-old sister was close to completing her first year at Julia Richman High School. She'd elected to attend the all-girls school because the curriculum included classes that would prepare her to apply for nursing school. Once she graduated, Delores planned on attending Bronx Community College of the City of New York to pursue a nursing degree.

"If I wasn't going to a wedding with Mami and Papi, I would tag along with you, because I'm willing to bet there will be some good-looking Italian boys there, I could talk to."

"You're just boy crazy, Delores," Ray spat out.

Carmen Torres shook her head. "You should concentrate on your books, not boys," she said in rapid Spanish. "You will have more than enough time to think about them after you become a nurse."

Delores pursed her lips as if she were expecting to be kissed. "The only thing I think about is becoming a nurse and marrying a doctor."

"What makes you think doctors marry nurses?" Ray asked his sister.

Delores's expression grew serious. "Don't they?"

Ray picked up a bottle of cologne with a small amount his father had given him, poured a drop onto his palm, rubbed his hands together, and massaged it on his throat. Papi had cautioned him never to douse himself with cologne or after-shave, because some women found it overpowering. Although he wasn't shaving, he still wanted to look and smell nice.

"You've been reading too many nurse-doctor books, Delores." His sister had read the *Sue Barton* nurse series over and over, and then one day announced she wanted to become a nurse. Delores wanted to be a nurse, and Ray had planned to become a doctor.

Enrique and Mariana had three boys and three girls, of which Ramon and Delores were the oldest and were lectured to continuously about how they had to be good examples for their younger siblings. Both parents worked out of the house, with Enrique as the foreman in a Bronx dress factory. Mariana had secured a position as a nurse's aide at a nursing home in upper Manhattan, after her mother-in-law moved to New York from Puerto Rico to look after her grandchildren. Mariana worked from midnight to eight in the morning, then rushed home in time to see her children washed, dressed, and fed breakfast before they left for school. Then she went to bed and slept until the afternoon, and with Carmen's help, prepared dinner for her family.

Ray knew his parents worked hard to support their kids, and he'd made certain to stay out of trouble, because he didn't want to disappoint them. He didn't smoke or cut classes like some other boys in the neighborhood. He also tended to avoid girls, who openly flirted with him. His father had cautioned him to keep his fly zipped until he was ready to accept the consequences of becoming a father.

He picked up a jacket off a hanger in the wardrobe. "I have to go now, because Frankie's cousin is supposed to pick me up downstairs at two." Ray left the apartment and walked down the stoop at the same time a four-door, powder-blue Chevrolet with a navy-blue top maneuvered up to the curb.

Frankie waved at him through the open passenger-side window. "Come, get in."

Ray opened the rear door and slid in next to Kenny. They shared a smile. "Thank you, sir, for giving me a ride," he said to the driver.

Anthony Esposito shifted in his seat and smiled over his

shoulder. The sun had darkened Frankie's cousin's complexion, and it was only slightly lighter than Ray's. The man's lips parted in a smile, but the gesture did not reach a pair of large dark eyes under inky black, thick eyebrows. Ray didn't know what it was, but there was something sinister about the man. His grandmother, who claimed to be a *bruja*, would've been able to discern something about him with a single glance.

"There's no need to thank me. If you're friends with my little cousin, then that's all I need to know."

Ray wanted to ask Kenny if there was something about Frankie's cousin that also made him uncomfortable, but looking at his friend, who appeared completely relaxed, Ray realized his imagination was getting the best of him. Frankie told him Tony was a cop, so that meant he couldn't be a gangster. He stared out the rear side window at the passing landscape as the vehicle went uptown on Central Park West before turning east on 110th Street toward the East Side. The ride ended when Tony Esposito stopped on Pleasant Avenue near 108th Street.

"You all can get out here and walk, while I drive around to find some place to park." His three passengers got out and had barely shut the doors when the Chevy sped off.

"We only have to walk a few blocks," Frankie said, as he reached up and pushed back a wave that had fallen over his forehead.

"Are you sure your cousin is a cop?" Ray asked Frankie as they began walking.

"Yeah. Why would you ask me that?"

Ray lifted his shoulders. "I don't know. He didn't look like a cop to me."

"How is a cop supposed to look?" Kenny asked.

"I don't know," Ray repeated. "I guess he would look different if he were wearing his uniform."

"My cousin is a detective, so he doesn't wear a uniform when he's on or off duty," Frankie explained.

Ray felt better. He'd accused his sister of reading too many nurse-doctor books, while he was guilty of watching gangster movies and reading crime stories in the local newspapers. He'd find himself glued to the television as he watched Joseph Valachi testify before the U.S. Senate Committee on Government Operations that the Italian American Mafia actually existed. It was the first time a member had publicly acknowledged its existence. His testimony had violated *omertà*, breaking his blood oath, while he had provided many details of the history, rituals, and operations of the Mafia. When he asked Frankie if any of his relatives were in the Mafia, his friend denied knowing any. Then he talked his friends into becoming blood brothers like the ritual mobsters made once they were inducted into the *Cosa Nostra*. They'd made small cuts on their fingers with a penknife, and mixed their blood, thereby becoming blood brothers.

Frankie stopped midway along a tree-lined block with brownstones and four-story apartment buildings. "We're here."

Ray shared a hint of a smile with Kenny as they followed Frankie up the steps to a three-story brownstone.

CHAPTER 10

Kenny felt as if he'd been doused by a bucket of ice-cold water when he walked into the first-floor apartment with what appeared to be wall-to-wall people. There had to be at least twenty people standing around in small groups talking, laughing, smoking, and drinking. There was even a priest, who was engaged in conversation with an elderly man. First of all, he'd never seen so many people crowded into one living space, and second, all conversation had ceased, and everyone was looking at him as if he had two heads and six eyes. They weren't only staring at him, but also Ray, and he wanted to ask them what was their problem. There was no doubt they'd seen Blacks and Puerto Ricans before. After all, they were in East Harlem, better known as *El Barrio*. A tall man sporting a light-brown crew cut and brilliant blue eyes in a deeply tanned face broke away from the others and approached him, Ray, and Frankie.

"You're here!" he said in a loud voice that appeared to be amplified in the hushed silence. He hugged Frankie, then kissed him on both cheeks.

A slight flush suffused Frankie's face. "Uncle, these are my friends I was telling you about. Kenny and Ray, this is my uncle and godfather. I was named after him, but everyone calls him Frankie Delano."

The older Francis rested an arm over his nephew's shoulder. "It's a pleasure to meet you. My nephew can't stop talking about his good friends, so I was finally able to convince him to invite you to my home. Welcome." He smiled, exhibiting a mouth filled with large, white teeth. "There are too many folks to introduce you to, but I want you to feel comfortable while you're here. Frankie, take your friends into the kitchen, where your Nonna will give them something to eat to tide them over before we sit down for the evening meal."

Conversations started up again when Kenny and Ray followed Frankie down a hall and into an enormous kitchen, where three women were busy filling platters with sliced meats, olives, cheese, peppers, and other foods he couldn't recognize.

An elderly woman wearing a net over her snow-white hair stopped stirring a large pot on the stove with a wooden spoon. Picking up another spoon, she scooped up a small portion of red sauce and blew on it until it was cool enough to taste. Smiling, she said, *"È pronto."*

"How long has it been cooking for it to be ready, Nonna?" Frankie asked his grandmother, speaking English.

Gianna D'Allesandro turned when she recognized her grandson's voice. The bright blue eyes she'd passed down to her sons and grandson widened when she saw him standing at the entrance to the kitchen. "It's so good to see you," she said in her heavily accented English. She wiped her hands on a towel, then kissed Frankie on both cheeks when he approached her. "I see you came with your *amici.*"

Frankie beckoned Ray and Kenny closer. "Yes, Nonna. These are my good friends, Kenny and Ray. This beautiful lady and the best cook in the world is my grandmother."

Gianna waved a hand. "You too much like your uncle. They say things they think you want to hear." She peered closely at Kenny. "My, my! You are a beautiful Colored boy. Your mama must be happy that she has such a pretty boy." Her eyes shifted to Ray. "And you, so handsome. You must have a lot of girlfriends."

Ray quickly shook his head. "No. I don't have a girlfriend."

Gianna grunted. "You're going to be a young man soon, so you should have a girlfriend. If you want, I will find you somebody."

Frankie shook his head. "Nonna, this is not the old country, where families arrange marriages for their children before they become adults. Here in America, we wait—"

"You wait until you are too old to take a husband or wife," she said, interrupting him. She threw up both hands. "What's with men waiting until they are thirty before they marry. And some wait until they are forty." She shook her head. "*Così triste.*"

"It's not sad, Nonna," said a woman cutting cheese into little cubes, "because men want to establish a career before they marry and start a family. It's the same with women. My girls say they want to finish college before they decide if they want to marry."

"Your girls act like men. Wearing pants all the time. *Lesbiche!*" Gianna spat out, angrily.

"My daughters are not lesbians!"

Frankie ushered Kenny and Ray out of the kitchen and into the living room before his grandmother and cousin began arguing. Whenever they got together, it was as if Nonna and her niece were unable to remain in the same room without exchanging words. His parents and sisters had arrived, and he noticed the girls were subdued, almost withdrawn. It was obvious his father's threat to take them out of public school and enroll them in a parochial school had tempered their sometimes out-of-control behavior. Knowing Giovanni D'Allesandro as well as he did, Frankie knew that the threat wasn't an idle one. Come September, his three sisters would go to school wearing the same uniform. His family would be paying Catholic school tuition and have another baby on the way, so Frankie knew economically things would get even tighter at home, and he decided rather than hang out with Kenny and Ray over the summer vacation, he would help his father in the store. That way, Gio wouldn't have to close for a few hours daily to make deliveries to loyal customers who refused to buy from the local supermarkets.

"Did you and your friends get something to eat?" his uncle asked.

"No, because Nonna and Patricia were arguing with each other."

"Go into Nonna's sewing room, and I'll bring you a plate."

"How big is this place?" Ray asked Frankie, as he led him and Kenny through a wide hallway, past a sitting room with love seats and armchairs, and finally into a small room with a trio of floor-to-ceiling windows. A round table with four pullup chairs was positioned in a corner opposite a built-in shelf with bolts of fabric and plastic bins with spools of thread.

Frankie met Ray's eyes when he sat across from him. "There are three floors with two apartments on each one. Each apartment has three bedrooms, but there is also one with five bedrooms. My grandparents raised my father and uncle and aunts on the first floor, while renting out the other apartment to my grandfather's brother and his family. Various relatives rent apartments on the second and third floors. Some of the old folks have passed away, but their children and grandchildren still live here."

"Why doesn't your father live here?" Kenny asked Frankie.

Frankie averted his eyes as he stared out the window. "My grandfather didn't approve of my father marrying my mother, because she's Irish."

"You're kidding?" Kenny and Ray chorused at the same time.

Frankie shook his head. "No, I'm not. My grandfather clung to the old ways, where you marry your own kind. Italians marry Italians, and Colored people marry Coloreds. It didn't matter that my mother was Catholic. She just wasn't Italian. Poppa defied him and married the woman he loved. My grandfather refused to attend the wedding and threatened to disown anyone in the family who did."

"Did they?" Ray asked.

Frankie shook his head again. "No one was willing to challenge him, so only my mother's family witnessed the wedding. Even after my grandfather passed away, Poppa refused to move back."

"Does your godfather live here with his family?" Kenny asked.

"Uncle Frank never married. I'd heard rumors that he was in love with a Black girl who lived in Harlem, but it ended when her family discovered they were sneaking around seeing each other. That's when her father sent her South to live with relatives."

Ray grunted. "Italians aren't the only ones who are racist and bigoted. That's why I intend to marry a Puerto Rican girl."

"It's the same with me," Kenny said. "If I do marry, it will be to a Black woman." He paused. "What about you, Frankie? Do you want to marry an Italian girl?"

"Probably, because I don't want to repeat what my parents had to go through."

"What if she's Irish like your mother?" Ray questioned.

"It wouldn't matter, because I refuse to deny that I'm half Irish."

Frankie's uncle walked into the room, carrying a tray with

small plates and three glasses of lemonade. "I tell anyone that I'm proud of my half Irish nephew, because once he becomes an accountant, he's going to help keep the taxman from snooping into my businesses every couple of years."

Kenny lowered his eyes. It was obvious Frankie's uncle had overheard them talking about who they wanted to marry. Even though he was attracted to girls, he hadn't done anything to let any of them know that he liked them. There was one girl in particular in his English class that he thought was the most beautiful girl in the school. Hemlines were now above the knee, and he'd found himself staring at her long, shapely legs when he should've been staring at what had been written on the blackboard. However, he'd found it hard to concentrate on his schoolwork when girls he'd known in grade school who had been flat-chested now had breasts, some proudly displayed whenever they wore tight sweaters.

He would turn thirteen at the end of the month, and then he'd be a teenager. A teenager who was going through puberty, and who wanted to experience what it would feel like to have sex with a girl. The first time he woke up to find his thighs coated with semen, he realized he didn't have any control over his body. Kenny was certain his mother would see the stains on the sheet, so he'd begun placing a towel between his thighs when going to bed, hoping it would absorb some of the nocturnal emission. He'd found it odd that he could control his body during the day, but it was different at night. When he woke to find he had an erection, at first he thought it was because he had to empty his bladder, but later discovered it wouldn't go down until he masturbated. Thankfully his mother had already left the house to go work when he was able to stand in the tub and jerk his dick until he ejaculated. The pleasure was so exhilarating that he was left feeling slightly lightheaded. Then he showered, got dressed, ate his breakfast, brushed his teeth, and left the apartment to meet Ray and Frankie to walk to school together. That was their time to talk about things they wouldn't have been able to say in the company of others. And it was always about sex. Kenny picked up a toothpick and speared a green olive and a cube of cheese. He'd never eaten olives and wanted to know if he would like them. He popped them into his mouth, slowly chewing the salty olive and hard cheese that was so different from the sharp cheddar cheese his mother used to make baked macaroni and cheese.

"Do you like it?" Frankie asked, as he picked up a small piece of marinated artichoke.

"I do. This is my first time eating olives."

Frankie smiled. "Hang out with me and my family, and after a while you'll become an unofficial Italian."

"What do you call this?" Kenny questioned, pointing to the plate with some food that was unfamiliar to him.

"Antipasto salad. We usually serve it before the main meal. It's made with chunks of Italian cold cuts, provolone cheese, green olives, pickled giardiniera, which are vegetables and pepperoncini."

"It's delicious," Kenny said, filling a small plate.

"I agree," Ray said, after he'd swallowed a mouthful of the salad. "What else are we eating for dinner?"

Frankie smiled. "Of course, there's going to be pasta with gravy and meatballs."

A slight frown appeared between Kenny's eyes. "You put gravy on pasta? Why not tomato sauce?"

Frankie's smile grew wider. "Italians call sauce gravy. Nonna starts making her sauce on Saturday afternoon, and by Sunday, she has enough for dinner and leftovers for the rest of the week."

"You have pasta every night?" Kenny had asked Frankie yet another question.

"Yes. It's like a side dish, like rice or potatoes."

"Your grandmother is like mine," Ray said. "She does most of the cooking for my family, because my mother works. I love her rice and beans, and my favorite is *pernil,* which is

Puerto Rican roast pork shoulder. But the best part is the crispy skin we call *chicharrón*. Whenever she makes it, the whole apartment smells like pork for days."

"When are you going to invite us to your house?" Frankie asked, laughing.

"I'll have to ask Mami and Papi if I can invite my friends over during the summer. She has two weeks' vacation, and she always takes one week in the summer and the other in December."

"Kenny doesn't have to ask his mom, because whenever we come over to study, she always feeds us," Frankie said. "Your mother makes the best fried chicken, macaroni and cheese, and cornbread I've ever had."

Kenny nodded, smiling. Justine Russell told him she didn't want his friends to go back and tell their parents that she wasn't hospitable enough to feed their children after they had spent hours in her home.

He'd always told her in advance that they were coming over, so she would cook enough for everyone.

"Don't forget her peach cobbler and sweet potato pies," Ray added.

"You're right, Ray," Frankie said. "You guys will get to taste my Nonna's cooking, and the only one left is Ray's grandmother's."

"*Abuela* loves to cook, so I'm sure she wouldn't mind having two more kids around the table."

Kenny stared at Ray. "Are you certain? After all, your folks have six kids."

"Two more is not a big deal. Frankie's grandmother makes a big pot of sauce, and my *abuela* makes rice in a large *caldero* that will last for days. Rice, beans, plantains, and some meat is all you need to feel full."

Kenny pointed to Ray. "Your house is next." He turned to look at Frankie. "I meant to ask you if your grandfather is still alive."

Frankie drained his glass of lemonade. "No. The mean,

old sonofabitch died seven years ago. No one, and I repeat, no one cried at his funeral. Not even Nonna. My mother refused to come here when he was alive. She allowed my father to bring us for family gatherings because she wanted her children to know the other side of their family."

Ray slowly blinked. "He was that bad?"

"May God forgive me, but I hated him," Frankie said, as he made the sign of the cross over his chest. "He was known as Sal the *Serpente*, because he was like a snake who would strike without warning. I don't know why he was so mean, especially to his four daughters. Poppa told me his father changed when his oldest daughter died from diphtheria. Then he began to beat the others because he claimed he didn't want them to grow up to become *puttane* or whores. What he did was drive them away. One joined a convent to become a nun; another got hooked on drugs and eventually overdosed. The police found her decomposing body in an abandoned building in West Harlem."

Kenny gasped. "Oh, how horrible!"

"Her death really hit Nonno hard, and my father said he wouldn't let anyone say her name in his presence. The youngest girl met a boy on Mulberry Street during the Feast of San Gennaro, and when my grandfather discovered they were meeting in secret, he threatened the boy. He didn't know the boy was the nephew and godson of an underboss in the Lucchese family."

Kenny hadn't realized he'd been holding his breath when listening to Frankie talk about his family until he felt tightness in his chest, which forced him to exhale. "What happened?" he asked, breathlessly.

Frankie let out an audible sigh. "I've only heard people whisper that Nonno had been set up, and whoever killed him wanted it to look like a robbery. His body was found along the East River Waterfront, not far from the Fulton Fish Market. He'd been stabbed in the throat and heart."

Kenny felt a chill race over his body. His mother told him

that his father had been killed in an attempted robbery. Former Army Private Kenneth Russell was left to die along a deserted street not far from the Bowery, where he worked in a beer factory. He'd lost his life for less than seven dollars in his pocket. "Was there any evidence it had been a robbery?"

Nodding, Frankie said, "His watch, wallet, and a gold St. Christopher medal he always wore around his neck were missing."

Ray leaned forward. "What do you think happened, Frankie?"

"I don't know, Ray. I suppose, like everyone else I believe, he'd messed with the wrong person."

"What happened to his daughter?" Kenny asked. "Did she end up with her boyfriend?"

"No. She met some Greek kid from Astoria, married him, and went to work in her husband's family diner."

"It sounds like mob justice to me," Ray said under his breath.

"I can't say if it was or wasn't," Frankie countered. "I just know that if he had still been alive, my mother would not have stepped foot here." He paused. "It was different with her parents, because when Poppa began dating their daughter, they welcomed him like a son."

Kenny stared out the window facing the rear of the brownstone. There was a picnic table, benches, and several more beach-type webbed chairs positioned in a corner. A small space was set aside for a garden with green stakes for growing tomatoes and peppers.

I wonder if they would have been so welcoming if her boyfriend had been Black? There was no doubt Frankie's Irish grandparents would have been just as threatening as his Italian grandfather had been. That's why I plan to stick with my own kind.

Although he didn't want to think about race, Kenny realized he'd been unable to ignore it completely, because his mother always talked about what Black people had to go through in the United States to grasp a tiny piece of the so-called American dream. Earlier that year, heavyweight boxer Cassius Clay had announced that he was changing his name to Muhammad Ali after converting to Islam. Then Malcolm X, the spokesman for the Nation of Islam who'd been suspended from the organization, announced he was forming a Black nationalist party. Kenny recalled his mother crying after hearing that an all-White jury in Jackson, Mississippi, trying Byron De La Beckwith for the murder of NAACP field secretary Medgar Evers, was unable to reach a verdict, resulting in a mistrial.

All of the ongoing talk about Kennedy's assassination, the growing anti-segregation demonstrations, and the recent news of twelve young men publicly burning their draft cards as an act of resistance to the Vietnam War, made it difficult for Kenny to focus on his schoolwork. Newspapers, magazines, and televised news constantly bombarded everyone with nothing but bad news. He was just a kid who shouldn't have to worry about wars, demonstrations, and civil unrest.

He wanted to go to school and hang out with his friends in Central Park. It was there they could be themselves as blood brothers who liked and wanted the same things. They all had professed to wanting to go to college, fall in love, marry, and have families of their own.

Kenny had decided he wanted to become a social worker, because he'd witnessed the ones who'd given his mother the assistance that she needed to raise him after losing her husband.

Ray talked constantly about going to medical school to become a doctor. Not only would he become the first one in his family to graduate college, but also the first Dr. Torres.

And it was obvious that Frankie would become an accountant, because he was a math genius.

Kenny's two friends had discussed taking the qualifying test to get into the Bronx High School of Science, while he wasn't certain which high school he would apply to. However, he had two more years in which to make that decision. And when he, Frankie, and Ray had made their blood oath to become brothers, they had also agreed to become friends for life.

They'd eaten most of the antipasto salad when they were summoned to come into the dining room for the dinner meal.

CHAPTER 11

Kenny felt overwhelmed when seated at a long table with so many people. There were sixteen, including himself, when he'd been instructed to sit on Frankie's grandmother's left. There was something about the elderly woman he liked. Perhaps it was because he didn't have a grandmother that he felt drawn to her. Nonna sat at the head of the table, with her eldest son Francis at the opposite end facing her. Kenny shared a slight smile with Frankie's youngest sister Carolina, who had inherited her mother's bright red curly hair, brown eyes, and freckles.

Everyone's gaze was on Father Morelli, waiting for the young, newly ordained priest from the local parish to begin the benediction, when a stocky man entered the dining room. There was something off-putting about him, and it wasn't because of his all-black attire, but rather the fact that he had one brown and one blue eye. A frown appeared between his strangely colored eyes when he met Kenny's.

"I spend eight years in the joint eating with niggers, and now I have to share a table with one," he spat out angrily. His outburst was followed by a chorus of gasps.

Frankie Delano stood up. "*Abbastanza*, Pasquale!"

"Enough, Frankie Delano. It will never be enough for me. You promised to take care of me, your cousin, when I went to the joint, but not once did I hear a word from you. Yet, you sit here like the fucking pope, holding court for niggers, spics, and half-wop and half-micks' kids, while your own Italian flesh and blood rotted in a jail cell for eight stinking years!"

A rush of color darkened Frank's face even more than it normally was. "You come here and disrespect my home, my mother, brother, his wife and children, and their friends, and Father Morelli, and you want me to feel sorry for you?"

"No! Pasquale shouted. "I just want you to make up for what I lost when I got locked up. My wife and kids had to go on welfare."

Giovanni D'Allesandro and Anthony Esposito rose at the same time. "Sit down, Gio. I'll handle this," the police detective said, in a soft voice that was barely audible. "Either you walk out of here now, or I'll call some of the boys at the station house and have them lock you up. And you know what that will do to your probation. You'll be violated, and you will have to serve out the rest of your sentence."

"Fuck all of yous!" Pasquale screamed. "Especially you, Frankie Delano! I will get you back if it's the last thing I do. You will pay for what you did to me." Turning on his heel, he walked out. He slammed the door so hard, the sound reverberated throughout the first floor.

Kenny, who had been holding his breath, was finally able to draw a normal one when the man Frankie's uncle called Pasquale left. Although he'd directed his anger at Frankie Delano, Kenny had also become an object of his rage, because he was Black.

Nonna placed her hand over his. "Do not worry about him. He is a little crazy in the head," she said in accented English.

Kenny smiled at the elderly woman, hoping to ease her distress when the tears filled her eyes. "It's okay, Nonna."

He'd told her it was okay when it wasn't; not when he was constantly bombarded with news about the country's racial unrest. Although Pasquale had referred to him as a nigger, Kenny understood that most of his anger was directed at Frankie's uncle, and he wondered what he had promised to do after Pasquale was sent to prison. Kenny glanced across the table and saw Frankie staring down at the tablecloth. He wasn't sure if his friend had been embarrassed by his cousin's outburst or because his mother was crying. Tears were streaming down Kathleen's face as her husband attempted to comfort her.

"I can't believe that SOB came here to ruin our Sunday family get-together," Gio mumbled under his breath.

"We must pray for him," Father Morelli said, in a quiet voice.

"Pasquale needs more than prayer, Father," Frankie Delano countered. "What he needs to learn is respect. Respect for himself and for the family. We invite everyone over the first Sunday of the month to stay connected, and this *asino* decides to show up and ruin it because he's feeling sorry for himself. He committed a crime, got caught, and was sent to prison. That should've been the end of it. But he wants to blame everyone but himself." A beat passed as he looked at everyone sitting around the table. "As of today, Pasquale Festa is no longer welcomed here. Father Morelli, will you please say the benediction?"

The tension in the dining room dissipated after the priest finished his prayer and dishes were passed around the table. Kenny filled his plate with sausage and peppers, lasagna Bolognese, linguine with garlic and oil, and a meatball. He stared at Nonna when she scooped a spoonful of something covered with melted cheese and placed it on his plate.

"It's eggplant parmigiana," she said.

"I've never eaten eggplant." Kenny had admitted not eating it, because not only did his mother not cook it, but it was a vegetable that was as foreign to him as artichokes.

"Taste it. It's very good."

Picking up his fork, he took a small portion and popped it into his mouth. It literally melted on his tongue. "Wow. That's good." He took another bite. "This is really delicious."

"You want to know how to make it?" Nonna asked.

Although he'd never had any interest in cooking because his mother cooked for him every day, his learning to cook something she'd never eaten before would definitely surprise Justine Russell.

"Yes."

Nonna patted his hand again. "Then I will teach you. Ask your mama if you can come here, and I will teach you all about Italian food."

Kenny smiled. He liked pizza, spaghetti, and meatballs, but that was the extent of his knowledge of Italian food. Accompanying Frankie to his grandmother's home had exposed him to foods he was unfamiliar with, because it was his first time eating olives, pepperoncini peppers, and marinated artichoke.

Even though he would ask his mother, Kenny knew she wouldn't approve of him going to East Harlem. At least not alone or on public transportation. "I promise to ask her."

"*Buono*, now eat up."

It wasn't until he sampled small portions of linguini with garlic and oil, asparagus with pecorino romano, baked ziti, and Nonna's spaghetti and meatballs that Kenny knew for certain he wanted to learn to cook Italian dishes. The sauce, called gravy, was different from his mother's because it wasn't as sweet. Despite the tartness, it was the garlic that made the marinara not only flavorful but delicious. It was the same with the tender meatballs seasoned with garlic and cheese. He'd found himself mimicking everyone when he tore off pieces of homemade bread to sop up the remaining sauce on the plate. His first trip across town, despite the intrusion of Pasquale Festa, was one he would remember all his life. Kenny didn't want to believe dessert would follow a meal that had left him unable to swallow another morsel of food. It was coffee with panna cotta, anise and orange biscotti, cannoli, and tiramisu. Once he sampled the affogato—espresso poured over a scoop of gelato—Kenny knew he would never eat ice cream again.

He managed to unbuckle his belt under the table and loosen it, because he felt as if he were going to burst. When he glanced over at Ray, he knew his friend was experiencing the same. Both had eaten too much.

Dinner ended when the women cleared the table and took platters and dishes into the kitchen. They'd made quick work of filling containers with leftovers and placing them in shopping bags. Kenny wasn't certain what his bag contained, but whatever it was, he knew it would be something he'd enjoy.

He met Ray's eyes and smiled when his friend showed him his bag. It was obvious the Torres family would get to sample some Italian food, too. Frankie Delano had volunteered to drive Kenny and Ray home, while Frankie would go back with his parents and sisters.

He approached them when they were prepared to leave. "Ray, I'm going to drop you off first before I drive Kenny home."

He led them outdoors to his car parked in front of the brownstone. Kenny sat on the rear seat of the car—it had seen better days, and he wondered why Frankie's uncle, who'd professed to being a businessman, drove what he thought of as a jalopy. Most businessmen, even if they weren't that successful, drove nice cars, if only to enhance their image.

Frankie Delano dropped Ray off, waited until he disappeared into his building, then executed a U-turn and drove four blocks, parked along Central Park West, and walked with Kenny to his apartment building.

Kenny stopped in front of his stoop. "Thank you for driving me home."

"I'd like to come up and ask your mother if it's okay with her if I can pick you up and take you to my mother's house for cooking lessons." He almost laughed when he saw the boy's jaw drop, his mouth gaping. "You do remember talking to her about learning to cook Italian food."

Kenny lowered his eyes. "Yes, but I didn't think she was that serious."

"My mother never says anything she doesn't mean to say."

"Okay. I live on the second floor."

Frank followed Kenny up the staircase to his apartment. The building was old, but clean. The lingering scent of disinfectant and pine lingered in the air. A business associate who had cultivated a connection with a member of the city council told him that certain neighborhoods along the West Side were slated to undergo urban renewal. And that meant residents would be forced to relocate, many into public housing.

Kenny unlocked the door and walked in. "Mom, I'm home."

Seconds later, a woman appeared, and it was Frank's turn for his jaw to drop. He suddenly felt as if he'd been punched in the gut when he stared at Kenny's mother. She looked much too young to have a teenage boy. Not only was she incredibly slender, but it was her face that held him enthralled. She was beautiful. She styled her straightened hair in a ponytail that made her look like a high school student.

She smiled and extended her hand, shattering his entrancement. "I'm Justine Russell. And thank you for seeing my son home safely."

Frank took her hand, holding it longer than necessary before releasing it, but not before he spied the gold band on her left hand. His nephew had mentioned that Kenny's father was dead and his mother a widow, and he wondered why she continued to wear a wedding ring.

"I'm Francis, and the pleasure is all mine, Mrs. Russell."

"I believe we can be less formal with each other if my son is best friends with your nephew."

"Mom, I have leftovers I'm going to put in the fridge," Kenny said, interrupting the interaction between his mother and Frankie's uncle.

"Okay, Kenny," Justine said. "I'm sorry, but I'm forgetting my manners. Can I get you something to drink?" she asked Frank.

He wanted to ask if she was kidding because he'd eaten and drank his fill, but there was something about Justine that made him want to spend time with her. Frank didn't know why he'd always found himself attracted to Black women. There had been only one time when he'd acted on it—but with disastrous results. Her parents had discovered them together, and her father had sent her miles away to keep her away from him. It had been his first and last time he'd attempted to form a relationship with a woman who wasn't Italian.

Frank did not think of what he shared with women as relationships but liaisons. They were women he saw, slept with, and then walked away until the next time. He'd told them if they wanted marriage, then he wasn't the marrying kind. Those who did want marriage rejected him, and those who didn't were resigned to share a bed and enjoy the occasional gifts he gave them for Christmas and their birthdays.

"If you don't mind, I'll have coffee," he said, smiling.

Justine smiled, bringing his gaze to linger on her lush mouth. "Please come into the kitchen and rest yourself."

Frank stared at her hips in a pair of white capri pants. Justine Russell, although slender, wasn't what he thought of as skinny. He smiled when noticing she'd tied the hem of a sleeveless white blouse at her waist, one he'd be able to span with both hands, leaving a display of skin at the small of her back. He felt a stirring in his groin, and he knew he had to sit before Justine noticed what would become an erection.

He sat down at the kitchen table and swallowed a groan. *What the hell is wrong with me? I'm not some randy teenage boy who can't control his body. And it couldn't be Kenny's mother, because it was just last week that I'd spent the entire weekend with a woman who was insatiable.*

Frank didn't know what it was about Kenny's mother that had turned him on so much, and he was curious enough to find out why. He glanced around the kitchen as she filled a coffee pot with water, filled the basket with coffee grounds, and put it on the stove to brew. Everything was immaculate, from the kitchen table to the floor. Even the windows were sparkling behind a pair of white ruffled curtains.

"You don't look old enough to have a teenage boy." He'd spoken his thoughts aloud.

Justine gave him a sidelong glance as she reached into an overhead cabinet to take down cups and saucers. "I had Kenny at eighteen. And before you ask, I did graduate high school."

Lines fanned out around Frank's eyes when he smiled. "Why do you think I would ask you that?"

Justine gave Francis a direct stare. "Because that's something I hear every time I tell folks when they ask how old I was when I became a mother."

"Did I ask you, Justine?" he questioned, saying her name for the first time.

She shook her head at the same time she lowered her eyes. "No, you didn't. Please forgive me for being presumptuous."

Frank laughed, and it came out more like a chuckle. "There's nothing to forgive."

"How do you like your coffee?"

"Black."

Justine nodded. "Black it is. I only drink black coffee when I need to stay awake."

"Do you work at night?" Frank asked.

"No. I have a day job, but I have a second one typing papers. And I do those at night after I make dinner and prepare what I need for the next day."

Pushing back his chair, Frank crossed one knee over the over. "Tell me about it."

Justine didn't know what it was, but she felt comfortable telling him about how she'd taken on a part-time job as a typist for college students and their professors. "The extra money comes in handy, because I'm able to buy things I wouldn't have if I depend on my regular paycheck."

"What did you buy with your extra money?" Frank questioned.

"A television. Now, I'm saving up for an electric typewriter. I've been typing on an old manual that has seen its better days. Oh, don't get me wrong, it has done what I need it to do to get the job done, but I would type a lot faster on an electric model."

"You really deserve a medal for what you've had to sacrifice to raise your son alone. He really impressed my mother, who wants to teach him how to cook Italian food. But that means he would have to come to her home at least once a week."

Justine shook her head. "That's not possible."

"Why not?"

"Because I don't want him going across town by himself, and Kenny knows he must keep up with schoolwork."

"What about the summer? Do you have anything planned for him during the summer recess? I could pick him up and drop him off if you don't feel comfortable with him taking public transportation."

Justine gave Francis a long, lingering stare. It was the first time she'd invited a man into her home, other than the building superintendent to make repairs, and never a White man. She had made it a practice not to get involved with any of the tenants in the building. She'd nod and smile, but that was it. If they thought her stuck up, then so be it. However, there was something about her son's friend's uncle that had put her at ease with him. If his mother wanted to teach her son to cook, then it was a skill he could possibly use in the future. Much like her typing and shorthand skills that afforded her the ability to make money off the books.

"Are you certain that won't put you out?" she asked.

"I wouldn't volunteer if it would put me out."

Justine smiled. "Okay."

Frank also smiled. "I'll tell my mother to expect him once the school term is over."

The smell of brewing coffee filled the kitchen, and Justine turned off the stove. She opened the refrigerator and took out a container of cream for herself. "I don't know what you gave me for leftovers, but I'd like to return the favor and offer you several slices of a praline-pecan sweet potato pie to take to your mother."

"Would you mind if I sample a slice here?"

Justine had baked the pie earlier that morning, because it was Kenny's favorite. She poured coffee into two cups, then cut a generous slice of pie for Francis. After adding cream to her coffee, she sat down at the table watching Francis eat.

"Damn, woman! This is delicious," he said, then clapped his hand over his mouth once he realized the curse had slipped out. "Sorry about that."

"It's okay. I've heard and said worse."

"This is the best sweet potato pie I've ever eaten."

Justine inclined her head. "Thank you. I usually make it when your nephew and Ray come to study with Kenny."

"You feed them, too?"

"Of course. There's no way you can concentrate when your belly is rumbling because you need to eat."

Frank slowly nodded. "Teenage boys can eat you out of house and home. I remember when me and my brother would come home after playing baseball or basketball and clean out the refrigerator. And forget about juice or soda. My mother would punish us because we would drink out of the bottle or container rather than pour it into a glass."

"That's so nasty," Justine said, scrunching up her nose.

"We didn't think so at the time." Frank finished eating and drank the coffee. "Thank you so much for the pie and coffee."

Pushing back her chair, Justine stood. "Don't leave yet. I'm going to pack up some pie for your mother." She cut half the pie and placed it in a glass dish with a cover, then slipped it into a brown paper bag.

He stood up and took the bag, smiling. "Thank you. I'll be in touch."

Justine smiled up at him. "Thank you for bringing my boy home safe."

Frank nodded, then turned. Justine followed him to the door. She closed and locked it behind him.

"What did you say, Mom?"

She turned to find Kenny standing several feet away. It was apparent he'd waited in his room until Frankie's uncle left. "I told him you could take cooking lessons once the school term ends."

"Yes!" he shouted at the top of his voice; then he pumped his fists.

Justine smiled. It wasn't often that she'd witnessed her son this excited. The only other time was when he discovered she had purchased a television. She'd limited his TV viewing during the week when he had school but allowed him more time on weekends and holidays.

"After you learn to cook, I'm going to expect you to cook for your mama every once in a while."

"That's for sure."

"I know you're probably full, but there's sweet potato pie if you want some."

Kenny shook his head. "I'm past full. I'm going into my room to read over a chapter in my science book. Then, I'm going to bed."

Justine watched his retreat, her chest filling with pride.

Not only was her son growing up, but he was also becoming the young man she'd wanted him to be. He was studious, polite, and obedient. She hadn't known when he'd drawn his first breath that he would make her proud to be his mother. She loved him with all of her heart and would willingly sacrifice everything, whatever it would take to raise him to adulthood.

CHAPTER 12

Ray sat on the sofa with his brothers, while his sisters occupied other chairs in the crowded living room. He could not remember the last time his father had called a family meeting, and he assumed this one was important, because when Enrique returned home from the wedding of a coworker, he told his children he needed to talk to them.

I hope Papi and Mami aren't splitting up. There are times when I hear them arguing, but they never talk loud enough for me to hear what they are saying. Ray shook his head as if to banish the thought. His parents were Catholic, and they didn't believe in divorce.

Enrique Torres stood with his back to the windows, his hands clasped tightly in front of him. He wasn't a tall man, but his ramrod-straight posture made him appear taller than he actually was. He rarely raised his voice, but when he did, his kids knew they were in trouble.

"Your mother and I have had long conversations about you kids, and we've decided that once school ends, we're sending you to my cousin's farm in Puerto Rico for the summer."

"All of us, Papi?" Delores questioned.

"Yes."

Ray felt his heart beating a double-time rhythm in his chest. "But why, Papi?"

"It's because me and your mother plan to work a lot this summer to save enough money to buy a house. Mami has been approved to work double shifts, while I found a weekend job delivering newspapers."

"Where are you buying the house?" Ray asked.

Mariana walked into the living room and sat on the arm of a chair next to her youngest daughter. "We're thinking about a nice neighborhood in the Bronx. There are some two-family homes with front and back lawns and enough room where all you boys and girls won't have to share the same bedrooms."

"When are we moving, Papi?" asked the youngest girl.

"Not for two years. It's going to take us that long to save up enough money for a down payment, closing costs, and if we have to make repairs."

Ray met his father's eyes. "Are you saying we have to spend two summers in Puerto Rico?" He was six when his parents took him and his older sister to the island to visit with relatives who owned a farm. The days seemed to fly by when he woke to the sound of a crowing rooster. Then he would scramble out of bed and go to the chicken coop to gather eggs that were still warm and bring them back to the house for breakfast. All of the food grown on the farm seemed to taste better than what he'd eaten on the mainland. His fourteen-year-old cousin would settle Ray in front of him on a horse as they rode along unpaved dusty roads where people had erected makeshift outdoor structures to roast whole pigs.

It was the last time he'd visited his island relatives, because once Mariana had another four more children in rapid succession, she claimed it was impossible to travel with so many babies, some who still were wearing diapers. Now that all of the Torres children were school age and becoming more self-sufficient, they were ready to visit the island of their ancestors. Although he was looking forward to going back to Puerto Rico, Ray knew he had to tell Kenny and Frankie that they would have to scrap their plans to spend the summer together.

"I signed up to get working papers so I could get a job this summer," Delores said, frowning.

"You'll have plenty of time to work once you finish school, but right now you're going to Puerto Rico to help look after your brothers and sisters," Enrique stated firmly.

"But that's not fair, Papi," she retorted.

"What's fair is you helping out when needed. Right now, your mother and I need everyone's cooperation, and that means doing whatever we tell you to do."

Mariana nodded. "I'm going to fly down with everyone and see that you get settled before coming back."

"What about *abuela*?" Ray asked.

His mother met his eyes. "She will stay here. Not taking care of you kids will give the break she needs for a couple of months."

"What's going to happen when we come back? Will you still be working double shifts?" Delores asked her mother.

Mariana shook her head. "No. I will go back to my regular schedule, and so will your father. It is only during the summers that we will work overtime. Hopefully by the time you are ready to graduate high school, we'll be living in our new home."

Delores huffed. "Will I have my own bedroom?"

"Yes," Enrique, confirmed. "As the oldest girl—and Ramon, as the oldest boy—you will have your own bedrooms. Juan and Carlos will share a room, and Bianca and Elena will share another."

Ray quickly counted in his head the number of bedrooms needed for the entire family. "You're going to need to find a house with five or six bedrooms because where is *abuela* going to sleep?"

Enrique smiled for the first time. "If the house has a basement, then we'll convert a portion of it into a bedroom for your grandmother. That's why we have to save enough money to find a house big enough for everyone. And that's why I want a two-family. We can rent it to another family and use that money to offset the mortgage, utilities, and repairs."

"Papi, will we have to share our house with the new people?" ten-year-old Elena asked.

"No, *mija*," Enrique said, shaking his head. "They will have their own home."

Ray looked at Delores, and they shared a smile. Both had complained to each other that nine people living in a three-bedroom apartment where no one had any privacy was a problem. He'd had to wait for everyone to go to bed to sit up in the kitchen and do homework, or study for an exam. There were times when it was past midnight before he got into bed, and once the alarm clock went off, he'd felt as if he hadn't gotten any sleep. If his parents had been arguing, it was about wanting better for their children.

"Okay, Papi. Let me know what you need me to do to help us move to a house," Ray told his father.

"The only thing you need to concern yourself with is staying in school and out of trouble. And I don't want to repeat myself when I say I don't want to find out that you were smoking, drinking, and messing around with girls. One slip-up, and I'll send you to my cousin Pedro who lives in the mountains, and he will work you like a slave."

Ray felt a rush of heat in his face, and he knew his father wasn't issuing an idle threat. Pedro owned a banana plantation and had earned the reputation of mistreating his workers for the least infraction.

"I know, Papi."

Enrique glared at him. "As long as you know, then everything is okay. It's getting late, so it's time some of you kids need to go to bed, because there's school tomorrow."

Ray sat on the sofa long after his parents and siblings left the living room. He knew his mother and father worked hard to pay rent, buy food and clothes for their children. They'd also preached relentlessly about them doing the right thing so they could stay out of trouble. And by trouble, his father meant staying away from drugs.

Ray didn't understand all that was going on in the world, because his social studies textbook hadn't caught up with what was being reported by television news journalists or in daily newspapers. The words *counterculture* and *anti-establishment* were just words that hinted of some upheaval that had nothing to do with him. He knew there was a war going on in the jungles in a country called Vietnam and that American soldiers were being sent there to fight, yet he remained unaffected because no one he knew had been drafted or sent overseas. He just wanted to finish high school, go to college, then onto medical school so he would become the first in his family to become a doctor.

He got up every morning, went to school, then came home to do homework, eat, then prepared to go to bed in the bedroom he shared with his two brothers. He went to mass with his family on Sundays and served as an altar boy every other Sunday. He also went to confession every Saturday to tell the priest what he'd done wrong and said the prayers he needed for absolution. Ray would occasionally admit to fighting with his younger brothers, but he was reluctant to tell the priest that he liked masturbating. That was a secret he would keep to himself. Even when Frankie and Ray had mentioned they engaged in the practice, Ray had lied and told them it was something he wouldn't do because it was a sin. They would laugh and call him Father Torres, because they said he was better suited for the priesthood than medicine.

Ray waited until he knew his younger brothers would be asleep in their bunk beds before going into the bedroom and readying himself for bed. He lay in the darkened room, his mind filled with memories of his first visit to the Caribbean island. He recalled his mother telling him she was taking him and Delores to Puerto Rico because she'd wanted them to experience their ancestral roots. Ray had believed she was talking about a plant until she opened an old family bible to a page listing the names, births, and deaths of people in her family going back four generations. It wasn't until he was much older that Ray realized he'd come from a long line of people who had survived slavery, being targeted for death or imprisonment from political opponents; although many of his relatives still lived in Puerto Rico, they were American citizens.

Inasmuch as he wanted to spend the summer on a tropical island, Ray was disappointed about the plans he, Kenny, and Frankie had made for themselves. They'd made a promise to see one science fiction, horror, western, and the latest James Bond movie that summer. They'd also talked about going to Times Square, but then dismissed the idea, because they knew the consequences if their parents found out they were going there to see if they could get into some of the peep shows.

He finally fell asleep, and when he saw Kenny and Frankie the next day, he would have to tell them of the plans his parents had made for their family.

"Are you really going to spend July and August in Puerto Rico?" Frankie asked Ray, as he and Kenny shared a table in the school's cafeteria during lunch.

"Yeah. We're leaving the first week in July and coming back the last week in August."

"Did you guys do something for your parents to punish you by sending y'all away?" Kenny questioned.

Ray shook his head and met Kenny's eyes. "No. Why would you say that?"

"Because my mother said when she was growing up, if Black kids acted up, then their parents would send them down South as punishment."

"We're not being punished," Ray told Kenny. He explained why the Torres kids had to stay on the island for the next two summers. He'd felt a measure of pride when his best friends appeared surprised that his parents were planning to buy a house. "Once we move in, you guys can come over whenever you want."

Frankie combed his fingers through his thick black hair. "Even if you weren't going away for the summer, we still wouldn't be able to do all of the things we planned, because I told my father that I'm willing to work in the store with him this summer."

Kenny set down his milk container. "What did he say?"

"I think I shocked him, because he didn't say anything. It was my mother who thanked me for helping him. My dad is a proud man who would never ask anyone for help, and that includes asking Nonna if we could move into one of the apartments in her brownstone so he could have more space for his family. But my mother refused to live under the same roof with a man who controlled the very lives of those who went along with rejecting her because she's Irish."

Ray wiped his hands on a paper napkin. "If my mother was in your father's position, she would have moved her family in right after her husband's father was in the ground."

"But the difference," Kenny said, in defense of Frank's father, "is your grandfather wouldn't have rejected your father's choice of a wife because she's Puerto Rican. Frankie's mother has every right to feel the way she does after being alienated because of who she is. It's the same with Black people. Folks judge us by the color of our skin and not because we're either good or bad."

A beat passed before Frankie said to Kenny, "This is the first time I've heard you talk about race."

Kenny closed his eyes for several seconds. "I don't talk about it much, because it upsets me with all that is going on in this country about Black people wanting to be accepted as equals. My mother talks about us being here for hundreds of years, and we still don't have the same rights as other people. Folks who came here for a better life forget that they were discriminated against in their country but do the same to my people."

"You sound like a militant," Frankie said, accusingly.

"I'm not militant," Kenny countered. "I just want what I'm entitled to as an American. It hasn't been that long since people didn't want to hire immigrants. They'd put up 'No Irish Need Apply' signs when it came to employment. And your father's people, Frankie, were and are still called dagos and wops. And forget about Spanish-speaking people being called spics. All of us were victims of that yesterday when your cousin Pasquale lost his temper."

"My cousin is an asshole," Frankie spat out.

"Asshole or not," Kenny continued, "he meant what he said. And it was enough to make your mother cry."

"You're right," Frankie agreed. "We don't have to go through that again, because he's been banished from the family."

Kenny smiled. "Talking about family. Once I begin cooking lessons with your grandmother, will I become an unofficial member of your family?"

Frankie stared at Kenny with wide blue eyes. "You're really going to let Nonna teach you how to cook Italian food?"

"Yup. My mother said it's okay because your uncle will pick me up and bring me back home."

"My uncle is part owner of a restaurant on Second Avenue, so if you're really good, maybe you can work there on weekends—that is, if they need extra help."

Smiling and nodding, Kenny said, "That's something to think about." If his mother made extra money typing, then he could do the same working in a restaurant's kitchen. And if he were able to master certain dishes, it was something he could do on weekends as a high school student as long as it didn't interfere with his grades. Not only did he need the grade average, but also had to score high enough on the SAT to get into a public college as a matriculated student. If he were to apply to private colleges, then he would have to rely on scholarships to cover tuition. Paying for room, board, and books would have to come from either savings or his having to work part-time while at the same time attending classes.

"Well, it looks as if we won't be able to hang out together during the summer over the next two years, and by that time, we'll be ready for high school," Ray said after a comfortable silence.

"Once we're in high school, we can take the first Saturday in each month for breakfast at our favorite coffee shop on Broadway," Frankie volunteered.

"I like the sound of that," Kenny said. He placed his hand palm down on the table. "That's a promise."

Ray placed his hand over Kenny's. "That's a promise."

Frankie did the same when he covered both hands. "Me, too."

The bell rang, signaling it was the end of the lunch period, and the three got up to empty their trays before leaving the cafeteria for their next class.

CHAPTER 13

It was Saturday, and Justine wanted to take advantage of having the apartment to herself for most of the day. Kenny had gone to the library to work on a book report before joining up with a group of his classmates to see *The Pink Panther.* It was a little after noon when Kenny rushed back to leave his books, then took off again, leaving Justine time to strip and remake beds, clean the bathroom, mop the kitchen, and sweep and dust floors. She seasoned a roasting chicken, made up a casserole dish with macaroni and cheese from the night before, and put the chicken in the oven on the lowest temperature to slowly cook over several hours.

Justine decided to forgo eating lunch, because she wanted to see how much she could accomplish typing the dissertation for an African exchange student who was pursuing his doctorate at Columbia University. She had become totally engrossed in his research on the rise and fall of ancient African civilizations.

Although she hadn't enrolled in college, Justine felt as if she had whenever she typed a paper for a student or professor. The knowledge and information she gleaned from what she'd typed had proven to be invaluable to her even before becoming a college student. Kenny was only a month away from completing the seventh grade, and in another five years, it would be his high school graduation. Her son had teased her saying they both would become college freshmen at the same time. Kenny would attend during the day, while Justine planned to enroll for night classes. She would continue to work at the hospital until she earned her degree. Then, her focus would be securing a teaching position.

She'd just removed the cover from the typewriter when the telephone rang. Whenever the phone rang, Kenny answered it, because the calls were from friends. The ones for her were from her typing clients. Pushing back her chair, she walked out of the room she had set up as an office and into the living room to answer the phone before it rang a third time.

"Russell residence."

"Good afternoon, Justine. Why so formal?"

A slight frown creased her forehead once she recognized the caller's voice, wondering why he was calling her when she hadn't exchanged more than a dozen words with the man whenever she encountered the hospital orderly. She didn't want to believe he'd actually asked the operator for her number.

"Norman?"

"So, you know who I am," came his reply.

"Why are you calling my home?"

There came a pause before he said, "I just wanted to tell you that I liked what you were wearing yesterday. I didn't realize you had such great legs."

"Goodbye." Justine hung up, unable to believe the man was flirting with her over the telephone. Even if she'd found the man attractive, which she didn't, she still wouldn't have entertained his overtures. Most of the hospital staff members were aware that she was a widow who had refused to take off her wedding ring. That had become a signal for the single men to keep their distance, but it was apparent Norman Robinson hadn't been one of them.

Seconds later, the phone rang again. When she picked up the receiver, she wasn't given the opportunity to announce herself when she heard Norman's voice again. This time when she disconnected the call, she left the receiver off the hook.

"Idiot," Justine said under her breath as she went into the spare bedroom to begin typing.

She'd lost track of time when the chiming of the doorbell shattered her concentration. Smothering a groan, she got up to see who was ringing her bell. If it wasn't the telephone, then it was the doorbell. It was as if disruptions had conspired against her because she didn't have Kenny to interrupt her when she least expected.

She peered through the security eye on the door, and the person looking back at her was someone she hadn't expected to see for another month. Justine opened the door and forced a smile. "I wasn't expecting to see you for a while."

"I would've called to tell you I was coming over, but I kept getting a busy signal."

She opened the door wider. "That's because I didn't want to talk to someone who was annoying me. Please come in, Francis."

The man she called Francis looked like the consummate businessman in a navy-blue pin-striped suit, white shirt, dark blue tie, and highly polished black wing tips. She waited until he walked in to close the door, then led him into the living room, where she hung up the phone.

Frankie Delano removed his sunglasses, his gaze taking in everything about the woman who unknowingly had occupied his thoughts since meeting her for the first time a week ago. He tried recalling everything about her and failed. A few strands had escaped the loose bun she'd secured on the top of her head, and he tried imagining what her hair would look like spread over his pillow after he made love to her.

He shook his head, banishing his traitorous thoughts when she continued to stare at him with a pair of large dark eyes. "I came to bring back the dish you gave me with the pie." He handed her a small shopping bag.

"You didn't have to come all this way to bring it back. You could've waited until it was time to pick Kenny up for his cooking lesson."

Frank smiled. "It's not only the dish, but I also wanted to bring you something else."

"What are you talking about?" Justine asked.

"Wait here, and I'll be back. Don't lock the door. I have to get something from my car."

It took Frank less than five minutes to remove a box from the trunk of his car parked outside the apartment building and carry it up two flights to the Russell apartment. When he'd made the purchase, he wasn't certain if Justine would accept his gift, but hopefully he thought she would. And it wasn't as if she didn't need it.

He knew he'd shocked Justine when he walked in, closed and locked the door behind him, and set the box on the floor. Frank held up a hand when she opened her mouth. "Please, Justine, don't tell me you don't want it."

Justine placed a hand over her mouth at the same time that tears filled her eyes. "I . . . I," she stuttered, blinking back tears. "Why, Francis?" she finally asked when recovering her voice.

"Why, Justine? Didn't you say you could type a lot faster if you had an electric typewriter?"

"Yes, but not because I wanted you to buy one for me. Let me know how much you paid for it, and I'll give you the money."

Frank met the large eyes shimmering with unshed tears. "I don't want your money. Think of it as a gift."

"A gift for what?"

A hint of a smile lifted a corner of his mouth. "For your birthday. Didn't you just have a birthday in March?"

Justine nodded. "Yes, but how do you know that?"

"My nephew and your son are good friends, so it made it a lot easier for me to find out."

"Do you buy gifts for all the mothers of your nephew's friends?"

Frank slowly shook his head. "No. Just the special ones."

Justine sat on the sofa; her eyes were fixed on Francis as he sat on a matching chair. She was beginning to feel uncomfortable with the man who'd not only come to her home unannounced, but with a gift she hadn't asked for but sorely needed. Then, there was her limited interaction with men. She hadn't had a boyfriend in high school, and after what she'd experienced with Dennis Boone, she wanted nothing to do with the opposite sex, other than her son. She just wanted to raise Kenny to become a productive, independent adult.

"What makes me special, Francis?"

He crossed one trousered leg over the opposite knee and gave her a direct stare. "You were widowed at a very young age, yet you have decided to raise your son on your own."

"That's a choice I wanted to make."

"Why?"

"Because once he was born, I made a vow to myself that it would be just he and I."

"You never thought that your son would need a man in his life?"

"Do you think Kenny having a man in his life would make him any different than he is now? He's a good student, an obedient son, and I trust him not to get into trouble," she added, answering her own question.

"You have beaten the odds, Justine, because even kids who have both parents in the home can end up in trouble. I apologize if you think I was saying that you were unable to raise your son on your own. You really deserve a medal, because Kenny is a fine young man who has made quite an impression on my mother."

"What about you, Francis? Has my son also impressed you?"

Frank smiled. "Yes. Your son and his mother."

What Justine had suspected, yet she hadn't wanted to acknowledge, was that Francis D'Allesandro was interested in her. If certain circumstances in her life hadn't occurred, she would have been flattered by his attention. There were a few men who'd flirted with her even though she was wearing a wedding band. It was different with Francis, because he was aware that she wasn't married.

"What exactly do you want me to give you, Francis?"

He slowly blinked. "What makes you think I want you to give me anything?"

Justine sighed and shook her head. "Maybe that came out all wrong."

Frank laced his fingers together, bringing the forefinger of his left hand to his mouth. "My giving you the typewriter isn't a tit for tat. And if I'm going to ask you for anything, it would be for us to become friends. I'm going to give you my business and home telephone numbers. I want you to call me if you need my help with anything."

Justine's eyebrows shot up. "That's it?"

"Yes, Justine. That's it. What . . ." His words trailed off when her telephone rang.

"Excuse me, but I need to answer the phone." Justine scooted over on the sofa and picked up the phone off an end table. "Russell residence." She went still when she heard Norman's voice again. "Can't you take a hint that I don't want to talk to you? And I want you to stop calling me." She started to hang up but then found her wrist trapped between Francis's fingers.

"Give me the phone," he whispered.

Justine complied and released the receiver.

"Is there something wrong with your hearing?" he asked

Norman. "She told you to stop calling her. If you don't, then maybe I'll have to convince you that she means what she says. Yes, man, I'm threatening you. Stop or you'll find yourself in more trouble than you can get out of. Now fuck off!" He slammed down the receiver. "Who the hell is this creep who believes he has the right to annoy a woman who wants nothing to do with him?"

"Norman Robinson, an orderly, and we work at the same hospital."

"Has he ever bothered you at work?"

Justine shook her head. "Never. He will stop by my office and wave, but nothing beyond that."

"If he bothers you again, then let me know. Maybe he needs a face-to-face to convince him I mean business."

Justine couldn't ignore the rush of panic making it impossible for her to draw a normal breath. Francis's voice was low, his words lethal. "Because he's never made a pass at me at work, I don't think he's going to call me again." What she didn't tell Francis was that she prayed Norman wouldn't call her again, because she didn't intend to spend her life monitoring annoying telephone calls.

She'd allowed two women to manipulate her in the past, but that was when she was a frightened seventeen-year-old girl. Fast-forward almost twelve years, and now that she was thirty, she had no intention of repeating that phase of her life. It had been the reason why she didn't want to marry. She didn't want a man telling her what she could or could not do. There were occasions when she realized Kenny did need a male figure in his life, if only to teach him how to treat a woman. She'd felt guilty depriving him of a father whenever she saw him staring at other kids with their fathers. However, the guilt was short-lived whenever she recalled how and why she'd become a mother. Justine had tried to erase the memory of being blackmailed and humiliated when she surrendered her will to avoid going to jail, while she'd been forced to give up her virginity to a man she didn't love. Justine didn't blame Dennis Boone for getting her pregnant, but his manipulative wife and mother-in-law.

There had been a time when she'd become physically ill when she saw a photograph of Dennis and Precious Boone with their young son Michael in the *Amsterdam News*. It had taken her a while to stop staring at the boy she carried beneath her heart, whom she would never be able to claim as her own. However, her twins had compromised. Michael resembled his father, and Kenneth, his mother.

Reaching for Francis's hand, she gave it a gentle squeeze. "Thank you for running interference for me."

He brought her hand to his mouth and kissed her fingers. "There's no need to thank me." He released her hand and took off his suit jacket. "I think it's time we get your typewriter unpacked and set up."

"After that's done, what do I have to do to convince you to stay for dinner?"

Frank took a step, bringing them within inches of each other. "Call me Frank instead of Francis."

Now Justine was confused. "But you introduced yourself as Francis."

He angled his head. "That's because I was trying to be formal. Only my mother calls me Francis."

"Formal is boring," Justine countered, smiling. "I put a chicken in the oven before you arrived, so it should almost be ready in about a half hour. I've already made the mac and cheese that will also go in the oven."

Frank unbuttoned the cuffs to his shirt and rolled them over his wrists. "Do you cook like this every day?"

"During the winter months, I cook enough to last for at least three or four days, and when I come home, I just have to reheat dishes. It's different during the spring and summer, because having the oven on for so many hours heats up the entire apartment."

"I meant to tell you that your sweet potato pie was delicious. I thank you, and my mother thanks you."

"The next time I bake pies, I'll make certain to make one for you."

"Be careful, Justine."

"Of what?"

"Spoiling me. Then, you won't be able to get rid of me."

She smiled. "We'll cross that bridge when we come to it."

Justine didn't want to think of interacting with Francis other than his picking up Kenny and dropping him back home. She appreciated him buying the typewriter and interceding between her and Norman. He wanted friendship, and that's what she would offer and nothing beyond that. And the nothing wasn't about his race. It was about his gender. She didn't trust men, and she could not afford to become involved with one until Kenny went off to college.

CHAPTER 14

"How many words do you type a minute?" Frank asked Justine as he stood behind her, watching her fingers fly over the keys in a motion almost too quick for his eyes to follow as words filled the blank sheet of paper.

The space she had set up as her office also doubled as a sewing room. A sewing machine sat on a corner table, and several baskets filled with fabric were lined up against one wall. Reams of paper, a tape recorder, steno pads, and a cup with different-colored pencils were neatly stacked on the top of a two-drawer file cabinet. He glanced over at the books packed tightly onto shelves in several bookcases. Lacy curtains and the windowsill lined with plants had added a feminine touch to the room.

Justine's hands stilled. "The last time I was tested, it was over seventy-five."

"How long ago was that?"

She glanced up over her shoulder at him. "It was when I was in secretarial school. I enrolled after graduating high school."

Frank hunkered down next to the desk, his head level with

Justine's. "Had you planned on becoming a secretary?" She smiled and shook her head, and he noticed an elusive dimple in her left cheek.

"No. I'd planned to go to college to become a teacher."

"What happened to make you change your plans?" he asked softly, unable to stop staring at her.

"I wanted to start a family after graduating college, but fate intervened when I lost my husband two months after we were married, and then I discovered I was pregnant with his child."

Frank closed his eyes for several seconds as he'd tried imagining the trauma Justine had had to go through knowing she would have to raise her child alone. "How did he die?"

Justine lowered her eyes. "He was shot during an attempted robbery. He'd spent a year in the Korean War without being wounded only to come home and have someone shoot him in the head for seven dollars." She paused and met Frank's eyes. "That's all his life was worth—seven stinking dollars."

Frank placed his hand over hers and gave her fingers a gentle squeeze. "Seven million wouldn't be enough for a human life."

Sighing, she forced a smile. "Enough talk about death and dying. I did promise to feed you, so let's go into the kitchen."

Justine could not believe she felt as comfortable as she did with Francis D'Allesandro as he sat across the table in her kitchen sharing an early dinner. He was so easy to talk to that she felt as if she'd known him for years, rather than a few hours.

"Why haven't you remarried?" he asked her after swallowing a mouthful of macaroni and cheese.

She stared at him over the rim of her iced tea glass. "I didn't want some man believing he was doing me a favor by marrying me and that he felt he could discipline my son where it would become abusive. I've never had to hit Kenny, but that's

not to say I don't punish him when he does something wrong."
Justine took a sip of the tea. "You know all about me, but I
know nothing about you."

Frank lifted sandy-brown eyebrows. "I'm thirty-seven, single, and I don't have any kids."

"Were you ever married?"

He shook his head. "No."

"So, you are content being a bachelor?" Justine teased.

"I like being a bachelor," Frank countered.

"Is it because you don't want the responsibility of being a
husband and father?"

Placing his fork beside his plate, Frank wiped his mouth
with a napkin. "It has nothing to do with not wanting to be
responsible. It's because I haven't found a woman I want to
share and spend my life with." He paused. "There was someone many years ago, but her father didn't want her to have
anything to do with me." He held up a hand. "And before
you ask, we were teenagers, so her family packed up her
things and sent her down to Georgia to live with relatives."

Leaning back in her chair, Justine gave him a long, penetrating stare. In that instant, it dawned on her why he'd
bought the typewriter, and why he was sitting at her table.
"She was a Black girl?"

He nodded.

"You like Black women."

Frank gave Justine a look that made men who knew him
fear for their lives, but it was lost on her. "Do you expect me
to deny it?"

"No, Frank. I don't. You can't help what you like."

He slowly blinked. "And what about you, Justine? What
men are you attracted to?"

"Black men, but that doesn't translate into me being a
racist. I'm troubled about what's going on in our country
when it comes to race. I keep asking myself why my people
are begging for the same rights given to them by the Constitution that all citizens have by virtue of their birthright. We

always find ourselves at the bottom of the ladder whenever other groups come here for freedom or a better way of life."

"Black people aren't the only ones who have faced discrimination, Justine. My people have been called wop and goombah more times than I can count. And then there are certain neighborhoods where we aren't allowed to live."

"As they say, Frank, you are preaching to the choir. It's the same with Black folks, and that's why people congregate in ghettos, so they can feel comfortable living with others who not only look like them but share a similar culture. Black people have fought and died in wars even before this country became the United States, and yet when people see someone who looks like Kenny's father, they tell him he can't live where he wants or he can't sit at a lunch counter with White folks, even though he risked his life to fight in Korea to stop the spread of Communism. Where is the justice, Francis?"

Frank noticed her eyes filling with tears, and something wouldn't allow him to get up and comfort her, because he knew instinctively, she would resent it. He'd heard it said over and over to stay away from talking about religion and politics, while they'd ventured into the dangerous waters of the latter.

"I'm not going to apologize for being attracted to Black women, but hopefully that won't encroach on our friendship." A hint of a smile touched the corners of Justine's mouth, one he wanted to kiss just once to assuage his curiosity whether it would be as soft as it looked.

"You don't have to apologize. If my son and your nephew can be friends, then it shouldn't be any different with us."

Frank exhaled an inaudible sigh of relief. It had been more than twenty years since he'd had his heart broken when the girl with whom he had fallen in love was sent into exile because her family didn't want her involved with an Italian boy.

"I'm glad you said that."

"By the way, were you and your girl dating openly?" Justine asked.

"No. We shared a few classes in high school, but we managed to get together for a couple of after-school clubs. It was when my best friend saw us together, he decided to tell my father, and then all hell broke loose. Word got back to her parents, and that's when they decided to send her away. I'm certain my father would've attempted to beat me like he did my sisters, but by that time, I was a lot taller, and my body was filling out, so I was ready to retaliate if he raised his hand. Once he found out she was no longer in the school, he let it go. I waited several days after graduating to teach my friend a lesson about opening his mouth."

"What did you do?"

"Just say I cured him of gossiping."

"What did you do to him, Frank?" Justine repeated.

"I punched him in the mouth."

What he didn't want to tell her was that he'd beat the living shit out of him; he'd broken his nose and knocked out a few teeth. It had been his first street fight, and it had left him feeling invincible. The word went out in the neighborhood not to mess with Frankie Delano, because he was as vicious as an attack dog.

"If he hadn't said anything about you and your girlfriend, would that have changed anything?"

Frank nodded. "We'd made plans to go to Canada after graduating. Once in Montreal, we'd get married and start a family, because we both knew it wouldn't be easy living here in the States as an interracial couple."

Justine slowly shook her head. "I'm sorry it didn't work out for you and your girlfriend."

A wry smile twisted Frank's mouth. "Some things are just not meant to be. Like you losing your husband before he could celebrate becoming a father."

Justine didn't know why, but at that moment, she felt like a hypocrite and that she was going to be punished for being so deceitful. She'd lied to Pamela Daniels, and now she was lying to Francis D'Allesandro, two people who didn't deserve her insincerity. Pamela, who'd been there for her before and after she'd had her son, and now Frank, who'd gifted her a typewriter that would make it a lot easier for her to type papers for those paying her for her skills.

Then there was her son, who didn't know he had a twin brother, and who believed his father had become a victim of a crime before his birth. Justine wondered how much longer she would have to carry the burden of lies and guilt before it all became too much for her to continue where she would be forced to reveal the truth.

She hadn't felt the guilt with Pamela, because she knew their friendship had a time limit; however, it was different with Francis. Justine couldn't just pick up and move so she could keep her secret, because she'd have to come up with another reason or excuse why she couldn't continue to live where she was. Local officials were talking about an urban renewal project that would raze four blocks to put up co-op apartment developments, and her tenement building was part of the projected plans. She was barely able to pay her rent and knew there was no way she could save enough money to purchase an apartment, even one as small as a studio unit. The other alternative was to move into public housing, something Justine didn't want. And if she was forced to move, then she hoped it would be after Kenny completed the ninth grade. Then he could go to a high school where he could make new friends.

"I've gotten used to it being just me and Kenny," she said after a lengthy pause.

"Are you saying you're never lonely?" Frank asked, his blue eyes boring into her.

"Lonely how?" Justine didn't know why she continued answering his query with a question. "Are you talking about male companionship?"

Frank nodded.

"I don't miss what I don't have. It's been more than a decade since I shared a bed with a man."

"Don't you have urges?"

This was a question Justine didn't how to answer. She'd slept with Dennis Boone twice, and at no time had she felt a modicum of passion when he'd had sex with her. However, there were occasions when her body betrayed her, and it was several days before she saw her menses. It was when her breasts were more sensitive, and she was unable to ignore the pulsing between her legs that made her bite her lip to keep from moaning.

"Yes, Frank. I have urges."

"But you don't do anything about them." His question was a statement.

"No."

"Why not?"

"I can't."

"Why can't you?"

"Because I promised myself I wouldn't get involved with a man until Kenny goes to college."

"But that's another five years."

Justine almost laughed when she saw an expression of shock sweep over Frank's features. There was nothing remarkable about his face, and his appearance would have been nondescript if not for his eyes. They were an odd shade of blue. They weren't sky blue, or sapphire, but what she thought of as a medium blue mixed with a small amount of green. She'd purchased fabric with the same color labeled *cornflower*.

"Almost thirteen down and five to go," she said jokingly, and laughed. Frank's laughter joined hers, and both were unaware when the front door opened before they realized they were not alone.

"Mom?"

"Kenny, I didn't hear you come in." Justine saw her son staring at Frank, who stood up.

"Hello, Mr. Dee."

Frank nodded. "Kenny."

"Mr. D'Allesandro came to bring me a—"

"That's okay, Mom," Kenny said, interrupting her. "You don't have to explain why he's here. Frankie told me his uncle likes Black women. So, it's all right with me if he wants to date you."

Justine stared at Kenny as if he were a stranger. She had no idea he'd known of his friend's uncle's proclivity for Black women. "We're still eating, so do you want me to fix you a plate?" she offered, after finding her voice.

"No thanks. After the movie, we stopped and ate pizza. I'm going to change my clothes, then watch television. It's nice seeing you again, Mr. Dee."

Frank was grinning like a Cheshire cat when he said, "Same here, Kenny."

Justine retook her seat. "Sit down, Francis, and stop gloating."

He sat, his smile still in place. "Oh, it's back to Francis? Does it bother you if the man of the house gave me permission to date his mother?"

"Kenny is not the man of this house."

Suddenly his face went grim. "Kenny is physically a man, isn't he?" Justine nodded. "I know he's not going to be considered an adult until he's eighteen, but I believe he's mature enough to know what he would like for his mother."

"And what is that?"

"He doesn't want to see you alone."

Justine replayed what Frank had just told her. It was obvious Kenny and his friends traded secrets, and she wondered if he was worried that she hadn't remarried or that she didn't have a boyfriend.

"I'm not alone. I have my son."

"Why are you being so stubborn, Justine? Can't you spare a few hours to go out to dinner or take in a movie every once in a while?"

She met his eyes. "With you?"

His expression softened. "Yes. Why not with me."

"Won't it bother your friends for you to be seen with me?" Frank counted slowly to ten so he wouldn't let loose with a stream of curses in English and Italian that would ruin his chances of seeing Justine again. He gave her a lethal stare. "No. My friends know better than to say anything about who I see and if I were to find out about it."

"What are you going to do, Francis? Punch them in the mouth?"

"No, beautiful. I wouldn't punch them." He knew Justine was ambivalent about going out with him when she chewed her lower lip. "I'll understand if you're not ready. And if you decide you don't want to go out with me, then no hard feelings."

"Will we still be friends?" she asked.

"Of course."

"I'm not ready to say no but are you willing to wait to the beginning of summer. By that time, I won't have many typing projects unless someone is taking summer classes."

Frank wanted to tell Justine that he'd waited more than twenty years, and waiting another two months was like the blink of an eye. "Of course I don't mind waiting." He picked up his fork to finish eating the roasted chicken that was so tender, he didn't need a knife to cut it.

"One of these days I'm going to return the favor and cook for you."

"You cook?"

"Of course. My mother taught all of her children to cook."

"What do you make?" Justine asked, before she took a bite of chicken.

"Everything. The only thing I don't attempt is her marinara sauce, because it takes too long. But I do know how to make it." Although he realistically knew what he'd hoped to share with Justine Russell would not lead to marriage, he was willing to accept whatever she offered.

"I'm really looking forward to that."

"If you want, I can bring all the ingredients here and cook for you, if you're still not ready to come to my apartment."

Justine laughed softly. "You are really determined that we spend time together."

Frank placed a large hand over his heart. "Guilty as charged."

"Okay, Francis. If you're free, then you can come by next Saturday. Just call to let me know you're on your way."

She was back to calling him Francis, and he wasn't going to correct her. She could call him whatever she wanted, as long as he could spend time with her. Why Justine Russell and not some other woman? Frank didn't know, nor did he care. He knew if his father had been alive, it would've set off another family war, and this time Sal the *Serpente* would lose. He was a thirty-seven-year-old man, not a sixteen-year-old boy, and now the head of his family.

"What do you think you're doing?" Justine asked when Frank stood and began clearing the table.

"I'm helping you with the dishes before I leave."

"No," she said, taking the plate from him. "You go and tell Kenny you're leaving and let me clean up *my* kitchen."

Frank towered over her, making Justine aware that his height eclipsed her by at least six inches. "Are you sure?" he questioned, staring down at her under lowered lids.

"Very sure."

Ducking his head, he kissed her cheek, then rolled down his shirt cuffs and buttoned them. "Thank you for dinner. It was delicious."

Justine felt as if she'd been holding her breath the instant she opened the door to find Francis D'Allesandro standing there. And now she could exhale. She had to ask herself what there was about him that had her agreeing to share a tiny portion of her life with him. She wasn't looking for a husband or lover, and definitely not a stepfather for her son.

Kenny had a father—a man he didn't know, one who hadn't known he'd fathered twin boys.

However, Justine had to admit she'd felt comfortable telling Francis about her sexual urges. And it was not to imply she needed him to assuage them. It had taken her a while to acknowledge she was a normal woman who had begun to recognize her own physical needs.

There were so many things she missed when she'd moved from the Bronx to Mount Vernon. She hadn't had a boyfriend; she'd never been kissed; she didn't attend a senior prom; and now, at thirty, there was the possibility that she would have her first date with a man who didn't share her race.

Justine hadn't lied to him about not being a racist, because it was her own people who'd altered her destiny. There would come a time when Precious Boone would pay for her deceit and blackmail once Justine exposed her as being a fraud.

She would wait until Kenny was old enough to deal with the circumstances surrounding his birth, and why his mother had to do what she did to protect him from the woman who'd conspired to have a young girl sleep with her husband, have his baby, then claim it as her own.

CHAPTER 15

Justine found Kenny sprawled on the living room sofa, watching television. Staring at him made her aware that he was growing up right in front of her eyes. He'd grown several inches since the beginning of the year, his voice was deeper, and his body was filling out. When Francis had asked if Kenny was physically a man, she had acknowledged he was, because several months ago, when she'd stripped the sheets from his bed, she saw stains she knew was semen.

She waited a few weeks before approaching him with what she'd discovered, and Justine was more embarrassed talking about it than her son. He told her he'd read about puberty and what he had to expect and that even at twelve, if he had sex with a girl, there was the possibility that he could get her pregnant. He wasn't ready to become a father, because there were a lot of things he wanted to accomplish before assuming that role.

Kenny got up, turned off the television, then returned to the sofa. "I know you want to talk to me about Mr. Dee."

Justine met a pair of eyes that were so much like her own. "Yes, I do."

Kenny lowered his eyes as he stared at his clasped hands. "I'm sorry if you felt I was out of line for telling him he could date you."

Reaching over, Justine covered his hands with her own. "I don't ever want you to apologize for saying what you feel, because it's coming from your heart. Now, tell me why you want me to go out with Mr. Dee?"

"First of all, I like him."

"And not because you know that he likes Black women?"

Kenny bit his lip. "That, too. But Mom, it's more than that." He told Justine about the incident at the D'Allesandro home when the ex-convict cousin had disrupted Sunday dinner and Francis's reaction to his cousin's racist tirade.

"He banished his cousin from his family because of what he'd said about you and Ray?" she asked.

"Yup," Kenny said. "And don't forget that Frankie is half Irish. If Mr. Dee was willing to stand up to his cousin for me, then that makes him okay in my book."

Justine gave him a sidelong glance. "Okay enough for him to take your mother out?"

"You never go out, Mom. You go to work, then come home to cook, clean, and type. When was the last time you went to the movies? Or out to a restaurant to eat?"

She wanted to tell her son she couldn't remember. She'd gone to the movies when she was a girl living with her mother in the Bronx, and it was so long ago she could hardly remember which ones they were. And forget about eating in a restaurant. Takeout joints weren't restaurants with tablecloths and a waitstaff.

Typing had opened doors for Justine she knew she never would've been permitted to enter without enrolling in college. Not only was she exposed to disciplines she would eventually take as a college student, but also to lifestyles granted to a select few when she typed a manuscript for an aspiring writer who'd grown up on Long Island's Gold Coast. His fictional novel had pulled back the curtain he'd created about a young immigrant man who had fallen in love with a girl from a wealthy family and was forced to learn how to navigate a new world where social etiquette had become a priority for acceptance.

She had lived vicariously through the protagonist when he was forced to learn the protocol of which fork to use at a formal dinner, or when to wear a white or black tie. Typing for others had offered her an education she didn't have to pay for but paid her. Precious Boone may have altered the course of her life, but Justine had to thank her and her mother for providing her with the opportunity to attend secretarial school to develop skills that afforded her the opportunity to earn extra money.

"It's been a while, Kenny," Justine admitted.

"That's why you should let Mr. Dee take you out."

"I'm thinking about it."

"What is there to think about, Mom?"

She gave him a look that said he'd crossed the line in challenging her. "That's enough, Kenny."

Kenny unclasped his hands and sat up straighter. "Why do you always shut me down when you don't want to hear the truth? You know you spend too much time alone, and what's going to happen when I go to college? Will you still be here in this apartment growing old and alone?"

Justine's hand curled into tight fists to keep from slapping her son. How dare he talk to her about her life, when she had sacrificed everything to raise him—alone. She'd lied and continued to do so about his existence and a world she created where she could continue living a lie that had become so real she didn't have to think of what to say.

"What you don't know is that I've had to go through a lot of shit to get you to where you are today." Justine knew she'd shocked her son, because she rarely cursed in his presence. "So, don't you sit here and tell me what I should and should not do when it comes to *my* life when I'm responsible for you and not the other way around. If I decide to go out with your Mr. Dee, then it will be my decision, not because you want it for whatever your reason is. And if I decide not to see him, then that's because I have my personal reasons for keeping him at a distance."

"Is it because he's White, because you're always talking about what White folks are doing to our people?" Kenny continued, refusing to back down.

Suddenly it hit Justine that Kenny was right, because most of her conversations with him were a recap of the nightly news with reporters talking about the Vietnam War or the Civil Rights Movement, unaware that as a teenage boy, he shouldn't be bombarded with the horrors going on in the world when his focus should be going to school and hanging out with friends, regardless of their race or religion.

She'd made a grievous mistake when exposing her teenage son to events better left for adults. Perhaps if she hadn't moved from Harlem, then Kenny would have been exposed to the demonstrations boycotting F.W. Woolworth because of their White-only lunch counters in Southern cities. Justine was raising Kenny in a racially diverse neighborhood, where he attended school with kids from different races and ethnicities.

"It has nothing to do with him being White or Italian, Kenny," she said in a softer tone. "Frankie's uncle is a nice man, and I like him and—"

"Like him enough to let him date you?" Kenny said, cutting her off.

"Why are you like a damn dog with a bone, Kenny?" she countered angrily, "That won't let it go?"

"And why are you cussing so much, Mom, when it's something you never do?"

His reprimand suddenly hit Justine. She'd preached to Kenny that folks used profanity when they couldn't come up with the appropriate word for something. But she wasn't about to apologize to him, not when he continued to challenge her.

And as a child, that was something Justine refused to accept. She was the adult, and he wasn't.

"I'm going to say this, then this conversation is over," she stated firmly. "If I decide not to go out with your Mr. Dee, it has nothing to do with his race, because it's Black folks who have hurt me far worse than Whites. That's something I will tell you about in the future. Right now, we've agreed to be friends like you, Ray, and Frankie. He will come here to eat, and if I feel comfortable enough with him, I will go to his place for dinner. Our friendship will never lead to marriage, because that's something neither of us want."

Her explanation seemed to please Kenny when he flashed a wide grin. "That's cool."

Justine leaned over to kiss his cheek, then pulled back at the last moment. He wasn't a little boy who enjoyed his mother hugging and kissing him, but a young man capable of making her a grandmother.

"Yeah, real cool," she said, smiling. "I've got more typing to do before I turn in for the night."

"Don't stay up too late," Kenny teased.

She smiled. It was something she always told him. "Same to you."

Justine moved off the sofa and walked to her home office. To say the day was filled with surprises was an understatement. First, there were the annoying telephone calls from Norman Robinson, then Frank's unannounced arrival with a typewriter she'd been coveting for a long time. Then her invitation for him to share dinner with her, his request to take her out, and her ambivalence in giving him the response she knew he wanted. And in the end, they had agreed on friendship, because there was no place in her future where she could envision spending it with Francis D'Allesandro. He would become someone just passing through her life, and it was impossible to predict whether she would be left with good or bad memories of him.

What had really thrown her for a loop was her son questioning her about her life. That he was concerned she was going to grow old and be alone. She hoped to grow old, and even if she ended up alone, she hoped to spoil the grandchildren Kenny would give her. She wanted his life to turn out differently from her own when he'd fall in love, marry, and have a family where she would be able to spoil her grandbabies.

"Are you certain you want to work with me in the store this summer?" Giovanni D'Allesandro asked his son.

Frankie stared at his father. "I told you before that's what I want to do, Poppa. Why are you asking me again?"

Gio shared a smile with his wife. "Because I've decided to close the store for two weeks and take your mother and the girls to Italy for vacation."

Frankie slowly blinked. "What about me?"

"You can stay with your Nonna if you want, or come with us."

Suddenly it dawned on Frankie that his father was joking with him. There was no way he was going to take his family to Italy and leave his son behind. "I think I'll go with you guys."

Kathleen rested a hand on his back. "There was no way we were going to leave you here. Remember when we all went to the photographer to have our pictures taken because I said my mother wanted updated pictures of her grandchildren?" Frankie nodded. "That's when I had him take photos for everyone's passports."

Frankie recalled his father telling his wife that the store was losing money; since the supermarkets opened, he'd lost a number of his customers. The ones that had elected to shop with him were the ones to whom he'd extended credit. He had kept a running tab of their purchases, and whenever they received their paychecks or government checks, they would pay their bill. And unlike loan sharks, his father didn't charge them interest.

"Aren't you going to lose a lot of money if you close for two weeks, Poppa?" he asked.

Kathleen stared at her husband. "You need to tell him, Gio."

"Tell me what, Mama?"

Gio cleared his throat. "I'm planning to close the store for good when we come back. I've finally convinced your mother that we should move out of this apartment and into the brownstone with Nonna, because now that she's having another baby, this place is too small for five kids. Nonna is giving us the top-floor apartment with five bedrooms."

Frankie felt a fist of fear squeeze his heart. He didn't want to move, because he didn't want to leave his friends. "Where will you work, Poppa?"

"I have a cousin who has a butcher shop on Second Avenue."

"What about my friends Kenny and Ray?" Frankie asked, as he struggled not to cry. If he was moving to a new neighborhood, then he would have to go to a new junior high school.

"They can always come over on weekends. There will be enough room in the apartment where they can spend the night."

Knowing he wouldn't have to lose contact with his friends made Frankie feel a little better. Moving across town meant living in a larger apartment, seeing his grandmother every day, and his extended family for dinner the first Sunday of every month. Knowing he was going to visit Italy for the first time was beyond exciting. Realizing it would be his first time on a plane and meeting relatives he never knew were things he was looking forward to.

"I hope Mama has a boy, because I don't need another sister."

Kathleen rolled her eyes at him. "It's not what you need but what the good Lord gives us."

"Your mama is right," Gio said. "All children are gifts from God."

Frankie wanted to tell his father that his daughters were probably from the devil because, despite the threat they would have to go to parochial school, they'd continued to fight with one another.

Things were happening that he hadn't anticipated when Ray told him that he and his siblings would spend the next two summers in Puerto Rico, so his parents could work more than one job to save enough money to buy a house in the Bronx. Now his family was moving across town while Kenny would continue living in an apartment half a block from Central Park. Frankie knew he would miss walking to school and sharing classes with Kenny and Ray. However, he knew they wouldn't lose touch with one another because not only were they friends, but also blood brothers. They'd sworn an oath to stay together, regardless of where the road of life would take them.

"When are we leaving for Italy?"

"The middle of July," Gio said. "When we come back the first week of August, I'll start packing up the apartment for the move. I want everyone moved in before the Labor Day weekend. Meanwhile, your mother will see that school records will be transferred to your new schools. It's going to take a while before I sell out everything in the store, so I'll be back and forth until that's done. What I don't sell, I'll give away to some of my most loyal customers."

"It's going to be a wonderful start for this family when we move into our new place with enough room for everyone," Kathleen said, smiling. "And come Christmas, not only will we celebrate the birth of baby Jesus, but our own little blessing."

CHAPTER 16

Frank entered the butcher shop to pick up the ingredients he needed to make his Bolognese sauce. He'd called Justine the night before to let her know he would be coming to her apartment Saturday morning around ten o'clock to make an authentic Italian dinner for her. The sauce, made from scratch, would take at least five hours to cook, and that meant he would be able to spend most of the day with her.

He still hadn't figured out why he felt so drawn to her and knew it only wasn't because of her race. What confused him was he didn't think of Justine solely as someone with whom he could have sex, because he enjoyed talking and sharing a meal with her, while discovering her to be more interesting than any other woman he'd encountered before. Since becoming sexually active as a teenage boy, he'd slept with women, and not once had he permitted himself to become romantically involved with any of them. They'd become mere receptacles for his lust.

However, unlike his father, Frank never mistreated a woman because of what he'd witnessed when growing up. It was as if Sal took pleasure in punishing his daughters for what he considered the slightest infraction. If they came home ten minutes late beyond their curfew, they were punished. If they didn't cook the sauce to his liking, they were punished. None were permitted to date because he feared they would sleep with boys and become *puttane*. The only female exempt from his tyrannical behavior was his wife. He was meek and almost subservient to her. What Frank and Gio didn't understand is why Gianna D'Allesandro had allowed her husband to come down so hard on her daughters when her sons were exempt.

When Justine asked if he liked being a bachelor, Frank hadn't lied to her when he answered in the affirmative. He was able to run his businesses, come and go at different hours of the day and night, and not have to answer to anyone but himself. With each passing year, Frank realized he was becoming not only more selfish, but also more discriminating when it came to whom he wanted to interact with. He'd become a successful businessman who was the complete opposite of CEOs of large corporations. He wasn't transported around in chauffeur-driven limousines, had no standing reservations at the finest restaurants, and didn't own penthouse apartments high above the city's noise and streets. He was Francis Michael D'Allesandro, better known in the neighborhood where he'd been raised as Frankie Delano, someone who was respected by many and feared by those who were equally afraid of Salvatore, the *Serpente*, D'Allesandro.

Frank didn't drive a flashy car or own gaudy jewelry, and he favored casual attire. The exception was a suit whenever he had a meeting with an investment broker. He rented a two-bedroom apartment on the second floor above a laundromat and checked in on his mother every day. After a long conversation with Gianna, he had decided to accept her advice to move his brother and his family into the brownstone, where they could have more space for Gio's expanding family. Gianna would get to see her grandchildren every day, and her younger son would be there to check in on her.

It was early morning, and there was only one customer in the butcher shop. Frank nodded to the elderly man behind the counter lined with fresh meat. *"Buongiorno!"*

"Buongiorno. What can I get for you this morning?" he asked Frank after his customer walked out.

Frank smiled at the man, who'd come to work for his father when he owned the shop, and had continued after Sal had passed away. "I need a pound of ground beef chuck, pork shoulder, lamb shoulder, and a half pound of chicken livers, sausage with garlic and fennel, and pancetta," he said in Italian.

Guillermo raised bushy white eyebrows. "So, someone is making Bolognese," he replied in the same language.

Frank nodded. It had been a while since he'd made the sauce which happened to be his favorite, second only to marinara. But only if his mother made the marinara. Not only would he make Bolognese but also an Italian white bean and sausage soup. He waited patiently as Guillermo removed a pork shoulder from the freezer showcase, cut off a portion, then placed it in a scale lined with butcher paper, grinning when it weighed exactly sixteen ounces. Frank didn't know how the elderly butcher did it, but he was able to visually measure whatever a customer requested to within ounces. Guillermo put the meat in a grinder labeled PORK ONLY, ground the meat and wrapped it in paper, then wrote what it contained with a short nubby pencil.

A young man wearing a bloodstained apron came from the back of the shop, carrying a tray of center-cut pork chops. Guillermo told Frank he'd recently hired the man because he needed someone to assist him in butchering large cuts of meat after he'd strained his back lifting a whole hog.

Several bells jangled when the door opened, and a man walked in and stood at the counter. In a motion almost too quick for the eye to follow, Guillermo's assistant handed the man something, and in exchange, he pocketed what Frank knew was money.

Moving quickly, Frank stood with his back to the door, preventing any escape. "What's in the hand!" he demanded in a dangerously soft voice.

The man, who looked barely out of his teens, shoved his hand in the pocket of his jeans. "Nothing, man."

Frank, at six-two, was a full head taller and weighed at least forty pounds more than the man who'd just lied to him. "If you don't take your hand out of your pocket, I'm going to have Mr. Guillermo call the police, but that's after I beat the shit out of you and then tell them you tried to rob the store. As they say, the ball is in your court. You can decide what is best for you. Now!" he shouted.

The man obeyed and held out his hand with a glassine packet Frank knew contained heroin. He didn't want to believe Guillermo had hired someone who was selling drugs in the shop. He stepped aside and opened the door. "Get the hell out of here and never come back." Waiting until the junkie disappeared, Frank glared at the man behind the counter, whose eyes were now big as saucers, while all of the color had left his face, leaving it a ghostly white. *"You, in the back!"* he ordered. *Please, Lord, don't let me murder this man with my bare hands,* he prayed as he walked around the showcase and opened the door to the walk-in freezer.

Once the door closed behind them, he grabbed the front of the man's apron and shook him like a large dog would a chihuahua. "What the fuck do you think you're doing dealing drugs in my cousin's shop?"

"I'm sorry, I didn't know it belonged to your family."

Frank couldn't believe what he'd just heard. "You thought it would've been okay if it didn't belong to my family?"

"I . . . I didn't mean it like that," he sputtered.

"Do you know what folks in some Middle East countries do when they find someone stealing?"

The younger man shook his head.

"They cut off his hand. And if he's found to be a liar, then they cut out his tongue. You've done both. My cousin gave you a job, and you stole from him by selling drugs rather than meat. And there's no doubt you lied to get this job because he was old and wouldn't pay attention to what you were doing. But it ends today. Where do you hide your drugs?"

"It's . . . it is on the top shelf in my locker."

Frank cursed under his breath. He didn't want to believe the butcher shop had become a stash house for a dealer. "Who did you buy the shit from?"

"I have contacts with some of Bumpy Johnson's people over in Harlem."

"How much did you pay for it?"

"A hundred dollars?"

"Do you owe them any money?" Frank asked. The man shook his head. Frank smiled, the gesture more sinister than benevolent. "And because I'm in a good mood today, I'm going to flush your drugs down the toilet and give you what you paid for them. I want you to answer one more question for me and that is, why have you become a drug dealer?"

The man's Adam's apple bobbed up and down as he swallowed. "I don't make enough working here because the landlord who owns the building where I live just raised my rent. Me, my wife, and two kids live in a studio apartment, and the greedy bastard decided to raise my rent from twenty dollars a week to thirty because I don't have a lease. I'm dealing to save enough money to move into a place with at least one bedroom."

Frank's eyebrows rose a fraction. "How much more do you need to cover the increase?"

"Forty dollars a month."

"I'll have Guillermo give you a ten dollar a week raise to cover the increase. You should be glad you caught me on a day when I'm feeling compassionate; otherwise, your wife would be putting flowers on your grave."

"Are you going to fire me?"

"No, because Guillermo needs you, and it's not easy finding a good butcher. My brother will be taking over the shop this summer, and I want to warn you that if he'd known you were dealing drugs, he would cut your heart out while you were still breathing, then sit on your body to eat his lunch. What's your name and where do you live?" The man told him what he wanted to know. Frank nodded. "Now go and get your stash."

Frank took out a money clip from his pocket and counted out one hundred dollars, as he watched Guillermo's assistant open a locker and remove a paper bag from the top shelf. There was a time when Guillermo had so many assistants that Frank couldn't keep up with their names. Most were unable to deal with Guillermo's grumpy personality and, on occasion, quick temper. Most of his customers ignored his irritability because he'd earned the reputation of selling the best meat in East Harlem.

Frank gave him the money he'd paid for the drugs, took the paper bag into the small bathroom, opened three glassine packets, and emptied the white powder into the toilet, flushed it, and then washed and dried his hands. He knew a lot of money could be made selling drugs, but it was something Frank refused to contemplate, because it was the poison that had cost his sister her life.

By the time he returned to the front of the shop, Guillermo had completed his order and was waiting on two women. He whispered in his cousin's ear that he had straightened out his assistant and that he should increase his salary to ten dollars a week. "I'll explain everything later," he said loud enough for the customers to hear. Reaching into the pocket of his slacks, he left two large bills on the counter next to the cash register.

"*Addio cugino,*" he said, picking up the paper sack with his meat order.

"*Addio,*" Guillermo repeated, smiling.

It wasn't until he stepped outside on the sidewalk that Frank replayed in his head what had happened in the butcher shop. If he hadn't come in when he did, there was no doubt Guillermo's employee would've continued selling drugs without his boss's knowledge. Not only was Guillermo getting older, but he also wasn't as alert as he'd been a year ago. Most times Frank dropped off a written order, then returned the next day to pick it up.

He had to thank his mother for suggesting Gio move to East Harlem and take over running the butcher shop; he knew he had to tell his brother about what he had witnessed with the exchange of drugs and money, and his decision to keep the assistant on the payroll. Frank knew his brother wouldn't have let the man off so easily; he'd taken their sister's overdose harder than anyone in the family, because he and Donella were only eleven months apart, and they were almost inseparable. There were a few times when Gio had admitted to Frank that he'd planned to kill their father for his mistreatment of their sisters, yet had been spared from murdering him when someone else did it for him.

Frank walked the four blocks to his apartment building, and up the staircase to the second floor. He didn't mind living above a laundromat, because he had come to savor the smell of clean clothes spinning around in the dryers. He unlocked the door to his apartment and elbowed it shut.

He'd never invited any of his business associates into the apartment, because it had become his private sanctuary that he'd made known only to the members of his immediate family. And his sexual encounters were always conducted in hotel or motel rooms. Sleeping with a woman at her apartment was a no-no for Frank. It was too personal, and for him, personal translated into a commitment.

He stored the meat in the refrigerator and then crossed off some of the list of ingredients he'd left on the kitchen table. The list was complete, because he picked up fresh sage and parsley leaves from his mother, who grew them indoors during the colder weather. During late spring and summer, her outdoor garden was a cornucopia of different varieties of peppers, tomatoes, squash, melons, eggplant, herbs, carrots, zucchini, and cucumbers.

Frank emptied his pockets of his keys and money clip, leaving them on a shelf in a kitchen cabinet, then ran a hand over his face. "I'm losing it," he whispered, as he made his way into his bedroom. If he hadn't met Justine Russell, he knew he would've reacted differently to the man dealing drugs out of one of his family's businesses. If he hadn't beaten him to a bloody pulp, then he would've had someone much more accomplished do it.

It had been a while since he'd had to resort to physical violence, and the older he became, the more he'd come to abhor it. Exacting revenge and retribution were now a part of his past, and that was where he wanted it to stay, because the last time he'd physically hurt another human being, he'd been sickened and repulsed by his actions for weeks. Then, he vowed never again would he allow himself to cross the line where he would be responsible for whether someone lived or died.

It had become a wake-up call for Frank that he was turning into his father where physical violence solved all of his frustrations. He was becoming more tolerant, and he enjoyed settling down to do what he wanted to without anyone else's approval. If Pasquale Festa had shown up at the family's Sunday dinner a year before with his outburst, Frank would've ignored everyone in the room and strangled him where he stood. Then he would have had Father Morelli give him the last rites as he drew his last breath.

Smiling, he walked into the bedroom, slipped out of his shoes, then stripped off his clothes before he lay completely nude across the bed and closed his eyes. Suddenly he was tormented by confusing emotions, wondering if he should've let the assistant butcher off so easily. Just because he'd been caught dealing drugs, there was no assurance he wouldn't do it again, and if he were caught by the police, then his family business would be implicated. Guillermo needed an experienced butcher, but not one ballsy enough to deal drugs out of the shop.

Frank opened his eyes and stared up at the ceiling. Becoming involved in the trafficking and sale of drugs was risky, because when a person was caught, it meant long prison sentences. Even if his sister hadn't overdosed on heroin, Frank still wouldn't have become involved in drugs, no matter how much money could be made.

Sitting up, he reached for the telephone on the bedside table and dialed a number. Frank didn't know why, but he couldn't shake the feeling the drug dealer couldn't be trusted. He spoke in rapid Italian when a familiar voice answered the phone, telling him what he wanted him to do. The call lasted less than fifteen seconds, and when Frank hung up, he felt better than he had since walking out of the butcher shop.

It took a while for him to relax completely, and when he fell asleep, his dreams were filled with the image of a slender woman with large eyes in a flawless nut-brown complexion who was smiling and holding out her hand to him. But when he reached out to take her hand, she disappeared as if she were an apparition. He saw himself running and searching for her, but she was nowhere to be found. Then he stopped running, and she reappeared. This time she wasn't smiling. She was yelling at him, but he couldn't hear what she was saying. Then she was gone again. This time for good.

Frank woke up, his body drenched in sweat. The room was warm enough for him to turn on the air-conditioning unit he'd recently installed in the bedroom window. Then he realized he hadn't had a dream, but a nightmare. The woman in his dream was Justine Russell, and like the girl with whom he'd fallen in love in high school, she would only be in his life for a brief moment—and when she left, he would only have memories of what they shared.

Times were different.

He was different.

Frank smiled. He wasn't a sixteen-year-old boy pining for a girl, but a thirty-seven-year-old man who was ready to accept the inevitable. And that was there would be no future with him and Justine Russell.

CHAPTER 17

Frank leaned forward, and using his elbow, rang the bell to Justine's apartment. He'd managed to carry a large picnic basket and two shopping bags up the staircase in one trip. If he'd been able to park closer to her apartment building, then he would've gone downstairs a second time, but he hadn't wanted to waste time. He hadn't been able to shake the images in his dream where he'd lost Justine—forever. And if it was meant to be, then he wanted to spend as much time with her until she'd cease being a part of his life.

The door opened, and Justine looked at him as if she'd never seen him before. "What on earth are you carrying?" she asked, stepping back and opening the door wider.

"Everything I need for our dinner," he said, walking in and heading for the kitchen.

"Can I at least take one of the bags?" Justine said, following him.

"No, doll. I have this." Frank set the picnic basket on the table, then slowly lowered the shopping bags on the floor.

Every time he saw Justine, she looked different. Today her hair was a mass of tiny curls framing her face and falling around her shoulders. It was the first time he'd seen her wear a dress—a flower-sprigged sleeveless A-line shift ending at her knees. Frankie forced himself not to stare at her shapely bare legs and slender feet in a pair of black flats.

He'd called her doll, and that was how he had started thinking of her. A delicate, beautiful, Black doll who'd unknowingly spun a web from which there was no escape, because he didn't want to wake up from the sensual spell that had held him captive the instant he first laid eyes on her.

Frank winked at Justine before he opened the basket and took out the ingredients for his Bolognese and soup. "Your hair looks amazing."

She smiled. "Thank you. I went to the beauty shop early this morning. I was lucky, because I was the first one in line before they opened up."

He gave her a sidelong glance as he continued to empty the basket. "What happened to making an appointment?"

"This shop doesn't take appointments. It's first come, first serve."

"Where is it?" he asked.

"It's in *El Barrio* near One-Eighteenth."

"I thought you didn't go to East Harlem."

"I don't want Kenny to go to East Harlem."

"Why, Justine? Do you think it's more dangerous than West Harlem?"

"No. I don't want him to go to either Harlem. At least not until he's older."

"What about when he goes to high school, Justine? There's no doubt he'll have to take the bus or the subway to get where he has to."

Justine crossed her arms under her breasts. "I'll cross that bridge when I come to it."

Frank's head popped up and met her eyes. He wanted to tell Justine that she was overly protective of her son; that she had to allow him the freedom to explore new places. If not, then she would stunt his maturing into a confident man able to withstand the ups and downs of life.

Knowing instinctively that she wouldn't appreciate his questioning her decision as to how she'd chosen to raise her son, he smiled. "By the way, where's Kenny?"

Justine lowered her arms. "He's in his room, sulking."

Frank's hands halted. "If you don't mind my asking, but what is he sulking about?"

"He feels as if he's losing his friends. He told me about Frankie moving across town and that Ray's family is planning to move to the Bronx. I tried talking to him, but he just stared at me as if I was speaking a language he didn't understand. This is the first time I've felt as if I'm losing my son."

"You're not losing him, Justine. He's probably going through things he can't talk to you about."

"And you think he would feel comfortable talking about those things to you?" she asked.

Frank bit back a smile. Justine had just given him the opening he needed to run interference between her and her son. "Probably," he said. "There was a time when I, too, was a teenage boy who refused to talk to my mother about what was bothering me."

"Did you talk to your father?"

Shaking his head, he said, "No. He believed that children should be seen and not heard."

"Who did you talk to?" Justine asked.

"My favorite uncle, and when he wasn't around, an older cousin."

"Kenny doesn't have an uncle or cousins, so I would really appreciate it if you would talk to him."

"I can't promise a miracle, but I will try." He held up a hand. "I'll finish unpacking everything when I come back."

"Francis."

Justine had said his name so softly that for a moment, he thought he'd imagined it. "Yes, Justine."

"Thank you."

Frank nodded. He didn't know if she was thanking him for being there for herself or because he'd volunteered to intervene between her and Kenny. He hoped it was the former. He walked out of the kitchen, through the living room, down a narrow hallway past a bathroom and bedroom he assumed was Justine's because it was decorated in pastel yellows and greens. Across the hall from hers was a bedroom with a closed door. Raising his hand, he knocked softly.

"I told you before I don't want to talk to you," came the reply to his knock.

"I'm not your mother."

It was a full minute before the door opened, and Frank smiled at Justine's son. "May I come in?"

Kenny opened the door, and he walked in, his gaze sweeping around the room, noting the unmade bed, a pile of discarded clothes in a corner, and stacks of books on a table doubling as a desk. The boy moved quickly to remove a loose-leaf binder from a chair. "Please sit down, Mr. Dee."

Frank pointed to the bed. "After you."

Kenny sat and stared at his hands sandwiched between his knees. "I suppose you were talking to my mother."

"That's where you're wrong, Kenny. She just told me that you weren't talking to her. And what could be so bad that you can't open up to her about?"

Kenny's head popped up. "She doesn't understand that I'm losing my friends, because she doesn't have any."

"That's where you're wrong, Kenny. She has me. I'm her friend whose cares about her."

"I'm not saying you're not her friend."

"Then, what are you saying?"

A beat passed as Kenny stared up at the ceiling. "It's different with Frankie and Ray, because they have a family when it's only Mom and me. I don't have a brother or sisters or even cousins I know about, so when I met Ray and

Frankie, they became my brothers that I could talk to about different things."

Frank's expression was impassive. "Things like sex and girls?"

Kenny appeared shocked when he said, "How did you know?"

"I was once a teenage boy going through the same things you, Ray, and my nephew are experiencing. The first time I had a hard-on that wouldn't go down, I thought there was something wrong with me."

"What did you do?" Kenny whispered.

A chuckle rumbled in Frank's chest. "I jerked off, and it felt so good that I thought my head had exploded."

"The same thing happened to me, Mr. Dee; then I got scared, because I'd heard somewhere that jerking off a lot could cause blindness."

"That's nonsense, Kenny, because more than half the world's male population would've lost their sight. The alternative to masturbating is having sex."

"At what age did you first have sex?"

Frank knew he'd scaled a hurdle with Kenny, because he felt comfortable talking about sex with him. Something he probably hadn't done with his mother. "I was sixteen."

Kenny's large eyes grew even larger. "Was it with a girl in your school?"

"No. It was with an older woman. My uncle took me to this woman who told me she was going to give me the best birthday present I would ever have, because once she finished with me, I would be a man."

"Were you?"

He didn't want to frighten Kenny with all the details and how frightened he'd been once it was over. That the woman had done things to him he never could've imagined after she'd put her face between his legs.

"Yes. My uncle thought it was better that I sleep with a

prostitute than the girls in the neighborhood, because he didn't want any of them to accuse me of getting them pregnant."

Kenny leaned forward. "Have you ever gotten a girl pregnant?"

"No, Kenny. When it comes time for you to sleep with a woman, then you must always use a condom if you don't want to get her pregnant. And always use your own, because there are some women who will put a tiny hole in their condom to trick you into getting them pregnant. Then, you may be forced to marry them, even if you're not ready for marriage."

"What if I'm in love with her?"

"If you love her that much, then you should marry her."

"I'm going to ask you a question, Mr. Dee, and you don't have to answer it if you don't want to."

"What makes you think I won't answer it?" Frank asked.

"Because it's about my mother," Kenny countered.

"What about your mother?"

"Are you in love with her?"

Frank slowly shook his head. "No, Kenny. I'm not in love with your mother. And even if I were, I wouldn't marry her."

Kenny glared at him. "Why not?"

"Because she told me she doesn't want to get married again. And I would never force a woman to do something she doesn't want to do."

"But what if she changes her mind?"

Frank wanted to tell the boy there were too many complications that wouldn't permit him and Justine to exist in a peaceful environment as man and wife. Not with the escalating conflict of race relations going on in the country. "I doubt if your mother is ever going to change her mind, Kenny. It's okay with me if we just remain friends. It shouldn't be any different with you, Frankie, and Ray. Just because you will eventually go to different schools, that doesn't mean you can't remain friends. You may not share the same school or classes, but you can always get together on weekends or when school is on recess. I still have the same friends I had in high school and college."

"You went to college?"

Throwing back his head, Frank laughed when seeing Kenny's shocked expression. "Yes. Why did you think I hadn't?"

Shrugging, Kenny said, "I don't know. Where did you go?"

"I went to Rutgers University in New Brunswick to major in business. My father wanted me to go to a college here in the city, but it was the one time I defied him. I told him if I didn't go away to college, then I wasn't going. Meanwhile, he'd bragged to all of his friends that his son was going to be the first one in the family to go to college, and in the end to save face, he relented."

"Why did you want to go away?"

"That's another story you don't need to hear." He didn't want to explain to Kenny that he needed to get away from his tyrannical father. "Now, I want you to do me a favor."

"What's that, Mr. Dee?"

"Go and apologize to your mother, and then I want you to be my assistant when I make my Bolognese sauce and white bean and sausage soup."

"I thought Mom was going to help you."

Frank stood up. "This time, us men are going to give her a break in the kitchen, because she's always cooking for you."

Kenny scrambled off the bed. "You're right. It's time for her men to take over the kitchen. But, can you wait for me to make my bed and pick up my clothes? Mom would have a fit if she saw my room like this."

"Five minutes, Kenny. That's all the time I'm giving you."

Frank would've begun prepping the ingredients he needed to make the sauce if he hadn't had to play stepfather to Justine's son.

He hadn't expected Kenny to ask him about marrying his mother. That wasn't even a thought when he doubted whether she would ever permit him to make love to her. It had been more than a decade since she'd slept with a man, and she admitted that she didn't miss what she didn't have.

Kenny made quick time making his bed and scooping up the clothes and putting them inside a bathroom hamper. Frank followed him as they made their way to the kitchen, where Justine sat at the table, drinking coffee while flipping through a magazine.

She set down her cup and stood up. "I thought I was going to have to send out a search party for you two," she teased, smiling.

"It's all right, Mom," Kenny said. "Mr. Dee and me had a man-to-man discussion about a lot of things, and I'm sorry about not talking to you."

Justine smiled. "It's okay, as long as you solved your problem."

"I hope you don't mind if Kenny and I take over your kitchen to cook today," Frank told Justine. "I want to teach him how to make Bolognese sauce before my mother shows him how to make her gravy."

"Italians call tomato sauce gravy," Kenny said quickly.

"I don't mind. So, you two do your thing," Justine said.

Frankie rested a hand on Kenny's shoulder. "Let's go, chef, because it's going to take a long time before the sauce is ready. Then, there's still the soup."

"How long, Mr. Dee?"

"It will take about five hours for the sauce and another hour and a half for the soup."

"I could do a lot in five hours," Justine said, as she emptied her cup and left it in the sink. "If anyone is looking for me, I'll be in my room in the back."

Waiting until she left, Frank reached into one of the shopping bags and took out two bibbed aprons, handing one to Kenny, and then putting on the other. He didn't want to tell Justine that cooking for her was special, because it was the first time he'd cooked for a woman, other than his mother.

As an adult, he lived his life adhering to a set of strict cardinal rules: he didn't invite women to his apartment; he always used his own condoms when sleeping with women; and he never kissed them on the mouth.

However, he was willing to break those rules with Justine. If they were to share a bed, he would continue to use a condom with her, because an unplanned pregnancy would be catastrophic for both their lives. Justine had plans for her future, and those didn't include having another child, while he doubted if he offered to marry her, she would accept his proposal. And he wondered if that was what he'd dreamt about. That she was carrying his child, and she was screaming at him to leave her alone. He closed his eyes and shook his head as if to banish the images that had continued to plague him, even after he'd awoken from the nightmare.

"Are you all right, Mr. Dee?"

He smiled at Kenny. "I'm good, son. Let's start cooking."

CHAPTER 18

"I'm not ashamed to say that I could eat this every night," Justine said after she'd finished her second helping of Bolognese with fresh-made tagliatelle.

Smiling, Frank raised his glass of red wine. "You have enough leftovers to last you for several days."

Not only had she eaten too much, but Justine was also feeling slightly tipsy, because it was her first time drinking wine. It wasn't sweet, but slightly dry, and when paired with the meat sauce, it was the perfect complement.

"I'm definitely going to heat the soup and put it in a thermos for my lunch."

"Mr. Dee, you should have been a chef," Kenny said, after swallowing a mouthful of pasta.

"I'll probably say the same to you after my mother teaches you how to cook. And if you're really good, then I'll try to get you a position in the kitchen of one of my cousin's restaurants several blocks from where I grew up. You can work there on the weekends once you're in high school or college."

"Really?"

Frank nodded. "Yes, really," he said, "but only if it's all right with your mother."

Justine met Frank's eyes over the rim of her wineglass, and there was something in his expression that challenged her not to deny her son the opportunity to travel to East Harlem, where he would earn money she wouldn't have been able to give him.

"It's more than okay if it doesn't conflict with his school-work."

"Why do you always say that, Mom?" Kenny asked, frowning.

"It's just to remind you of your priorities."

"I know," he huffed, "keep my room clean and pass all of my classes."

"That doesn't sound like too much to ask," Frank said, agreeing with Justine.

"I should know," Kenny said under his breath, "that grown folks always stick together."

Justine smiled, mouthing a *thank you* when Frank winked at her. She didn't know why he'd come into her life at this time, when her son was beginning to not only challenge her, but had begun asserting himself.

For far too long, she'd thought of him as a little boy who needed her to not only tell him what to do, but also think for him. Now she was forced to acknowledge that he was a young adult who still needed her, but not as much as he had in the past. She trusted him to get up and get himself ready for school without her checking to see if he'd showered, brushed his teeth, and put on clean clothes. And whenever he closed the door to his bedroom, she had gotten into the practice of knocking before entering before he told her to come in, because she now allowed him a modicum of privacy.

There were times when she wondered if her life would've varied vastly if she'd given birth to a daughter. The advantage would be renting an apartment with one bedroom rather than two, because they would be able to share the room. The disadvantage would be having a promiscuous daughter who could possibly make her a young grandmother. Fate had given her what she needed—a son who had made her proud to be his mother.

Watching Kenny interacting with Frank had her thinking perhaps she'd made a mistake not allowing a man in his life. Perhaps he did need a man he could talk to about things he hadn't felt comfortable discussing with her; a man who would take him to baseball games; a man to show him how to treat a woman with love and respect.

Justine refused to dwell on how giving Kenny a stepfather would impact her life, because she wasn't ready to share hers with a man. The only personal interactions she'd had with men were her shell-shocked, alcoholic uncle and the bombastic, narcissistic Dennis Boone. They were not what she thought of as good examples. There were boys in high school who wouldn't have anything to do with her because they thought she was stuck-up, and the ones who claimed they liked her but wanted to cheat off her test paper.

Then without warning, like an unpredictable thunderstorm, Francis D'Allesandro had swept into her life, making her feel things she didn't want to, while also making her acknowledge how predictable her day-to-day existence was. Kenny was right. She got up; went to work; came home and prepared dinner; then, if time allowed, she'd type or sew, before going to bed and turn around the next day to do the same thing. Weekends were no different, when she cleaned the apartment, went grocery shopping, and every other week emptied the hamper to take dirty clothes to the laundromat. It didn't matter if others thought her life boring, or her existence parochial; Justine had no intention of changing it, not until Kenny was emancipated.

"Are you certain you don't want to take any of the leftovers with you?" she asked Frank.

"No, because I usually share dinner with my mother. That will probably change once my brother and his family move in with her."

"When is that happening?"

"Gio wants the move to be final before the Labor Day weekend. He wants his kids to get used to the neighborhood before they go to their new schools."

Now Justine understood why Kenny was so upset about losing his friend. She'd never had that experience. Even in grade school, she hadn't formed any close friendships with any of the girls in her classes. She would see girls congregating in small groups, and at no time was she bothered she hadn't been included. She told herself she didn't need friends because of what she'd witnessed with her mother, aunts, and their so-called friends during their weekly card games. One day they were best friends; then they were cursing one another out and repeating gossip that should've remained within the group.

However, it had been different with Kenneth, Frankie, and Ramon. They had attended the same elementary and junior high schools, and even though they talked about going to different high schools, they'd made a pact to remain friends for life.

"Mr. Dee said I can get to see Frankie on weekends—that's if it is okay with you, Mom."

Justine slowly shook her head as she rolled her eyes, wondering why her son wanted her to look like the bad guy with his Mr. Dee. "Yes, it will be okay."

She had to understand the older Kenny became, the more he'd want to explore the outside world, and that meant loosening the reins to allow him to mature. What her son didn't understand was her fear that so many young kids were ruining their lives because of drugs. The articles she read in the *Amsterdam News* about Black folks overdosing in alleys, on rooftops, and in vacant lots and buildings made her blood run cold. She didn't know if the stories were written for shock value or as a warning to the Negro race that taking drugs was nothing more than another form of slavery. That they would only be able to break free from the chains of addiction once they were dead.

Her fear of Harlem wasn't in her imagination. It was as real as the neighborhood's documented history, even before the Great Migration of Negroes coming north to find employment or to escape Jim Crow. Before there were Negroes, Harlem had become a destination point for diverse European ethnic groups that included Germans, Jews, Irish, and Italians.

She'd typed a thesis for a student who had researched the history of gangsters in Harlem from the turn of the century to post-World War II. It was as if he'd been an eyewitness to the criminal activity of people he had known intimately. Justine had found herself transfixed by the names of gangsters who'd set up lucrative rackets to make money that included prostitution, loan-sharking, bookmaking, gambling, extortion, and even murder. The ringing of the telephone shattered her musings as Kenny jumped up from the table to answer it.

"Should I assume that you don't get that many calls?" Frank asked, smiling.

Justine nodded, returning his smile. "You assume right. If the phone rings six times a day, five of them are for Kenny."

"Wait until the girls start calling," he teased.

"Please, Frank. That's something I'm not looking forward to."

"You have to know it's only a matter of time when he will take a real interest in girls."

"I know."

"That doesn't bother you?" Frank asked.

"I'm not going to lie and say it doesn't, but hopefully he'll wait until he's more mature and responsible when it comes to sleeping with girls."

"I don't think . . ." Frank's words trailed off when Kenny rushed into the kitchen.

"Mom, that was Ray. He and a few other guys are going to the park to play baseball. Can I go with them?"

"Yes, but don't forget to wear some old jeans. I don't need you putting holes in your good ones when you decide to slide into a base. And remember, I want you home when the street-lights come on."

"Thanks, Mom. See you later, Mr. Dee."

"What are you smiling about?" Justine asked Frank when Kenny left.

"You," he said softly.

"What about me?"

"Even though you told Kenny he could go and hang out with his friends, you're still struggling about letting him go off on his own."

"That's where you're wrong," she said defensively. "I allow Kenny to hang out with his friends, but I need to know where he's going so if something were to happen to him, I could tell the police where he'd been. I'm not one of those mothers who will go to bed while their kids are still in the streets getting into who knows what. I don't need the police knocking on my door telling me they found my son dead in some alley from an overdose of drugs, or that he's been arrested and locked up for something he shouldn't have been doing."

"I doubt that's going to happen to Kenny."

Justine's eyebrows lifted slightly. "Why, Francis? Because you say so?"

Frank realized Justine only called him Francis when she was upset with him. What he couldn't figure out was what he'd said to upset her. She deserved a medal to have raised a boy who exhibited all the signs that he would grow up to make her proud to be his mother.

"Yes, I say so, Justine. I don't have kids, but I've seen and been around enough of them to know if they're going to make their mothers proud or weep for them. It isn't easy raising kids in a city where they are exposed to so much negativity before they even reach adulthood."

"There is one thing in particular that I worry about when it comes to Kenny," she admitted. "And that's drugs."

Frank nodded. "I know, because my youngest sister died from a drug overdose."

Justine gasped, then bit her lip. "I'm so sorry."

Suddenly his face went grim, and Frank chided himself for telling her about his sister. It wasn't something he liked talking about, and especially not to someone who wasn't family. Despite his growing feelings for Justine Russell, he knew she would never become a part of his family. Not because he didn't want it, but because she didn't.

He'd told her that he and his high school girlfriend had planned to move to Canada to marry and start a family, but that was two decades ago. Fast-forward more than twenty years, and he now found himself in a similar situation where he found himself falling for another Black woman. He constantly had to remind himself not only was she different, but times were different. He just couldn't pick up and move to another country, because he had obligations that bound him to his family's businesses. His great-grandfather had come from Sicily to the United States in 1881 with three dollars, two changes of clothes, and a dream to make a living in his new country. He'd found life tough and the welcome to Harlem unpleasant, where he experienced racist backlash from other immigrant groups. However, he endured when he worked two and sometimes three jobs to make enough money to send for the wife he'd left in Italy. Life for future generations of D'Alessandros improved, and now with Sal's death, Frank had become the head of his family.

"The only thing I can say is that she's in a better place, because her addiction had turned her into someone I didn't recognize as my sister." He forced a smile. "Enough talk about drugs. Are you ready for coffee and dessert?"

"Francis!"

"That's my name," he teased. "I'm as full as a tick, and here you're talking about having dessert."

Throwing back his head, Frank laughed with abandon. "Every once in a while, you come out with these expressions that are funny as hell."

Justine smiled. "Southerners have their own unique sayings that will make you laugh until you cry."

"Southerners aren't the only ones who have their own sayings. Roman philosopher Lucius Annaeus Seneca said: *manus manum lavat*, which translates to 'one hand washes the other,' while modern Italians say, *Una mano lava l'altraed entrambe le mani lavano il viso.*"

"Oh, my goodness. You speak beautiful Italian. Now tell me what you said."

"I said one hand washes the other, and both hands wash the face."

"It's so true about both hands washing the face. It sounds so much better in Italian," Justine said.

He winked at her. "That's why it's called a romance language."

"I'll see you guys later," Kenny called out as he ran past the kitchen.

"Did you grow up speaking Italian?" Justine asked Frank.

"Yes. My mother spoke Italian to her children, while my father spoke English, so by the time I entered the first grade, I was completely bilingual."

"I took four years of Spanish, and I got an eighty-five on the Spanish Regents."

"That's really good. Are you fluent?"

Chuckling softly, Justine shook her head. "No."

"Do you want to learn to speak Italian?"

Her expression changed, becoming serious. "Why would I want to speak Italian?"

"You said that you want to become a teacher."

"And?"

"Have you thought of teaching a foreign language?"

Justine shook her head. "No. I want to teach elementary school children."

"Reading, writing, and arithmetic," he said in a singsong voice.

Pushing back her chair, Justine stood. "I'm going to clear the table and put the dishes in the sink to soak before I put up a pot of coffee for our dessert."

Frank also stood. "I'll help you."

There wasn't much to clean up, because he and Kenny had washed everything as they were cooking. It was a technique he'd learned from his mother, who wanted to spend the least amount of time in the kitchen once dinner was over. And the pots and utensils he'd brought over were clean and stored in the picnic basket.

He stood behind Justine, waiting for her to fill the sink with hot water, then add a liquid detergent, before reaching around her to put plates in the sink. Frank heard her suck in her breath as he pressed his chest to her back. "Are you okay?" he whispered in her ear.

"I don't know," she said breathlessly.

Justine didn't know because although she'd found him to be too close, she wasn't repulsed by it. Her heart was beating so fast, she felt it in her chest and her ears. The warmth of his body and hypnotic scent of his masculine cologne sent her nerve endings racing erratically throughout her body.

"Francis," she whispered.

"What is it, doll?"

She smiled. It was the second time today he'd called her

the endearment. "You're too close," she said, recovering full use of her voice.

He took a step back. "Is that better?"

"Better, but still too close."

She didn't have time to react when his hands went around her waist and turned her to face him. Justine didn't know if it was the fading afternoon light coming in through the kitchen curtains, but Frank's eyes seemed to darken until they were a shade of blue jeans. She didn't know how it happened, but lyrics to The Crystals' hit "Then He Kissed Me" played in her head as Frank's head slowly came down, and he kissed her.

It was the first time a man had kissed her, and she felt as if she were melting, not only against him but into him. Her emotions whirled and skidded as she struggled to get closer when seconds before she'd told Frank that he was too close for comfort. Her mouth was on fire, and she quivered at the sweet tenderness of his kiss.

The sensual spell was suddenly shattered when she felt the bulge in Frank's groin, his hands gathering the hem of her dress, baring her thighs, and his labored breathing as he became more and more aroused.

"No, Francis! Please don't."

Justine's strident plea tore and penetrated the web of longing that had held Frank captive the instant he saw her. Not only had he frightened her, but he had broken one of his cardinal rules. He'd kissed a woman on the mouth. Then he had to remind himself that Justine Russell wasn't a prostitute he paid to take care of his sexual frustrations, but a woman with whom he wanted to openly date, but only if she agreed.

She was standing there looking at him like a deer caught in the blinding glare of a vehicle's headlights. "I'm sorry, Justine. I shouldn't have done that," he said, breathing heavily.

"You're right, you shouldn't have kissed me. Now, will

you please go." It hadn't been his kiss in as much as it was his hands moving up her inner thighs to touch the place where her body had betrayed her. Her response to Frank had frightened her, because she knew if she hadn't stopped him, she would've shamelessly pleaded with him to make love to her so that she could experience what it really meant to be born female.

"Justine, please let me explain."

She shook her head. "There's nothing to explain. Please go and don't come back again until it's time for you to pick up Kenny for his cooking lessons."

Frank felt pain squeeze his heart when he realized the images in his nightmare had manifested. Justine had extended her hand in friendship, and instead of honoring it, he had overstepped and allowed his base instincts to treat her like the women he paid to slake his lust.

She was sending him away, and he would go, yet all was not lost. He promised to come back and pick up Kenny at the end of the school year. Hopefully that would give Justine time to forgive him for his brutish behavior.

He nodded. "Okay, Justine. Take care of yourself."

She smiled. "You, too."

Turning on his heels, Frank left the kitchen, picked up the picnic basket, opened the door, and walked out of the apartment. He was glad he hadn't found a parking space near the apartment building, because walking gave him the time to clear his head.

What the fuck is wrong with me? How could I have forgotten that she's nothing like the other women I mess around with? She is a single mother struggling not only to make ends meet, but also raising a son on her own, and I treated her like a whore who was willing to do whatever I wanted because she was expecting payment for her services.

Frank unlocked his car and set the basket on the rear seat before getting in and slipping behind the wheel. He stared through the windshield. Justine telling him not to come back until the end of June, he thought, was a reprieve, because she hadn't told him to *never* come back. Hopefully the next six weeks would be enough of a cooling-off period where Justine would forgive him, and it was more than enough time for him to atone for his treatment of her.

CHAPTER 19

Justine covered her mouth with her hand as she stared at the images on the television screen of what reporters were calling ghetto riots in which hundreds of students were protesting the killing of James Powell, a fifteen-year-old student who'd been shot and killed by police Lieutenant Thomas Gilligan in front of his friends and more than a dozen other witnesses.

There were conflicting reports from officials in the police department who said Gilligan had killed the student in self-defense. He claimed he'd been attacked by the young male student with a knife. Powell, who was from the Bronx and in the ninth grade, was attending summer school at Robert F. Wagner Sr. Junior High School on East 76th Street, across the street where he was shot.

Whenever a Black boy was killed, the press had a field day when they interviewed people who claimed the kid had a troubled past. Powell was purported to have gone wild after the death of his father, while he'd had prior run-ins with the law when he attempted to board a subway and bus without paying, and he'd also been accused of breaking a car window in an attempted robbery, but had been cleared of those charges.

There was less talk about Lieutenant Gilligan, who prior to killing Powell, had shot a man he claimed was trying to push him off a roof. He also shot a young man he said was burglarizing cars in front of his apartment. The *New York Daily News* reported six-two, two-hundred-pound Gilligan had disarmed suspects in the past, so why hadn't he been able to disarm five-feet, six-inch Powell, who weighed a mere one-hundred twenty-two pounds?

The protests that had begun on Thursday escalated into a riot on Saturday, and when Frank called to her to say he was coming to pick up Kenny, Justine told him she was keeping her son in the house until it was safe for a Black person to walk the streets. People were swept up in the chaos as they exited the subway and local businesses, while some did not realize why they were being pursued by police.

Frank had tried to tell her Kenny would be safe in the car with him, but she wasn't willing to listen to anything he had to say. Justine told him emphatically that Kenny was her son and therefore her responsibility, and then she hung up the phone. Not only was she concerned about her son staying away from drugs, but also the police, who seemed not to differentiate whether a Black person was young or old, a criminal, or a law-abiding citizen when they drew their weapons to fire without discretion, while claiming self-defense.

"But Mom, nothing will happen to me if I'm with Mr. Dee," Kenny said, who'd watched her during her conversation with Frank.

Justine fisted her hands and mumbled a prayer not to lose her temper with her son. "Don't you watch the news, Kenny? Didn't you see the police arresting members of CORE, an organization dedicated to peaceful protesting? They were just demanding that Gilligan be suspended, and now they're being treated like criminals. If Black folks see you riding in a car with a White man, they will assume he is the police and what do you think would happen if they decide they need to rescue you? Cops aren't the only ones who have guns, Kenny. Black folks own a lot of guns, too."

Kenny flopped down on a chair. "Okay, Mom. I'll stay home."

"Don't sound as if you're doing me a favor, Kenneth Douglas Russell, because I'm trying to keep your Black ass out of jail or the morgue."

Kenny glared at his mother. "I don't know what happened between you and Mr. Dee, but I hope you work it out, because you're always mad with me for no reason."

"Nothing happened between us."

"Yeah, right."

Justine threw up both hands. "I want you to go into your room and stay there, because if you keep mouthing off, I'm going to call Francis D'Allesandro and tell him he's never to knock at my door to take you anywhere. Do you understand what I'm saying, Kenneth?"

Kenny bowed his head, nodding. "Yes, Mom."

"Now go!"

Slumping against the sofa, Justine tried to calm the runaway beating of her heart. She didn't know how to get a thirteen-year-old fatherless boy to understand that every time he stepped out of the apartment, he had a bullseye on his back when it came to a rogue or racist cop, who viewed Black people as less than human. Negroes had come north to escape Jim Crow, but unfortunately, it was waiting for them even before they arrived. On the morning after the shooting, when CORE—the Congress of Racial Equality—demanded a civilian review board to discipline the police, they were met by fifty officers holding nightsticks. So much for peaceful diplomacy.

Justine felt a band of pain tightening around her forehead that made it impossible for her to focus, and she realized she was having a migraine. It had been a while since the last one, which had been so debilitating that one of the doctors at the hospital had written a prescription for pain medicine that had helped to ease the discomfort after she'd spent hours in bed in a darkened room.

Going into the bathroom, she retrieved the bottle with the pills, and took two with a glass of water, then went into her bedroom, lowered the shade, changed out of her clothes and into a nightgown, and got into bed. It took nearly half an hour before the pills kicked in, and she was able to drift off to sleep.

Frank realized he was losing his concentration after he'd counted the stacks of bills in denominations ranging from fives to fifties at least three times before filling out a deposit slip for a night drop at his local bank. The telephone call with Justine was just as disturbing as the conversation he'd had with his police detective cousin. Anthony Esposito had called Gilligan a fool for killing the kid rather than wounding him, because his name and reputation would always be linked to the city's racial unrest.

He'd driven Gio and his family to the airport for their flight to Italy a day before the Powell kid was killed, so they were spared of the chaos going back home. And when he'd spoken to Justine about picking up Kenny, he'd tried to reassure her he would take another route to her apartment in an attempt to avoid the Tactical Patrol Force, who'd been called in an attempt to break up the crowds of protesters. But everything he'd said had fallen on deaf ears. She just wasn't hearing it. He wanted to understand her reasoning, and because he wasn't a parent, he'd been forced to acquiesce.

There was one bit of good news he'd received that morning. Guillermo's assistant had been truthful about his landlord raising his rent, and he had stopped dealing drugs out of the butcher shop.

Frank smothered a curse when the temperature in the kitchen became unbearable. The temperature was predicted to go above ninety, and the cool air from the unit in his bedroom didn't reach the kitchen. He picked up the bag with the cash and secured it next to a registered handgun in the floor safe in a bedroom closet. It was too hot to go out, so he decided to wait until Monday morning to make the drop. After cranking up the air conditioner to the highest setting, he went into the bathroom to shower.

The telephone was ringing when he emerged from the bathroom. Walking quickly into his bedroom, he picked up the receiver. "Hello."

"Mr. Dee, you need to come quickly. Mom's in bed, and I can't wake her up."

Frank felt his knees buckle as he sank down to the mattress. "Is she breathing?"

"Yes-ss. But I tried to wake her up, but—"

"I'm on my way," Frank said, cutting him off.

He didn't remember getting dressed or running to where he'd parked his car, or how fast he was driving to make it across town; he found a spot close to Justine's apartment building and took the stairs two at a time. His pulse had slowed to a normal rate by the time he rang the doorbell.

The door opened, and he saw fear in the eyes of the teenage boy he unconsciously thought of as his own. A son if he'd married Justine and they'd had a child together. "Stay here," he said, closing the door.

Frank walked into Justine's bedroom and sat on the side of her bed, watching the rise and fall of her chest under a cotton nightgown. Leaning over, he smelled her breath to see if she'd drunk something. He didn't detect alcohol, and then he spied the bottle of pills on the bedside table. He picked it up and read the label. It was a prescription for migraine headaches, with directions for her to take one pill every eight hours as needed for pain. A slight frown creased his forehead. Had she exceeded the dose, and that's why Kenny couldn't wake her?

He set the pill bottle on the table, then went into the bathroom to wet a cloth with cold water. By the time he returned to the bedroom, Kenny was standing there watching him as he placed the cloth on his mother's forehead.

"Is she okay?"

Frank gave him a reassuring smile. "She will be when she wakes up. She had what is called a migraine, and she took some medicine to relieve the pain."

Kenny slowly blinked. "I know she sometimes gets headaches, but she will take a couple of aspirins, and they will go away."

"Migraines are ten times worse than a headache, Kenny."

"Have you ever had one, Mr. Dee?"

"Thankfully, no. And I don't want one. I'm going to sit here with your mother until she wakes up, if that's okay with you?"

Kenny smiled. "Of course it's okay. That's why I called you."

Frank gave Justine's son a long, penetrating stare, wondering if the boy may have had an ulterior motive to get them back together. After the incident in the kitchen when he'd attempted to make love to Justine, everything between them changed. They'd become polite strangers whenever he came over to pick and drop off Kenny every Saturday morning since the school year ended.

However, when Frank picked up the phone and registered the fear in Kenny's voice, he realized the boy had reached out to him because he was his mother's friend. And as her friend, he had come to see about her.

"I'll be in my room," Kenny said.

"And, you know where to find me."

Frank sat on the side of the bed, watching Justine sleep, then got up, took off his shoes, and lay beside her. It was something he knew he wouldn't have been able to do if she had been awake. The room was so quiet, he could detect her measured breathing. He turned over with his back to her so he wouldn't have to stare at the roundness of her breasts under the delicate white nightgown.

He lay there thinking about what could've been if things were different between them before he, too, succumbed to the comforting arms of Morpheus.

Justine opened her eyes and went completely still when she stared up at Francis D'Allesandro sitting up in the bed next to her. She reached down to pull up a lightweight blanket to cover her chest when she saw the direction of his gaze.

"What are you doing here?" She didn't recognize her own voice, because her mouth hadn't caught up with her brain.

"I was waiting for you to wake up, Sleeping Beauty." Frank smiled at her under lowered lids. "Don't go and get your cute nose out of joint. I'm here because Kenny called and told me he couldn't wake you up."

Justine groaned as she sank back down to the pillows under her head. "That's because I took something for my headache."

"Headache or migraine?"

She closed her eyes, grateful the medication had worked. "Migraine."

"How often do you have them?"

"Not too often."

"Have you always had them?" Frank asked.

Justine opened her eyes, noticing the stubble on his chin and jaw. It was the first time she'd seen him unshaven. "No. They started right after I began taking an oral contraceptive."

His eyebrows shot up. "You're on birth control?"

She nodded. "Yes. My doctor recommended it to regulate my menstrual cycle."

"Have you always had a problem with it?"

Justine sighed. "No. Before I had Kenny, it would come like clockwork."

"Can't you stop taking the pill if you're having migraines?"

"Hopefully the migraines will stop now that I've been prescribed the lowest dose." She smiled, her expression appearing more like a grimace. "Thank you for coming and allaying Kenny's fear that he'd lost his mother."

"There's no need to thank me, Justine. I'm just glad I can be here for you and Kenny."

"How's he doing with his cooking lessons?"

Frank shifted and sat at the foot of the bed. "He's a natural. My mother is also teaching him Italian."

"That's a skill he'll be able to use if he does get a part-time position in an Italian restaurant."

"I told you before that I'll make certain of that once he's in high school."

"That all depends where we'll live," Justine said, meeting his eyes. "I got a notice from the city's department of buildings that they're going to demolish this entire block of buildings in the coming year. I spoke to my social worker about moving, who gave me a choice of several public housing projects in Manhattan and in the Bronx."

For the second time that day, Frank found difficulty in drawing a normal breath. He was aware of the urban renewal project slated for Justine's neighborhood, and he wanted to believe it would take at least another three, maybe even four years for it to begin.

"Which one have you selected?"

"The Amsterdam Houses. They are on the southeast corner off Sixty-third and West End Avenue. Kenny can take the number one train on Sixty-Sixth Street directly to One Hundred Third and Broadway, then walk three blocks to his school."

Frank's anxiety eased when he realized Justine would continue to live on the Upper West Side. Although he was realistic enough to know he would never recapture the easygoing relationship they'd had before he crossed the line from friendship to something more than she wanted, he hoped they would always remain friends.

"When do you anticipate moving?"

"Not until next spring when my lease is up here. Kenny will have completed most of the eighth grade before we move."

"What about the ninth?" Frank questioned.

"He'll probably stay and complete the ninth before going to high school. He's been talking about going to George Washington High School in Washington Heights, then from there to City College."

"It looks as though your son doesn't want to leave Manhattan," Frank teased.

"Look who's talking, Frank. You still live and probably work in the same neighborhood where you were born and raised. Meanwhile, this Bronx girl lived in Mount Vernon for a while before moving to the Big Apple."

"I did leave home when I went to college in New Jersey."

"Princeton?"

Frank laughed. "Surely you jest. My grades and SAT scores weren't high enough for me to get into an Ivy League college. I went to Rutgers as a business major."

She smiled. "So, my good friend is a college grad."

"Are you saying I've been promoted from mere friend to good friend?" he teased.

Justine's expression grew serious. "You will always be a good friend, because you are my only friend, Francis D'Allesandro."

"It's the same with me, Mrs. Russell, because you hold the distinction of being the only woman with whom I've had a friendship."

"I suppose that makes us special," she said in a quiet voice.

Frank nodded. "Very special."

She smiled again. "I don't know what Kenny pulled you away from, but would you like to stay and share dinner with us?"

Frank felt as if he'd been given a reprieve. It was the first time since that disastrous Saturday, after when he'd cooked for Justine, that he would share a meal with her. "There's nothing I would like better."

Moving off the bed, he walked out of the room, closing the door behind him. It had taken him a while to understand that, while he'd lived his life adhering to a certain set of rules, it had been the same with Justine, and he had to respect hers. It didn't matter what he wanted, and if he'd hoped to continue to accept what little of what Justine was willing to share with him, then he was okay with it. She had the responsibility of raising a child, and had hoped to educate him and herself, while his only responsibility was to himself and the viability of his family's businesses.

Frank sat on the sofa in the living room and picked up *Ebony* magazine off the coffee table. There were also copies of the *Amsterdam News* and the *Daily News* on the table. There was no doubt Justine was an avid reader. She'd joked about being twice as old as most night school students once she attended college, and she would probably be in her early forties by the time she graduated. He knew if their relationship had been different, then he would've supported her financially while she attended day classes to achieve her dream of becoming a teacher.

Even if he'd broached the subject hypothetically, Frank knew she would've rejected it. However, he knew it would be different with Kenny. He'd wait; wait until the boy graduated high school to repay his mother for her friendship.

PART THREE

LOSS OF INNOCENCE

CHAPTER 20

Justine Russell felt as if she'd scaled Mount Everest when she saw her son walk across the stage to accept his high school diploma. Kenny had exceeded her expectations as a son and student when graduating in the top ten percent in his class. Tall, standing several inches above six-foot, and broadshouldered, he cut a handsome figure in his cap and gown. It had taken some effort for Justine to get his cap to fit over his Afro while she complained that he'd let his hair grow too long.

Their move into public housing was a smooth transition from where they'd lived so close to Central Park. Kenny continued to attend the same junior high school, where he maintained his friendship with Ray before the Torres family finally moved into their house in the Bronx. The move for Ray was perfect, because he passed the entrance exam to attend the Bronx High School of Science, while Frankie had enrolled in the LaSalle Academy, a private all-boys' Roman Catholic College prep school in the East Village.

The three boys remained close friends throughout their high school years, and once again they would attend separate colleges. Kenny had chosen to attend City College; Frankie, Baruch College; and Ray had been awarded a full scholarship to attend Columbia University as a pre-med student. They'd kept their promise to get together the first Saturday of every month to share breakfast at their favorite coffee shop.

There were times when Justine envied their friendship because of the lack of her own. She'd divorced herself from her family following her grandmother's death, and she waited until Kenny was three before she sent her mother a Christmas card with a note telling her she was now a grandmother of a three-year-old boy. The envelope was returned weeks later stamped with: MOVED and no forwarding address. That had made the break complete.

As promised, Frank had gotten Kenny a job working in the kitchen at his cousin's pizzeria/restaurant. He'd begun as a dishwasher before graduating to assisting the cooks, making everything from sauce to specialty dishes. He was fluent in Spanish and Italian, which shocked many of the older residents in the neighborhood when he would occasionally fill in as a server to take their orders. He'd saved his wages and tips, depositing them in a savings account at a local bank.

Justine knew he'd become involved with several girls when they began calling the house asking for him. The weekends he didn't work, he would meet Frankie, and they would go to house parties. He would come home smelling of cigarettes, declaring he wasn't smoking while admitting he would occasionally have a small amount of wine whenever he shared dinner with the D'Allesandro extended family the first Sunday of every month. Frank had extended an invitation for her to join them, but after declining several times, he stopped asking.

He also had stopped coming to her apartment to pick up and drop off Kenny once he attended high school, saying if her son was old enough to take public transportation to and from school, it was no different when traveling across town to East Harlem.

The commencement exercise ended, and she was waiting on the sidewalk when Kenny met her. "Congratulations!" she said, grinning from ear to ear.

Dipping his head, Kenny kissed her cheek. "Thank you, Mom. I couldn't have done it without you." His eyes, behind the frames of a pair of round, black-rimmed wire glasses, were shimmering with excitement, glasses that were necessary once he complained of not being able to see what had been written on the blackboard.

Reaching up, Justine rested her hand on his clean-shaven jaw. "Don't say that. You've put in the work, so accept your success."

"Your mother's right," came a familiar voice behind Justine. Turning slowly, she saw a smiling Francis D'Allesandro, dressed in a tailored suit that was the perfect fit for his tall, slender physique. It was apparent he'd lost weight since the last time she saw him. For a man in his early forties, he'd aged like fine wine. His gray-streaked sandy-brown hair was longer and brushed off his forehead, while a network of lines fanned out around his eyes whenever he smiled.

"What are you doing here?" Justine asked, smiling.

"I came to see my best friend's son achieve a milestone."

Kenny extended his hand to Frank. "Thank you for coming, Uncle Dee."

Frank took the proffered hand, then released it to reach into the breast pocket of his suit jacket to retrieve an envelope. "Here's a little something to help you with your college expenses."

Kenny looked at the envelope, then took it as his eyes filled with tears. He threw both arms around Frank's shoulders as the older man kissed him on both cheeks. "Thank you," he whispered, then turned and walked away.

"Did I embarrass him, Justine?" Frank asked her.

Her eyelids fluttered wildly, because she'd never seen her son this emotionally demonstrative. There were times when she thought him too serious for his age. "I don't think he's embarrassed. There are times when it's difficult for Kenny to show what he's actually feeling."

"I've said this before, Justine, but you deserve a medal, because Kenny has become a spectacular young man. And if I did have a son, I'd want him to be like Kenny."

"It's still not too late for you to have one," she teased.

Frank slowly shook his head. "No, Justine. I can't imagine myself becoming a father at my age. If it had happened five or six years ago, then maybe. But definitely not now."

"It's the same with me. At thirty-five, I couldn't think of having another baby when my son is old enough to make me a grandmother."

"At least you can look forward to becoming a grandmother when I'll always be an uncle."

Justine wanted to tell Frank that was a decision he'd made for himself, just like when she'd decided not to marry and have another child. She knew she'd turned a corner in her life when she had finally taken off the gold band she wore on her left hand. When Kenny had mentioned it to her, she told him it was time for a new beginning, that she was tired of living in the past.

"Did you attend your nephew's graduation?"

"Yes. When my brother enrolled Frankie at La Salle, he complained constantly that he didn't want to go to an all-boys' school, but that's what he needed to keep his mind on his studies rather than on girls. I told him there will be plenty of time for girls once he completes his education. I don't know what it is, but something tells me that women will be my godson's downfall."

"We all have to live and learn, Frank. If I hadn't moved from the Bronx to Mount Vernon to live with my grandmother, I wouldn't have ended up a widow with a baby on the way, because I never dated boys in the Bronx."

"Are you saying you regret marrying and having your son?"

"Oh, no," she said quickly, as she watched Kenny talking to a curly-haired girl. There was no doubt the girl was entranced with him because of the way she was smiling up at him. "I don't regret having Kenny; he is the reason for me becoming who I am today."

"And you know how much I like who you've become," Frank said, winking at her.

Justine moved close to him. "You're still a silver-tongued devil when it comes to compliments," she whispered.

A hint of a smile tugged at the corner of his mouth. "That's because you're the most beautiful woman I've ever known." His smile faded. "I know I've never said it, but I fell in love with you years ago, and nothing has changed. I loved you then. I love you now, and I will love you forever."

Justine put her hand over her mouth as she struggled to control her emotions. What she'd suspected for years was now apparent. Francis D'Allesandro was in love with her, while she denied loving him. Although she'd told herself that she wasn't in love with him, there were so many things she loved about him. He'd become the surrogate father Kenny never had, and there were a few times when her son said he hoped Frank would become his stepfather.

Frank reached into the pocket of his suit trousers and gave her his handkerchief. "I'm sorry if I upset you."

She blotted her eyes, careful not to smear her eyeliner and mascara. "You wait until we're surrounded with hundreds of folks to tell me this."

"When would be a good time, Justine?"

"I don't know."

"Neither do . . ." His words trailed off when Kenny came over with the girl clinging to his arm.

"Mom, Larissa wanted to meet you."

Justine smiled at the petite, pretty Black girl with large brown eyes and a head full of curly black hair. "It's nice meeting you, Larissa."

"And this is my uncle," Kenny said, introducing Frank.
Larissa's expression mirrored confusion. "I . . . it's nice meeting you, too."

Kenny laughed. "Tell her that you're my uncle," he said, speaking Italian.

"*Ha ragione,*" Frank replied in the same language. "I am his uncle," he confirmed, switching to English.

Larissa appeared even more confused as she stared at Kenny. "I didn't know you spoke Italian."

"That's because I only speak it when I'm with my uncle's family."

"Well," Larissa drawled smugly, "I happen to be half Italian on my father's side. That's where the name Rossi comes from. Mrs. Russell, my parents have invited some of my classmates to come to our house for a barbecue. I told Kenny I'd like him to come, but he said he had to ask his mother."

Justine looked at Kenny. She wanted to tell him that she didn't know anything about Larissa's parents—where they lived, or what they did for a living. And as much as she tried not to, she still found herself watching over Kenny as if he were a little boy. He was eighteen, and she allowed him a lot more freedom than she had in the past; but unlike mother birds who would push their fledglings out of the nest when it came time for them to fly, Justine had found it more difficult for her.

"I'd like to talk to your parents before I give Kenny permission to join you."

Larissa smiled. "Of course." She beckoned to her father. "Dad, this is Kenny Russell's mother and uncle."

The tall, swarthy man wearing a three-piece tan linen suit extended his hand to Justine. "My pleasure, Mrs. Russell," he said in slightly accented English. "I'm Matteo Rossi."

Justine inclined her head. "It's nice to meet you, Mr. Rossi." She shared a glance with Frank. "And this is Kenny's uncle," she continued, with Kenny's pronouncement that Frank was his uncle.

Frank offered his hand, smiling. "Franco D'Allesandro," he said, introducing himself, using the Italian derivative of his first name.

Matteo's sweeping black eyebrows lifted. "*Un paisano?*"

"*Sì*. My nephew said you've invited some of his classmates to your home," he continued, speaking Italian. "I'd like to know where you live and what time I can come and pick him up."

Justine's gaze went from Frank to Kenny and then Larissa's father, because she hadn't understood a word they were saying. Frank turned to her. "The Rossis live in Riverdale, and he said they plan to end the gathering around eight. I have the address, so I'll pick him up."

She saw the expectant look on Kenny's face. It was obvious he liked this girl, and she, in turn, liked him. "Okay."

Kenny took off his cap and gown, handing it to Frank, then gave Justine the envelope with his diploma and Frank's gift. "I'll see you guys later," he said, as he and Larissa went to join their classmates.

"Not to worry, Mrs. Russell. Your boy will be safe in my home," Matteo said.

Frank put his arm around Justine's waist. "He's going to be all right," he whispered in her ear. "Kenny is aware that we're going to pick him up."

"But you didn't write down the address."

Frank tapped his forehead. "It's up here. I have what folks call a photographic memory, so there's never a need for me to write down numbers."

Justine wanted to tell him he was full of surprises, like confessing that he was in love with her. "Larissa is lovely."

"That she is," Frank agreed, "but Kenny will meet a lot more lovely girls before he decides to settle down."

Justine hoped Kenny would wait until after he finished college before deciding to settle down. "I planned to take him out for dinner, but it looks as if he has more exciting plans."

Frank tightened his hold at her waist. "That doesn't mean we can't go out for dinner."

"I just realized something."

"What's that?" he asked.

"That we've known each other for five years, and we've never been out on a date."

Frank angled his head. "That's because you didn't want to date."

"It wasn't because I didn't want to date. I just wasn't ready."

"Are you ready now?"

"I'm working on it."

Throwing back his head, Frank laughed with abandon. "While you're working on it, I'm going to take you to Peter Luger Steak House in Brooklyn. But first I need to find a phone so I can call to make a reservation."

Justine wasn't given a chance to object when Frank took her hand. They stopped on Broadway, where there was a phone near the corner. She watched as he deposited coins in the slot and dialed a number. It was obvious he'd memorized it when he made a reservation for two for later that afternoon.

She waited until he hung up to ask Frank, "Do we have time to stop at my place to change my clothes?" She had selected a navy-blue linen gabardine pantsuit with a white silk blouse to wear to Kenny's graduation ceremony, and with the rising temperatures and humidity, she needed something much cooler.

Frank reached for her free hand. "Of course. I made the reservation for five, so we have a lot of time to do whatever you want."

She smiled. "Right now, I want to get out of this suit."

"After we go to your place to change, we'll go to mine so I can also change."

Justine nodded. She'd known Francis D'Allesandro for five years, and during that time, she'd never been to his apartment—

and, aside from his nephew and namesake, she'd never met anyone in his family. He'd come to her apartment when she moved into public housing a few times, but after a while, he would call and tell her he was waiting downstairs when it came time for him to pick up Kenny for his cooking lessons. And once Kenny entered high school, he'd stopped picking him up.

So many things had happened in five years that Justine felt as if it had passed by at warp speed. She'd secured a better-paying job working at Bellevue Hospital in their billing department once her typing projects dwindled to less than three a year. And she was able to finally get off welfare. She'd also changed her attitude about living in public housing, because there was always heat and hot water, things that were occasionally missing when she lived in the tenement building. The Amsterdam Houses weren't the towering monstrosities housing tens of thousands of residents like so many public housing developments in New York City. There were playgrounds, a nursery, gymnasium, and a community center for the residents, and if she hadn't initially been so opposed to moving into the projects, the Amsterdam Houses would've been the perfect place to live and raise Kenny.

Frank led her to his car. It was a more updated model than the one he'd had when she first met him, but still not the latest model.

Frank opened the passenger door for Justine. He waited until she was seated, then rounded the vehicle and opened the driver's door. He removed his suit jacket and placed it on the rear seats before getting in behind the wheel.

Putting the key into the ignition, he started the engine, then maneuvered away from the curb and into the flow of traffic. When he'd gotten up that morning, he debated whether to attend Kenny's graduation, then decided it was something he wanted to do. There was nothing he wanted more than to stay in the boy's life and his mother's. The boy was growing older and more independent, while Frank felt as if he and Justine were growing further and further apart.

They rarely saw each other over the past three years, and there were times when he believed he'd forgotten what she looked like. He realized a lot of things had changed, and there were issues he knew upset her. Kenny told him his mother was worried about the escalating war in North Vietnam, because at eighteen he would have to register for the draft.

Racial unrest had swept across the country like a lighted fuse attached to a stick of dynamite with riots in Watts, Newark, and Detroit. The latter, known as the 12th Street Riots, decimated Black neighborhoods, and was eventually stopped when over twelve thousand federal troopers and National Guardsmen were called in. Kenny said his mother couldn't believe that their government had called for soldiers to round up American citizens as if they were the enemy.

Frank had found himself glued to the television after the news that civil rights leader Dr. Martin Luther King, Jr. had been assassinated in Memphis, Tennessee, and then two months later, it was presidential candidate Robert F. Kennedy in Los Angeles, California. It was now the middle of 1969, and he wondered if the civil rights and turmoil that had plagued the 1960s would spill over to the next decade.

If Kenny was apprehensive about being drafted, it was also the same with Frankie and Ray Torres. They were eighteen and worried that their number would come up and they would have to report to their nearest draft office. Frank had tried to allay their fears, because as college students, they could request a deferment.

"Now that Kenny is headed for college, are you ready to follow him?" Frank asked Justine.

"Yes. I submitted my application, sent in my high school transcript, and now after nearly eighteen years, I'll find myself sitting in a classroom once again."

"You're good, doll, because I don't think after being out of school for that length of time, I would have the patience to sit in a classroom or lecture hall again."

"That's because you've done it, Frank. College is very different from high school, where you attend classes every day. I'm going to begin taking two courses this upcoming semester, then register for more during the spring. Don't forget, I have a day job, so I'm going to have to monitor my time wisely."

"Are you still typing papers?"

"Not as much as I did in the past. I'm lucky if I have three, and once I begin my classes, I'll stop completely."

"Don't you need the extra money?" Frank asked her.

"Even though I could use it, I don't need it as much now, because I'm making more money working at Bellevue than I did at St. Luke's."

Frank stared out the window when he came to a stop at a red light. "You know you could've always asked me for money if you needed it."

Justine shook her head. "No, Frank. That's something I would never do, because I'd rather go without than beholding to some man."

He clenched his teeth to keep from spewing curses he knew would sever their friendship—forever. "Since when did I become just *some* man to you, Justine? I don't know who you dealt with in the past, or even now that we haven't seen each other since Kenny went to high school, so please don't lump me in with the other men who wanted to use you."

Shifting on her seat, Justine met his eyes for a brief second. "There were no others, Francis. You and my son have been the only men I've had to deal with, and that makes for a very uncomplicated existence. I've finally been able to cross off a number of things on my wish list and so far, so good."

"Is companionship one of those things on your list?"

"It's not written down, but I've been considering it."

"Like having a male friend?"

"I already have that, Francis. I have you."

Frank chuckled, the sound rumbling in his chest. "Damn, doll. I had to wait five long years for me to take you out on a date, because you wanted to wait for Kenny to graduate high school."

"Something like that," Justine said, smiling.

Frank's hands tightened on the steering wheel, and he knew he had to tell Justine something he'd asked Kenny never to disclose to his mother. "If we're going to continue to see each other, there's something you should know about me."

CHAPTER 21

Justine felt as if she'd been doused by a bucket of cold water, despite the heat of the sun coming through the windshield. There was an ominous tone in Frank's voice that frightened her. "If what you want to tell me is upsetting, then I don't want to know what it is."

"I lost a kidney two years ago," Frank said, ignoring her objection. "I was experiencing pains in my back," he continued, "and when they became unbearable, I finally went to a doctor, where he discovered one of my kidneys wasn't functioning properly. It was removed, and when it was biopsied, the pathologist found cancer. I underwent chemo and radiation. I lost all of my hair, and there were days when I wasn't able to keep food down. I lost over thirty pounds, and once my oncologist said I was cancer-free, I was able to eat solid food again."

Justine closed her eyes. She'd believed his weight loss was from dieting. She opened her eyes and glared at him. "Why did you wait until now to tell me this? You could've told me when you were first diagnosed."

"I told Kenny and made him promise not to say anything to you."

"Why, Francis?"

"Because I knew it would upset you, and I didn't want you worrying and hovering over me like you do with Kenny."

"I thought we were friends," she spat out.

"We *are* friends, Justine. But there are times and situations when friends have to sit it out. My cancer ordeal was something I had to go through alone."

"But you didn't have to be alone," Justine said, as she continued to debate the issue.

"It's over, so can you please let it go?"

A beat passed. "How are you now?"

"I'm still here, doing okay with one kidney. But I did have one lingering side effect from all that chemo. It left me sterile."

Her jaw dropped, and Justine couldn't imagine what that would do a man's psyche and his virility. "I'm so sorry, Francis."

Frank smiled, attractive lines appearing around his luminous eyes. "It's okay. I've had plenty of years to sow my wild oats. I'd also planned not to father children." He paused. "And it's been a while since I've been able to achieve an erection."

She couldn't believe he was joking that cancer had been instrumental in stopping his tomcatting. "Do you miss not having sex?" Justine questioned.

He shook his head as he turned off Broadway and headed in the direction of Amsterdam Avenue. "I remember you saying you don't miss what you don't have, and it's the same with me. And the answer is, no, I don't miss it."

What Justine didn't miss was having had meaningless sexual intercourse with Dennis Boone. As a young girl, she had been robbed of her virginity. It had taken her a long time not to feel guilty about touching herself. The first time she had an orgasm, she lay savoring the sensation, relishing having been born female. She usually waited until Kenny was out of the apartment for an appreciable amount of time to close the door to her bedroom and assuage her sexual needs. Knowing what she knew now about the pleasure of masturbating, she thought back to the time when Frank had kissed her in the kitchen and why she'd stopped him from making love to her. Initially it was her fear of getting pregnant, then being overwhelmed with guilt that she'd slept with a man who thought nothing of seducing a woman when her son, without warning, could've walked back into the apartment.

"I suppose that makes us kindred spirits," she teased.

"We're like priests and nuns who have taken vows of celibacy," Frank said, chuckling.

Justine reached over and rested her left hand on his right on the steering wheel. "That's why we are friends."

Reversing their hands, Frank gave her fingers a gentle squeeze. "Not knowing whether I was terminal has allowed me a new perspective on life, and that's when I decided I needed a will. I've made provisions to leave you and Kenny something."

"No, Francis."

"Yes, Justine. I don't have a wife or children, so why not?"

"What about your nieces and nephews?"

"Gio has enough to take care of his family after he sold his grocery store and took over the butcher shop. He makes enough to send all his kids to private school."

"Gio's family, unlike me and Kenny."

"That's where you're wrong," he argued softly. "You and Kenny are the best things to have come into my life in a very long time. I'm a businessman who occasionally will do things I must do to keep my businesses solvent."

With wide eyes, Justine stared at his impassive expression. Something told her he was alluding to criminal activity. "Whatever it is, I don't want to know about it." It was the second time she had denied wanting to know what he was going to say.

"I know what you're thinking, but I'm no different than a chief executive officer of a major corporation who will do whatever it takes to maintain profits. It's called free enterprise."

"Are you saying that heads of Mafia families are CEOs?"

"They operate on the same principles as General Motors, Ford, or General Electric. It's all about supply and demand."

"Are you in the Mafia, Francis?"

He slowly shook his head. "No, Justine." There came a pause before Frank said, "Would it make a difference to you if I was?"

"Yes, because it's responsible for drugs that are polluting Black and Spanish neighborhoods."

"You talk about Black and Spanish neighborhoods. You act as if White kids don't take drugs. You don't see them because they're not waiting in doorways or on street corners, waiting for pushers to sell them a nickel- or dime-bag of shit. They live in nice suburban enclaves and wait for couriers to deliver their drugs. They have the money where they don't have to steal from their parents or hit an old woman over the head to get her purse to get enough for their next fix. And don't forget, it is Black people who sell drugs to their own people," Frank continued with his monologue.

"That still doesn't make it right, Frank," Justine argued softly. "Drugs are like a plague that's going to spread across this country like a pandemic, and I don't believe it when government officials claim they don't know how to stop the flow of drugs coming into this country when they are able to identify every foreign spy living on American soil. Profits from drugs is what is propping up our economy, and if they were able to eradicate it, companies like Ford and General Motors would go out of business, because it's the criminals who buy expensive cars, purchase expensive homes, and fill bank vaults with drug money."

"As you say, Justine, you're preaching to the choir. I would never touch the stuff or get involved with drugs, because I saw what it did to my sister."

"How old was she when she died?"

"Nineteen."

Justine slowly shook her head. "So young."

"I'd like to ask you something," Frank said when they were a block from her building.

Justine extricated her hand from his. "What is it?"

"Will you go away with me for a week?"

His question was so unexpected that Justine was unable to say anything for several seconds. "When and where?" she asked, answering his question with one of her own.

"When you have vacation time coming to you, I'd like to take you to Puerto Rico."

Excitement eddied through her, because she'd never been on a plane or traveled out of the country. Something told her Frank also had a wish list of things he wanted to do because of what he'd gone through after being diagnosed with kidney cancer.

"What about Kenny?"

"What about him, Justine?"

"Do you think it will be okay to leave him here alone?"

"Dammit, woman! The boy's eighteen and old enough to go to war and make you a grandmother. I can't believe you're worrying about leaving him alone. If that's your only concern, then I can drop him off to stay with Gio. He and Frankie can hang out together for a week."

"He probably would resent having someone chaperone him while I'm away."

"You have to learn to trust him, Justine. It would be the same if he were to go away to college."

Justine knew she had to accept the fact that Kenny was an adult. "Okay."

"Okay what?"

"I'll go away with you. I've put in for a week's vacation the last week in July."

"Give me the exact dates so I can order airline tickets and make a reservation for a hotel."

"Francis."

"What is it, Justine?"

She smiled. "Thank you."

Frank parked along West End Avenue, then turned to look at her, his eyes making love to her face. "I'm the one who should be doing the thanking. You have no idea of how much I need you in my life . . ."

Justine placed her fingers over his mouth, stopping his words. "Don't, Francis. You need me and I need you, but for very different reasons. So, let's enjoy the time we've been given."

"You know that I love you."

"I can recall you telling me that before." She knew he was waiting for her to tell him that she also loved him, but her love for Francis D'Allesandro was more of a need to help her learn to trust without prejudice.

"Come upstairs with me," she said, "so I can change out of this suit."

Justine waited in Frank's living room as he changed his clothes. His apartment was the quintessential bachelor pad, with navy-blue leather seating and solid oak end tables. The highly polished parquet floors in a herringbone design were covered with blue and white area rugs with geometric designs. Either he was obsessively neat, or he had someone clean his apartment.

When she got up that morning to prepare to attend her son's graduation ceremony, she hadn't anticipated meeting up with Frank. But then, she shouldn't have been that surprised, because even when she and Frank had stopped seeing each other, it was different with Kenny, who continued to go to East Harlem to work in his cousin's restaurant. He'd also joined Frank's extended family for dinners on the first Sunday of the month. Kenny was equally proficient speaking

Spanish and Italian. He claimed he conversed in Italian with Frankie and in Spanish with Ray. Kenny had stopped calling Frank "Mr. Dee" and now chose "Uncle Dee," because it was something Frank had insisted on.

Justine crossed her ankles and stared at her feet in a pair of navy-blue espadrilles, wondering how Kenny would react once she informed him that she was going out of the country for a week with Frank. It would be a first for her, going away with a man and leaving him completely on his own. However, she found Frank's disclosure that he'd had cancer to be more shocking than his revelation that he loved her. She didn't understand why Kenny hadn't told her that Frank was ill, despite his promise to Frank that he would keep his secret. Didn't he know she cared enough to be with him when he had to go for his chemotherapy? She didn't want to believe that Frank had been so vain that he hadn't wanted her to see him bald and emaciated.

Frank came out of the bedroom in a pair of black linen slacks, matching jacket, white linen short-sleeved shirt, and black loafers. He wore a watch with a black alligator band on his left wrist. "Ready whenever you are," he said, smiling and extending his hand to help her off the sofa.

She returned his smile, her eyes meeting his. There was something about the older, slimmer Francis D'Allesandro she found more attractive than the one she'd first met five years before. In the past, he'd projected a restless energy that made it impossible for her to completely relax around him. That was then, and now there was an air of supreme confidence that indicated he was in total control of himself and the world in which he navigated.

Going on tiptoe, Justine brushed her mouth over his, knowing she'd shocked him. Frank sucked in his breath. "Ready," she whispered.

"Damn, doll," he groaned. "You wait until I can't get it up to start something I can't finish."

"Not all relationships are based on sex, Frank."

He squeezed her hand. "I've never been the relationship type of guy, but I know it's going to be different with you."

Justine wanted to tell him that even if he'd been able to achieve an erection, she still wasn't ready to have sex with him, because despite their knowing each other for five years, they still were strangers. Strangers who would have to learn to trust each other. And if he had trusted her, then he would've confided in her when he had been diagnosed with cancer two years ago.

Smiling, she said, "It's going to be different for both of us."

"Have you ever been to Brooklyn?" Frank asked Justine, as he closed and locked the door to his apartment, then led her down the flight of stairs.

"Yes. Once when I took Kenny to Coney Island to ride the roller coaster. He loved it, but I was scared to death when it picked up speed and came down so fast that I nearly lost the contents of my stomach."

"I get the same feeling whenever a plane picks up speed before takeoff."

Justine gave him a sidelong glance as they walked hand-in-hand to where he'd parked his car. "Have you done a lot of traveling?"

"Not as much as I would've liked to. But hopefully that will change if I can convince my favorite girl to accompany me," he said, wiggling his eyebrows when she looked up at him.

"Have you forgotten that I have a job?"

"No. But whenever you have vacation or decide to take a couple of days off, we can go away together and just relax."

Frank was making plans for their future, when she was someone who lived one day at a time. Yes, she had a wish list, but those were things she wanted to accomplish over ten-year increments of time. Then she realized he couldn't plan that far ahead, because he never knew when his cancer would return. His life had become a virtual ticking time bomb, and he wanted to go and see as many places as he could before it exploded.

"I'll let you know once I get my school calendar," Justine told him. "I'll have a break between the fall and spring semesters, and I'll put in for vacation at that time."

Curving an arm around her waist of a loose-fitting white-and-blue-striped tent dress, Frank pulled her closer to his side. "That's when we can fly down to Florida and take a cruise to the Caribbean."

"I can't believe I have my own personal genie."

Lowering his head, Frank dropped a kiss on her hair. "I'm different from other genies, because you don't have to rub me to make me appear or grant your wishes."

"Lucky me," Justine drawled.

"No, doll. Lucky me."

CHAPTER 22

Justine chewed a piece of thinly sliced steak. It literally melted in her mouth. It was obvious why Frank had suggested coming to Peter Luger, which had earned the reputation of being one of the best steakhouses in the city. The aged porterhouse had been grilled to perfection, and after sampling it, she knew she'd been spoiled.

Frank smiled at her across the table. "Do you like it?"

She smiled. "It's delicious." He had ordered it medium well, because he knew she didn't like rare meat. "Thank you for suggesting we eat here."

He inclined his head. "Remember, I'm your personal genie, and when and wherever you want to go, somehow just let me know."

"You're spoiling me, Frank."

"I remember my telling you that what now seems so long ago."

Justine tilted her head and flashed a sensual smile. "Yes. It was when I offered to make a sweet potato pie for you."

Frank's expression changed, becoming a mask of stone. "Why did we waste so many years when what we have now, we could've had then?" he asked. His tone was layered with a hint of reproach.

"What we have now couldn't have happened then, because we were different people at that time, Francis," Justine countered. "You wanted more from me than what I could give you because my sole responsibility was raising my son. As a single mother on welfare, my priority was keeping a roof over our heads, food on the table, and shoes on my kid's feet. And having a man in my life wasn't even an afterthought."

"But you could've had a man willing to give you not only what you needed, but also whatever you wanted."

Justine leaned back in her chair and gave Frank a long, penetrating stare. "And what would I have become for you?" she whispered. "A woman who'd willingly open her legs just to get what she wanted?" She continued in a hushed tone. "That would've made me your *whore*." She was fortunate their table was positioned far enough away from other diners not to overhear their conversation.

Frank glared at her. "You're wrong about that!"

"I know what happened when my mother got involved with a man who was able to give her what she wanted, and the day she told him she was pregnant with me, he walked out on her. But not before he told her he couldn't marry her because he was already married."

"The difference between me and your father is that I'm not married."

"You're not married, and we'll never marry, Francis. That's just a fact we have to live with." An audible sigh slipped past her lips. Justine didn't want to ruin what was an enjoyable evening with Frank by arguing. "I like you and you'll always have a special place, not only in my life, but also in my heart."

The second hand on Frank's watch made a full revolution before he asked, "Like, or love, Justine?" There was something in his eyes that challenged her; that he was waiting for something not what he wanted but needed to hear.

How could she tell Frank that she didn't know how to love him because she'd never had a relationship with a man? That she'd been caught up in a web of lies from which she hadn't been able to escape, even after eighteen years. That she'd never been a widow. That she'd been blackmailed into having a man's baby he pretended to have conceived with his wife. And that she'd fooled the unscrupulous blackmailer because she was unaware that she'd carried not one, but two of her husband's babies beneath her heart.

There was a part of her that loved Francis D'Allesandro because of her son. He'd shepherded Kenny through adolescence, allowed him to learn a skill that would be useful if he needed a part-time job as a cook. Frank had taught her son to drive and accompanied Kenny when he took the test to obtain his driver's license, all the while being a positive role model for a young Black boy growing up in an urban jungle.

"Yes, I do love you, Francis D'Allesandro," she lied, adding it to the many others she'd told and continued to tell, wondering when and if they would ever stop.

A slow smile spread over his features. "You are an incredibly beautiful liar."

Justine's jaw dropped. "Why would you say that?"

"Because you took too long to answer my question."

She lowered her eyes, staring at the food on her plate. Not only did he have a photographic memory, but he was also exceedingly perceptive. She had taken time to form her thoughts to give him an answer because she feared blurting out the truth that she was a fraud. That she'd managed to fool everyone who had ever interacted with her.

"I do love you, but it's not what I think of as a romantic love," she said in a quiet tone. "Perhaps if we'd continued to see each other over the years and had slept together, then it is yes. I love you for being the friend that you are. But more importantly, I love you because of Kenny. You've become the father he not only wanted but also needed. And for that I will be eternally grateful."

* * *

Frank stared across the table at the woman who continued to intrigue him. He didn't want her gratitude. He wanted her to love him. He'd had a lot of experience with women to assess who they were and what they wanted from him within minutes of their introduction. However, it had been different with Justine Russell. It was as if she'd erected an invisible wall around her and wouldn't allow anyone to get close enough for them to scale it. Not only had he wanted to scale it, but he'd wanted to become a part of her life behind that wall.

He wanted to tell Justine he hadn't done what he did for Kenny because he wanted to get close to his mother. He truly liked the boy. Kenny was bright, polite, and ambitious. Kenny's cooking lessons with Gianna D'Allesandro during summer and school recesses had turned him into a very marketable chef. Frank's cousin who owned the restaurant said Kenny's cooking skills had surpassed some of the cooks who'd worked with him for years.

What Frank could not tell Justine was that if he'd had a son, he wanted him to be like Kenneth Russell. Over the years, they'd become co-conspirators sharing secrets. When Kenny told him he was ready to lose his virginity, Frank took him to a woman who was the best when it came to deflowering young boys. And he'd felt confident enough to tell Justine's son about his family's businesses, knowing he would not repeat what he'd disclosed to him.

Frank had recognized a change in Kenny's demeanor when he appeared to be withdrawn and monosyllabic during his last year in high school. Once he was able to get him to open up about what was bothering him, Kenny revealed that he'd applied to Howard University in Washington, DC, and had been offered a partial scholarship; however, he was forced to decline, because he didn't have the money to offset the cost of tuition, books, room, and board. He told Kenny that he was willing to underwrite the cost of his college education as a gift to him, but after endless debates, Kenny told him in no uncertain terms that he would not accept a gift he knew he wouldn't be able to repay. It was then Frank realized he should not have said *gift* but *endowment*. It was also the first time he saw another side of Kenneth Russell's normal laidback personality when he spewed profanities that because he'd grown up on welfare and lived in the projects, he didn't want to continue his life accepting the White man's handouts. Not only were Kenny's words sharp and hurtful, but Frank felt as if Justine's son was ungrateful, when he'd done everything he could to improve his life and hopefully secure a future where he didn't have to live in public housing or raise his kids on welfare.

It took nearly a month for him to approach Kenny and admit that he loved him like a nephew, and as his stand-in uncle, he saw it as his responsibility to help pay for his college education. Kenny appeared remorseful when he apologized and said he was proud to be thought of as his nephew like his blood brother Frankie. It was the last time he'd called him Mr. Dee. He was now Uncle Dee.

Not only was Kenny a masculine version of his mother, but he had also inherited her stubbornness. He was as unflexible and proud as Justine. She was too proud to accept any financial support from him when she'd become a professional typist to earn extra money and made her own clothes.

Francis D'Allesandro wasn't wealthy, but he had enough resources to purchase a house for Justine and Kenny in a suburb with good schools and low crime rates. He would've done it for her while only asking for a small portion of her life.

He smiled at Justine. "You have to know how I feel about you has nothing to do with Kenny," he said after a long pause.

Justine nodded. "I know that. I knew that the first time you brought Kenny home after he joined your family for

Sunday dinner and you stared at me. It was much later that I realized it wasn't so much curiosity as it was lust. You wanted me then, and fast-forward five years, and you still want me."

Frank angled his face toward her. "True. But the difference is, I can't act on that lust. Yes, I feel desire, but my body refuses to synchronize with my head."

"Maybe it's more mental than physical," Justine said.

"That's no longer a priority in my life. Staying healthy is." Justine pointed to his plate. "Now that we've established how we feel about each other, you should eat something."

Picking up his knife and fork, Frank smiled. "Yes, Mama."

Frank was glad he and Justine had scaled that hurdle. She'd agreed that they would see each other and occasionally vacation together. He'd taken a sip of Merlot, and before he could set the wineglass on the table, he went completely still when recognizing the man approaching his table. Pushing back his chair, he stood up.

"Hello, Pasquale."

"*Buona sera,* Frankie Delano," Pasquale Festa said in greeting before staring down at Justine. "I don't want to disturb you while you're eating with your lady, but do you think you can set aside time for us to talk about a business venture?"

Frank wanted to tell his cousin that he was disturbing him but decided not to make a scene like the one Pasquale had made what now seemed so long ago, when he'd been banished from attending all and any D'Allesandro family dinners.

"Meet me tomorrow at Jimmy's Bar. I'll be there at one."

Pasquale nodded, smiling. "Thank you."

Frank waited for Pasquale to walk away and join two other men sitting at a corner table, before retaking his seat. If he hadn't been eating with Justine, he would've told Pasquale to fuck off. Despite sharing blood, he never liked his mother's nephew, who wanted to believe he was a throwback to old-school gangsters, who felt it was his right to intimidate and physically abuse anyone who stared at him too long because of his different-colored eyes.

"Sorry about that," he said to Justine, who met his eyes.

"Something tells me you don't like him."

"Why would you say that?"

"Because you looked as if you were ready to detach that poor man's head from his body."

Frank's smile resembled a sneer, the gesture not reaching his eyes. "There was a time when I wanted to do exactly that but didn't because it would upset my mother. He happens to be her nephew."

"What's the expression. We can pick our friends and not our relatives."

Frank picked up his wineglass and drained it. "I've never heard you talk about your relatives other than your mother and grandmother."

"That's because I was never close to them. My uncle's wife left him when he returned home shell-shocked after World War II and took his four children with her when she moved to Detroit, while both my unmarried aunts never had any kids."

"Are you still in touch with your mother?"

Justine shook her head. "Once I left to live with my grand-mother, she accused me of thinking I was too good to live in the Bronx because her mother had gotten a position as live-in cook for a well-to-do family in Mount Vernon. I sent Mama a Christmas card a few years ago, but it came back that she'd moved and left no forwarding address." A wry smile twisted her mouth. "So now it is just me and Kenny."

Frank wanted to tell Justine it didn't have to be just her and Kenny. That he also wanted to be a part of her life. He'd tried every way he could to convince her that he wanted them to be together exclusively. It had taken a brush with death for him to realize if Justine had changed her mind about marriage, he would marry her within days of their filing for a license.

Then he would buy a house in the suburbs, where she wouldn't have to work so she could concentrate on earning her college degree at the same time Kenny earned his. And he would ask her if he could legally adopt Kenny, give the boy his name, and make him heir to his estate. Frank realized he was becoming delusional. There would never be a Mr. and Mrs. Francis D'Allesandro and son. It was something he had to get used to and accept.

He picked up a forkful of creamed spinach and winked at Justine when she smiled at him. Aside from Pasquale's unexpected intrusion, their first date was nothing short of perfection. He had to admit to himself that he liked the more mature Justine Russell. She'd cut her hair. It was now parted in the middle and tucked behind her ears, the straightened strands covering the nape of her slender neck. Her jewelry was a pair of tiny gold hoops in her pierced lobes and a wristwatch. Everything about her was simple and elegant.

At the end of their dinner, they both opted for coffee rather than dessert. When Frank left Brooklyn to drive back to Manhattan, his mood lightened appreciably when Justine told him she had enjoyed going out with him and wanted to do it again.

There were so many places he wanted to see with her, yet he knew it would have to be at her convenience. Not only did she have a full-time job, but she was also planning to attend classes at night at the same college where Kenny would enroll as a full-time student.

He walked her to her apartment door and brushed a light kiss over her lips. "I'll call you in a couple of days to see if we can get together again."

Justine stared up at him under lowered lids, unaware how sensual it was. "You know where to find me."

Frank left the building, returning to where he'd parked his

car. He thought about stopping to check on his mother, then changed his mind. Ever since Gio had moved into the brownstone with his family, Kathleen spent practically every hour with her mother-in-law. Gianna doted on her latest grandson, to whom she only spoke Italian. Even Gio's daughters had begun to speak the language and had become almost as fluent as their older brother, Frankie.

Frank still worried about his godson, who appeared to have a new girlfriend every few months, and found his "love them and leave them" attitude disturbing. When he had broached the subject with Frankie, his namesake told him most of the girls he dated didn't want to have sex, so it was onto the next. It was when Frank predicted that one day he would fall in love with a woman who would break his heart because she wouldn't sleep with him unless he married her. His nephew, who had turned women's heads because of his resemblance to movie heartthrob Tony Curtis, laughed and said it would never happen. Frank hoped and prayed he was wrong.

He arrived home, tossed his keys and money clip on the kitchen table, and then walked into his bedroom and changed, wondering what business venture Pasquale wanted to discuss with him. If he hadn't been blood, he would've dismissed him like someone waving away an annoying fly buzzing around his head. But Pasquale was family, and he owed it to him to listen to what he had to say.

Frank stripped down to his underwear and lay across the bed. Exhaustion had swept over him like a fog rolling in off the water. Fatigue, a common side effect of his cancer treatments, continued to plague him when he least expected it. There were times when the voice in his head told him he was dying—but then, wasn't everyone from the instant they drew their first breath?

He was forty-two, and he wasn't ready to die.

Not yet.

CHAPTER 23

Frank was sitting at a table in the back area of the bar when Pasquale walked in, minutes after one o'clock. His cousin knew his penchant for punctuality and had made certain to come on time. He stood up and motioned to the back door. "Let's talk outside."

Pasquale frowned. "Are you crazy, Frankie Delano? It's hotter than Jerusalem outside."

"I'm not talking business in here, so the decision is yours. Out or in?"

"Okay. Outside."

Frank walked to the rear door and opened it, heat hitting him in the face like a blast from a hot furnace. However, he had no intention of talking to Pasquale in a place that could've been bugged by law enforcement, who believed every Italian business was a front for illegal activity. There were several chairs positioned under beach umbrellas to shield them from the summer sun.

"I want you to unbutton your shirt before you sit down," Frank ordered Pasquale.

"What the fuck!"

"Just do it, Patsy," Frank said, calling his cousin by his boyhood name.

Pasquale slowly blinked. "You think I'm wearing a wire?"

"Just do it, or this meeting is over." He watched as Pasquale undid the buttons on his shirt and pulled it up to display his chest and back. "Satisfied?"

"Sit down," Frank said, not answering him. He took a chair opposite his cousin, who hadn't bothered to button his shirt. Looping a leg over the opposite knee, he laced his fingers together, bringing the forefinger of his left hand to his mouth. "I'm listening," he said in a quiet voice.

Pasquale glanced down at the red-and-white-checkered plastic tablecloth. "I've been approached to ask you if you're willing to move a couple of kilos for them."

Frank glared at Pasquale as if he'd lost his mind. He closed his eyes, counting slowly to ten. "I can't believe you're asking me to become involved with narcotics. Have you forgotten that your cousin Donella overdosed on heroin?"

"That was a long time ago, Frankie," Pasquale said.

"It's fucking not long enough to forget the shit was responsible for taking my sister's life. And you can tell whoever sent you that he's lucky it was you and not someone else asking me to become involved with drugs, because I would've put a bullet in their head, then cut it off and sent it back in a box."

"If Sal was still alive, he—"

"I'm not my father!" Frank said, cutting him off. "And you're wrong about him, because even before Donella died, he swore the D'Allesandro name would never be linked to drugs."

Pasquale leaned forward; his blue eye darkened until it was hard to tell it from the brown one. "Please don't tell me that you forgot how my uncle made his money?"

"Those days are over, *cugino*," Frank said softly. "I'm a legitimate businessman, and that's the way it will be from now on and for future D'Alessandros." He paused. "If you continue to fuck around with narcotics and get caught, you'll be locked up so long that you won't be around to see your grandchildren make you a great-grandfather."

"I should've known not to come to you with this, because you do more for your Black bitch's son than—" Pasquale's words died on his lips when Frank backhanded him across the face so hard that he fell over backwards in his chair.

Frank rose, stood over his cousin, and put his foot on his throat. "You're lucky you are my mother's nephew, because she would be devastated if I murdered her dead brother's son." He leaned down at the same time he removed his foot off Pasquale's throat. "We're done here."

Pasquale got up and buttoned his shirt, then walked back into the bar, Frank staring at his retreating back. It was as if he were reliving the scene five years before when recently paroled Pasquale Festa had stormed into his aunt's home, spewing venom. Gianna's brother had done his eldest son a disservice when he never disciplined him whenever he did something wrong. It had always been the other person's fault. When Pasquale had been picked up for robbing a drugstore, his father paid the owner for the merchandise and warned his son not to do it again. But he did do it again. By the time he was twenty, he'd begun shaking down Black number runners at gunpoint, taking their money and policy slips.

Then it came to an abrupt stop when he assaulted a police officer who'd stopped him in a stolen car. He was tried, convicted, and sentenced to serve ten years in the Sing Sing Correctional Facility. Frank's father would occasionally send Pasquale's wife money to appease Gianna after her brother passed away, but once Sal was buried, the money stopped. Frank refused to continue to take care of Pasquale's family once it was verified that his cousin's wife was sleeping with men to supplement her welfare check. And when she wrote her husband to tell him Frankie Delano had stopped giving her money, Pasquale told her he would make him pay for going back on his promise to take care of his wife and children.

Frank flopped down on the chair, ignoring the heat, when he should've returned to the bar. Sighing, he closed his eyes. He didn't know why, but he suddenly felt old. As if he'd lived two lifetimes in one, and that he was eighty-four rather than forty-two.

He needed a break. The last week in July, when he would go away with Justine, couldn't come fast enough. He planned to spend more than a week with her on an island, where he could forget everything going on back on the mainland.

Frank realized Pasquale had become like his kidney that had become so painful and diseased, it had to be removed. He opened his eyes to stare at the back of his right hand. His knuckles were bruised from backhanding his cousin. Pasquale didn't know how lucky he was, because if any other man had said to him what he did, he wouldn't have hesitated to crush his windpipe.

He got up and went inside the bar to order a cold beer. He smiled at the barmaid when she asked if he was okay. He reassured her that he was, but Frank wasn't certain about Pasquale Festa, who'd decided to become involved in narcotics because he realized he could make a lot more money than working in the city's Meatpacking District. Not only were narcotics dirty; it was also a dangerous business. It was inevitable that his cousin would soon find out.

Kenny opened his eyes and reached over to answer the telephone. It seemed as if he'd just gotten into bed to get some sleep when the ringing of the phone jolted him awake. If he'd thought about it, he would have turned off the ringer. There were times when he loathed asking his mother to install an extension in his bedroom because he was tired of going into the kitchen to answer the wall phone.

"Hello," he drawled.

"Kenny?"

"Yeah." A girl had called him.

"Kenny, it's me, Larissa. Did I wake you up?"

Going on an elbow, he stared at the clock on the bedside table. It was after eleven in the morning. "Yeah. I had to get up early this morning to drive my mother and her friend to the airport for a six o'clock flight to Puerto Rico." Frank had given him permission to use his car during his absence.

"How long will be they be away?"

"A week. Why?"

"Do you want to come up to Riverdale today and hang out with me?"

Kenny fell back on the pillows. He liked Larissa, and thought of her as the three B's: brilliant, beautiful, and brazen. She achieved a near-perfect score on the SAT and earned scholarships to Brown, Spelman, and Yale. She'd decided on Spelman, because her mother had graduated from Howard University, and she also wanted the experience of attending a Black college.

"Maybe another time, Larissa. I'm planning to stay in today."

"Do you want company? You don't have to answer that, because I'm coming."

Before Kenny could tell her no, he heard the dial tone, indicating she'd hung up. He tried calling her back, but after counting off ten rings, he placed the receiver on the cradle and then swept back the sheet.

Today he wanted to sleep in late and spend the rest of the day listening to music. Frank had given him two checks for graduation. One to purchase a turntable and speakers he'd been talking about, and the second to purchase books and what he called "ancillary things" to ensure a smooth transition from high school to college. Between his mother and Frank, Kenny had learned to budget his earnings, purchasing only what he deemed a necessity. And that necessity was adding to his record collection.

Twice a month, after his shift ended at the restaurant, he'd walk across town from East to West Harlem to stop at the Record Shack on 100 Twenty-Fifth Street to purchase records. His taste in music ranged from R&B, to soul, to pop. He'd purchased a few jazz records featuring Nina Simone, John Coltrane, Herbie Hancock, Eddie Palmieri, and Vince Guaraldi. His mother had teased him, saying he was too young to have cultivated a taste in jazz when he should've been listening to popular Motown artists like the Temptations, Four Tops, Martha and the Vandellas, the Supremes, Marvin Gaye, and Smokey Robinson and the Miracles.

There were a few times when he'd caught his mother dancing and finger-popping whenever he played Motown, and Kenny wondered if she had missed going to school dances and house parties because she'd married right after graduating high school. That was something he vowed to avoid at all costs. He planned to enjoy going to college while earning both baccalaureate and master's degrees to become a certified social worker.

Kenny made up his bed, then went into the bathroom to shower before Larissa arrived. There was something about his former classmate he hadn't been able to figure out, because although they'd shared several classes, she hadn't indicated she was interested in him until six weeks before the end of the school year. She had sought him out in study hall and asked if she could copy his analytical geometry notes; she'd missed two classes because of a cold. He gave her the notes, and they exchanged telephone numbers with a promise to share notes whenever the other missed class. There were times when she stood a little too close for comfort, but Kenny hadn't thought much of it until he talked to Frankie and Ray during their monthly breakfast meeting.

Ray had asked if there was something wrong with him, because the girl was sending out signals that she liked him. Frankie agreed with Ray and told him that if she was willing to put out, then he should take her up on the offer. Kenny was reluctant to sleep with any of the girls at his school and had learned to ignore their flirtatious overtures, but Larissa wouldn't allow him to ignore her.

When he attended the barbecue at her parents' home, Larissa had clung to his arm as if she were an extra appendage. It had become so uncomfortable and embarrassing that he took her aside and asked her to stop hanging onto him. He'd regretted chastising her when her eyes filled with tears, but it worked when she didn't come near him again until Frank and his mother came to pick him up. She called him the next day to apologize, and they ended up spending more than an hour talking on the phone. It was the last week in July, and in another two, she would prepare to leave New York for Atlanta, Georgia, to move into her dorm at Spelman.

Kenny would continue to live at home and take the subway nine stops to and from City College. It was 1969, and City College of New York was a free public university; he'd promised Frank he would continue to help out at the restaurant every other weekend. He planned to take twelve credits his first semester, then sixteen or eighteen in subsequent semesters to graduate within four years. He knew it would take his mother as a part-time student much longer to graduate, but he also knew she was rooting as hard for him as he was for her.

He was dressed in a pair of jeans and a T-shirt when he opened the door for Larissa. Smiling, she held up a shopping bag wafting mouth-watering aromas, reminding Kenny that he hadn't eaten anything since the night before.

"Hey, handsome. I brought lunch for us."

Kenny opened the door wider. "Come in. It smells like Chinese food."

"I decided on Chinese because you said you eat a lot of Italian."

"Come into the kitchen," he said, staring at Larissa, who'd brushed her curls and secured them in a topknot, adding at least an inch to her petite frame.

"Your apartment is nice," she said as she followed him into the kitchen.

He wanted to ask her if it was nice for the projects, since she lived in a large single-family home in the Riverdale section of the Bronx with six bedrooms and bathrooms. Her father owned several car dealerships in the Bronx and New Rochelle.

"My mother tries to make the best of living in public housing."

Larissa stopped in the middle of the kitchen, setting her small purse and keys on the table. "Did I mention public housing, Kenny?"

He squinted, knowing he should've put on his glasses. "No, you didn't, but it did sound a little condescending."

"Please don't try to psychoanalyze me, because you really don't know me," she snapped angrily.

"And you definitely don't know me, Larissa. If you did, then you wouldn't have come here without an invitation."

Her eyelids fluttered. "Do you want me to leave?"

Kenny stared at her in what had become a stalemate. "No," he said, his tone softening. "You can stay, and thank you for bringing lunch."

She smiled. "Good, because I didn't drive all this way just to turn around and go back home."

Opening cabinets, he took down plates and glasses at the same time Larissa emptied the shopping bag. "What did you buy?" he asked her.

"Pork dim sum, barbecue spareribs, fried rice, deep-fried prawns, and spring rolls."

Kenny gave her an incredulous look. "You expect us to eat all of this for lunch?"

"We can have some for lunch and the rest for dinner."

He met her eyes. "Won't your folks expect you to be home for dinner?"

"No. They're spending the weekend in Boston. They took

my younger brother and sister with them for a family wedding."

"Why didn't you go with them?" Kenny asked as he took a container of fruit punch from the refrigerator and filled two glasses.

"I didn't want to go all that way to skin and grin at a cousin whose ass I can't stand. And she knows it."

"I'm sorry that y'all don't get along."

"It's all her fault, Kenny, because the bitch is a kleptomaniac. The last time we had a family reunion, she stole my mother's ring when she left it on the bathroom sink. I was waiting to use the bathroom, and I saw her go in and come out after my mother left. Then she swore by all that's holy that she didn't see the ring."

"Was the ring valuable?"

"Yes. It was my mother's birthstone—a ruby surrounded by diamonds. I told Mom not to wear any jewelry this weekend, because she'll definitely come home missing a piece."

Kenny had gone to house parties where doors to off-limits rooms were kept locked. He hadn't hosted any parties for his friends, and if he did, he would hold them in the residents' community center.

He set out spoons for them to select what they wanted from each container. "Do you need a fork?" he asked Larissa, when she set chopsticks on the table.

"Please. I still haven't gotten the knack of eating with chopsticks."

Larissa watched Kenny as he served himself, using chopsticks while she spooned portions from each container onto her plate. There was something about Kenneth Russell she'd struggled for months to ignore, until she decided it was getting close to the end of the school year, and if she didn't act, then she wouldn't see him again once they graduated.

She discovered him quiet, almost reserved when interacting with other students. Kenny was everything she liked in a boy. He was incredibly handsome, intelligent, aloof enough to appear mysterious, and respectful. He had what her maternal grandmother would've said was good home training. And he seemed oblivious to girls when they flirted with him. When asked whether he was attending the senior prom, he claimed he'd had a prior commitment on that night. It was then she decided on a different strategy when she followed him into the study hall and asked to copy his math notes.

Larissa had taken a chance inviting him for a backyard barbecue following their graduation and was shocked when he agreed to come. She was certain he could see her heart beating out of her chest when he introduced her to his mother and uncle. The way Mrs. Russell was staring at her had her wondering if the older woman knew that she'd had designs on her son.

She made it a practice to call Kenny when she knew his mother was at work, because a few times when Mrs. Russell had answered the phone, Larissa had changed her voice, pretending she had the wrong number. She hadn't realized she was going to hit the jackpot when Kenny answered the phone and told her that his mother was going to be away for a week. Her family was spending the weekend in Boston, and that meant she and Kenny could spend most of the day and night together.

"When your uncle came to pick you up, he told my father that his mother had taught you to speak Italian whenever you went to her house for cooking lessons." Kenny nodded. "How old were you when you began the lessons?"

Kenny, using chopsticks, picked up a prawn, meeting her eyes. "I was thirteen," he said, before taking a bite.

Larissa listened intently when he told her about going for weekly cooking lessons during the summer recess, then twice a month whenever school was in session. He was taking Spanish in junior high, so learning to speak and understand Italian had come easy to him.

"Don't you get confused when speaking Italian when it should be Spanish, and vice versa?"

Kenny smiled, tapping his forehead. "No. It's easy for me whenever I think in the language."

"I took French, and I still have to struggle for certain words and phrases."

"What made you decide to take French?"

"I like the way it sounds when someone speaks it." She slowly blinked when Kenny stared at her. "Do you think that's an asinine reason for taking it?"

"It doesn't matter what I think, Larissa. I've never been one to judge a person for what they decide to do or not do."

Larissa narrowed her eyes at the boy who was making it so difficult for her to get close to him. "You don't like me, do you?"

CHAPTER 24

Kenny set his chopsticks beside his plate, then rested his elbows on the table. He so wanted to tell Larissa that she was a spoiled brat, used to getting whatever she wanted, because her father doted on her.

"What gives you that impression?" he asked.

She lowered her eyes. "You came out and said in not too many words that you didn't want me to come here."

"That's because there were things I'd planned to do by myself while my mother was on vacation."

"Had you planned to have a girl over?"

A slight frown furrowed his forehead. "Is that what's bugging you? You think I'm involved with another girl?"

Larissa met his eyes. "Yes."

"What gave you that impression?" Kenny questioned.

"You didn't want me to touch you at the barbecue. You even told me to stop."

"That's because I couldn't move without you clinging to me. What were you trying to prove to the other girls? That I was your boyfriend?"

"No, Kenny. I wasn't trying to prove anything."

"Are you always so clingy with other guys?"

A secret smile parted her lips. "Only with those I like. And you have to know that I like you. A lot."

Kenny wanted to tell Larissa that she couldn't have been more obvious. It was something Frankie and Ray had confirmed when he told them about her. "And I like you, Larissa, but nothing's going to come of it, because you'll be heading for Atlanta in a couple of weeks."

"True. But can we see each other before I have to leave?"

"That all depends."

"On what?" Larissa asked.

"My job." Kenny told her about working in a restaurant kitchen in East Harlem.

"You're kidding, aren't you?" she questioned, her expression mirroring shock.

"Why would I kid about that?" He was hard-pressed to keep his increasing annoyance with Larissa out of his voice with each passing minute.

"Because it appears to be so beneath you to work in some kitchen."

"And what would be better than working in a kitchen?" he asked, raising his voice. In that instant, Kenny knew he was close to losing his temper. Something he rarely did.

"I could get you a position working at one of my father's car dealerships. He would be able to adjust your hours depending on your class schedule."

"Why would I want to work for your father when I work for my family? Yes, Larissa. The restaurant belongs to my uncle's family."

A rush of color suffused her gold-brown complexion. "I'm sorry. I didn't know."

"No, you didn't," he said facetiously. "That's because you don't know anything about me, Larissa."

Larissa knew Kenny was right. She knew nothing about him, and that made it difficult for her to get close to him. She knew he wasn't who her mother wanted her to get involved with. She had preached to her relentlessly about what type of man she wanted her daughter to marry. He had to be a college graduate, someone from a good family, and he must be a professional. The year her mother hosted a sweet sixteen celebration for her, Larissa decided it was no longer who or what Gladys Rossi wanted for her; it was who Larissa wanted for herself. And right now, she wanted Kenneth Russell, because she'd found him to be a challenge. And there was nothing she liked better than a challenge.

Peering at him through her lashes, she decided on another approach. "Why don't you tell me about you, so I can stop making a fool of myself."

Kenny smiled. "You're not a fool, Larissa. And there's not that much to tell you about me."

"I'm interested in whatever you choose to tell me."

Kenny was right, because she didn't know much about him other than he was an above-average student. She knew he lived with his mother, and it was his uncle rather than his father who'd come to the graduation ceremony.

She listened intently when Kenny revealed his father had died before he was born, and he'd been raised by his widowed mother. He'd grown up half a block from Central Park West before moving into public housing four years ago once his old neighborhood was slated for urban renewal. While in high school, he worked weekends at his uncle's restaurant as a cook and server, and had promised to work there every other weekend while in college.

"My mom and I will be going to the same college this fall. She married right out of high school and got pregnant right away, so she had to put off going to college until now."

Larissa laughed. "You're kidding."

"Nope. Mom will take night classes, while I'll go during the day."

"That is so cute." She picked up her fork and continued

eating. "It appears as if you and your mother have a very good relationship."

"We do. My mother is the best."

"Your mother was widowed very young. Didn't she want to marry again?"

"I asked her the same thing, and she said no."

"But your mother is so pretty, and men would be attracted to her."

Kenny agreed with Larissa. Men were attracted to his mother. And he was certain she would've accepted their advances if it hadn't been for Francis D'Allesandro. The man he called Uncle Dee had become an integral part of Justine Russell's life, and he suspected she was in denial about being in love with him. It was only after he'd graduated high school that his mother and Frank had resumed their friendship, where they were not only dating each other, but planning trips away together.

"My mother claims she's living her best life right now, and marriage doesn't factor into it."

"Good for her. I'm just waiting for the time when I can do whatever I want without having to answer to someone."

Kenny frowned. "You don't realize how lucky you are, Larissa. Your parents are sending you to a private university where they can write a check to cover all of your expenses for the next four years. Even after you graduate and have the career you want, you'll still have to answer to someone. The alternative is going into business for yourself."

"I'm definitely not going to take over my dad's business, because I'm planning on a career in politics." Larissa swallowed a mouthful of fried rice. "What had you planned to do if I hadn't come here?" she asked.

Kenny slowly shook his head. Larissa didn't want to work for her father, yet she'd talked about him working in one of his dealerships because she believed it was better than working in a restaurant's kitchen. It was obvious the girl was confused.

"I was going to listen to music."

"On the radio?"

"No. I'm developing a rather extensive record collection."

Larissa's eyes grew wide. "Can I see what you have?"

"Sure."

After he and Larissa finished eating, Kenny stored the cartons filled with leftovers in the refrigerator and washed the dishes and glasses, leaving them on a rack to air dry. Then he led Larissa into the living room to show her his record collection.

Sitting on the living room's area rug, Kenny took albums out of a wicker basket he'd stacked alphabetically, watching for Larissa's reaction to his taste in music. "I've just begun collecting jazz," he said after a comfortable silence.

Larissa shook her head. "I don't know what it is, but I can't get into jazz. All that improvising goes over my head."

Kenny stared at Larissa's delicate profile as she read the backs of the album covers. He liked her and would've liked her better if she hadn't been so aggressive. He preferred doing the chasing rather than the reverse.

"It has taken me a while to come to appreciate it."

Larissa picked up a 45, smiling. "This is more my taste. I love Motown." She handed him a record. "Can you please play this?"

Kenny took the record, got up, and removed the cover to the turntable. It was "My Girl," by the Temptations. Securing the plastic yellow adapter, he placed the record on the spindle.

"Don't turn it on yet," Larissa said, pushing to her feet. "I have to get something."

"What?"

"You'll see," she said, smiling at him over her shoulder.

Kenny didn't have to wait long to see what Larissa was holding in her hand when she returned to the living room. It was a marijuana joint and a lighter. Waves of shock slapped at him. Not only was he entertaining a girl in his home while his mother was away, but she was inviting him to smoke dope with her.

He'd smoked it for the first time the year before, when he, Frankie, and Ray had gotten together with some other boys in the basement of a building in *El Barrio* that was slated for demolition. The smoke had burned his eyes and chest before he felt a calming sensation that left him so lethargic, it had taken a while before he was able to stand upright unaided.

Although he enjoyed the effects of smoking weed, he'd never purchased it for himself, because he didn't want to risk being arrested and sent to prison. Frankie knew a dealer, and whenever Kenny felt the need to indulge, he gave his friend enough money for a few joints. He'd made it a practice never to smoke in the apartment, and prayed his mother would never discover that her son was an occasional pothead.

"I don't smoke in my house."

Larissa smiled. "But you do smoke?"

Kenny nodded. "On occasion."

Her smile grew wider. "I hope this is one of those occasions, Kenny Russell, because you don't have to worry about anyone seeing us." Larissa flicked the lighter and lit the joint. She took a drag, held the smoke in her mouth before slowly letting it out, then handed it to him.

Kenny sucked in a lungful of smoke, feeling its effects immediately. It was stronger than any herb he'd ever smoked. Then she was kissing him, and tearing at his clothes. Bending slightly, he picked Larissa up and headed for his bedroom.

"I'm on the pill," she whispered in his ear.

Kenny realized he was high, but not so high that he'd forgotten what Frank had lectured him about using a condom when sleeping with a woman. The only exception would be making love with his wife. Larissa wasn't his wife, and at eighteen, he had no intention of becoming a father. Pulling back the blanket, he placed her on the mattress, then walked over to a chest of drawers to retrieve several condoms he'd secreted under several T-shirts. Returning to the bed, he met Larissa's eyes as she watched him slip the latex sheath over his erection. Smiling, she extended her arms, and he got into bed with her.

Within seconds of joining their bodies, Kenneth Douglas Russell forgot almost everything he'd been warned about having girls in the house when his mother wasn't there. That underage drinking and smoking marijuana could lead to more addictive substances like heroin and cocaine. And she'd pleaded with him not to make her a grandmother until he was old enough to support a woman and his children.

Kenny felt himself floating, and he knew it was from a combination of drugs and sex. He buried his face against the column of Larissa's scented neck when her legs circled his waist, allowing for deeper penetration. It no longer mattered that he'd found her too aggressive for his liking, because she was offering him the best sex he'd ever had.

Larissa bit her lip when she felt the flutters in her vagina grow stronger and stronger before realizing she was going to experience an orgasm for the first time since having sex. She'd slept with boys since turning fifteen, but was left unfulfilled and wondering why she felt nothing with them. However, something told her the first time she smiled at Kenny, and he returned her smile, that still waters ran deep. That his aloofness was a foil for a sensuality that could turn a woman on with a single glance.

She could feel the heat of his body course down hers, from her head to her toes, as she moaned with the erotic pleasure that made her feel as if she'd been transported to a place she'd never been before. Then, without warning, the first orgasm came, followed by others overlapping one after another.

Larissa could not disguise her body's reaction to Kenny's lovemaking, when they climaxed at the same time. She didn't know how long they lay together, their bodies joined.

Kenny lay on Larissa, supporting his greater weight on his forearms. He knew he had to get up and discard the condom but loathed pulling out of her warm body. Larissa Rossi, drugs, and sex were a lethal combination. He was glad she was going away for college, because if she remained in the city, then he knew it would be impossible for him to stay away from her.

"Where are you going?" she asked when he pulled out.

"I have to throw away the condom." He had to dispose of it and clean up any evidence of their smoking and lovemaking.

Sitting up, Larissa caught his wrist. "Can I spend the night?"

Kenny looked at her as if she'd suddenly taken leave of her senses. "No."

"Why not?"

"Because I said you can't, that's why."

Her eyes grew wide. "That's the thanks I get for letting you fuck me."

He slowly shook his head. Kenny didn't want to believe that because they'd made love, he would give in to her demands. "That's where you're wrong, Larissa. You fucked me, not the other way around. You can use the bathroom to clean yourself; then I want you to get your things and leave."

"Fuck you, Kenny Russell!" she shouted.

He grabbed her shoulders in a firm grip. "Don't push me," he warned in a dangerously soft voice, "or I'll toss your naked ass out the door, and lock it behind you. What's it going to be?"

"I'm leaving."

"Good."

Kenny waited for her to go into the bathroom before he walked to the kitchen and discarded the condom in the garbage. Now, in hindsight, he realized he'd made a grievous mistake in opening the door for Larissa Rossi. He had to know she was clingy when he'd gone to her home after graduation. He'd been willing to spend the rest of the afternoon with her and then escort her to her car when it came time to leave. There was no way he was going to allow a woman to spend the night with him in his mother's house. If he wanted to spend a night with a woman, it would be at a hotel or motel.

He'd put on his boxers, jeans, and T-shirt by the time Larissa emerged from the bathroom fully dressed. Her eyes were red, and he assumed she had been crying. "I'll walk you to your car."

She shook her head, wayward curls moving with the motion. "That's okay. I'm not parked that far away."

"I'm sorry, Larissa," Kenny apologized.

She nodded, smiling. "It's okay, Kenny. I shouldn't have tried pressuring you to do something you didn't want to do. There are times when I know I'm too pushy."

"And clingy," he teased.

"That, too."

"Please call me to let me know you got home safe."

Larissa combed her fingers through her hair. "Does this mean we're still friends?"

Kenny wanted to tell her they were never friends. That they'd gone from former classmates to lovers. "Of course."

He waited for her to retrieve her purse, then walked her to the door. Lowering his head, he kissed her cheek. "Don't forget to call me."

Going on tiptoe, Larissa brushed her mouth over his. "I won't."

Kenny opened and closed the door behind her and exhaled an audible sigh. Now that Larissa was gone, he had to take a shower, get rid of what remained of the joint, strip his bed, and in a few days, take the bedding to a laundromat.

His phone rang forty minutes later, and when he picked up, it was Larissa telling him she'd made it home safely. "Can we get together again before I leave for Atlanta?"

Hell, no, girl, because you're nothing but trouble with a capital T. But if I do agree to see you again, then there can't be any weed or sex.

"Okay," Kenny said, when the voice in his head was calling him every kind of fool imaginable, telling him that Larissa Rossi was a master manipulator. "I'm not certain when I'll be called in to work, because the restaurant gets very busy in the summer."

"That's okay. I'm willing to wait until you have some free time."

Kenny wanted to tell her that if he did have some free time, then he didn't intend to spend it with her. There was no need to lead her on when he knew getting involved with her would be problematic. "Goodbye, Larissa."

A beat passed. "Goodbye, Kenny."

He hung up, knowing he'd deceived her. Kenny didn't want to believe that he'd used her for sex, because she'd been the one to initiate it. He knew if he'd been in his right mind, he would've rejected her. But the pleasure he'd derived from the marijuana had clouded his judgment, and the pleasure he experienced when he'd penetrated her was too intense to disregard. He'd admitted to his mother that he wasn't smoking cigarettes, but she hadn't mentioned marijuana.

Kenny didn't know what was in the joint he shared with Larissa that had triggered an instant high. Never again. He vowed it would be the last time he would ever smoke a joint.

CHAPTER 25

"Are you certain you only want juice?" Justine asked Kenny when he entered the kitchen.

"Yes, ma'am. I'm meeting Ray and Frankie for breakfast."

She gave him a warm smile. "Oh, now I'm a *ma'am*."

Kenny sat at the table and picked up the glass of freshly squeezed orange juice. His mother preferred making her own juice to buying those in cartons. "Mom or ma'am," he teased, "whatever fits."

His mother had returned from vacationing in Puerto Rico, her complexion several shades darker and with diamond studs in her ears. She said they were a gift from Frank, who claimed every woman should own a pair of diamond earrings during her lifetime. He didn't know if Frank and his mother were sleeping together, and if they were, it didn't bother him as long as she was happy. And Kenny hoped it was the same with Frank, because of what he'd had to go through after being diagnosed with kidney cancer. When he'd gone to see Frank after his undergoing chemo and radiation therapy, he'd begun crying and couldn't stop. Not only had Frank lost all of his hair, but he'd appeared emaciated. That's when

Frank made him promise not to tell Justine that he had cancer. There were so many times when he'd wanted to tell his mother, but he realized it wasn't his secret to reveal.

The telephone rang, and Kenny met his mother's eyes. "You answer it," he said.

Her eyebrows lifted questioningly. "Are you sure?" she asked when it rang a second time.

"Yes, and if it's for me, I'm not here."

Justine picked up the wall phone. "Russell residence. I'm sorry, Larissa, but he's not here. He has to work today. Do you want to leave a message? Okay. I'll let him know." She hung up the phone and glared at him.

"What's with you and that girl?"

Kenny took a sip of juice. "I don't want to see her."

"Why, son?"

"Because she's too clingy."

Justine set the plate with two pancakes and several strips of crispy bacon on the table. "You didn't seem to mind it when she was hanging onto your arm after your graduation. Or were you too enthralled with her to overlook her body language?"

"Maybe I was."

"What happened, Kenneth?"

He knew his mother was serious when she hadn't shortened his name. "She's just too aggressive."

Picking up a bottle of syrup, Justine poured it over her pancakes. "Explain aggressive."

"She's smothering, Mom. I know if I got involved with her, she'd want to control every phase of my life."

Justine gave him a direct stare. "I'm going to ask you something, and I don't want you to lie to me. Have you slept with her?"

Kenny stared at his mother behind the lenses of his glasses. They'd developed a relationship where she demanded complete honesty from him. She'd warned him not to lie to her, even if she didn't like what he said or did.

"Yes."

Justine slowly blinked. "How many times?"

"Once."

"That was one time too many, Kenny. If you knew in advance that the girl was going to be a problem, why would you have sex with her? Sleeping with her sent a message that she was a lot more than a friend."

"I know, Mom. I messed up."

"No, Kenny. You *fucked* up when you slept with that girl!"

"Mom!"

"Don't you dare 'Mom' me, Kenneth. No woman wants to be used, then discarded, when a man decides he's through with her. I'd like to think I raised you better than that. What happened to dating a woman for a while before you hop into bed with her? If you'd done that with Larissa, you wouldn't need me to run interference for you."

Kenny's hand came down hard on the table. "Like you and Frank? You make the man wait five years before you're willing to not only go out, but go away with him. If he'd been any other man, he would've walked away and not looked back."

"You don't know what you're talking about."

"Don't I, Mother? The man fell in love with you the first time he saw you. But you made up all kinds of excuses why you didn't want to marry him when you could've been with him when he was going through his cancer treatments. The day I walked into his apartment and saw him looking as if death was waiting to take him, I started crying like a baby. When he saw my reaction, he made me promise not to tell you that he was sick, because he didn't want to upset you. That's how much he loved and still loves you."

Justine stared at her son, who'd turned into a stranger right before her eyes. She knew he and Frank were close, but she had no idea how much Kenny had wanted them to be together. "There are so many things you don't know that I can't tell you," she said in a hushed voice.

"Why not?" Kenny challenged.

"Because it's not the right time."

"When will it be the right time?" he asked.

Justine closed her eyes and huffed a breath. There was no way she could reveal that she was a complete fraud. That her life was filled with lies that seemed to penetrate every phase of her existence, and she didn't know how to stop lying. The web of lies kept growing bigger and bigger until they'd turned her into someone she had come to loathe.

"Soon," she whispered. She'd waited eighteen years for her son to reach adulthood, and Justine knew it wouldn't take another eighteen before she revealed the circumstances surrounding his existence.

"I'm sorry for what I said about you and Frank."

"You don't have to apologize, because what you said about us is true. And Frank was right to hide his cancer from me, because I don't think I would've been strong enough to help him go through his treatments. Both of us are older and hopefully wiser, where we can truly enjoy each other's company."

"Does this mean you're going to marry him?"

"No, Kenny. Frank doesn't want to get married, and neither do I. That's something we can both agree on."

"So, it doesn't bother you to see him every once in a while, and then go on vacation together?"

"Of course not. We're not like some young couple who have to call and see each other every waking minute. I'm thirty-five, and Frank is forty-two, and we plan to have fun for how much time we've been given."

"I suppose I'll see life differently when I'm your age," Kenny said, smiling.

"I'm sure you will. Now, tell me if you want me to keep this girl off your back until she leaves for college?"

"Please, Mama."

"Oh, now it's Mama. And because I am your mama, I will answer the phone whenever it rings and tell her you're either working, sleeping, or out with your friends."

Kenny smiled. "Love you, Mom."

Justine nodded. "I know."

She sat at the table long after Kenny left the apartment to meet his friends. She didn't want to believe her son had slept with a girl he didn't like, then decided he didn't want to see her anymore. But how did he expect her to react? No woman wanted to be used for sex, then discarded like a piece of trash.

Justine knew from the way Larissa had been staring up at Kenny and hanging on his arm that she wanted more than friendship. Justine hoped that he'd used a condom when he had sex with her. One time she had been rearranging the clothes in his dresser and she'd discovered a supply of condoms. They indicated he was having or contemplating having sex, and their presence had eased some of her anxiety that he would get someone pregnant or come down with a venereal disease.

Kenny had been so adamant that he wanted her and Frank to marry, and Justine wondered if it was because he hadn't wanted her to grow old alone. Every once in a while, he'd talk about her being alone, and she knew it was something that weighed heavily on him. She didn't have any close friends, but there were a few times when she would join some of her coworkers at a restaurant for the retirement or birthday celebration of a staff member.

It was at one of the get-togethers that a Black pharmacist had asked her out. She'd agreed to meet him for brunch. Justine found him intelligent, charming, and articulate. Someone she wouldn't mind seeing again. Then everything changed when he began talking about his ex-wife. It was apparent he hadn't gotten over her leaving him for another man. When she suggested he seek counseling to deal with the dissolution of his marriage, he thanked her, because it was something he needed to hear. He then asked if she would see him again once he resolved his problem. Justine told him she would and wished him the best. They'd parted as friends, and whenever she would see him at the hospital, he would give her a thumbs-up sign. That was more than three months ago, before Frank had come back into her life.

Frankie and Ray were waiting for Kenny in front of the coffee shop when he arrived. The dining establishment had changed owners twice since they'd first begun eating there in the seventh grade, but the cooks had stayed on.

Ray, who'd let his curly hair grow, now sported a modified Afro. Frankie also stopped cutting his hair like so many young college students. Raven-black waves nearly reached his shoulders. They were eighteen, all had registered for the draft, and were fiercely opposed to the war in Vietnam. The three entered the coffee shop and sat in their favorite booth near the rear.

"What's up with the beard?" Kenny asked Frankie.

Frankie ran his fingers over the stubble on his face. "I'm trying to fit in with the hippies before I begin classes."

Ray grunted. "That's okay with me. Just make certain you shower every day."

Frankie laughed. "Not all hippies are dirty."

"Frankie's right," Kenny said, meeting his blue eyes.

With the emerging beard and longer hair, Frankie's appearance had changed from matinee idol leading man to villain. He said his mother complained about his long hair, but there wasn't much she could do about it now that he was an adult.

"My sister Delores came home a couple of days ago and announced she enlisted in the Army as a nurse," Ray said. "I thought it was the beginning of World War III. Papi went completely *loco*, and my mother cried so much she had to go to bed."

"Why did she do that?" Frankie asked.

Ray shook his head. "I don't know. It would be one thing if there wasn't a war going on, but to be shipped overseas to work in a jungle hospital is crazy as hell."

Frankie slowly shook his head. "She's going to a war zone while we're trying to keep our asses here, hoping to get a deferment as college students."

Kenny didn't want to think of being drafted and leaving his mother alone. Perhaps it would be easier if she had another child or children, but to bury her only child would prove to be devastating for her. Expressly since she refused to marry again.

"What if we marry and have some kids, then maybe we would be exempt from the draft," Ray joked.

"That was possible before that fucker LBJ rescinded the exemption for married men with children in 1965," Kenny spat out.

"That's because the motherfucker had us fully enter the war in 1965," Frankie stated. "If the French couldn't defeat the Vietnamese, then what makes these dumbass politicians believe the Americans can?"

"It was different in Korea and World War II, because we knew who the enemies were," Kenny said.

"How can an American soldier tell a North Vietnamese from a South Vietnamese when all the fuckers look alike?" Ray asked.

"You're right," Kenny said. "That's why we're going to lose the war. I have no intention of going overseas to kill people who haven't done shit to me. Even Malcolm X spoke out against the United States' involvement in Vietnam before he was assassinated. It was the same with Dr. King, who talked about the suffering of the Vietnam people, whose homes were being destroyed and their culture obliterated."

"You sound like a militant," Frankie said accusingly.

Kenny glared at him. "Maybe I am because of the way I'm feeling about a lot of things nowadays. I've been reading a lot about the Black Panther Party for Self-Defense, who are fighting for justice for African Americans and other oppressed communities in this country."

"The Black Panthers aren't the only group organizing against injustice," Ray added. "Late last year, the Young Lords, who were a former Chicago street gang, is now a civil and human rights organization. Their slogan is *Tengo Puerto Rico en mi corazón.*"

"I have Puerto Rico in my heart," Kenny translated.

"Speaking of Puerto Rico, Kenny," Frankie said. "I heard that my uncle took your mother to the island for vacation."

"I heard the same thing," he joked, smiling.

Ray waited until the server set menus on the table before he said, "Don't be holding out on us, Kenny. What's up with your moms and Frankie's uncle?"

"Nothing's up, Ray. They've been friends for years."

"*Amigos?*"

Kenny struggled to hold his temper. "Why are you asking me how they are friends, Ramon? They're grown and do whatever the hell they want to do."

"Whoa, Kenny," Ray said, holding up a hand. "I meant no disrespect."

Frankie elbowed Ray in the ribs. "If that's the case, then you shouldn't have said it."

"Sorry. I forgot that I was talking about your family." Ray studied the menu, mumbling in Spanish under his breath.

Kenny slowly shook his head. "You just can't let it go, can you?" he said in the same language. "You're talking about both my family and Frankie's."

Frankie looked at Ray, then Kenny. "Come on, guys, let's not start shit with one another when we have more important things to worry about. Playtime is over for us. If our number comes up in the draft, we're going to have to make the decision whether to report to the draft office or get in a car and drive across the border to Canada."

"That's something I can't afford to do," Kenny said. "The first thing the government would do when I come back is throw my Black ass in a federal prison and lose the key."

"I may be exempt because I have flat feet," Ray announced proudly. He gestured to Kenny. "You could also get an exemption if you can't pass the eye test."

"That's a probability." He never thought not having perfect vision would be his ticket out of military service.

Frankie blew out his breath. "I have perfect vision and don't have flat feet, so I don't really have an out. Vietnam is all about a rich man's war and a poor man's fight. Just think about the billions of dollars the government will pay these companies to manufacture tanks, guns, and fighter jets."

Kenny put up both hands. "Enough talk about the war. You can't turn on the television or open a newspaper or magazine and not be bombarded with news about Vietnam."

"I'd rather talk about pussy," Ray joked.

"You would," Frankie said, shaking his head.

"I know you're not talking," Ray countered. "Aren't you the one who has a little black book with names of girls in alphabetical order?"

Frankie blushed. "Not quite."

Kenny met Frankie's eyes. "Have you been holding out on me?" Whenever he went to East Harlem, he usually stopped to visit with him. And he'd continued the practice to join the extended D'Allesandro family for first Sunday dinner.

"No," Frankie admitted. "I broke up with the last girl I was seeing, because she was getting serious. Talking about wanting to get married. When I told her that I wasn't ready, she got into a huff and walked out. She came back to see me a week later, claiming she was willing to wait until I was ready. What I didn't tell her is she would have to wait a long time and that she'd better look for someone else."

"I don't think you'll ever be ready, Frankie," Kenny said, "because you don't know what you want."

"And you do, Kenny?" Frankie asked.

He shook his head. "No. But, I'm willing to wait. When the right one comes along, I'll know it."

"How long are you willing to wait, Kenny?" Ray questioned.

"For as long as it will take. It wouldn't matter if I'm twenty or thirty-five. Once I make that decision, I'll commit to being a faithful husband."

"You better get all you can before that, because all of the kitty cat that's out here will no longer be available to you," Frankie teased, winking.

Kenny didn't want to talk about sleeping with women because of what he'd just experienced with Larissa. It probably served him right, because he never should've had sex with her in his mama's house.

The server came over to take their orders, and all talk about the war and women was forgotten. The conversation segued to college and the courses they planned to take, as they shared bacon, sausage, pancakes, eggs, waffles, and coffee.

Two hours later they parted, with a promise to meet again the following month.

PART FOUR

1970s–1980s
THE ROADS NOT
TAKEN

CHAPTER 26

Ramon Torres closed the textbook and then walked over to the bed in the alcove of his basement apartment and flopped down on it. He was exhausted, his brain drained, and he prayed to make it through the next four months and earn his degree, then take the entire summer off to mentally recuperate before enrolling in medical school. The apartment had become his sanctuary, where he wouldn't have to interact with members of his family until it was time for him to eat. He'd asked his father if he could move out of his bedroom and into the basement, because he needed a quiet place to study. He had to maintain a certain grade average, because he didn't want to jeopardize losing his scholarship.

Although there was more room in the house than in their Upper West Side apartment, his brothers and sisters ran down hallways and in and out of rooms as if they were playing in Central Park. Once he threatened to move out and into residences belonging to Columbia University, Enrique agreed to let him move into the finished basement he'd planned to use as a rental. His parents had worked two jobs for two years to save enough to purchase a two-family house in a quiet neighborhood along a tree-lined Bronx street. Ray's full scholarship to an Ivy League college was a financial windfall for his parents. He'd made the Dean's list every semester and was scheduled to graduate with honors.

He'd just closed his eyes when he registered tapping on the door leading into the backyard. Swinging his legs over the side of the bed, he went to see who it was. Peering through the security eye, he recognized his girlfriend.

Ray opened the door and went completely still when he saw her face. She'd been crying. She fell against his chest, his arms going around her body. He closed the door and led her over to his bed.

"What's the matter?" Ray cradled the back of her head. "Come on, baby. Talk to me."

"I'm . . . I'm pregnant," she sobbed.

Ray went still, as if he'd been jolted by a bolt of electricity. "What!" She couldn't be. He'd always used a condom whenever they slept together.

Moisture spiked her lashes as she looked up at him. "I'm having your baby."

Ray shook his head. "No, Micky, that's not possible. Every time we slept together, you know I always used a condom."

Migdalia, or Micky to her family and friends, had become an obsession for Ray the first they shared a bed and, he'd found himself addicted to her. She'd become his drug of choice. And she hadn't been his first addiction. That was sex.

It was with the onset of puberty when he'd begun masturbating several times a day, but it hadn't been enough to quell the urges that would happen spontaneously whenever he saw a woman he found physically attractive.

Things changed for him when he met Migdalia Hernandez, who was working at a city hospital while studying to become a dietitian. She was the first girl with whom he'd been able to discuss politics and current events. They'd talked about the Vietnam War, and how drugs were ravaging and destroying Black and Spanish neighborhoods. When he first asked her out, she'd admitted she was seeing a boy who was very jealous, but eventually she agreed to come to his house whenever she wasn't working. She would come when his family had settled in for the night and stay with him until dawn. He never knew when she was coming, so he installed a telephone in his apartment so she could call before coming over. Once they begun having sex, after she'd broken up with her boyfriend, Ray found himself in over his head, because he found himself craving Micky like an addict looking for his next fix.

"It is possible, because this baby inside of me is yours and you have to marry me."

Ray shook his head. "If the baby you claim is mine, then we'll wait until after it's born to determine the paternity. Meanwhile, get it out of your head that I'm going to marry you."

Micky sucked in her breath, held it, then slowly let it out. "I'm good enough to sleep with but not good enough to become your wife. Thank you, Ramon Torres, for letting me know what type of man I fell in love with."

She was up and out the door before Ray could bring his thoughts into any semblance of order. He buried his face in his hands, unable to believe what had just transpired. They'd slept together less than a half dozen times, and there wasn't a time when he hadn't used a condom. Maybe her menses was late and she'd assumed she was pregnant. There were so many scenarios crowding his head that Ray felt like screaming at the top of his lungs to release his frustration.

The next day was the first Saturday of the month and his scheduled breakfast meeting with Frankie and Ray. He would wait and talk to his friends about his dilemma.

"We'll be graduating in another four months, so why do you look so down in the dumps?" Frankie asked Ray.

Ray forced a smile. His boyhood friend was right. It was 1973, and four years had gone by faster than he'd expected it would. Many things had happened during that time. Student protests at Kent State University in Ohio resulted in four students losing their lives and nine others wounded when the National Guard opened fire on them. There was a Constitutional Amendment lowering the voting age from twenty-one to eighteen. Newspaper headlines blared with the news that four men had been arrested for breaking into the Democratic National Committee headquarters in the Watergate office building in Washington, DC. And in the 1972 November election, incumbent President Richard M. Nixon had beat his Democratic challenger George McGovern, winning by a lopsided victory of five hundred twenty electoral college votes to McGovern's seventeen. The Vietnam War had ended in January, and he, Frankie, and Kenny had miraculously escaped the draft. The war was over, but at the expense of more than 58,000 dead American soldiers.

"I have a dilemma."

Kenny ran a hand over his bearded face. "We all have dilemmas at one time or another."

"Not the one I'm facing," Ray said.

"Talk to us," Frankie urged.

"How the hell can I support a wife when I'm still in college and living in my parents' house?"

Kenny adjusted his glasses on the bridge of his nose. "Why are you talking about marriage when you've never mentioned having a girlfriend?"

Ray told his friends about Migdalia and that she was carrying his baby. "I don't know if she's telling me the truth, but every time I slept with her, I used a rubber."

Frankie leaned closer. "How long have you been sleeping with her?"

"Not long. I met her around Christmastime, and we didn't begin sleeping together until a couple of months ago, and I doubt if we've been together more than six times."

"Well, it only takes one time, Ray," Frankie said quietly.

"She's asking that you marry her?" Kenny asked. Ray nodded. "Well, brother, I don't know what to tell you."

"Have you offered to give her money for an abortion?" Frankie asked. "In case she's not aware of it, abortions are now legal in this country."

Ray closed his eyes. Earlier that year, the US Supreme Court ruled in *Roe v. Wade* that women could not be prevented by a state in having an abortion in the first six months of her pregnancy. "No. And if she is having a baby, I can't begin to think of her killing it."

"A baby or *your* baby?" Kenny questioned. "Something tells me you don't believe the baby is yours."

Ray combed his fingers through his curly hair. "I don't want to believe it's mine. I told her I'm willing to wait until after she has the kid to determine whether it is mine or someone else's."

"Was she seeing someone else?" Frankie asked Ray.

"Initially she wouldn't go out with me because she said she had a jealous boyfriend, then everything changed when she'd come to my place at night just to talk. The first time she let me make love to her, I figured she'd broken up with him."

Kenny covered his face as he shook his head. "Ramon, were you so blinded by pussy that you were taken in by this girl? If she came to you at night, it was because she was still with her boyfriend. Maybe the dude worked nights, and that was when she was able to get away."

Leaning back against the booth, Ray closed his eyes. "You're right, because I never thought of that."

"That's because you were pussy-whipped," Frankie snapped angrily.

"How many times haven't we had this conversation?" Kenny asked, frowning at Ray. "You're smarter than me and Frankie put together, but you're a moron when it comes to women. You can dish out good advice to others, but you refuse to listen when me and Frankie tell you what you shouldn't do."

"I'm not telling you about my problem so you can beat me the fuck up. I need to know if my friends are in my corner."

"We are," Frankie and Kenny chorused.

"One thing for certain is I'm not going to marry her now. And if the kid is mine, then I'll try and provide whatever financial support I can until I graduate from medical school."

"So, you don't intend to marry her?" Frankie asked.

"I don't know, Frankie," Ray said. "I like her a lot, but not enough to marry her."

Reaching across the table, Kenny patted Ray's hand. "Maybe you'll change your mind after the baby is born. Kids have a way of melting the coldest hearts."

Ray knew his friends were right. Whenever they had a problem with a woman, he would tell them not what they wanted to hear but what they needed to do if it meant resolving their relationships. Kenny had become involved with a girl who was enamored with the Black Panther Party, and his increasing militancy was attracting the attention of college officials and also jeopardizing his draft deferment. Although Ray agreed with the organization's fight for justice for African Americans and other oppressed communities, the FBI had identified them as a radical subversive group.

When Kenny revealed she'd been pressuring him to marry her, Ray had questioned, what was the rush? Why couldn't she wait until after they graduated to tie the knot? When Ray had posed the same question to her, she was forced to tell him she was planning to move to Oakland to become a member of the Black Panthers, and she wanted him to come with her. Within days of Kenny telling her he wanted to put off marriage until graduation, she dropped out and joined a group of radical students heading for the West Coast. Kenny was heartbroken, but in the end he was thankful for the advice.

Frankie was dating a girl he suspected was stealing from him. He'd complained to Ray that whenever he went to her apartment, he would leave with less money than when he arrived. Frankie had admitted he would sometimes give her money to purchase something she wanted, yet that didn't explain how she'd managed to remove bills from his wallet without him being aware of it. When Ray suggested he mark the bills with an invisible ink that was only visible when it came into contact with a minimal amount of body heat, it did the trick when Frankie found red color on her fingertips. She was forced to confess that she'd come from generations of pickpockets, and it was something she did for a living.

When Ray thought about it, Kenny becoming involved with a girl who joined a militant group and Frankie falling for a pickpocket both paled in comparison to what he was facing. There was the possibility that he may have gotten Micky pregnant. Condoms and oral contraceptives weren't one hundred percent effective in preventing contraception. Only abstinence was.

Micky telling Ray she was carrying his baby was like a stop sign. He had to stop sleeping with women. It was time for him to revert to adolescence, when he was forced to assuage his own sexual needs.

"Thanks, guys, for hearing me out."

"If this turns out to be a false alarm, then make sure you keep your Johnson in your pants until you're ready to become a daddy," Kenny drawled.

"I second that," Frankie said. "But if it turns out to be the real deal, then I'm volunteering to become godfather to your son or daughter."

Kenny wrapped an arm around Frankie's neck. "That's not funny."

Frankie flung off Kenny's arm. "I'm serious. Both Ray and I are Catholic, so I would be the better choice for godfather than you, heathen."

Kenny glared at Frankie. "You call me a heathen while you two Catholic boys are out here fucking everything in a skirt. What happened to waiting until you're married to engage in sexual intercourse? And when was the last time either of you went to confession?" He held up a hand. "Wait, you don't have to answer that. You probably stopped after you made your Confirmation. So, y'all should be careful about who you call a heathen."

Ray leaned over the table. "There's no need to be so sanctimonious, Russell, because you're no choirboy."

Kenny smiled. "True, but at least I'm not a pussy gangster like my brother, D'Allesandro."

Frankie laughed loudly, causing several diners to turn and look in their direction. "One of these days I'm going to give up pussy," he whispered, "and settle down with a nice girl and start a family."

"One these days, all of us will give up our causes to become a part of the establishment we now disdain," Kenny said. "We'll cut our hair, shave our beards, give up our love beads, dashikis, and sandals in exchange for a Brooks Brothers suit, trench coat, wingtips, and a wedding ring."

Ray nodded. "As crazy as it sounds, I have to agree with you, Kenny."

Frankie massaged the nape of his neck. "I know I'm going to miss my long hair when I have to get a position at an auditing firm before I take the CPA exam."

"Same here when it comes to shaving," Kenny said, running his fingers down his bearded face. "My mother keeps complaining that I look like the Wolfman with my hair and beard."

Frankie shifted on his seat to meet Kenny's eyes. "You mentioning your mother."

"What about her?"

"Are she and my uncle still together?"

Kenny shook his head. "I really don't know. There are long stretches of time when they don't see each other; then he'll come and take her out to dinner. Mom doesn't have much free time with work and school. She just earned enough credits to become a junior, so she's focused on graduating and becoming a teacher."

"Good for her," Ray said, smiling. "You must feel good that your mom decided to go back to college at her age."

"She's not going back," Kenny told Ray. "She put off going to college because she married right out of high school and got pregnant with me a few months later. But she never gave up on her dream to become a teacher. Whenever she's home, she has her head in a book, so I end up tiptoeing in and out so not to disturb her."

"Is it weird that both you and your mother are going to the same college?" Frankie asked Kenny.

"Not at all. I suppose it would feel weird if we were in the same classes. But she goes at night, so our paths rarely cross."

"Are you still planning to go to graduate school?" Ray asked Kenny.

"Yup. But I'm going to take a year off before starting. I need to give my brain a rest before opening more textbooks. Meanwhile, I'm planning to apply to several city social service agencies for a caseworker position. And if I'm hired, then I'll keep my day job and go to social work school at night, because I want to save enough money to move into my own place."

Frankie smiled at the waitress when she placed cups of steaming coffee on the table. "I'm calling it quits after I graduate, because once I get my CPA license, I don't plan to sit in another classroom."

Ray took a sip of coffee, staring at Frankie over the rim of the cup. "Do you still plan to take over your uncle's business?"

"Yeah. He wants me to keep it in the family."

"You and Kenny will be able to take a breather from school, while I have many more years ahead of me before I'll be able to add Ramon Torres, MD as my signature."

"Dial back the bullshit, Ray," Frankie drawled. "In another ten years, me and Kenny will be bringing our kids to your office for medical checkups for school and sleepaway camps."

"I don't remember telling you yokels that I was going to specialize in pediatrics."

"Yes, you did," Frankie said.

"I did?" Ray asked, looking confused. "I was sure I mentioned gynecology."

"Forget about that, Ray," Kenny said, grinning. "Being around that much snatch will only get you in more trouble than you are now."

"That's not funny, my brother," Ray snapped.

Kenny's expression changed, becoming serious. "What you're now facing isn't funny. So, it's time you get ready for the fallout. And whatever the outcome, remember me and Frankie are your brothers. We'll always be here for you."

Ray nodded. "Same here." He placed his hand palm down on the table. Kenny placed his hand over his, and then Frankie did the same with Kenny's. "Brothers for life," he said in a hushed whisper.

"Brothers for life," Kenny and Frankie repeated.

CHAPTER 27

The incessant ringing shattered Kenny's sleep, and he reached over to the bedside table to answer the phone. He'd gone out to a bar with several of his classmates to celebrate the end of their undergraduate education, and against his better judgment had drunk more than he should have, and was forced to hail a taxi to bring him home.

"Hello."

"Kenny, it's Frankie."

He was suddenly alert when he heard the panic in Frankie's voice. "What's up?"

"Ray is in Lincoln Hospital. Someone beat the shit out of him, and right now it's touch and go with him."

"Come and pick me up. I'll be downstairs when you get here." He slammed down the receiver, not giving Frankie the chance to accept or reject his command.

Getting out of bed, he raced to the bathroom to brush his teeth and shower. Twenty minutes later, he stood on the corner, waiting for Frankie to drive up. He and Frankie had attended Ray's graduation commencement two weeks before, and Ray had accompanied him when they went to Frankie's.

It would be another three days before he would walk across the stage to receive his own degree. He scribbled a note for his mother, leaving it on the kitchen table to let her know he had to leave in the middle of the night to go the hospital because Ray had been in an accident. But Ramon Torres didn't have an accident. Frankie said someone had assaulted him, and Kenny did something he hadn't done in years. He prayed.

He spied Frankie's dark blue Mustang when it skidded to a stop, and within seconds of Kenny getting into the car, Frankie executed a perfect U-turn and headed uptown. It had only been months before that they'd talked about getting haircuts and shaving beards. As it came closer to graduation, they visited their respective barbershops to cut off the hair they'd coveted during their college years.

"How did you find out that he'd been beaten?" Kenny asked Frankie.

"His sister Delores, who is a nurse at Lincoln Hospital, called me, saying the police had brought her brother in after they found him on a corner in Hunts Point."

"What the hell was he doing in Hunts Point?"

Frankie shook his head. "I don't know." A beat passed. "Do you know what I think?"

Kenny stared at his friend's distinctive profile. "What?"

"It had to do with a woman."

"No, Frankie. Don't say that, man."

"What else could it be, Kenny? We both know Ray can't stay away from the ladies, so maybe he was trolling the area looking to pick up a whore, and if he got into it with one of the girls, then her pimp probably kicked his ass to teach him a lesson."

"I hope you're wrong."

"So do I," Frankie agreed.

Kenny stared out the windshield trying to process that a boy he'd known from grade school was in a hospital fighting for his life when his dream was to save lives. It was only weeks ago he'd graduated cum laude, and in the coming months would enroll in medical school to train to become a doctor.

"I'm not going to stop until I find out who the mother-fucker is who put Ray in the hospital."

Kenny felt as if he'd been dunked in a frozen lake when he registered the venom in Frankie's voice. There never had been a question as to their loyalty to one another; Kenny knew he would willingly give up his life for his blood brothers, and it was obvious they would do the same for him.

He'd stopped questioning himself why he, Ray, and Frankie had remained friends for so long. Their personalities were as different as their appearances, yet it was as if they were of one mind. Kenny was quieter, more reflective, while Frankie tended to be vocal and volatile. Ray was the dreamer, roman-tic, and pragmatic; the one they could go to with their prob-lems and get honest feedback that wasn't judgmental.

"Don't you think you should let the police do that?"

Frankie shook his head. "Do you really think the police are going to put any energy in finding out who beat up a Puerto Rican kid who was in the wrong place at the wrong time? Get real, Kenny. If Ray had been some rich White kid from Jersey, they would have every cop in the Bronx looking for his attacker. I know people who have their way of finding out things the police overlook, so it's only going to be a mat-ter of time when we find out what sonofabitch beat up our brother."

Frankie found a parking spot a block from the hospital. When they approached the admissions desk, they were in-formed that Ray was in ICU, and right now, only family was permitted to see him.

"We are family," Kenny said, challenging the woman. "Page Nurse Delores Torres and let her know we're here to see Ramon. Our names are Kenneth and Francis."

"You can wait over there," she said, pointing to a row of plastic chairs, "while I call Nurse Torres."

Fifteen minutes later, the former Army nurse met them in the reception area. Delores hugged Frankie, then Kenny. "Come with me."

"How is he?" Kenny asked her once they were in the elevator.

"Not good. He came out of surgery a couple of hours ago, and there was extensive damage to his skull and one of his eyes. He has a broken ankle, ribs, a collapsed lung, and a ruptured spleen."

"What are his chances of survival?" Kenny questioned, giving Ray's sister a long, penetrating stare.

"Right now, it's sixty-forty. We'll know better once he's able to breathe on his own."

"How did you know to call me?" Frankie asked Delores.

A hint of a smile parted the lips of the pretty brunette. "My brother couldn't stop talking about his blood brothers, so when you guys came to Ray's graduation, he gave me your phone numbers, because he wanted me to call you. Papi is planning a party on July Fourth to celebrate Ray going to medical school, and he wants to invite my brother's friends."

"How are your parents taking this?" Kenny asked Delores.

"I told them not to come tonight, because I didn't want them to see Ray like this. I tried to downplay his injuries and said he was in a hit-and-run accident and that he would have to stay in the hospital for a couple of days."

"You know all hell is going to break loose once they see him," Kenny told Ray's sister.

"I'll deal with it when it comes. I've had more than enough experience dealing with parents when they come to a VA hospital to see their sons for the first time with missing body parts. It will be the same with my parents."

The elevator doors opened, and they followed Delores down a hallway to the ICU. Kenny thought he was prepared, but when he saw Ray in bed, his head and face covered with bandages, his vitals monitored by machines, and the sound of the ventilator helping him to breathe, he felt his knees buckle, and he had to hold onto the wall to keep his balance. He closed his eyes for several seconds and when he opened them, he saw that Frankie's reaction was similar to his. Frankie stumbled for a chair, sitting down heavily as tears streamed down his face. That's when Kenny lost it completely, breaking down and crying without making a sound. *They're dead. Whoever did this is a dead man. I will kill him with my bare hands.* Kenny wanted to stop the voices in his head, but they continued to taunt him, and after a while they left him alone long enough to get up and walk out of the room. He was back in control when Frankie finally joined him.

"Whoever did this to Ray is a dead man walking," he said to Frankie.

"If he knows what's good for him, he better leave the country before my people find him."

My people. Kenny chanced a sidelong glance at his friend. He'd never heard Frankie utter those two words. It was as if he were the head of a mob family who had people working under him, willing and ready to do his bidding. And to his knowledge, the D'Alessandros weren't involved in any mob or criminal activity. Or were they?

It wasn't his concern one way or the other, but if Frankie knew people who could ferret out who'd assaulted Ray, then Kenny was all for it. And Frankie was right about the police not putting any great effort in trying to find out who had beat up a Puerto Rican kid whose name would be added to the list of the city's crime statistics for assaults.

"Kenneth, I hope you're not going to sit around the house all day doing absolutely nothing when you should be looking for a job."

Kenny stared at his mother. He'd tried explaining to her he

didn't want to leave the house until Frankie called to let him know they'd found Ray's attacker. "I've mailed out résumés to different city agencies, and now I'm waiting for someone to call me. And I have a job. I still work at the restaurant."

"Why didn't you say that before?"

"You didn't ask."

Justine rested her hands at her waist. "There's no need to get snippy with me, Kenneth."

He noticed the abundance of gray in her hair. She was in her early forties and graying at an alarming rate. There was no doubt her hair would be completely white by the time she was fifty.

"I'm not, as you say, snippy. I'm still worried about Ray."

Justine walked over and sat opposite him. "How is he doing?"

"He was discharged from the hospital last week, and now he has to undergo rehab to help him walk, because they had to put a plate and screws in his fractured ankle. He's lost almost all his vision in his left eye, so he's given up his dream of becoming a doctor."

"That poor kid. All that brilliance going to waste. Have the police found out who assaulted him?"

Kenny shook his head. "Not yet. And chances are they're not putting in any effort to find out."

"Why would you say that?"

"Because to the police, Ray is just another spic who got what he deserves for soliciting hookers."

Justine's jaw dropped. "I know I didn't hear you say what you just did."

"Yeah, Ma. I did. Do you think they would lose any sleep if someone mugged me and left me for dead? No," he said, answering his own question. "Just another nigger who was in the wrong place at the wrong time. And if they catch the perpetrator, he wouldn't get as much prison time for assaulting his own folks than he would if he assaulted some White

CEO riding around in a limo whose company's profits include laundering drug money for the mob."

"Where is all this talk coming from?" Justine asked.

"It's reality, Mom. It's the same with politicians who look out for their fat-cat friends at the expense of working-class chumps who applaud when they're given tax breaks that are pittance when compared to the corporations and millionaires who use scams to hide their money from the taxman."

"It's apparent you still haven't gotten over that fake-ass activist girl who left you because you weren't militant enough for her. What she was going to do was get you killed with all that rhetoric she was spouting."

Slowly leaning back in his chair, Kenny stared at his mother until she dropped her eyes. They'd argued ad nauseum about the girl who had become the love of his life. He knew his mother would never accept her as her daughter-in-law the first time she laid eyes on her. But that hadn't mattered, because she was going to marry him, not his mother.

"You just had to bring her up, didn't you?"

"Yes, I did," Justine retorted, "because she turned you into someone I don't know or recognize, because now you are always so angry."

"Maybe as a Black man in America, I have a lot to be angry about. It's 1973, and we still have to fight for equality. How much more blood do we have to shed to become equal citizens in a country where our ancestors were used as free labor to enrich those in power? Are you aware that twelve presidents owned slaves? Did you also know that even Benjamin Franklin owned slaves?"

Justine closed her eyes and clutched her chest. "Enough, Kenny."

He sat up straight. "Are you all right?"

She opened her eyes and smiled. "Yes. It's just a little indigestion. I shouldn't have put those onions in last night's salad."

"Are you certain it's only indigestion? Maybe you should go for a checkup?"

"Have you forgotten that I work in a hospital, and I get a complete physical every year."

"Just checking."

"There's no need to check on me. I know you're worried about Ramon, but if he's made it this far considering his injuries, he's going to be okay."

"When I spoke to him the other day, he was talking about going into the priesthood."

Justine smiled. "Do you think he would be a good priest?"

"I do, because whenever Frankie and I had a problem, we would go to Ray. He would listen without saying anything, then whatever he would tell us is what we needed to hear."

"How long will it take him to become an ordained priest?" Justine asked.

"Almost as long as it takes to become a doctor. He already has a Bachelor of Science degree, so he'll have to study another two years for a Bachelor of Philosophy. After that, there's another three or four years of instruction, then six months of becoming a deacon, then after that, he can become ordained."

"That's a lot of schooling."

"It is," Kenny agreed.

Once Ray had made up his mind about becoming a priest, Kenny knew his friend would put in the time and effort to accomplish it. Ray wasn't only smart, he was a genius, and would've become an exceptional doctor.

"I was thinking about taking a few summer courses, then changed my mind," Justine said, sighing.

"Who or what made you change your mind?"

"It's not a who, mister busybody."

Kenny smiled. "Did I mention his name?"

"No, but I know who you're thinking about."

"Since when did you become a mind reader?" Kenny asked, teasing his mother.

Justine massaged her neck before rolling her head from one side to the other. "My decision not to take summer classes has nothing to do with Francis D'Allesandro."

Kenny pointed at Justine. "Gotcha! You said his name."

She smiled. "Frank is like an old shoe. Not only is it a perfect fit, but it's also very comfortable."

He wanted to ask his mother if Frank was a perfect fit when they made love, but he knew she would shut him down and not speak to him for days, because she'd accuse him of crossing the line; that despite his being an adult, he wasn't her equal.

Not only did he love his mother, but he also worried about her. She still was spending too much time alone, and it was only when Frank came to see her that she would turn into a younger version of herself and laugh and tease him like an adolescent girl. And he hadn't missed the longing looks Frank gave his mother, and his love for her was as obvious as the nose on his face.

They were good for each other, even if they vehemently denied wanting to marry or live together. Social mores had relaxed where couples were sharing free love, living together without the benefit of marriage, and women opting to become single mothers.

He didn't think of Frank and Justine as dinosaurs, but it was as if they weren't willing to let go of the rules of the prior generation, when women had to remain virgins until they married, or if a boy got a girl pregnant, they were forced into shotgun marriages.

Pushing off the sofa, Kenny stood up. "Do you plan on going out this afternoon?" he asked his mother.

"No. Why?"

"Because if anyone calls about setting up an interview, could you please take the message?"

"Of course."

"I'm going out for a walk. I'm getting cabin fever cooped up in this apartment."

"Do you want me to wait on you for dinner?"

"No thanks, Mom. I'll grab something outside." Kenny went into his bedroom to get his driver's license, keys, and a small amount of cash. It was as if his life was in limbo, knowing everything would change once he secured employment.

CHAPTER 28

It was the first time his godfather had invited him to the apartment he'd heard about but never visited. He'd grown up believing the man with his same name lived in the brownstone's street-level apartment.

"Come in and sit down," Frank said.

Frankie had taken one look at his godfather's expression and knew he wasn't happy about something. He walked into the living room and sat on a butter-soft navy-blue leather sofa. He was twenty-two-years-old, yet he felt like twelve being summoned to the principal's office.

Frank sat on a matching chair, facing him. "Do you know why I asked you to come here?"

Frankie shook his head. "No."

"A couple of weeks ago, you approached me with the news that your friend had been assaulted in the Bronx, and you wanted me to find out who did it."

"Yes, sir."

Frank crossed a leg over the opposite knee, laced his fingers together, and rested his hands on his lap. "I made a few inquiries and found out who did it."

Frankie leaned closer. "You did?"

"Are you questioning me?"

"No, sir."

He didn't know why he feared his uncle more than he did his father. Maybe it was because he now was the head of the family, and there was a lot of responsibility resting on his shoulders. Hopefully, he would lighten some of that responsibility now that he was an accountant.

"My people uncovered talk about some kid who got his ass kicked because he'd been messing with a girl whose boyfriend is the leader of a street gang. When she told her boyfriend she was pregnant, he went crazy and threatened to give her a hot shot because he knew the baby wasn't his."

"He was going to shoot her up with heroin?"

Frank slowly nodded. "He knew she'd lied because he'd gotten into some trouble in Westchester County and was sentenced to six months in a county jail. Then she lied again and said that Ray had raped her, and she was afraid to say anything but then she discovered she was pregnant."

"So, the baby is Ray's?"

"Yes. But you can never tell him. Once she revealed Ray's name and address, her boyfriend and his brother stalked him, waiting until they found him alone. They forced him into a car, took him to an abandoned building, beat him, then dumped his body in Hunts Point."

Frankie pressed his fist to his mouth. "Sonsofbitches."

"Street thugs will spill their guts if they're offered enough money, and it didn't take long before the brothers found themselves in the same situation as Ray. Hanging from meat hooks like pieces of slaughtered beef can take its toll on one's mind and body. One was left in Brooklyn and the other near the Bowery. It's going to be a very long time before they'll be able to walk, talk, piss, or shit without experiencing extreme pain. I'm telling you this because I never want you to come to me ever again asking me to help you get retribution for anyone. I'm not my father, and when he died, I left that life behind."

"I understand, uncle."

"Wrong answer!" Frank shouted. "I don't think you do, because if you did, you never would've come to me with this shit. We are not murderers, and if one of the fuckers would've died, then his death would've been on my conscience. Not yours!"

Frankie nodded, because he was too scared to say anything. It wasn't often that his uncle lost his temper, and this was one of those times. He'd heard stories about his grandfather, who would put fear in someone's heart with just a look, and he was experiencing the same with Frankie Delano.

"One of these days, you will head this family, and it's time for you to begin your lessons."

"Isn't my father in line to take over after you, Uncle Frank?"

"No. Gio has no head for finance. Prepare yourself, because this summer I'm going to teach you everything there is to know about how I run my businesses. When you're ready, you will use this apartment as your base of operation. You will never hold meetings here. And more importantly, never bring a woman here. I don't want you to learn the hard way that you shouldn't shit where you eat. I own this building and the laundromat. You will be responsible for maintaining separate books for the butcher shop, restaurant and pizza shop, shoemaker, Jimmy's Bar, and the laundromat. And like any smart accountant, I have two sets of books. There's a floor safe in one of the bedroom closets with the actual accounting, and the other set is in a file cabinet. That's the set you make available if there is an internal revenue audit.

"I also have a loaded gun in the safe. I have a license for it, because there are times when I have to pick up cash from the various businesses. You'll have to apply for your own gun license. Now that we're legitimate, I'd like to keep it that way. If anyone comes asking you to get involved in narcotics, do not entertain them, because if you're caught trafficking in drugs, you'll be facing a mandatory minimum sentence of fifteen years to life. Can you imagine not seeing your family for fifteen years?"

"No."

"And another piece of advice. Don't get caught up in the mob. Once you're in, it's for life, because you're not allowed to walk away. And whatever I've told you today stays here. You are never to breathe a word to Ray that his attackers were punished for what they did to him."

"What about Kenny?"

"No. Definitely not Kenny."

"Why? Because you're still involved with his mother?"

"I'm going to pretend I didn't hear you ask me that."

"You're just like Kenny. He gets very touchy whenever I mention you and his mother."

"That's because you should mind your damn business! You're going to have enough on your plate once you begin working for an auditing firm. Then there's the CPA exam. And I shouldn't have to warn you that in order to keep your head on straight, you'll have to stop fucking around with women. They're like trains. There's always one leaving the station."

Frankie digested what his uncle had revealed to him. He would be in his mid-twenties when it came time for him to take control of the family business. All he had to do was listen, follow orders, and not question authority to ensure a smooth transition from one Francis D'Allesandro to the next-generation Francis D'Allesandro.

CHAPTER 29

New Year's Day—1983

Kenneth Russell celebrated the New Year with his mother, sitting with her and watching television as the world welcomed in the third year of a new decade. It had been ten years since he graduated from college, and it had taken Justine even longer to finally earn her degree. She'd just begun her junior year when she got up one morning complaining of chest pains. At first, she'd attributed it to indigestion, but when he finally was able to convince her to go to the emergency room, she was immediately taken into surgery.

He'd waited for hours, and when he finally met with the surgeon, he was told that his mother's aorta had ruptured and that she would have to remain in the hospital up to ten days, and it would take another four to six weeks at home for her to fully recover.

She dropped out of college and focused on regaining her health and strength. Once she was medically cleared, she returned to work on a part-time basis. However, it had taken her longer to re-enroll for classes. She'd celebrated her fiftieth birthday in March, and two months later, she proudly walked across the stage to receive her degree.

Justine patted Kenny's hand. "I've decided not to teach."

Easing back, he stared at her. "You're kidding me, aren't you?"

"No, I'm not kidding. At my age, I realize I don't have the patience to deal with a lot of little kids. The exception would be my grandchildren, because if they got on my nerves, I could always send them back to their parents. Earning a college degree was on my wish list, and now that I have it, I can cross it off."

Kenny wondered if his mother was still mourning the loss of her friend. Frank D'Allesandro's cancer had returned six months ago, and it had been so aggressive that he died three weeks later. Justine had refused to attend the funeral and the reading of his will, when he bequeathed her enough money for her to live comfortably for the rest of her life. Within days of receiving the money, she transferred most of it to Kenny's bank account, because she didn't want to face the risk of having to move because her assets exceeded the income threshold for living in public housing. She'd gotten used to the neighborhood within walking distance to the Lincoln Center. Frank had also left Kenny enough for him to move out of his Greenwich Village studio rental to purchase a two-bedroom co-op in an East Harlem high-rise with views of the East River and bridges spanning the boroughs of New York City.

"What other surprises are you hiding from me?"

"I'm going to quit my job in June."

"And do what, Mom?"

"Travel."

"Travel where?"

"I'm going to take an around-the-world cruise. There was a time when Francis asked me what would I do if I had enough money to do whatever I wanted. I told him I wanted to travel and see the world."

"And he left you a shitload of money to do that."

"More than I would ever need living here. That's why I gave you most of it to use when you finally decide to settle down and start a family."

"I'm not certain when that's going to happen," Kenny said.

"I don't want you to call me a meddling old woman, but aren't you seeing someone?"

"If I was, then I wouldn't be spending New Year's Eve with my mother."

"I'm not that gullible, Kenneth. I know you're seeing women, so don't try to pull the wool over my eyes. And I'm not going to have a meltdown if I bring in the new year alone."

"Do you realize this is the first year you won't celebrate it with Uncle Dee since you two got back together?"

Justine wanted to tell her son that she didn't like talking about her friend, because she truly missed him. And he'd been a true friend to the end. When she was discharged from the hospital, he'd paid for a nurse to take care of her until she regained most of her strength. Then, he chartered a yacht to sail down to St. Thomas, where they spent more than a week in the sun before returning to New York. She didn't know if her life would've been any different if she'd married or lived with Francis. She did know that he was a faithful and loyal friend to the end.

"Yes." Even when there were long stretches of time when they didn't see each other, he would come over and celebrate the new year with her.

"I still think you should've married him."

She gave Kenny a prolonged stare. A couple of years ago, he'd traded his glasses for contact lenses. Justine liked seeing him with glasses, because they made him appear bookish. "You're beginning to sound like a scratched record that got stuck in a groove. How many times are you going to repeat yourself?"

"As many times as it takes for you to admit that you should have married him."

"Francis didn't want to get married."

"That's not what he told me."

"Now, you're calling a dead man a liar?"

"No, Mom. He told me he'd changed his mind and was getting ready to propose to you, but he got sick and that he didn't want to be a burden to you."

"He wouldn't have been a burden, Kenny. He got cancer, and I had a heart attack. So, we would've been a pair of invalids you would've had to ship off a nursing home."

"That would never happen. There's no way I'd put my mother in a nursing home, where she would be neglected or abused."

"What would you do if I got too old to take care of myself?"

"Hire a live-in nurse like Uncle Dee did when you were recovering from your heart attack."

"Let's hope I don't get to that stage," Justine said.

Francis had admitted ignoring the pains in his back, while she'd ignored the pains in her chest. When Kenny carried her into the ER with pains knifing her chest, she knew then it wasn't indigestion. Then when a doctor placed the stereoscope against her chest, within seconds she was strapped onto a gurney with doctors and nurses sprinting toward the operating room.

After surgery, she was in intensive care, where she floated in and out of consciousness for several days. Once she moved into a room, the first face she saw was Kenny's. He'd whispered in her ear that she had scared the shit out of him and never again would he listen to her self-diagnose her pain. He'd come every night directly from CPS—Child Protective

Services—where he'd been promoted as a casework supervisor. There were visits from some of her coworkers, and when she was finally discharged, Francis was waiting in her apartment with a private-duty nurse. He admitted he couldn't come to the hospital because it was a reminder of what he'd experienced as a cancer patient.

Her eyelids fluttered as she blinked back tears. Her dear, dear friend was gone, and she would never get to see his face, hear his voice, or enjoy his gentle touch. She hadn't been able to attend his funeral mass, because she feared experiencing an emotional breakdown; when Kenny had come to her apartment to tell her Francis had passed away, the pain in her chest had returned, and she feared having another heart attack. Kenny called her cardiologist, who suggested she come to his office for a battery of tests, all of which, thankfully, came back negative. He told her she probably had a panic attack and should avoid upsetting situations.

"Do you still meet your friends for breakfast every first Saturday of the month?" Justine asked Kenny, deftly changing the topic.

"No. The last time I saw Ray was when he assisted Father Morelli, who is the D'Allesandro's family priest, at Uncle Dee's funeral mass."

"Does he like being a priest?"

"Ray says instead of healing bodies, he's now healing souls. He's currently assigned to a parish in the Bronx as an assistant pastor."

"What about Frankie? You haven't mentioned him in a while."

"It's been a while since we've gotten together. The last time we spoke, he said he was up to his eyeballs taking care of his family's finances. And . . ."

"And what, Kenny?" Justine asked when he didn't finish his sentence.

"He's been running around with this girl who is messing with his head. I told him to stop seeing her, but he claims he can't."

"Why not?"

"I don't know, Mom. Maybe he doesn't want to stop seeing her."

Justine angled her head. "I hope you're not having a similar problem with the woman you're seeing."

"Nope, because I'm not seeing anyone at the present time." Kenny paused. "I've decided to take a break from dating and especially from getting into a relationship. I like not having to share the apartment with another person. I go to bed when I want, get up when I want, and I don't have to answer to anyone as to where I've been."

"That sounds a little selfish, son."

"It's your fault that I was an only child, and I've never had to share what belongs to me with anyone."

"That's where you're wrong, Kenny. There was a time when you, Ramon, and Frankie shared everything. Y'all changed after Ramon was assaulted."

"I think that was the point when we grew up, Mom. We were in our early twenties, believing we were invincible. That there wasn't nothing we couldn't do or accomplish. Seeing Ray in that hospital bed covered in bandages and hooked up to machines that were keeping him alive was the scariest thing I'd ever experienced in my life. That if they'd disconnected his ventilator, he would've stopped breathing. It was a wake-up call that life is as fragile as a single sheet of tissue paper. Everything Ray had worked for up to that point was futile, because with the loss of sight in one eye, a fractured ankle, collapsed lung, ruptured spleen, and crushed skull, his injuries were so severe that everyone knew he would never make it through medical school."

"And because life is fragile and time fleeting, don't you think it's time for you to reunite with your friends? Invite them over to your place for a weekend get-together. I'm certain they would appreciate you cooking for them."

Kenny's smile was dazzling. "I kinda like your suggestion, Mom."

"Don't kinda like it, Kenny. Just do it. It's probably what you need to get you out of your funk."

"I didn't realize I was in a funk."

"Well, you are," Justine countered. "Every time you come to see me, you bring a bad vibe with you."

"Maybe it has to do with my work. You can't imagine what some parents do to their kids before we're forced to remove them from their homes."

"That's why you need a distraction in your personal life. Reconnect with your friends and find a woman who makes you laugh. One whom you'd want to spend more than a few hours with. And it wouldn't hurt if y'all were friends for a while before you decide on something more serious."

"Define serious, Mom."

"Sleeping together."

"What about living together?"

"Even though I'm not that old, I am old school about shacking up. What's the expression? *Why buy the cow when you can get the milk for free?*"

"A lot of women who claim to be liberated say they don't want to be married because they want the freedom to control their own destinies."

"Women say a lot of things, Kenny, because it sounds good. There are very few women out there who prefer to live their lives as single women."

"Are you talking about lesbian women?"

"There's no doubt that even lesbians want life partners. But that isn't possible, because same-sex marriage is illegal in this country."

"Do you believe in same-sex marriage?"

"I believe people should be able to marry who they love."

Kenny wagged a finger. "You're not answering my question."

Justine successfully concealed her annoyance with a saccharine smile. "I thought I did, so let's drop the subject."

She knew for certain she would've married Francis if he had been Black. However, with the state of race relations in America, their union would've been fraught with derision and ridicule. Black folk would call her a sellout for marrying out of her race, while White women in particular would probably insult her to her face for taking what they'd deemed belonged to them.

"Do you want me to sleep over so we can go out for breakfast in the morning?" Kenny asked.

Justine shook her head. "No, sweetie. Go home and get some sleep. I'll be all right here."

"Are you sure, Mama?"

She angled her head, smiling. "Of course, I'm sure. Be careful driving because you know folks use any holiday to act a fool. And don't forget to ring my phone twice, then hang up so that I know you got home safe."

Leaning over, Kenny kissed her cheek. "Love you."

"Love you more." She was still sitting in the spot when the door closed behind Kenny. Then she heard him lock it. Even after he'd moved out, he held on to the key to the apartment. And respecting her privacy, he'd never come over unannounced. The exception was after she was discharged from the hospital following her heart attack.

It was the first day of a new year, and for the first time in her life, Justine Russell decided to make a New Year's resolution. She was going to put down in words how she'd become a pawn for two selfish women and how it had altered her life. She'd kept the secrets and had lied so often that they were beginning to keep her from a restful night's sleep.

Kenny had a right to know where he'd come from in order to know where he had to go, and who his mother actually was. Before she embarked on an around-the-world cruise, Justine decided she would chronicle her life, beginning with what she could recall growing up with her mother, aunts, and uncle in a cramped apartment in a less-than-desirable Bronx neighborhood. Rather than talk to a priest or a therapist, she would tell her story on the pages of a journal for her son to read when she felt it was the right time. She knew it had to be soon, because she needed to unburden herself and break the chains of deceit that had controlled, and continued to control, her life.

CHAPTER 30

Father Ramon Torres thought he was hallucinating when he met the large dark eyes of the little boy staring up at him as he hesitated placing the communion wafer on the little outstretched tongue. The boy was his mirror image at that age. It was only when he glanced over toward the head of the woman standing behind the child that he knew exactly who she was.

Migdalia Hernandez hadn't lied when she said he'd gotten her pregnant. Without a doubt, the boy was his. He had to be at least ten, because he'd slept with Migdalia Hernandez a couple of months before his graduating from college, and that was in 1973. His hand trembled slightly as he placed the wafer on the child's tongue, then met the eyes of Migdalia when she stepped in front of him.

"The body of Christ," he said softly as he repeated the gesture with her.

Migdalia smiled. "Amen." She was still smiling when she lowered her eyes and escorted her son back to their pew.

Ray didn't want to believe his volunteering to perform mass for a priest at another parish would bring him face-to-face with his past. Even after he'd recovered from the savage beating, he continued to deny that Migdalia was pregnant with his baby, because of what his attacker told him within seconds of being abducted off the street in broad daylight. *"You're going to pay for fucking with my lady."* The threat told Ray that Migdalia was probably sleeping with him and her boyfriend at the same time, and he was the better marriage prospect because he planned to become a doctor.

Once mass concluded, he retreated to the rectory, where he went into a room and closed the door to change out of his vestments and into the quintessential black suit with the white collar identifying him as a member of the clergy. If he hadn't stepped in for an ailing colleague, Ray knew he probably would have spent the rest of his natural life unaware that he had produced a child. Studying for the priesthood had made him a changed man. Over time, prayer and abstinence had curbed the sexual urges that had at one time controlled his very existence. The first year he struggled not to touch himself; then, after a while, it was as if the very act had become distasteful. He was an eager divinity student and enjoyed the hours of solitude where he devoured the works of religious scholars and philosophers.

Ray had found a new home at the seminary, and even when he was allowed privileges to visit with his family, he preferred spending hours in the chapel praying and meditating. Once he felt that he'd achieved the spiritual healing that had eluded him, he would call his mother to let her know when to expect him to come home. It wasn't until after he had emerged from the drug-induced coma that he was told his grandmother had passed away and his parents had accompanied her body to Puerto Rico for her burial. His sisters and brothers were young adults, and his older sister had married a hospital social worker, and after a couple of years, he decided to reconnect with his blood brothers.

Ray's reunion with Frankie and Kenny made him aware of the strong bond that still existed between them. A bond that was stronger than it had been before the assault that had left him partially blind in his left eye. He teased Kenny that he was better-looking in his glasses because of the slightly tinted blue lenses that concealed the damage to his cornea.

He joked with his friends, saying they had become sellouts because now they were a part of the establishment they'd once railed against. Missing were the long hair, beards, and loose-fitting attire favored by flower children. They had agreed to disband their first-of-the-month Saturday breakfasts but promised to keep in touch.

The last time he saw Frankie and Kenny was at Francis D'Allesandro's funeral mass when he assisted Father Ralph Morelli, who'd come to the hospital to see Ray and give him the sacraments of Anointing of the sick, Reconciliation, and the Eucharist. Six months later, the priest had become Ray's confidante, confessor, and mentor.

Seeing Migdalia with his son reminded Ray that he had to call his friends and ask for their advice, something he hadn't done in a very long time. He was reaching for his topcoat when he heard a knock on the door.

"Yes?"

"Father Torres, there's someone here who wants to talk to you."

"I'll be right out." Ray put on his coat, scarf, and hat, making certain the brim was turned down all the way. Checking his pocket for his car keys, he opened the door and saw Migdalia standing next to an elderly nun.

"Thank you, Sister Agnes." Waiting until the nun walked away, Ray nodded to the woman who still had the power to make his heart beat a little too quickly. "Hello, Micky."

A hint of a smile touched Migdalia's lush mouth, one he remembered doing wicked things to him he'd never experienced before.

"So, you do remember me," she whispered.

Ray slowly blinked behind the lenses of his glasses. "How could I forget the woman who bore my son?"

"A son you denied even before he was born."

Ray registered the resentment in his son's mother's words. "Is there some place we can go so we can talk about this?"

"You can come to my place. Micah went home with my mother."

"You gave him a name from the Bible?"

"No, Ramon. I named him after my grandfather."

"Where do you live?" Ray asked her.

"I have an apartment in Washington Heights. I come to the Bronx on Sundays to see my parents and let Micah hang out with his cousins."

Ray nodded. "My car is in the back."

He waited for Micky to put on a knitted cap, then walked with her out of the rectory to the church's parking lot, where priests were assigned reserved spots. He unlocked the passenger door, waiting for her to get in before rounding the vehicle and slipping behind the wheel.

There were so many things Ray wanted to ask her. First, he wanted to know if she'd married, and if she had, where was her husband? And what had she told her son about his biological father?

He started up the car, then glanced at her profile as she stared out the windshield. "You need to tell me your address."

Migdalia gave Ramon her address as she struggled to keep her emotions in check. When she stood in line with her son waiting to receive communion, never in her wildest years could she have imagined that the priest wearing a pair of tinted glasses would be the one who'd made her a mother. She had arrived late and had to sit in the back of the church where she couldn't see the officiant's face clearly, but that changed when she went up to the front of the church to take the Eucharist.

Whenever she came across town to see her parents, she'd always accompanied them to Sunday mass before returning to her apartment to catch up on things she'd neglected to do during the week. Micah enjoyed spending time with *abuelo* and *abuela* and his many cousins until it came time for her to come back to the Bronx to pick him up. He also looked forward to school holidays and recess when he could stay over longer.

She did not want to believe the only man with whom she'd fallen in love was now a priest who'd taken vows of poverty and chastity. However, she was only able to let go of the rage she'd carried long after he rejected her once she gave birth to a little boy who looked exactly like his father.

"You can park over there," she said, pointing to an empty space at the end of the block facing Riverside Drive.

Ray maneuvered into the space with minimal effort. "Do you live alone?"

"I'm not married."

His hand halted removing the key in the ignition. "That's not what I asked you," he said softly.

"No, Ramon, I'm not married." She knew he was recalling the time when she told him she wasn't with her boyfriend. It wasn't entirely a lie, because Hector had been locked up in Westchester County after being arrested for shoplifting at a mall, and the judge had sentenced him to six months in a county jail.

"Don't move," Ray said as he shut off the engine. He got out and came around to open her door to assist her out.

She smiled. He was still the gentleman she remembered, and that's why she'd found herself so taken with him. That and because he was a pre-med student at Columbia University who was studying to become a doctor. She worked at a hospital kitchen, hoping to become a dietitian, and she was in awe of the doctors in their white coats treating patients and giving orders to nurses and members of hospital staff as if they were royalty and expected to be obeyed without question. Migdalia couldn't believe that she'd fallen in love with Ramon, and one day she would be a doctor's wife and the mother of his children.

But her fantasy world imploded when she discovered her period was late, despite Ramon using a condom. At first, she believed her cycle was off, but after not seeing her period for two months, she went to the hospital lab for a pregnancy test. When it came back positive, she panicked. She hadn't slept with Hector since he'd been incarcerated, and there was no way she could pass the baby off as his, and she was forced to tell Ramon that she was having his baby.

She walked back up the block to her building, waiting for Ramon to open the door to the lobby. Reaching into the pocket of her coat, she took out a set of keys and unlocked the door leading into the vestibule. It had taken her a while to rent a two-bedroom apartment in a building on a clean tree-lined street in upper Manhattan.

"This is a nice building," Ray said.

"It will stay nice until the drug dealers decide to use it as a place where they can stash their drugs," Migdalia said over her shoulder as she led the way to her first-floor apartment.

Ray removed his hat and ran a hand over his close-cropped hair. "Drugs have become a plague in this country."

She unlocked the door and pushed it open. "A plague that's so out of control, it's impossible to eradicate despite First Lady Nancy Reagan's 'Just say no' campaign. She would've made more of an impact if she said to dealers and traffickers that they are going to jail for life without parole if they get caught selling or bringing drugs into this country."

Ray hung up his hat and coat alongside Migdalia's on a tree stand in a corner near the door. "Not even stiff prison sentences are enough to deter those bent on amassing enormous fortunes from products that destroy lives."

Migdalia turned to look at him. "Are you an advocate for the death penalty?"

"You should know better than to ask me that."

"Is it because you're a Catholic priest and don't believe in the death penalty?"

"It has nothing to do with religion, Micky. I don't believe any man has the right to take another man's life, regardless of the crime. And yes, life mandatory sentences may work, but it's not a cure-all in this country."

"Where would they work?" she asked, glancing at him over her shoulder as they walked down a hallway into the living room.

"In countries where the culture is based on a religion."

"But those religions are usually extremely inhibiting."

Ray waited for Migdalia to sit on a sofa before he took a matching armchair, looping one leg over the opposite knee. The living room furnishings weren't fancy, but functional. He noticed that everything was in its proper place, like arranged pieces in furniture showrooms. "Not to someone who grows up in the culture. What we may find inhibiting, they would see as encouraging social behavior that will eventually corrupt a society."

"Give me an example, Ramon."

"We're hypocritical when it comes to the human body. We visit museums and stare at statues of the naked body that are considered priceless masterpieces, but our puritanical biases blur the lines between art and pornography. Hollywood has placed ratings on movies shown in conventional movie theaters, while untold millions are made selling porn flicks in seedy neighborhoods all over the country."

Migdalia kicked off her shoes and pulled her legs up on the sofa. "You don't talk like a priest."

"How is a priest supposed to talk?" he asked.

"Not about pornographic movies."

"Why? Because depicting lovemaking on the screen is dirty and sinful?" Ray realized what he was saying had shocked Migdalia because she wasn't thinking of him as a man, but a priest.

Her eyelids fluttered wildly. "I don't know how to answer that."

"I can, because it is a discussion I have with a lot of people who come to me for counseling. And it is the same discussion I had with another priest before I finally made the decision to join the seminary."

Ray knew he'd shocked his son's mother once he revealed he had an addiction. Not to drugs, but sex. That it had nearly taken over his life, and if he'd been able to control his carnal urges, he never would've slept with her.

Staring at her under lowered lids, he continued, "You were the only girl I met that I wished I hadn't slept with because I wanted to save you for marriage."

"Are you saying we wouldn't have made love until our wedding night?"

He nodded, smiling. "That's exactly what I'm saying. There are some women men sleep with and others they don't until they're married. You fell into the latter category."

"Why me, Ramon?"

"Why not you, Migdalia? Remember when we first met, all we did was talk. There wasn't a subject we couldn't discuss."

"You're right. And there were a few on which we could never agree."

"True. But you were the first girl who didn't bore me to tears. And that made you special."

"Were there any special ones after me?" she asked.

Ray pressed his head to the back of the chair and closed his eyes, feeling as if he were about to enter the confessional to reveal what he had and hadn't done. "No, Micky. You were the last woman that I lay with."

CHAPTER 31

Migdalia stared across the space at the man who had changed her inside and out. Watching him gripping the arms of the chair, as if he were girding himself for something he knew was coming but hoped he'd be able to avoid. He hadn't said *made love to*, but *lay with*. Was he talking about sleeping with men?

"What happened?" she whispered.

Ray opened his eyes. "I almost lost my life because I slept with you."

She leaned forward, her heart beating a double-time rhythm. "What are you talking about?"

"I was abducted by your boyfriend and his brother, then beaten and left for dead."

"No!" She hadn't realized a primal scream had slipped past her lips until it was out.

"Yes, Micky."

She listened intently as Ramon told her that while he was walking to a bus stop, someone hit him on the back of his head and shoved him into the rear of a car. Stunned and bleeding, he was bound, gagged, and blindfolded. He lost consciousness, and when he woke up, he was in an abandoned building and beaten repeatedly with bats and pipes.

Migdalia covered her mouth, and her eyes filled with tears when Ramon told her the injuries he sustained were so severe that there had been the possibility he wouldn't survive. "Why did they do it?" she asked, recovering her voice.

"It was to teach me a lesson for, as your boyfriend put it, 'fucking with his lady.' So instead of going to medical school to become a doctor and save lives, I went to seminary to become a priest to save souls. Not knowing it was my soul that needed to be saved."

"I'm so sorry," she repeated over and over as guilt enveloped her like a weighted blanket that made it impossible for her to draw a normal breath.

It was because of her that Ramon had become the object of her ex-boyfriend's vengeance. She'd broken up with Hector once he was arrested and incarcerated, but everything changed once she discovered she was pregnant and Ramon didn't believe he was the father. If he had married her as she pleaded with him to do, then she never would've gone back to the neighborhood to face Hector, who'd been released from jail and saw that her body had changed. And she did what she'd been forced to do to save her life.

She lied to him.

"I lied and told Hector you raped me, because if I didn't tell him whose baby I was carrying, he threatened to inject me with enough heroin to kill me and your baby."

"It's all in the past," Ray said softly.

"It may be in the past for you, Ramon, but the lie will haunt me for the rest of my life."

"Are you asking for absolution, because if you are, then I forgive you, Micky. And I need you to forgive me for not believing you when you came to me saying I'd gotten you pregnant."

"There's nothing for me to forgive you for, Ramon. You reacted the way you did because you probably felt I was trying to trap you into marriage."

"I didn't know what I was thinking at the time. It had nothing to do with you. I was months away from graduating college and going to medical school. Becoming a father at that time was not part of the equation. Meanwhile, you had to deal with a crazy ex who'd threatened your life and my baby's."

She stared, tongue-tied when Ramon called Micah *my baby*. It had only taken seconds for Ramon to look at the boy waiting to receive the Eucharist for him to acknowledge that Micah was his son. "It was either street justice or karma that paid Hector and his brother a visit they will have to live with for the rest of their lives."

A slight frown furrowed Ray's forehead. "What happened?"

"I heard rumors that they were taken somewhere and tortured for days. Word is they were kept in a freezer and hung on meat hooks, where someone pulled out all their teeth, fingernails, broke their kneecaps, and abused them internally. I ran into someone from the old neighborhood a couple of years ago, and they told me Hector has to use a wheelchair to get around, while his brother has crutches to help him walk."

Ray made the sign of the cross over his chest. "That sounds like mob activity rather than street justice."

"Why would you say that?" she asked him.

"Pulled teeth, fingernails, and broken kneecaps are more in line with mob retaliation if they're owed money."

Migdalia slowly shook her head. "It's so sad how people mess up their lives. To my knowledge, he wasn't into anything illegal when we were dating. He was possessive and jealous, but at that time, I thought it was because he wanted me all to himself. And for a nineteen-year-old girl, that was exciting. What he managed to hide from me was that he headed a small gang of thieves who were shoplifting and fencing stolen goods. They got away with stealing in the Bronx, but their luck ran out when they left the Bronx and went up to a mall in Yonkers and were caught stealing sunglasses. When I heard he was in jail, I told his sister to let him know we were through."

"What did you tell your parents when you found out you were pregnant?"

"I told them the truth. That I'd met this boy, and when I told him I was having his baby, he denied it was his. So, I left him."

"Do you know why I didn't believe you?"

"Yes, Ramon. Because you always used a condom. I was taking an oral contraceptive when I was dating Hector, but I stopped after he went to jail. If I had continued to take it, things would've been different between us."

"Even if you weren't pregnant, your ex wasn't willing to let you go."

"You're probably right." Migdalia continued to stare at an older, more mature Ramon Torres, and she wanted to see his eyes behind the tinted lenses. There was something about his features that was reminiscent of the faces of Roman busts in one of her history books.

Ramon was right about them being able to talk about everything because she always had been a voracious reader. It was as if she had a thirst for knowledge she found impossible to quench.

"I forgot to ask, when do you have to be back to your parish?"

"I'm finished for the day. I came down to fill in for Father Shelton, who's recovering from dental surgery."

"Where's your parish?"

"It's in Soundview."

"Do you like it there?"

Ray smiled. "Yes. I've been there for two years, and I'm familiar with most of the parishioners."

"Is it true that they move priest from parish to parish every couple of years?"

"No. Priests usually rotate parishes every five to seven years. There are some who stay longer or are transferred when there is a new bishop."

Migdalia glanced at her watch. "May I offer you something to eat?"

Ray lowered his leg, planting both feet on the floor. "Will you join me?"

"Of course. I made empanadas yesterday, so we'll start with those as appetizers."

"I was thinking about taking you out to eat."

"It's okay, Ramon. I prepared everything earlier this morning, so it's no trouble to heat it up."

"Are you sure, Micky? Because I don't want you to go through any trouble."

"Yes. I'm sure. And you're definitely not who or what I consider trouble."

CHAPTER 32

R ay touched a napkin to the corners of his mouth and
shared a smile with Migdalia. He was glad they hadn't
gone out to eat, because what he would have ordered couldn't
compare to what she had prepared. It was as if he had gone
back to his childhood when his *abuela* cooked for the family.

Migdalia had prepared beef empanadas with the crust so
flaky that it literally melted on his tongue. And her *arroz con
gandules* and baked chicken reminded him of the two summers he and his siblings had spent in Puerto Rico when, after
working long hours on his farm, he'd wash up and come into
the house to sit down for the evening meal. He was a growing teenage boy, and it was as if he couldn't get full, no matter how much he ate. Every night there was rice, beans, fried
or sweet plantains, and meat that varied from chicken, to
pork, and steak and onions, avocado, and soup. At the end
of the first summer, he was ten pounds heavier, two inches
taller, and his complexion two shades darker. The year he
turned eighteen, he was an even six foot and weighed one
hundred sixty-five pounds of lean muscle.

He stopped growing by the time he entered college, and his

weight dropped to one-fifty before graduating, because he'd spent long hours studying while neglecting to eat. After he was assaulted and spent nearly a month in the hospital, he was down to a hundred and thirty pounds. He refused to look in a mirror, because he didn't recognize the image staring back at him. Rehabilitation was slow and painful, and as his body healed, so did his resolve to enter the seminary to become a priest.

Now he was Father Torres, with a ten-year-old son he'd never met before but now wanted to get to know. "You're an incredible cook. I'm glad we didn't go out."

Migdalia lowered her eyes, the gesture so demurely sensual that Ray found he couldn't look away. "Thank you. I like to cook."

"You need to be prepared for that in a few years, because Micah will eat you out of house and home."

"And also drink out of the juice container instead of getting a glass."

"How do you know that?" Ray asked, laughing.

"Because it's something my brothers used to do, and I bet you did it, too."

Ray held up a hand. "Guilty as charged." His expression changed, as he studied the face of the woman who had the power to make him feel things he wasn't allowed to feel. Not at this time in his life. "What have you told Micah about his father?"

Migdalia knew the question would eventually come up. It was if they'd danced around the subject, and now it had to be resolved. "I told him the truth, Ramon."

"And that was?"

"I'd fallen in love with this boy, and we broke up before he was born."

Ray rested an elbow on the table. "You didn't tell him that I wanted to wait until after he was born to have a paternity test?"

"No! Why would I tell my child his father didn't want him?"

"It's not that I didn't want the child, Migdalia. I just wanted to make certain he was mine."

"And what if we'd stayed together and he wasn't yours?" she questioned, angrily. "Would you still have claimed him as your son?"

"Of course."

"Why *of course?*"

"Because if I loved you enough to marry you, then I would've accepted anything that came from you."

A rush of color darkened her face. "What about now, Ramon? Has everything changed because you now know Micah's yours and not some other man's?"

"Yes, Migdalia. Everything's changed, because I've changed."

"How?"

"I want my son in my life."

Migdalia tried to suppress a giggle. "Do you hear yourself, Ramon? You're an ordained Catholic priest who wants to have a relationship with his bastard son."

Ray's hand came down hard on the table, rattling dishes and serving pieces. "I don't ever want you to utter that word in my presence again."

Migdalia half-rose from her chair. "Or what, Ramon? Or should I say Father Torres!"

Pushing back his chair, Ray stood up, walked out of the kitchen, and stood at the living room window, staring out on the street and waiting until he felt his anger wane and he was back in control.

He knew Micky blamed him for deserting her when she needed him most. If he'd been a different person at the time, there was no question that he would've married her and given his son his name. Even if he hadn't been able to afford to take care of a wife, he would've asked his parents if she could live with them until he completed medical school.

He returned to the kitchen to find Migdalia crying, and he recalled her weeping before she walked out on him. Now that seemed like eons ago. Ray walked over to her, eased her from the chair, and cradled her against his chest.

"It's going to be okay, Micky. I'm going to take care of you and our son."

"How are you going to do that?" Pulling back, she stared up at him. Light from a ceiling fixture illuminated a face the color of burnished gold, and he noticed a sprinkling of freckles over her cheekbones that weren't there years ago.

"You are going to marry me."

"The blow on your head must have left you with some brain damage. You're a priest and forbidden to marry."

"I'm not forbidden to marry, Micky. I took a vow not to marry. That's a choice I made before I realized I had a child who needs to grow up with his mother and father."

"What about love, Ramon?"

"What about it?"

"Couples who marry usually love each other."

"Didn't you just say that you told Micah that you'd fallen in love with a boy and that we broke up before he was born?"

"Yes, but—"

"No buts," Ray said, cutting her off. "Or are you ready to lie again?"

"When . . . when did I lie?" Migdalia sputtered.

"When you told your boyfriend that I raped you."

"I said it to save my life," she retorted.

"It was a lie that saved your life and almost cost me mine." Ray sucked in a lungful of breath, held it for seconds before letting it out. "We'll talk about this again after I meet Micah."

"When?"

"Whenever it's convenient for you, Micky. I'll give you my number to the rectory, and if I don't pick up, then leave a message with the secretary, and I'll get back to you. In the meantime, I suggest you let your son know that he has a father who wants to meet him."

Migdalia nodded as she sniffled. "Okay."

"I'll help you clean up here before I drive you back to the Bronx."

Migdalia felt as if she was on an emotional roller-coaster ride. She didn't want to believe Ramon was willing to give up his vocation to marry her and legitimize his son. Where was the love? Or was it all about possession? There was a part of her that still loved her son's father, but it wasn't the all-consuming passion that had her seeking him out all hours of the night. The first time Ramon had made love to her, she knew she was a changed woman. His lovemaking made her believe they would be together for the rest of their lives. That she would grow old in his arms with their children and grandchildren to remind them what they'd had when they were young.

But it had been a fairy tale that didn't end with a happily ever after. She'd come to him with the news that she was carrying his child, and he rejected her because he either didn't believe she was pregnant, or that she'd slept with some other man and wanted to trick him into marrying her.

If he'd changed, so had she, because she wasn't a frightened nineteen-year-old girl fearful of telling her parents that she'd been sleeping with a man who'd gotten her pregnant. She was twenty-nine, soon to be thirty, and a registered dietitian who'd completed a master's degree program, a year of internship, and had passed the CDR exam. She earned enough to support herself and Micah without assistance from anyone. She didn't need a husband as much as Micah needed a father in his life.

That was something Father Torres would have to accept. If not, then his recourse would be to sue her for visitation. And she was certain his bishop would not look favorably on the young priest who had fathered a child out of wedlock.

Ray spent a miserable week waiting for Migdalia to call him for a date and time when he could meet his son. He knew he'd made a serious faux pas when he insisted she marry him. The demand was out before he could censor himself.

He knew his demand was to absolve himself of the guilt that he hadn't believed her when she'd come to him with the news that she was carrying his child. He also had been inflexible because he believed she couldn't get pregnant if he'd always used a condom when having sex with her. The only thing that made conception impossible was abstinence, something he'd practiced for the past ten years.

The phone in his bedroom rang, and Ray picked it up before it rang a second time. "Hello."

"Hey, buddy. Do you have time to come into the city and hang out with me and Frankie?"

It was Kenny, not Micky. "When and where?"

"At my new place."

"I've never been to your new place."

"That's why I'm inviting you. I know you have obligations and are on call twenty-four-seven as a priest, but can you spare a couple of hours to reconnect with your brothers?"

"I'm free Saturday afternoon. But I have to be back on Sunday, because I'm responsible for the Spanish mass."

"What time is that?"

"One o'clock."

"If that's the case, then pack an overnight bag. I'll put you in my spare bedroom and get you up in time to get back to the Bronx before you have to say mass."

"That's a bet. See you Saturday. Is there anything you want me to bring?"

"Yeah."

"What, Kenny?"

"A couple of bottles of your communion wine. I heard that it's really good."

"It is. Are you sure all you need are two bottles?"

"Two is enough. I can't have you breaking the Eighth Commandment. Thou shalt not steal."

Throwing his head back, Ray laughed loudly. "What do you know about the Commandments?"

"Enough, Father Torres, even though Frankie still believes I'm a heathen."

"Do you want me to baptize you?"

"I'll let you know when the time comes."

Ray stared at the crucifix on the wall. "Don't wait too long, my brother. We don't know the day or the hour when God decides he wants to take back the breath you were given, because we're all here on borrowed time."

"Goodbye, Ray."

"Think about what I've just said, Kenneth."

A cold shiver swept over Ray as soon as he hung up. It felt as if he were falling through a frozen pond, and something was holding him down as he fought to get to the surface, where he could fill his lungs with precious air.

Ray moved off the bed, picked up his rosary beads, and knelt to pray. He didn't know what it was, but whenever he felt the bone-chilling cold invade his body it foretold tragedy and eventually death. He'd experienced it last year, weeks before Frankie called to tell him that his uncle had passed away earlier that morning.

"No, not Kenny," he whispered. He could not imagine his friend dying. At least not now. He prayed the entire rosary and when he finished, he felt better.

CHAPTER 33

Ray reclined on a chaise in the living room of Kenny's twelfth-floor co-op, staring out wall-to-wall windows with views of the East River. His friend had come a long way from the small, cramped Greenwich Village studio apartment he'd decorated with secondhand furniture.

"This is really nice, Kenny. You did good, brother."

Kenny handed Ray a wineglass. "Thanks. I have to admit, I had a lot of help from Frankie's uncle, who left me a little something in his will."

Frank, holding a wineglass, walked over and sat on the leather sectional. "My uncle left Kenny and his mother more than a little something. He left them almost all of his estate."

Ray turned to stare at Frankie. "Do I detect a hint of jealousy or resentment in your tone?"

Frankie shook his head. "Hell, no. My uncle left me the D'Allesandro business, and I've increased profits by more than fifty percent in less than five years than my uncle made in nearly twenty years."

"That's because you're an accountant, and your uncle wasn't."

"It's more than that," Frankie said softly. "I've decided to diversify, because I discovered Uncle Frank was much too conservative when it came to investing."

Ray took a sip of wine, staring at his friends over the rim. He knew he had to tell them that he'd fathered a child and he wanted to marry the boy's mother. "Kenny, I'm glad you arranged this get-together, because I need to tell you and Frankie something I hadn't known anything about a week ago."

Rising slightly, Frankie removed a handkerchief from the pocket of his slacks and wiped his nose. "Come on, Father Torres. Spit it out!"

"I have a son." The words, though softly spoken, had the impact of a stinging right hook to the jaw. The expression on the faces of the two men registered shock.

"When?" Kenny asked, when he recovered from Ray's revelation.

Ray set his glass on a side table, then told them everything about recognizing the boy with the last woman with whom he'd had a sexual relationship as his son, to the details of his conversation with Migdalia Hernandez.

Kenny smothered an expletive under his breath. "You've made the decision to leave the priesthood to marry her and legitimize your son?"

Ray nodded. "She hasn't agreed to marry me, but that doesn't matter. I intend to have a relationship with my boy, and I can't do that if I'm totally committed to the Church."

"Have you talked to the boy?" Frankie asked.

"No. I'm waiting for Micky to contact me for a time and place when that can happen."

"So, she wasn't lying when she said she was carrying your baby," Kenny said, meeting Ray's eyes behind the lenses of his own glasses.

"No. But I refused to believe her, because we never had unprotected sex."

"I could've told you that you had a son," Frankie announced, smiling.

"Either the coke or the wine has gotten to you, Frankie, because you're talking crazy," Ray said, accusingly.

Kenny sat up straight. "What the hell are you talking about, Ray?"

"You don't know, Kenny?" Ray asked.

"Know what?" Kenny retorted.

"That our brother is a cokehead. He's snorted so much that he can't stop his nose from running. And don't you dare tell us that you have a cold, Francis D'Allesandro, because we're not dumb or stupid!"

Frankie held the handkerchief to his nose. "I'll admit to snorting a few lines every once in a while, whenever I'm stressed out."

Kenny moved closer to the end of his seat. "You were so stressed out that you come to my home high, Frankie? And I hope you don't have any of that shit on you, because if you do, then I want you to walk the fuck out of here and get rid of it!"

Frankie buried his face in his hands. "I swear I don't have any on me."

"What kind of stress are you having?" Ray asked him.

Frankie lowered his hands, blue eyes shimmering with unshed tears. "I really love this girl, but she won't let me touch her. She says she won't sleep with a man unless she's married."

"What's wrong with that?" Ray questioned.

Frankie glared at him. "Everything. I'm not going to marry a woman, then find out she's no good in bed."

"Marriage isn't all about sex."

"Spoken from a man who hasn't seen or touched pussy in ten years," Frankie spat out.

"That's enough, Frankie," Kenny warned. "Either you respect Ray's chosen vocation, or you can leave. I invited everyone here so we can catch up on what has been going on in our lives since Uncle Dee's funeral, not to attack or insult one another."

Frankie glared at Kenny. "One thing I can take is a hint, because this is the second time you've talked about showing me the door. You wouldn't have this place if my uncle hadn't given you and your mother a shitload of money. You're the son he always wanted, and your mother the wife he could never have."

Spittle had formed at the corners of his mouth when he glared at Ray. "And you want to know how I knew about your son? Well, I'll tell you. I went to my uncle and asked him if he could find some people to take out the guys who beat you the fuck up, and he did. He paid them, and they did what they had to do to make certain they would never hurt anyone ever again. That's when he told me the girl had your kid, because her boyfriend was locked up for six months when she was fucking you. But he made me promise never to say anything about the dudes who took care of your attackers or about the kid. And didn't you wonder why you'd been beaten up and left for dead?"

"I know why I was assaulted, Frankie. Because one of my attackers told me it was retribution for, as he put it, 'fucking with his lady.' It was because I was sleeping with Migdalia Hernandez, who'd been his girlfriend before he was locked up. You didn't have to say anything, because when I saw her last week, she told me everything." Ray paused, slowly shaking his head. "You're not to be trusted, Frankie. You broke your promise to your uncle."

"Don't you dare preach to me, Father Torres! Or judge me. Yes, I dabble in drugs, but I asked my uncle to do something he didn't want to do because of you, Ray. When I saw you lying in that hospital bed with tubes and machines keeping you alive, all I thought about was getting revenge on those who'd put you in that bed. My godfather did it because if anyone else had asked him what I did, he would've turned his back on them without a backwards glance. My uncle wasn't a gangster, but in that instance, he became one when he paid people to exact revenge for *me*, and I know it was something that bothered him for years. Something he told me he'd confessed to Father Morelli before he died."

Kenny groaned. "Damn, brothers. I thought us getting together wouldn't turn into a gripe and therapy session where we're divulging things that are better left unsaid."

Frankie managed a lopsided grin. "Blame it on the coke."

"Spoken just like a junkie," Kenny accused. "And don't you dare deny you're not addicted to the stuff. Have you forgotten, number man, that I'm a social worker who will encourage clients to go into rehab if they hope to regain custody of their children. And the ones who really want their children will do it, and those who are ambivalent will continue to abuse, because they're afraid to face reality when they're clean and sober. The fact is that your girlfriend isn't the only excuse why you're using, so if you don't want to lose her, then I suggest you seek counseling."

"Can I come to you?" Frankie asked Kenny.

"No, Frankie. We're too close, and I don't think you'd want to listen to what I have to tell you. My becoming your therapist would destroy our friendship."

"So, we're still friends?"

Kenny smiled. "We're brothers to the end."

"Brothers to the end," Ray repeated.

"Ditto," Frankie drawled.

Kenny stood up. "I've spent most of the morning cooking, so I hope you dudes brought your appetites, because I don't like leftovers."

Ray rose, extending his hand to Frankie. "Come on, brother. Let's go and get our eat on."

Frankie took the proffered hand and wrapped his free arm around Ray's neck. "I'm going to need you to pray with me," he whispered.

Ray kissed his cheek. "Any time, Francis. Just let me know the day and time."

Frankie nodded. "I'll let you know after I talk to my girl-friend. There's a lot I need to tell her."

"Are y'all coming?" Kenny called out from the dining room.

"Yes," Ray and Frankie answered in unison.

CHAPTER 34

Frankie paced the floor as he waited for Sophia Toscano's arrival. It was time for him to clear his conscience. He had to tell her everything, because he didn't want to lose her. Ray was right that sex wasn't everything when it came to love. And he'd been with enough women to know what he felt for Sophia was love. As real as the love he'd witnessed over the years between his parents, who in a few years were planning to celebrate their thirty-fifth wedding anniversary.

Ray was also right when he said he couldn't be trusted because he had broken a number of promises he'd made to his uncle. It wouldn't be the first time he would invite Sophia to meet him in the apartment above the laundromat because it was more intimate than the street-level one in his family's brownstone.

The chiming of the doorbell shattered the silence, and he went over to the intercom and tapped a button. "Yes?"

"It's me. Sophia."

"Come on up," he said, tapping another button to disengage the lock on the door leading out to the street.

He didn't have long to wait when he saw her coming up

the staircase. Frankie had taken one look at the young woman with a pair of hazel eyes and hair the color of roasted chestnuts and knew there was something about her that had appealed to him as no other had. When she told him her mother was Irish and her father Italian, he knew immediately they were ancestral kindred spirits. They were destined to meet.

Frankie knew it had to be fate when he walked into his family's restaurant and saw her sitting alone at a table. He approached her, asking if he could share her table because he was dining alone. At first, she was hesitant, but then invited him to join her. When he mentioned that he didn't recall seeing her come into the restaurant before, she told him she freelanced part-time to gather historical information for writers whose names she wasn't free to divulge because she was bound by a non-disclosure agreement. She'd recently moved to Manhattan and had secured the part-time position to supplement her salary, because rents were higher in Manhattan than in her old Queens neighborhood.

Not only was it easy for them to carry on a conversation, but Frankie was captivated by her natural beauty. At some urging, she finally told him she'd been raised by her father after her mother passed away the year she'd turned thirteen, and that's when her father had become overprotective to the point where she felt smothered. It was only after she'd finished college and got a job with a small publishing house that she was able to move out on her own. Now, at twenty-six, she was not only emancipated, but also in control of her life and destiny. When he asked if he could see her again, she accepted his phone number but held back giving him the number to her home and office, saying she would be in touch whenever she had a free moment.

The moment stretched into more than a month when she returned to the restaurant to share dinner with him. Frankie was forthcoming when he told her the restaurant had been in his family for three generations, and it was a favorite to long-time neighborhood residents. Unfortunately, she had come to the restaurant on the weekend Kenny wasn't scheduled to come in, because he'd wanted to ask his friend what he thought of her.

Their next official date was to the New York Botanical Garden, followed by a trip to the Cloisters, because she loved history. He'd lost track of the number of museums they had visited that summer, followed by brunch at sidewalk cafés, and Frankie knew he'd fallen in love and wanted Sophia to be the last woman in his life.

At first, he thought she was frigid, because she would allow him to kiss her, but nothing beyond that. When he asked her why, she said she'd promised her dying mother that she would remain a virgin until married, because Bridget Cunningham was forced to marry a man once she discovered she was pregnant when she'd slept with him after two dates. Her mother had drilled it into her head that she was to refrain from premarital sex until married.

One time, he became so aroused that he put his hand up her skirt, and she freaked out, spewing expletives and screaming that she never wanted to see him again. He had arranged for a florist to send candy and flowers to her office every day until she called him and asked that he stop. He told her he would stop if she accepted his apology and that he would never pressure her to do something she didn't want to do. Sophia accepted his apology and said she would see him again. That was weeks ago.

"Hey, you," he crooned, curbing the urge to lean over and kiss her.

Sophia smiled. "Hey, yourself." She rubbed her hands together. "I feel like it's going to snow."

Frankie sandwiched her hands between his, warming her cold fingers. "Why didn't you wear gloves?"

"I misplaced them, and I forgot to buy another pair."

Frankie reached over and closed the door. "I'll get you a pair lined with fur."

Sophia removed her ski cap, shaking out her naturally

wavy hair. She took off her peacoat and handed it to Frankie to hang up. "I don't need a pair with fur."

"Can I get you something hot to drink?"

"No, thank you. I'm not going to be here that long, because I promised my father I would spend some time with him."

"How is he?"

"He's good. I keep telling him that he's working too much, but whatever I say goes in one ear and out the other. He claims if he can find a mechanic who is as good as he is, then he'll cut back on his hours. I know Daddy is just talking out the side of his neck, because he doesn't believe anyone can be as good as he is."

Reaching her hand, Frankie led her into the living room. "How long has your father had his shop?"

"More years than I can count. Remember, I told you the garage belonged to a cousin, and my father began repairing cars when he was still in high school. Once his cousin retired, Daddy took over."

"That sounds familiar, because I took over the family business even before my uncle passed away."

"There's something to keeping it in the family," she said, smiling.

Frankie stared into the large gold-green eyes framed by long black lashes. "I want—no need—to talk to you about something that may affect whether you're willing to continue to see me, or if this will be the last time we'll be together."

A slight frown creased Sophia's smooth forehead. "You're scaring me, Francis. What are you trying to say?"

"I'm trying to say that I love you and that I'm willing to wait, if you agree to marry me, and not make love to you until our wedding night."

She lowered her eyes. "What brought on this epiphany?"

"I met with some friends, who set me straight about things I'd done in my past life that should remain there."

"Like sleeping around?"

"Yes," Frankie admitted.

"And abusing drugs?"

He looked at Sophia as if she were a stranger. "Why would you say that?"

"I may be innocent when it comes to sex, but I'm not that naïve when it comes to drugs. And no, I've never indulged, but I know people who do." She looked at him as if she dared him to refute her accusation. "Cocaine?"

Frankie knew he was between the proverbial rock and a hard place. If he hoped to have any kind of future with her, he had to be open and honest about his life. "Yes, babe. I've snorted cocaine."

Her eyebrow lifted slightly. "Snorted or still snorting?"

He nodded. "I did a few lines last night."

"Why, Francis? Why do you feel the need to medicate yourself with drugs that will eventually destroy you? There's no way I'm going to agree to have a future with a man who can't stay away from drugs. Do you think I want our children to see their father high all the time?"

All he heard was "our children," and realized Sophia was seriously thinking about marrying him. "I'll stop."

"You better, or there's no way I will consent to marry you. And by the way, who do you buy your cocaine from?"

"I don't buy it from anyone."

Sophia shook her head. "I don't believe you. And if you fucking lie to me, Francis D'Allesandro, it will be the last time you'll ever see me after I put my coat on and walk out that motherfucking door."

It wasn't often that Sophia used profanity in his presence, and when she did, he knew she was enraged. He'd witnessed her explosive temper once and vowed to do everything he could not to see it again.

"After I tell you what I'm going to confide in you, if you want to walk, then I won't stop you. But you ever repeat what I'm going to tell you, then I'll hunt you down and blow your brains out." His lips twisted into a cynical smile. "And it won't be the first time that I had to shoot someone."

Sophia sat up straighter. "You're sick when you talk about loving and shooting me in the same breath."

"I do love you, Sophia. It's something I've never said to another woman. And I would willingly give up my life to protect you and the children I hope to have with you."

"Protect me from what, Francis?"

"I've been living a double life."

Sophia rested a hand over her throat under a bulky green turtleneck sweater. "I want you to tell me everything, and please don't leave anything to my imagination."

Frankie knew he was about to break another promise to his uncle when he told Sophia everything that he'd become involved with and concealed from his godfather. Once Frankie Delano relinquished all responsibility of running the family business to him, he'd reestablished the connections his grandfather had before his eldest son decided to take the business in another direction. He'd become known as the incarnation of Salvatore—the *Serpente*—D'Allesandro, who was feared by anyone who dared cross him.

When he finished telling Sophia what he'd vowed never to disclose, he waited for her reaction. She was just looking at him with those beautiful hazel eyes, and he wanted to know her inner thoughts. He wanted to shake her and tell her to say something.

The seconds ticked until they became minutes before she said, "I will never repeat what you just told me."

Frankie slumped and huffed a groan. "Thank you, babe."

"Now that we've gotten that out of the way, we should talk about our relationship."

He smiled at her. "What about it?"

"I want you to check yourself into a drug rehab program. And once you're cleaned, we can get engaged. I want a long engagement."

"How long, babe?"

"More than a year and less than two years."

He frowned. "That's a long time."

"It's not as long when compared to what we'll spend together as husband and wife."

Frankie's frown vanished when he smiled. "You're right about that. Now can I kiss you?"

Sophia shook her head. "Not until you're drug-free."

"You're a hard woman, Sophia Toscano."

"That's because my man has a hard head." She stood up. "I have to go now, because I told my father I would meet him before he closed his shop."

Frankie helped her into her coat and watched as she walked out of the apartment, feeling freer than he had in a very long time. He knew he had to kick his cocaine habit, but there were times when he needed to experience the euphoria that made him feel invincible. He had a few grams lying on the bedside table he would save for later when he needed to feel good again. Then when it was gone, he swore it would be the last time he would use, because he'd promised Sophia he would get off the drug.

CHAPTER 35

Labor Day Weekend—1985

"It's finally come to this," Frankie whispered in Kenny's ear. "Now that Ray's living in Connecticut, it means we have to break up the band."

Kenny gave his friend a sidelong glance. He, Ray, and Frankie were the same age, but time hadn't been as kind to Francis D'Allesandro. He'd struggled with his addiction, relapsing over and over until Kenny found a residential rehab facility on Long Island that had helped him to get and remain clean for the past three months. Frankie had earned enough credits to leave the facility to come to the Bronx to see Ray, his very pregnant wife, and son before they returned to their home in Connecticut. Kenny knew it wasn't easy for Frankie to stay drug-free once his girlfriend left him following his second relapse.

Ray had resigned his role as a Catholic priest to accept one as pastor and teacher at a Lutheran school in Fairfield, Connecticut. He'd married Migdalia a week after resigning from the Catholic Church and legally changed his son's name to

Micah Alexander Hernandez Torres. It was a mouthful for a twelve-year-old to say, but it was a tradition for Spanish kids to have a lot of names.

Many things had happened in two years. His mother had retired and went on an around-the-world cruise, meeting up with a group of retired women, who had invited her to join them on future ventures. When Justine wasn't traveling, she divided her time volunteering at a senior citizens' community center, teaching dressmaking. Occasionally she would ask him who he was dating, and the answer was always the same. He was going out socially but there wasn't any special woman in his life. Kenny knew his mother wanted grandchildren, but he wasn't willing to bring a child into the world without marriage just to pacify her.

Kenny hugged Ray, thumping his back. "Stay in touch, Father Ray."

Ray kissed him on both cheeks. "That's a promise. I need to get on the road before I run into holiday traffic. Or before Micky decides to go into labor on our way home."

"It would serve you right if you have to pull over and deliver your own baby because you decided to drive down here instead of us coming up to your place."

"We only came down because Frankie isn't allowed to leave the state, and there was no way I wanted to miss seeing my blood brother before taking on a new position and with a baby that's due any day now."

"Once he graduates, I'll drive up with him but only after you guys have completely settled in."

Ray smiled. "The door will always be open to you and Frankie."

Kenny nodded. "I know that. And if you need anything, don't hesitate to let me know."

"I have everything I need, Kenny. A loving wife, wonderful kid, and another on the way. Now I wouldn't mind you becoming godfather to my son or daughter, but first you have to be baptized."

"The day I find a woman I want to marry, I will allow you to put water on me. Then after I have kids, you can baptize them, too."

"Sounds good, Kenneth."

Kenny knew Ray was serious when he called him by his full name. "Now go and drive carefully. You're carrying precious cargo."

He watched Ray help his wife into the minivan and then his son, waiting until they'd secured their seat belts, then rounded the vehicle to get in behind the wheel. He watched as it vanished from sight, then walked over and nodded to Frankie.

"Let's go, buddy. I have to get you back before six."

Frankie slowly nodded. "I don't know why, but I thought you would be the first one to marry and have kids, because you didn't chase as many skirts as me and Ray."

"Chasing skirts is tiresome, Frankie. I can honestly say that I'm ready to look for a special woman to marry and start a family."

"How special does she have to be?"

"Special enough to put up with me. The older I get, the more set in my ways I become."

"That's because you don't mind your own company," Frankie said, as he walked with Kenny to where his friend had parked on the street in front of the Torres house.

"I can't fight with myself, Frankie."

"That's the difference between you and me. I can't stop fighting with myself. It's as if there's a war going within me that I sometimes feel I'm losing."

Kenny draped an arm around Frankie's shoulders. "You've been winning the battles these past three months, so you're not losing."

"Three down and nine to go," Frankie drawled.

"You're going to make it, brother, even if I have to drive more than a hundred miles to come see you every week instead of twice a month."

"That's not necessary, Kenny. I have to confess, this is the first time in years that I've been clearheaded enough where the cravings have stopped."

Kenny wanted to tell Frankie that although people who are addicts may change their behavior, they will relapse if they don't change what's going on in their heads. "Good for you. Let me know what you want to listen to on the way back." Kenny had established a ritual of playing music instead of talking whenever he was in the car with Frankie, because he didn't want to slip into the role as a counselor. They were lifelong friends, and that's the way he wanted and liked it.

CHAPTER 36

*February 5, 1987—Woodlawn Cemetery—
the Bronx, New York*

Kenneth Russell ignored the sleet beating down on his bare head as he stared at the mound of fresh dirt covering his mother's grave. He still hadn't come to grips that she was gone, and he'd never see her again. His only solace was that she'd been buried close to Francis Michael D'Allesandro. It had been her wish to be with him in death when it hadn't been possible in life. It was the second week in the new year when he picked up the phone to call Justine to let her know she was about to get her wish. He'd met the woman with whom he believed he wanted to share his life and future, but when she didn't answer the phone, he became alarmed, because she hadn't scheduled any trips until later that summer.

He continued to call her, then decided after leaving work to stop by his mother's apartment. When he walked in, he found her on the kitchen floor, her breathing shallow. Forcing himself not to panic, he called 911 and asked the operator to send an ambulance. When the EMTs arrived, they were able to stabilize her enough to transport her to the nearest hospital. Kenny alternated praying and pacing until a doctor told him Justine had suffered a stroke from an undiagnosed aneurysm, and they would have to wait to see if she would recover.

Kenny took a leave of absence from his job and spent every waking moment at his mother's bedside. Ray had come down from Connecticut to be with him for several days, but it was Frankie who'd never left his side. They were truly brothers to the end. One day merged into the next when he'd go back to his apartment to shower and then fall into bed to sleep for at least four hours before getting up to return to the hospital.

One morning when he walked in, he felt a spark of hope. Justine had opened her eyes. She was trying to talk, but he couldn't hear what she was saying, so he bent down until his ear was mere inches from her mouth. She kept repeating the same phrase; then he understood what she was trying to tell him.

I want you to pay the bitches back for ruining my life. I don't care how you do it. Just do it!

Kenny didn't know who the *bitches* were his mother was rambling about. Then the machine monitoring her heart stopped. She flatlined. Seconds later, the room was crowded with doctors and nurses, as they tried to resuscitate her. He stood outside the room, and the last word he remembered was the doctor calling the time of death before he collapsed on the floor weeping uncontrollably. He was still sitting on the floor when Frankie found him, managed to get him up, and take him to the hospital chapel, where they sat side by side, not talking for a long time.

The next few days were a blur when he had to make funeral arrangements for his mother. He found an envelope inside the desk she'd used when they lived in the tenement, with typed instructions for what she wanted if she were to pass away before him. She wanted a graveside service, and she had included a paid invoice for the plot, signed by Francis Michael D'Allesandro. It was obvious they'd discussed wanting to be buried next to each other.

"Let's go," Frankie said in his ear. "You're going get sick standing out here, and I'll be damned if I want to go to another funeral any time soon."

Kenny nodded. It was less than three months ago that Frankie had buried his Nonna. Gianna D'Allesandro had never recovered from losing her eldest son, saying over and over that mothers weren't supposed to bury their children.

"I'm ready."

Kenny knew he was kidding himself, because he refused to believe his mother was gone and never coming back. He would miss talking to her several times a week or stopping by to watch her favorite television shows with her and occasionally bringing over food when she didn't feel like cooking.

Frankie followed him in his car as they headed across town. Kenny could remember, as though it was yesterday, when his mother didn't want him to go East Harlem, and much to her chagrin, he'd made the neighborhood his home. He'd come to love the energy that came from residents speaking languages he understood. He was able to segue from English, to Spanish, and Italian with equal facility. There were times when he'd walk into the restaurant's kitchen, slip on an apron, and assist the cooks after he'd been away for months.

He maneuvered into his assigned space outside his building and parked. His mailbox in the lobby overflowed with mail he hadn't picked up in days. Kenny gathered magazines, bills, and junk mail and walked to the elevator. The doors opened, and he walked into the elevator, punching the button for his floor. The elevator rose swiftly, stopping on the twelfth floor. He made his way down the carpeted hallway to his apartment, and he opened the door to the ringing of the telephone. Picking up the receiver on the entryway table, he mumbled a greeting as he slipped off his boots.

"Kenneth, it's MacKayla."

At any other time, he would've enjoyed listening to Mac-

Kayla Harrison's sultry voice, but he'd just buried his mother, so he wasn't up for chitchat. "Hi, MacKayla."

There came a pause. "Is something wrong?"

"No. I'm just tired," he lied.

He'd met the high school teacher at an afterwork mixer he attended with some of his coworkers. She was his boss's sorority sister, and they'd hit it off within minutes of being introduced to each other. After a couple of drinks, they exchanged telephone numbers with a promise to keep in touch. They played phone tag, and with Kenny spending so much time in the hospital, he wasn't inclined to return anyone's call.

"Look, Kenneth, if you don't want me to call you, I don't have a problem forgetting your name and number."

"Please don't," he said quickly. "I buried my mother today, so—"

"I'm so sorry," she apologized, stopping his words. "Call me when you feel like talking."

"Thank you."

"Is there anything you need?"

Kenny wanted to say yes. Her. But he didn't know her like that. They'd only met once, and it was enough for him to know there was something special about her. "No, but thanks for asking. Please be patient with me, because I'm going to be busy cleaning out my mother's apartment. Once that's done, I'll call you, and hopefully, we can get together."

"You know where to find me. And again, I'm sorry about your loss."

"Thanks, Mac. Talk to you soon."

Kenny hung his damp topcoat on a hook of the closet in the entryway, not bothering to close the door. Even though he turned the heat in his place to the highest setting, he was still chilled. He hadn't bothered to draw the wall-to-wall drapes, because he liked the river views and watching the change of seasons. The apartment was as quiet as a tomb, so picking up a remote device, he turned on the stereo and tuned it to a station playing cool jazz.

He would celebrate his thirty-fifth birthday later that spring, but lately he was feeling much older. There was a time when Kenny believed he would have his life together by that age. That he would be married with children, and maybe even purchase a house in the suburbs where his children would attend good schools, and not be exposed to some of the social ills that befell city kids.

After a shower and a mug of hot chamomile tea, he got into bed and slept soundly for the first time in weeks.

The incessant chiming of the phone woke him before dawn, and Kenny quickly picked it up. "Hello."

"Kenny, the FBI are here with a warrant to arrest me."

"What!" Now he was fully alert.

"Look, I can't talk, because if I don't open the door, they're going to knock it down. I'm entitled to one call to my lawyer. I'll tell him to call you with all the details. I . . ." There was only the sound of a dial tone. Frankie had abruptly hung up.

Kenny knew he couldn't go back to sleep. He wondered why the FBI would want to arrest his friend? What had Frankie gotten into?

He knew Frankie had been addicted to cocaine, but since graduating from the drug treatment program, he'd managed to stay clean. He ran a hand over his face. "What the fuck were you doing to have the feds come after you?"

Kenny wanted to call Ray to let him know their brother had been arrested, then decided to wait until Frankie's lawyer called him to let him know what his friend had been charged with.

CHAPTER 37

Francis Joseph D'Allesandro was charged under RICO with running a criminal enterprise. He was charged with drug trafficking, money laundering, and attempted murder. They seized all his assets, and liens were placed on all his businesses and the brownstone. He pled innocent to all of the charges, and when his attorney asked that he be released on bail, the judge denied it.

When told that Sophia Toscano was an undercover DEA agent who bugged his phones and was wearing a wire the day he'd told her everything about his family business, he refused to believe her deception. Ray had come down to visit Frankie in prison and relayed to Kenny that Frankie was a broken man, and if he'd been released on bail, there was no doubt he would've gone back to abusing drugs.

During one of his telephone calls with Frankie, his friend said it would take a year and maybe even longer for the prosecutors at the Southern District of New York to collect evidence to bring it to trial, because they were going over thousands of hours of wiretaps. Meanwhile he would have to remain behind bars during that time.

It had taken Kenny several months to go through all of his mother's possessions in her apartment to either throw or give away. He would come for a few hours after work to box up books and clothes, electing to keep personal mementos.

He had reconnected with MacKayla, and while he'd found her geographically undesirable because she lived in New Jersey, that hadn't become a deal-breaker for him. He recalled what his mother said about becoming friends before lovers and had cautioned Mac, as he'd begun calling her, that he wanted to take it slow. She was in agreement, because she'd just gotten out of a long-term relationship where she and her ex had lived together.

Kenny had no idea his life would eventually change dramatically when, on a top shelf of a closet in his mother's bedroom, he found a box filled with her journals. He would've missed it if he hadn't stood on a stepladder to replace a bulb in the ceiling. He took the box to his apartment with the intent of reading what she'd written whenever he had a lot of spare time, storing it in a footlocker in the closet of his spare bedroom.

His relationship with MacKayla was so angst-free that Kenny could not believe he'd finally found his soulmate. He took her with him up to Connecticut to visit Ray and his family. Migdalia had given birth to a baby girl, and a year later, another boy. Ray admitted they'd talked about having one more child to make it an even number, but then his wife claimed she was done pushing out babies. He had watched MacKayla with Micky's children and knew there would come a time when she'd talk about wanting children.

He and Ray talked about Frankie and the mounting charges that, if he were found guilty, would send him away for a long time.

"His lawyer is still working to see if he can be released on bail," Kenny said to Ray when they'd gone for a walk away from the house.

"How much do you think the judge would set the amount?" Ray questioned.

Kenny shook his head. "I don't know, but it has to be around at least half a mil."

Ray clasped his hands behind his back as he continued walking. "I can't even count that high."

"I can," Kenny said, deadpan.

Ray stopped and met his eyes. "What are you saying?"

"Frankie's uncle left me and my mother a lot of money."

"If you don't mind my asking, how much did he leave you?"

"Try a million each."

"You're kidding?"

"No, Ray. I'm not kidding. My mother transferred most of her share to me, because she wouldn't be able to continue living in public housing claiming that much money. I used a portion of my inheritance to purchase the co-op and deposited the rest in treasury and tax-free municipal bonds. So far, I've been fortunate enough not to touch any of it. And if Frankie needs money for bail, I'm willing to give it to him. Now that we're talking about money, I'm thinking about drawing up a will, and if anything were to happen to me, I'd like for you to inherit whatever I own."

"No, Kenny. What if you marry, shouldn't your wife and kids be the beneficiaries?"

"Right now, I don't have a wife or kids. And if I do marry, then I'll add a codicil, leaving everything to her. Better?"

Ray smiled. "Much better. I like her," he said as they began walking again.

"Are you talking about MacKayla?"

"Of course I'm talking about her. She's so different from the other women you used to date."

"That's because she isn't a skirt I need to chase," Kenny teased.

Ray gave him a soft punch on his shoulder. "Good for you. Looks like you got some sense in that big head of yours before your hair turned completely gray."

Kenny ran a hand over the cropped salt-and-pepper strands. "I'm not as gray as Frankie."

"That's because you haven't lived the life that Francis has. When I went to visit him he admitted that if he'd listened to his uncle, he wouldn't be looking to spend the rest of his life in prison. He said Frank had predicted that women would be his downfall, and unfortunately it became a reality when he took up with the likes of Sophia Toscano. And that wasn't even her real name."

"Do you think I should pay someone to do a background check on MacKayla Harrison?"

"Stop it, Kenny! You know for a fact that the woman is a schoolteacher."

"Undercover agents can assume a lot of identities."

"Are you trying to sow doubt so you can extricate yourself from a relationship because you fear commitment?"

"No, Ray. Mac is the real deal, and I really like her." There was something about her that reminded Kenny of his mother in looks and temperament.

"Good. So let me know well in advance when you set a wedding date, so I can do the honors. But before that—"

"I know, Ray," Kenny interrupted, laughing. "I'll let you baptize me."

Ray rested a hand on Kenny's shoulder. "I'm glad you've become a mind reader."

Kenny patted the hand on his shoulder. "Let's start back before our women send out a search party for us."

CHAPTER 38

Christmas Eve, 1988—East Harlem, New York

Kenny opened the door and pulled Frankie into a rough embrace. "Welcome home, and Merry Christmas."

Frankie grabbed Kenny's shoulders and kissed him on both cheeks. "It wouldn't have been a merry anything if it hadn't been for you. Thanks for putting up the money for my bail. I did promise to pay you back."

"What are you talking about? I thought the feds seized all your assets."

"They missed one," Frankie whispered.

"Say what?" Kenny whispered back. He knew his apartment wasn't bugged, but understood Frankie was paranoid because of what Sophia Toscano had done to him.

"Do you mind if we go out on the terrace in your bedroom to talk?"

"Sure," Kenny agreed, even though the temperature had dipped well below freezing.

"Before I was released, I'd asked the judge for permission to stay in the apartment above the laundromat, and he said yes," Frankie said in normal tone as they stood outside in the bone-chilling cold. "I had someone come in and sweep the place for bugs, and they found all of them. When the feds came to take the file cabinet with a set of bogus accounting ledgers, they missed the actual ledgers and cash hidden in a safe under a false floor in a closet. Even though I spilled my guts to Sophia about what I'd been involved in, I never mentioned what my uncle had installed under the floor."

"How much cash, Frankie?"

"Try eight mil." Reaching into the breast pocket of his jacket, he removed an envelope and handed it to Kenny. You'll find the money you put up for the bail and a little extra for having to withdraw monies from your investments."

"But I'll get my money back once you go to trial. That's if you don't jump bail."

"Don't tempt me with the suggestion. I intend to stand trial and beat the charges. I hired a couple of barracudas for lawyers who convinced the judge to let me post bail. Eight million dollars is tempting enough to convince a lot folks to change their minds."

"Are you talking bribes?"

"You said it, I didn't," Frankie said, smiling. "You said you needed some advice about a situation that has to do with something that happened to your mother back in the day."

"Let's go inside, Frankie. I'm freezing my nuts off out here." Kenny closed and locked the doors to the terrace after they stepped back into the bedroom. He pointed to the journals stacked in a neat pile on the edge of a padded bench at the foot of the king-sized bed.

"What's in those?" Frankie asked.

"My mother's life. I packed them away after cleaning out her apartment and forgot about them until one day last week, when I opened the trunk to get a ski jacket and pants that I need to take with me when MacKayla and I leave for Colorado in a couple of days. Come in the kitchen with me, and I'll tell you what she wrote down."

"You're fucking kidding me, Kenny! You're a twin?" Frankie questioned, after Kenny gave him the unabridged version of what Justine had written.

"That's what my mother wrote, and there's no reason for her to pen lies."

Frankie ran a hand through his thinning gray hair. "But you're nothing like that pompous loudmouth who looks for every opportunity to have his face in front of the camera."

"That's because even though we have the same father, we were raised by different women, who are as different as night from day. The last thing my mother said before she died was that she wanted me to pay the bitches back for ruining her life. I had no idea of what she was talking about until I read her journals."

"There's no doubt someone needs to pay for forcing her to live a life of lies. And all along, you believed your father was murdered when he was sitting up in a big house in Mount Vernon with his duplicitous wife, pretending she'd given him the heir he wanted. Who the *fuck* does that?"

"Folks who believe that because they have power and money, they can get whatever they want. I decided to tell you and not Ray, because he would tell me to pray for them, and I'm sorry, but I'm not the forgiving type when it comes to people hurting those I love."

"Do you mind if I take the journals and read them myself before I come up with a solution to help you pay the bitches back for what they did to your mother? Now I know why she wouldn't marry my uncle. She was afraid he would find out about her past."

"There probably wasn't a day when she didn't live in fear that someone would uncover who she actually was. And that's why she wouldn't let anyone get close to her."

"No one but Uncle Frank. And there were times when she refused to see him. He would tell me he didn't understand why she kept pushing him away. It was only after he had cancer that they started to spend more time together."

"My mother was a complicated woman."

"She had to be, Kenny, to keep up the façade she had to play all of her life."

Kenny closed his eyes and shook his head. "That had to be stressful, and now I know that's why she died so young."

"Are you going to honor her dying wish and pay the bitches back for how they ruined her life?" Frankie asked.

Kenny opened his eyes. They were cold and unreadable as a stone. "Yes."

"That's all I need to know. And I'm not going to tell you how I'm going to make it happen, except that I know people who run a prostitution business and owe me a few favors. My soul is damned, and I know I'm going to hell, and there's no way I'm going to bring you down with me. So, whatever we talked about here stays between us. After I finish reading your mother's journals, I'm going to burn them. I hope that's okay with you?"

"It's okay, because I also planned to burn them."

Frankie stood up, Kenny rising with him. "I know you and your girl are planning to go away for Christmas, so I'm going to get out of your hair so you can get ready. Now that you've found your special lady, don't take too long to put a ring on her finger."

"That's what I've been thinking about, because she's been hinting that she wants to be a June bride."

"Are you talking about this coming June, Kenny?"

"No. That's too soon. Her birthday is coming up in July, so that's when I plan to give her a ring, and if she doesn't want to wait until the following June, then we'll marry sooner."

"Go get the journals, buddy, because I promised my father I'd be back in time to help him put up the tree. I don't know why he waits until Christmas Eve to get a tree, but I can't get him to change. I suppose it's because old folks get stuck in their ways, and it's hard for them to change."

"It's going to happen to us if we live long enough," Kenny said, smiling. "I'll be right back." He put the journals in a canvas sail bag and gave it to Frankie. "Merry Christmas, brother."

Frankie nodded. "Back at you, brother."

Kenny walked him to the door, closing it behind him. He felt a sense of relief now that he was able to share what his mother had written with another person. And whatever decision Frankie would come up with, Kenny would go along with it.

He had two things on his wish list for the coming year:

Buy an engagement ring.

And have Ray baptize him.

Epilogue

●

Newark Trauma Center—Newark, New Jersey—
August 8, 1989

Frankie walked back into the room and rested his hand over Kenny's. "Brothers for life."

That had been their childhood motto. It didn't matter what they had to go through; they would never desert one another. He had a flashback of another time, when he stood next to a hospital bed watching Ramon Torres fight for his life. Now it was Kenny.

He didn't understand why, despite the many sins he'd committed, he wasn't the one in a hospital bed hooked up to machines monitoring his vitals. He supposed he'd been spared because a higher power would punish him later for breaking a number of the seven deadly sins.

Frankie realized his entire life was based on lust for women, power, and money. And twice in his life, he'd been a party to devising a scheme to exact revenge. Something he knew he would have to atone for.

"Frankie?" He turned to find Ray dressed in clerical garb

with a purple stole around his neck. He held a small box in one hand. "What are you doing?"

"I'm here to give Kenneth last rites."

"No! You can't. I won't let you."

"Please, Francis. Don't make this harder on any of us. I love Kenny just as much as you do, and it's time we let him go where there is no more pain and suffering. He needs to be with his mother."

Turning on his heel, Frankie walked out of the room and saw Kenny's fiancée standing with her back against a wall. Her eyes were closed, and he knew she was praying. A large flawless emerald-cut diamond ring sparkled on her left hand. Some of the hospital staff had discovered the ring in Kenny's jacket after he'd been airlifted to the trauma center. They'd also found MacKayla Harrison, Ray, and Frankie in Kenny's emergency contacts in his wallet. They'd called MacKayla first, and she called Ray, who in turn had called him.

Kenny had been in a coma for a month, and she'd been by his side every one of those days. He had talked incessantly about finding his special woman, and once Frankie met her, he knew Kenny had chosen well. They were perfect for each other.

Ray exited the room, his expression unreadable. "You can go in now."

Frankie took MacKayla's hand, and together they returned to the room. He and MacKayla gasped at the same time. Kenny had opened his eyes. He tried smiling, but it appeared more like a grimace. MacKayla squeezed Frankie's hand. "He's going to make it."

Frankie was galvanized into action when he raced down to the nurses' station. "Kenneth Russell just woke up!"

Less than a minute later, two doctors and a nurse ordered everyone to leave as they tended to their patient.

Kenny moaned softly. He wasn't going crazy. The voices weren't in his head. They were the people in the room. He tried to talk but couldn't get his tongue to move. He lifted his hand and moved his fingers.

"Can you hear me?" a deep voice asked. "Nod your head if you can."

Kenny nodded. *Hell yeah, I can hear you. I've been hearing voices for days. Now, take this damn thing out of my throat.* A shuddering sigh echoed in the room when a doctor removed the trach.

"Thank you," Kenny whispered. Damn, his throat was on fire. "When can I go home?"

The young doctor patted his arm. "It's going to be after you go through a battery of tests, and if you pass them, then you'll be discharged."

He nodded. "I need to talk to Father Ramon."

The doctor turned to the nurse. "Please go get the priest."

Kenny closed his eyes, and when he opened them again, he found Ray leaning over him. "When you were praying for me, I saw my mother shaking her head when I started walking toward her. She wasn't ready for me to join her."

"That's because you have more living to do. I'm going to come back in a couple of days to baptize you. As soon as you're discharged, I want you and MacKayla to come up to Connecticut. There is no waiting period after you get your marriage license. I'll marry you two so you can start living your lives together."

"What about Frankie? Will he be there?"

Ray shook his head. "I don't know about his legal situation. Because he's out on bail and is restricted from leaving New York, his lawyer had to ask the judge for special permission for him to come and see you. He wasn't going to allow it until I asked to speak with him. There's something about the clerical collar that changed his mind."

"You were meant to be a priest."

"I know that now. Get some rest. I'll see you in a couple of days."

October 20, 1989—Fairfield, Connecticut

A small group of family and friends were on hand to witness the marriage of Kenneth Douglas Russell to Mac-Kayla Yvette Harrison, with Father Ramon as the officiant. MacKayla's sister stood as her maid of honor, and Francis D'Allesandro was Kenneth's best man.

The prosecutors representing the Southern District of New York were shocked when the jury found Frankie not guilty of all charges. His lawyers had worked their magic when they were able to convince the jury that undercover DEA agent Sophia Toscano had used entrapment to bring charges against their client.

Frankie knew he'd been given a second chance, and now strictly followed the rules his godfather had established to run the family businesses. What he hadn't disclosed to anyone was that the cash hidden in the safe beneath the false floor had decreased appreciably by more than half, most of it going for legal fees. He'd willingly given the barracudas what they asked for to get their client off.

Frankie was glad that both his blood brothers were happily married, and maybe one day, he would be lucky enough to find a special lady to share his life and future with. He was in no rush, because he wanted to take a couple of years to make amends for what he'd done when he straddled the line between good and evil. He smiled when Ray pronounced Kenny and MacKayla husband and wife.

After the reception that was held in the dining room of the manse concluded, Kenny and Frankie joined Ray in his study and hoisted flutes of champagne. They toasted one another, smiling because they were together again.

Brothers for life.

Discussion Questions

1. What impact did Precious Boone and Lillian Crawford's manipulation of Justine Russell change her from being an innocent teenage schoolgirl into the woman she would eventually become?

2. Do you believe Justine should have told Kenny about his existence earlier in the novel? How do you think it would have changed his life?

3. Do you believe it was anger and resentment that would not allow Justine to love or trust anyone other than her son? Explain your answer.

4. What was the common thread that made Kenny, Frankie, and Ray lifelong friends despite their racial and ethnic differences?

5. Discuss in detail the interactions Kenny had with his mother when growing up, and how it affected his relationships with women.

6. Frankie mentioned he was guilty of breaking a number of the seven deadly sins. Which ones do you think he was referring to?

7. Ray's lustful desires almost cost him his life. Was the incident the reason for him to go from saving lives to saving souls?

8. Do you believe Justine became a romantic substitute for Francis's unrequited love with his high school girlfriend? Or did he truly love her?

9. Describe how different Justine's life would have been if she had married Francis. Do you believe once they reconnected that they were able to share the intimacy that hadn't been possible before?

10. There are a few parallels and references to biblical events in the novel. Are there any you can connect with and why?

11. Discuss how the need for revenge, retribution, and forgiveness affected the lives of Justine, Kenny, Frankie, Francis, and Ray.

12. There were a few references to actual historic events. How many do you remember or you weren't aware of?

13. What about Between *Good and Evil* did you like or dislike? Did you find the ending satisfying?